PRAISE FOR T. KINGFISHER

"Dive in...if you are looking to be charmed and delighted."

— Locus

"...[A] knack for creating colorful, instantly memorable characters, and inhuman creatures capable of inspiring awe and wonder."

— NPR Books

"The writing. It is superb. T. Kingfisher, where have you been all my life?"

— The Book Smugglers

PALADIN'S STRENGTH

PALADIN'S STRENGTH

BOOK TWO OF THE SAINT OF STEEL

T. KINGFISHER

Paladin's Strength

Production Copyright © 2021 Argyll Productions

This is a work of fiction. All characters are fictional and anybody who says differently is itching for a fight.

http://www.tkingfisher.com

Published by Argyll Productions

Dallas, Texas

www.argyllproductions.com

ISBN 978-1-61450-530-3

First Edition Hardcover February 2021

Still for Kevin, but moreso

CHAPTER 1

Clara stood outside a stranger's tent, holding a naked sword in her hands.

She was not particularly afraid. She was aware that fear would be appropriate, but she had shoved it all down into the vague space inside her chest, where it could not interfere. It was the saint's will that she be where she was, and if that meant that she was going to stand here with a group of armed men a few feet behind her, waiting for a stranger to come out of his tent, then so be it. She might have preferred to be somewhere else, but the saint had put her here.

Let us hope, therefore, that it not be the saint's will that I be cut down by the owner of this tent before he realizes what is going on.

The tent was large but collapsible, and made of oiled cloth rather than leather. It had been pegged down somewhat loosely and no attempt had been made to secure it against weather.

Temporary lodging only. They plan to move on before the weather changes.

This struck her as a good sign.

There was a tent flap, but her hands were full of steel. Clara cleared her throat.

There were four tents in all, a wagon, and a trio of picketed mules.

She knew that the occupants of the others had already seen her and the armed men behind her.

"Boss..." drawled a voice from near one of the other tents, "they're back. And there's a woman out front with a sword."

"God's balls," said a voice from inside the tent, presumably "Boss." "Not another one!"

Clara rather suspected that they didn't expect her to speak their language, which was Harshek, from the south and west. There was no point in letting her future captors know how much she understood just yet, so she kept her face studiedly neutral.

"This one doesn't look like she plans to cut you just yet, Boss."

"Well, that's something."

She heard the sounds of a man moving inside the tent, the scrape of metal on metal as he drew a sword from a sheath.

Well, if I am going to die today, at least the weather is nice... The sky was clear blue, with only a few puffy white clouds. The air smelled of the pine trees that grew close around the road.

Clara had been very close to death twice in the last month. Once the air had smelled of burning buildings, and once of sickness and unwashed bodies. Pine was certainly preferable.

Oddly, the tent itself had a faint odor of whiskey. Clara wondered how much the inhabitant drank, if the outside smelled of it. A bold black sigil had been embroidered on the tent flap. A name? A rank? A ward against whatever misfortune might befall tents? *And what might those be? Windstorms or stampedes or avalanches?* This seemed like a great deal to place on one ward.

Behind her, the leader of the Arral war band shouted, "We bring the payment of victory!"

The man addressed as Boss threw back the flap and stepped outside. There was a sword in his hand, much finer than the one she carried.

He was tall and heavy-boned, taller than any of the men behind her, and he almost certainly expected to look down to meet a woman's eyes. That Clara had only to lift her chin a fraction to meet his clearly surprised him.

His gaze dropped very quickly, however, to the sword.

She dropped down onto her heels and held the blade out on the flats of her palms. She tried to make herself look as nonthreatening as possible, head bowed, while she studied him through her eyelashes.

His face was dark and seamed with scars, his hair black and fiercely curly, shot with gray at the temples. There were fine lines at the corners of his eyes, paler than the surrounding skin. Clara had seen lines like that in men who spent a great deal of time in the sun. It made him look older than he probably was, and he already did not look young. Nearly forty, perhaps.

He looked past her to the band of men standing twenty yards away. "*Now* what do they want?"

"They're not looking all that friendly, Boss!"

"Thank you, Galen. I could not possibly have figured that out for myself."

"It's what I do, Boss."

Clara said in War-tongue, very quietly, "Take the sword."

His eyes dropped down to hers. "What?"

"Please keep your voice down. I should not be talking. And take the sword. It belongs to the man you killed."

"I don't—" He swallowed, then lowered his voice to a fierce whisper. "I don't want his damn sword! I didn't want to kill him at all!"

Clara sighed. "If you don't take the sword, you are saying that his house still owes you. If you accept the sword, then you accept the price his house has paid and this will be done."

The men behind her were growing restless. Clara could hear them murmuring to each other.

"Why does his house owe me anything?"

"Because he claimed offense and challenged you. The gods clearly found against him."

"I would have just apologized if he'd explained!"

Clara prayed to St. Ursa for patience. "Take the sword. Please."

"Or what?"

"Or his uncles will have to get involved. That's them standing behind me."

"Saint's balls." The man rubbed his face. He was wearing worn leather gauntlets, only a shade darker than his skin. "All right."

He reached down and picked the sword up by the hilt. A sigh went through the watching men.

"Now what?"

"Now hold it up. Sideways, not point up."

He did so. "Ah...They're backing up."

"Good."

His eyes flicked down to her again. "What the *hell* is going on?"

"A very complex bit of social theatre. Put your hand on my shoulder." She was ordering him as if he were one of the novices, poor man. Well, there was no help for it. More lives than hers were at stake. "It's for the best," she said. "Truly."

He obeyed. A man used to taking orders as well as giving them. That was interesting. His expression was really quite indescribable. Frustration, she thought, and under that, a fine sense of the absurdity of it all.

"What are they doing now?" she asked, keeping her eyes on his face.

"They seem to be leaving."

"Now would be a good time to go back in the tent, then."

"There's one left."

"Yes, I imagine so. He is watching to make sure that it is concluded."

He glanced warily back at the man in the road, then down at her. She raised her eyebrows.

"All right. Err...thank you."

She nodded.

He stepped back into the tent. Clara shuffled forward on her knees.

"Annnnd you're coming in. All right. Ah...well, then."

"I will explain inside," she promised.

"Oh, *good.*"

4

She bowed her head even lower, partly for the benefit of the watcher and partly to hide her smile.

Once she was inside, the man let down the tent flap behind them. In Harshek he called, "Galen, I don't know what's going on here, but hopefully this woman can explain."

"What if she kills you, Boss?" called Galen.

"Then either avenge me or put her in charge. Your choice."

Clara was glad that she had experience keeping her face schooled to immobility or she might have given away her mastery of the language right there.

The inside of the tent was dim, lit by the open smokehole at the top. There was no fire burning, though, only a small brazier of coals, just enough to warm an equally small kettle. A hide tarp had been thrown down across the floor. It was warm enough outside that with the flaps closed, the tent might soon become stuffy.

Despite the dimness, she could see that the inside walls were a blaze of color, scarlet and carmine and sky blue. It was unexpected compared to the drab exterior. She wondered what that said about the man in front of her.

"All right," said the man. "I'm sorry I don't have any chairs to offer you. Would you like tea?"

She raised her head sharply. "I would commit a *venial sin* for a cup of tea."

It was his turn to raise his eyebrows. "That shouldn't be necessary." He stretched out a long arm to the kettle, rummaged two metal cups from a nearby pack, and poured hot water into each, then added a pinch of leaves from a tin. He sat down opposite her and set one cup in front of her and one in front of himself while they steeped.

"Do you have a name?" he asked.

"I do. Do you?"

His lips twitched. "Yes?"

"Excellent. We are both named beings." Clara picked up her cup and blew on it to cool it. The leaves swirled back and forth.

He pinched the bridge of his nose. "Istvhan, if it pleases you."

"Clara," she said. "Whether it pleases you or not, I'm afraid."

He lifted his teacup in salute. His expression was that of a man having a very trying day.

"Now," he said, "can you please tell me what in the name of the saints is going on here? We were passing through and I thought everything had been settled. I paid the Arral thanes for the use of their territory. And then the next thing I knew, this boy who was barely old enough to shave began screaming that I had offended him and came at me with a sword!"

"That would have been young Bastian," said Clara. She could imagine how it had happened. "Oh, dear."

"I tried not to kill him!" said Istvhan. "I tried very hard! I nearly threw my back out trying not to hit him! And I still don't know how I offended him in the first place!"

"It was nothing you did," she said. "He needed money."

His brows drew together in a fearsome scowl. "Someone paid him to attack me?"

"Oh goodness, no." Clara set her cup down. "They wouldn't take money for that. That would be to declare themselves hired killers — no, no."

"Technically *I* am a hired killer," said Istvhan dryly.

If he was expecting some kind of shocked response, he was disappointed. Clara took this in stride. "That's fine for *you*. You're not Arral."

He pinched the bridge of his nose again.

Clara folded her hands into her sleeves. "Let me try to explain this simply. Bastian's father is dead and he has — had — a mother and three sisters to support. He had no money for dowries, which means that he could not marry his sisters off. He was most likely hoping that if he challenged you to a duel, you would either try to buy him off, out of cowardice, or that he could kill you, in which case your men would pay a forfeit to him."

"A forfeit?"

Clara waved vaguely in the direction of the other tents. "Your swords and something of value from your house. One of your mules, perhaps."

"They just expected my men to say, 'Oh, you won, here's his sword and a mule?'"

"If you were Arral, they would have."

"I'm not Arral."

"No, which means you would not have a great many relatives to come after him if he killed you, so you were a safe target. At most, there would be your men here to deal with, not an entire angry household."

"But I killed him," said the man. "Mostly on accident. The damn fool practically ran onto my sword."

"Yes. From what little I observed in his house, Bastian was not terribly realistic in his expectations." The tea was finally cool enough to sip. It was strong and of reasonably high quality, but had clearly been sitting in the tin for quite some time. Still, Clara was thrilled despite the metallic undertaste. It tasted like home.

The taste was like a key, opening feelings that she had tried to lock away. *Home. My sisters. My life.* She felt a sudden tightness in her chest and shoved it down hard. This was not the time. It would not be the time for weeks. It could wait.

Istvhan took a deep breath and let it out. She was pleased to see that he had been sufficiently distracted by his own troubles that he had not noticed any lapse in her calm.

"So what happens now?" he asked.

"To you? Nothing," said Clara. "It's already happened. You killed him and his family paid the forfeit. You accepted it and no more is needed."

Istvhan leaned back and sighed with relief. "Well, thank the gods for that. And thank you for your assistance. May I offer you more tea before you go?"

Clara hid her expression behind her cup. He had, it was clear, rather the wrong impression. She had expected as much.

She took the moment to study him, now that her eyes had adjusted to the dimness. He was much darker than the Arral, but they were a pale, fair-haired people. Istvhan had an angular jaw, and his beard had been cut close to frame it. The scars on his face were mostly superficial, except for one across his cheekbone that stood out like a pale brand. A handsome man, she decided. Black eyebrows formed sharp wedges over dark, expressive eyes. At the moment, they expressed mostly weariness.

"I am afraid," she said, as gently as she could, "that I am not going anywhere."

"What?"

"You accepted the forfeit."

He wasn't slow. She could see the realization hitting.

"The sword and something of value from his house." Clara made a self-deprecating gesture at herself. "I'm afraid that would be me."

CHAPTER 2

"What?" said Istvhan.

The woman sitting before him, Clara, looked at him placidly. They might have been discussing the weather. "They had no money. It was either me or one of his sisters. His mother was very distraught, but she certainly would not give up one of her daughters when I was available."

"Available?"

"As a house slave." She drank the tea with every evidence of enjoyment.

"No," said Istvhan. "No. Definitely not. We do not keep slaves. *I* do not keep slaves." He could hear his voice rising and he clamped it down.

It was not good for a leader to lose his temper. It didn't inspire confidence. Admittedly, Galen had known him for years and was not going to abandon him for anything short of genocide, and the other men were being well paid for this trip, but it was a habit he didn't dare to get into.

It was also a very bad idea for Istvhan in particular to lose his temper, for reasons that had nothing much to do with the woman in front of him.

The kneeling woman seemed completely unbothered. "I'm glad

to hear it," she said. "Technically the Arral don't either, but it's a distinction without a difference in this case."

She was a big woman. Nearly as tall as he was, which put her well over six feet, with heavy breasts and belly, hips and thighs. Her shoulders were broad and she carried herself with the confidence of one who is used to being the most physically powerful person in the room.

Istvhan had carried himself like that once, though it had been beaten out of him a long time ago. There was always something bigger than you, no matter how big you were.

He wondered idly if he could take her in a fight. It seemed likely, but he wouldn't assume. Such assumptions had also been beaten out of him a long time ago.

"You'll go back at once," he said.

"I don't suggest that," she said. She had a low, husky voice, and though her tone was pleasant, it did not yield an inch. "They no longer have a man of the house. Bastian's oldest sister will swear as a son, I expect, and then he will take up the sword. But if you return me, then that means you have suggested that Bastian's forfeit was too high."

Istvhan could feel the situation spiraling out of his control. He had some vague notion of the Arrals' customs, but that had only been enough to convince him to stay out of their internal affairs completely. This dense web of forfeits and blood prices was nightmarish for an outsider to navigate, particularly an outsider who just wanted to pass through Arral territory and be on his way.

He thought he had navigated it. The Arral thanes had been more than willing to take money to let him pass through their lands. He had learned the polite forms of address for a stranger to use, he knew who to speak to and who to studiously not look at, and he thought that had been enough.

And now here was this woman kneeling in his tent, looking ridiculously calm, and telling him that she was part of a forfeit he didn't need from a duel he certainly hadn't wanted.

"Too high?" he asked weakly.

"Too high," Clara agreed. "And that would mean that you said his life was not worth what they thought it was. It will fall on the men of his house — in this case, the newly sworn son — to seek revenge for that insult."

Istvhan put his head in his hands. "You mean I'd have to duel his *sister?*"

"Well, his brother who had been his sister the day before. And as the Arral women do not handle weapons, his brother would have had about twelve hours to learn to use a sword."

Istvhan moaned.

Clara reached out and patted his arm kindly. "It's all right."

"But what am I supposed to do with you?"

"Well," she said. "You can take me with you. Or I suppose you could *try* to kill me."

He looked up, catching the emphasis. "Try?"

"Try." Her face was serene.

Istvhan kept his eyes from narrowing, although not without difficulty.

She's either utterly mad or knows something I don't...

"Let us assume for the moment that I don't kill strangers who aren't trying to kill me," he said.

"You *did* say you were a hired killer."

"Yes, but no one has hired me to kill *you.*"

"Then it would probably be best if you take me with you when you leave."

He shook his head. "No. Absolutely not. Out of the question."

"Don't be obstinate," she chided, as if she were not sitting in a stranger's tent, entirely at his mercy. "I'm quite useful. I was with the Arral long enough to make some sense of the finer points. I can keep you from giving offense."

"You're not Arral, then?" He wasn't surprised. Her robes were definitely not of Arral make, although she wore the shapeless hide-wrapped boots they all favored. Her hair was dark blonde and caught back in a neat braid, but her eyes were brown. The Arral mostly had blue eyes.

"No more than you."

He poured out more hot water, shaking his head. "I've no intention of staying with them for long. Only of passing through their lands. I have been hired to see a man and his goods through, that is all."

She smiled into her tea. "All will be well, friend Istvhan. The gods have brought us together. I was planning to escape myself."

"Then I'm glad to have been of service, and I wish you luck."

She laughed at that. "No, I'm afraid you don't get out of this so easily. You are going east, are you not?"

Istvhan met her eyes evenly, saying nothing.

"The men were talking about your deal with the thane," she said. "I'm not a mind-reader."

He raked his hand through his hair. Fighting a barely bearded boy had thrown him badly off his stride, and this maddening woman was not helping matters any. *Although she did keep you from making the situation with the Arral worse...or so she says...*

"Very well," he admitted. "We're going east for a little way."

"I, too, am going east." She sat back, looking as if she had resolved the situation to everyone's possible satisfaction. "My plan was to travel by night after I escaped."

"Then go," he said. "Light a candle for me when you reach your home."

For the first time, her smile slipped. "Ah," she said. Her eyes dropped to the tea, but not before he caught something flat and frightening in her eyes. "That, I fear, will not be so easy. My home was the convent of St. Ursa. It was burned some weeks ago, and my sisters kidnapped. It is their trail I follow."

Istvhan inhaled sharply.

"You're a *nun*?"

She made a dismissive gesture with one hand. "A lay sister, only."

A nun. Of course. Not a madwoman after all, although depending on who you asked, the distinction was very fine.

Istvhan closed his eyes.

He had to go east.

He had not *quite* lied. He was indeed a killer. It was merely that he was, or had been, a paladin of the Saint of Steel, and he had killed with the blessing of his god.

His god was dead. His order was dissolved, the paladins dead or mad. Only a few of them, like him and Galen, remained. He worked now for a temple that dealt in practicalities more than divinity, and he was on an assignment for them now, seeking the source of the strange clay men that had terrorized the city of Archon's Glory.

And if he did not turn aside and help a nun, his maternal relatives for nine generations would rise from their graves and come to his dreams to box his ears, with his mother at the forefront.

And Bishop Beartongue would be waiting to smack me senseless once their shades were done.

"Domina Clara," he said, bowing as he knelt so that his forehead nearly touched the ground, "I am your servant."

Clara looked at him with mild dismay. "Sister is fine," she said. "You don't need to bow. I'm really only a lay sister."

"I have found that with nuns, it is best to show respect." He straightened and gave her a smile that was open and charming and which Clara was certain was not half so open as it appeared to be.

He is not lying, she thought, *but there is a great deal going on behind his eyes.*

She weighed the ease of company in her travel across Arral territory against whatever might lie behind the mercenary's eyes, and came again to the same conclusion. It was almost always better to travel in a group than alone.

If things go south, I can leave them in enough disarray to get away. If I travel by night and avoid hunters... She grimaced. For a few hours, for a day, perhaps, but travelling that way for days on end held its own dangers. *It would be so easy to get lost. My sense of urgency never lasts.*

No, it was better to travel with the mercenaries as far as she could. This group was clean and professional-looking, armor in good repair, tents neatly assembled. They had attempted to talk their way out of the encounter with Bastian, and their leader seemed to respect women of the cloth. That respect would hopefully take her at least across Arral territory, and if St. Ursa looked kindly upon her, perhaps a little farther.

St. Ursa, I do not know if I am doing your will. You are not one to make Your wishes obvious to anyone. So I am doing my best, and if You need me to go in any particular direction, please make the arrangements as You see fit. It wasn't much of a prayer, but St. Ursa arguably wasn't much of a saint. A few dozen god-touched sisters and a passing mention when the locals were thanking every divinity that could conceivably be thanked. The nuns had gotten used to doing what they could and hoping things worked out for the best.

"Allow me to introduce the rest of my men," said Istvhan. He rose to his feet and held out a hand to help her up. She took it, amused by the courtesy, and then grudgingly impressed. She was not small and he took her weight with no sign of strain, barely shifting his feet at all.

"Galen you've met," said Istvhan, opening the tent flap and pointing. "My second in command." He nodded to the red-haired man waiting outside. She inclined her head to him, and Galen bowed dramatically over her hand.

"Domina Clara."

"Oh no," she said, laughing. "Just Clara. Sister Clara, if you must. I'm not listening to *Domina* from all of you. I'm only a lay sister. I've never aspired to take vows. My parents offered me to St. Ursa when I was young."

Galen's handsome face narrowed as he scowled. "Do you wish to leave, then?"

"It's been burned down," said Clara. "So that's moot, I'm afraid."

Galen blanched.

She took pity on him. She had wedged everything down into the dark place under her breastbone and his question had no power to hurt her. "That's why I'm going east. The raiders who kidnapped my sisters took them that direction. I need to find them again."

"And our fearless leader has graciously offered our services?" Galen raised an eyebrow at Istvhan.

"I grant you that I am a flawed man, Galen, but the day that I do not turn aside to help rescue a group of nuns…"

"If you say so, Boss."

"I do say so. Emphatically."

"Our business…" Galen trailed off eloquently.

"Will keep." Clara would have had to be very dense not to guess that there was a great deal of information being conveyed, but let it go. "This is Brindle, our mule driver," said Istvhan, clearly changing the subject. "A job-gnole."

The gnole by the wagon nodded to her. Clara had met the badger-like creatures on her trading jaunts up and down the canal. As a member of the job-gnole caste, Brindle would be referred to as *he*. He had a broad white stripe down his face and brindled fur elsewhere, though his fur was going salt-and-pepper gray over his eyebrows and along his muzzle.

"It's a pleasure to meet you," said Clara. "Do you know the gnole clan along Slicewater Canal?"

Brindle's ears flicked in a smile. "A gnole knows some, yeah. A gnole has far-cousins there."

Clara nodded. "I knew…ah…Shedding. And Cobbleclaw. Also mule drivers."

"Mules," said Brindle, with good-natured disdain. "A gnole prefers an ox." He glanced at the trio of picketed mules. "But temple says take mules, not an ox." He shrugged.

"Temple?"

"Rat-god Temple."

"Rat…oh!" Clara turned to Istvhan. "You're from the Temple of the White Rat?"

Istvhan shrugged. "We were hired there," he said. "They arrange things. They arranged Brant's barrels. We're supposed to come back with herbs for their healers or something."

Clara was glad to hear it. The Temple of the White Rat was that rarest of religious orders, one that simply found problems and solved them and tried to make life better for everyone involved. If they had hired Istvhan's men, then it was very unlikely that he was a murderous thug inclined to, for example, attempt to slit a nun's throat in the night. Still... "Barrels?"

Istvhan led her around the back of the wagon and tossed back the tarp. "Brant, this is Clara. Clara, Master Distiller Brant."

"You're escorting empty barrels?" said Clara, staring at the contents of the wagon.

"These barrels," said the small, balding man sitting on the back of the wagon, "are *Emperor Oak*."

He looked at her as he said it, clearly expecting her to recognize the name. Clara had been well-trained by nuns to admit ignorance when she had it. "I'm afraid I don't know what that is," she said.

"Emperor Oak! The greatest of trees! The greatest of all wood!" Brant waved his arms. "To age a whiskey in Emperor Oak is to confer grace upon it. These barrels are worth more than a palace."

"...I see."

"Brant's family keeps an Emperor Oak grove," said Galen, taking pity on her.

"*The* Emperor Oak grove." Brant's chest puffed up. "The only stand of the great trees in all the world."

"As rare as that?" asked Clara.

The little man deflated, his face almost a parody of sorrow, and yet Clara could see that it was genuine and deeply felt. "As rare as that," he said. "They were cut recklessly, and they grow only where they will, not where we wish them to. My family is the steward of the last grove. They are healthy now, but it is not enough. A single fire could wipe them all out. In summer, during lightning season, we do not sleep."

He turned abruptly and darted away, pulling something from his belt. As Clara watched, bemused, he jabbed his walking stick into the dirt, loosening it, then dropped a small object into the hole.

"Acorns," said Clara. "He's planting acorns?"

"Aye," said Galen. Brant moved ten feet away and dug another hole. "Everywhere we stop. He says that if even one in a hundred survive, it is another oak in the world."

Clara found that she was touched. "Now there is faith," she murmured.

She did not expect a mercenary to understand, but Galen nodded to her. "A faith that relies on neither gods nor priests," he said, and sighed. "Would that all faiths were so kind."

"Many of them are," she felt compelled to say, in defense of St. Ursa, who started no wars and asked for no sacrifice, and whose blessing upon her chosen was the purest kindness.

"And many of them are not," said Galen, his voice clipped. "Many would take all that a man is and leave him a husk."

Clara was still trying to think of a response when he turned and walked away.

"Don't mind him," said Istvhan. "We're about to break camp anyway, now that this...ah...unpleasantness is behind us. You may ride on the wagon, if you wish, or walk with us."

"I can walk."

He nodded and turned away, clapping his hands together, and shouting the orders to the men to break camp.

CHAPTER 3

They made rather more distance than Clara would have expected, given that they were traveling on foot with a wagon. The mules were clearly chosen for stamina rather than speed. She was impressed with the efficiency with which the mercenaries packed — eight troops, not including Galen and Istvhan, each loading up their personal gear and a tent and sliding it into one of the empty barrels lined with oilcloth. That explained the faint odor of whiskey she'd detected on Istvhan's tent.

Two of the troops were women. Clara confessed a certain relief about that. There was nothing about Istvhan that made her think that a woman would be in peril from men under his command, but one could never be too careful.

St. Ursa, it seems that You have guided me to a man who can help me, at least for travel through the mountains. Thank You.

All that said, it was still a long walk. As a matter of pride, she kept up, but her hip joints and her feet were less than pleased. Most of her travel selling goods for the convent was on foot or by barge, and she was no stranger to it, but she was also used to setting her own pace. (Arguably, she was also at the tail end of recovery from a fever so brutal that her captors had left her for dead, but Clara had gotten extremely tired of being sick and had decided a week ago that she was done with it. Her body did not necessarily agree, but Clara would be damned if she let it win.)

I suppose the marches will get longer, trying to catch up to the raiders. Ah, well. She put one foot in front of the other and concentrated on her breathing, telling herself that she did not feel lightheaded and anyway, she was a great deal better off than her sisters. She waited for Istvhan to call a halt, but he kept going until Galen said, "Boss? Getting too dark to see out here."

"I know, I know." He ran his hand through his hair. "I know. I was hoping to be past this particular thanedom, given everything, but I suppose it's not going to happen tonight."

"A mule is going to *trip,*" said Brindle accusingly.

"We should be safe enough," said Clara. "Bastian's attempt was considered...ah...in poor taste. They're not going to take revenge."

Istvhan shook his head. "You say that," he said, "and I believe you, but if manners are the only thing stopping them...well, I've seen plenty of men be very rude when it suited them. Rude and stabby."

He stood for a moment, clearly thinking, then turned to Clara. "Do you know how far the next thanedom is?"

Clara studied the horizon, trying to orient herself. Dark blue was creeping down the sky and black tree trunks rose to meet it. "Five miles," she said, "give or take."

"Too much for a mule in the dark," said Brindle, who apparently did not feel that respect for the chain of command applied to him.

"Right," said Istvhan. "No tents tonight. No fire, either. As far as we're concerned, this is enemy territory."

Clara heard a sigh sweep through the mercenary ranks, but no one argued.

The field on one side was flat enough that they could simply pull the wagon to the side of the road. Brindle slid off the wagon seat and began unhitching the mules.

"Don't get too comfortable, people," Istvhan called. "We'll be up at dawn and over the border. *Then* we can set up camp for a day or two while we talk to the next set of thanes."

"Boss," said Galen. And then, "Come on, you lot, you heard the man. Roll out your blankets. Waybread and jerky tonight, and we'll have something more substantial tomorrow."

Clara leaned against the wagon. She had neither food nor bedroll, and wondered if Istvhan had considered that, or if he simply expected her to fend for herself.

She need not have worried. The mercenary captain vanished around back of the wagon and then returned, carrying two waxed packages. He handed her one and opened the other himself.

The waybread was much the same as every travel bread ever baked: tough, faintly sour, and impervious to mold. The jerky was actually a pressed bar of meat with some kind of dried berries, and a great deal better than Clara was expecting.

"I know, right?" said Istvhan. "It's not half bad. I've had dried meat that was just on the edge of rancid and you had to wipe the mold off, but this stuff holds up remarkably well." He bit off half the bar and chewed, then swallowed. "Mind you, I won't cry if we can convince the next set of thanes to trade us some eggs."

Brindle walked past them, leading the two mules and talking softly to them in gnolespeech. Clara heard the wagon creak as the gnole climbed inside, and then rustling as he rummaged for something.

"Horses too much trouble?" she asked.

Istvhan nodded. "We're limited by the speed of the wagon anyway. Unless we wanted to use a dozen mules and change them out in teams, they won't go much faster than we'll walk. And this way we're only carrying a little extra grain for the mules, not a great load of food for a half dozen horses." He shrugged. "It's slower than I'd like, but no one's in a great hurry."

Clara *was* in a hurry, but not so much of one that she would seek a mount. Horses generally did not like her and she returned the favor.

"Lot of guards for some barrels," she said, testing the waters.

And now is the point where a lesser man would tense up, and then hurry to cover it up...

"Tell me about it," said Istvhan easily. "I told them we didn't need more than Galen and me, and maybe a third. This many people makes us look like a much richer target than we are." He shook his head. "But Brant's family has money, and they wanted half a regiment to guard their precious barrels, so here we are."

He trailed off. Clara looked over at him. The light had faded and the first stars were coming out. She could not make out his expression.

It all rang true and Clara had no reason to doubt anything he was saying. *And yet...and yet...*

She didn't press the issue. "Where are you going after you're out of the mountains?"

"The barrels are going to Morstone."

Morstone. Hmm. It was the largest city for a long way in any direction, an ancient trading hub along the sea coast. You could buy anything in Morstone, if you paid the right price. Clara had never been there, but she had heard all the stories...slave pits, charnel houses, pirate fleets.

"I've heard that's a very dangerous place."

"It is." His voice held nothing beyond the bare fact.

"Well. I do not know where my sisters have been taken, but perhaps you'll be rid of me before then."

"Mmm." Istvhan pushed away from the wagon. "There's a spare set of blankets," he said. "We'll be sleeping cold tonight, but if you want to sleep in the wagon, we can probably convince Brant to share."

"No need," said Clara. "I've slept on the ground many times. I thank you for your hospitality."

"It is the least we can do."

It was Galen who found her blankets and a spare mess kit — tin cup, fork, metal plate. "I'm grateful," said Clara, accepting them, "but I don't want to put any of your people out."

Galen shook his head. "You aren't," he said. "A long trip, somebody always loses part of their kit, or one of the blankets gets soaked and mildews, or someone falls in a river. It's just easier to keep a few spare sets so that no one spends half the trip having to share gear."

She had a long drink of water — the wagon held a water barrel as well, although not made of Imperial oak — and wandered off to relieve herself. When she returned, Istvhan gestured to the space under the wagon.

"A place of honor," she said, amused. The spot under the wagon would keep frost off and hold heat better than the open air.

"As befits your station, Domina," he said, and though she couldn't see his face, she could definitely hear the smile.

Clara rolled herself into the blankets. The ground was cold, but no harder than the floor of Bastian's house had been. She closed her eyes, extracted a rock from under her head, and was asleep before the rest of the camp had settled.

It was a cold morning. Frost coated the grass. Istvhan allowed a fire just long enough to heat water. They shared out tea so strong that it was bitter on the tongue, but it shocked everyone awake.

"A mule behaves," muttered Brindle to his charges. "A mule does what a mule is told, and a mule gets warm mash later." He rolled one dark eye at Captain Istvhan, as if daring the man to make a liar of him.

"As soon as we're across the border," agreed Istvhan. "Then we'll make a decent camp and see what the thanes have to say."

The thanes, as it turned out, were pleased to see them. They charged outrageously for passage through their territory — "I want to buy passage, not the entire town!" — and haggling it down was enjoyable for everyone.

"You could have gotten it for less," murmured Clara.

"Yes, but this way they think they've gotten one over on me, and it puts them in a good mood." Istvhan counted out coin and handed it to the thane's representative. The tall blonde man eyed the rest of the pouch and invited them all to the market the next day. Somewhat to Clara's surprise, Istvhan accepted.

"Is it safe, boss?" asked Galen, as the representative rode away.

"Markets are under truce," said Clara. "No one will challenge you to a duel. Otherwise people would get too fidgety and it would cut into profits for everyone."

"Good to know," said Istvhan. "And I'd like to ask around about a few things." He gave Clara a weighing look. "Would you be able to ask questions among the women for me? It's not a culture that looks kindly on strange men talking too closely with women."

"Certainly. What do you want to know?"

He and Galen exchanged a look. Galen murmured "Is this wise, boss?" in the language that Clara was still pretending not to know.

"Unexplained deaths," said Istvhan, ignoring him. "We were hearing some very unsettling rumors as we came north. I'd like to follow up on them."

Now that *is interesting.* "It's a hard country," said Clara. "People die all the time."

"The rumors were about decapitations, specifically. Which isn't normal, no matter how hard the country is."

Clara whistled. "Hadn't heard anything like that with Bastian's people."

"And if we're lucky, we won't hear anything here. I'd rather not have severed heads turning up in the soup." Istvhan folded his arms. "Nevertheless, the people we talked to were very concerned."

"I would be too, if people were turning up without heads."

Istvhan and Galen shared another brief glance. Clara wondered what they weren't telling her. *Had* she fallen in with a band of roving killers who were chopping off people's heads at random? It seemed unlikely, but you never knew. And it would be depressing. She rather liked Istvhan and Galen and would hate to have to kill them in self-defense. *St. Ursa, if you have sent me to be an instrument of Your vengeance, I wish that you would have waited until after I'd found my sisters...*

Fortunately, no one offered to cut her head off in the next few hours. They reached the agreed upon camping spot and Istvhan signaled a halt. "We'll be here for two days," he said. "If you've got any gear that needs mending, now's a good time to work on it."

Brant climbed out of the wagon and began planting acorns.

Brindle unhitched the mules and tethered them in a line. Clara turned back to Istvhan. He had a slight frown on his face, dark eyebrows pulled together. "I am sorry for the delay, Domina. I know that you are eager to reunite with your sisters."

Clara snorted. "It's been nearly a month, half of which I spent at death's door. You need not apologize. I have already accepted that there is no hope of catching up to them before they reach their destination. I only wish to learn what that destination is."

"And then?"

"And then I will find a way to get them back," said Clara. She cracked her knuckles. Istvhan's eyes widened just slightly, then he laughed.

"I pity the men who stand against you." He shook his head. "More immediately, I should ask if you mind sharing the command tent. I give you my word I will treat your honor as my own, but I will not be offended if your people do not let unwed men and women share sleeping quarters."

"Bah," said Clara. "I'm not so rude as to kick you out in the cold when you're being so gracious as to escort me across the mountains."

"It wouldn't be the cold," said Istvhan. "I'd make someone else share. They'd whine, but they'd live."

"Still seems unkind. And I suppose then I'd have to put the blasted thing up myself as well."

Istvhan laughed. "Actually two of the men are positive demons at tent building. They put all of them up and in return, they don't stand watches. They'll have the command tent up in ten minutes, while I'd still be laying out poles and trying to figure out which set goes where."

While Clara suspected that he was playing droll for her benefit, she had to admit that his men really had an uncanny knack for it. She went off to relieve herself just out of sight and when she returned, half the tents were erected and the pair was hard at work on the remainder. Istvhan held back the command tent flap and gestured. "Your palace, Domina."

"So kind."

He had already laid out his bedroll, which was a subtle bit of kindness. It let her place hers as far away as she liked, without making it awkward. She chose a spot halfway around the tent where nothing lay between her and the door. *And I wonder if he did that deliberately or if it was just a happy accident...*

Hard to say. It wasn't the sort of thing that most men ever had to think about. But there was more going on behind Istvhan's eyes than he let on, she'd bet money on it.

At the moment, what was going on behind his eyes appeared to be sleep. He was stretched out, using his bedroll as a bolster, eyes closed as if he was about to take an afternoon nap. Clara was reminded of the lynxes that prowled the forests near the convent — big, heavy-bodied cats with enormous paws and the same sense of lazy alertness. She'd seen pumas in the woods, which were undoubtedly larger, but they always seemed lanky to her, as if they had a hard time getting weight on. The biggest lynxes were almost spherical, with bunchy hindquarters and thick coats of fur.

This is probably not the time to be speculating on how bunchy the gentleman's hindquarters are. She swallowed a laugh. Nevertheless, the image stayed with her. There was a great deal of raw animal vitality to Istvhan, even when he was resting.

The tent was warming quickly from the brazier. The bright colors of the walls made it feel like summer. *Perhaps that's what he reminds me of, a cat in a sunbeam...*

"May I trouble you for some tea?" asked Clara. "I'll make it if you tell me where it is."

Istvhan opened his eyes a slit. "Metal tin on your left."

She was already reaching for it when she registered that he'd spoken in Harshek. She gave him a cross look and he smiled lazily.

"Well, blast," she said. "And here I was hoping to keep that to myself, in case you gave orders to murder me."

He chuckled, eyes closing again. "Clever, Domina. Do you speak any others?"

"Several, depending on how you count the various trade-tongues along the Slicewater. They've all got the same basic structure, but they take words from all over, so one end sounds different than the other. My monastery spoke Dryman, but we illuminate in Harshek."

"Ah, that's how you learned it."

"You?"

"A few. Harshek's my native tongue."

Clara let the tea leaves finish steeping and poured the tea out. She passed him a cup. He took it, rubbing his eyes with his free hand. "Dirt was a harder bed than I like, at my age," he said. "Particularly after a very awkward duel in the morning."

"I'm sorry. That couldn't have been pleasant."

"I don't mind killing," he said. "I don't enjoy it, but it's a thing I'm good at, so I do it as needed. But desperate young men..."

"It wasn't your fault."

"No, it wasn't." Istvhan gave her a wry look. "I'm not wallowing in guilt, Domina, if that's what you fear. I was doing my best to disarm him and he practically threw himself on my sword. Truly, there was nothing I could have done. Some people are going to be killed by the world, and it appears this time I was chosen to hold the blade. It's just such a damn waste, that's all."

Clara lifted her cup in silent acknowledgement.

She didn't quite know where to look, so she found herself looking down at her hands, and then at his hands on the tea cup. His were thick and powerful, the backs covered in dozens of short scars, the defensive wounds of any warrior. There was a particularly nasty puckered scar on the left one, right at the web between thumb and forefinger, as if he had been stabbed in the hand.

"It was a possessed peacock," he said.

She looked up, startled. "Beg pardon?"

"The scar you're staring at."

"I'm sorry, I didn't mean to stare." And then, because she couldn't possibly let it go, "A possessed peacock?"

Istvhan grinned. His teeth were very white. "Not truly possessed. A wonderworker whose peculiar talent was controlling poultry. We were hired to deal with him. He'd been using flocks of geese to terrorize a nearby town and demand protection money. He could only do domestic fowl, thank the gods, or he'd probably have sent swans and eagles after us."

Clara thought there was an almost infinitesimal pause before '*hired*' but it had been so slight that she might have imagined it. "So he attacked you with a peacock?"

"Drove its beak right into my hand. I was lucky. One of my compatriots took three geese to the head and we had to carry him out on a stretcher."

She lifted her teacup and frowned at him over it. "I am not sure how much of that story to believe."

"It is the god's own truth, Domina. I have been slightly nervous around certain shades of blue ever since." Istvhan drained his cup. "I'm for a nap," he said. "If you wish to wander, any of my men will accompany you if you ask."

"Is that an order?" she asked, raising an eyebrow.

"Not at all. You know as well as I do what the risks are here. You've lived through them." He rearranged the bolster and slouched back against it, closing his eyes. "It is as much for the benefit of my nerves as your safety, Domina."

"We must save your nerves at all cost," said Clara. "Never fear, Captain Istvhan, I could use a nap myself." She stretched out on her bedroll, and if he said something clever in response, she fell asleep too quickly to hear it.

CHAPTER 4

Istvhan dozed, but only lightly. It was the kind of nap that wasn't quite sleep, and he could have been on his feet with a sword in his hand in a matter of seconds.

As no one came through the door waving weapons and shouting that he had murdered their second cousin twice removed, he got perhaps an hour of rest. Occasionally, he would glance over and see Clara sleeping on her bedroll. She had curled on her side and reminded him of a hibernating bear. A large, powerful beast, currently at rest, and yet he had a suspicion she could be dangerous if roused.

He still didn't know how he felt about her. They were, at the moment, going the same direction, and she had not slowed his mission at all. And certainly his mission was not so time-sensitive that he could not turn aside for a convent of kidnapped nuns.

And yet...

There was something reserved about her. He had no doubt that her story was true, but she was telling him only so much as he needed to know. Which was...oh, not suspicious, not at all, you didn't fall into the lap of what appeared to be a mercenary captain and immediately blurt out your life story. It was just that when he looked at her, watching and weighing, she looked back and he was quite certain that she was watching and weighing him the same way.

Istvhan was pleasant and generally good-humored and because he was very large, he knew that people thought he must be stupid. They did not expect him to look any farther than his next meal or his next job or his next woman. He wondered if they thought the same of Clara, that because she was very large, she must be slow and not terribly bright.

And I wonder if that is as dangerous a mistake to make about you as it is about me?

She had spoken so blithely about escaping her captors and traveling by night. His first thought had been that such things were a great deal more difficult than civilians thought.

His second thought, however, was that Sister Clara did not strike him as a fool.

She sat up. He hadn't known that she was awake, and that, too, was interesting. She had a complicated expression, although it didn't seem to be directed at him.

"Are you married?" asked Clara abruptly.

Istvhan's first thought was that she was somehow propositioning him. His second was that she was a nun and that was just not a thing that happened. His third thought, somewhat belatedly, was that he wouldn't actually mind if she did. She was...interesting.

Interesting, my ass. She's built to the same scale you are, and that's rare enough to be fascinating. And she was cool as ice sitting on your doorstep with a sword and a lot of angry men behind her.

She also had great thighs. Istvhan had always quite admired women's thighs. And her breasts were built to the same scale as the rest of her, which meant that there was enough of them to fill even Istvhan's enormous hands.

She's also a nun. Bishops, yes, priests sometimes, nuns never. There are rules.

He took refuge in amusement. "No woman's been fool enough for that, I'm afraid."

Clara did not meet his eyes. She was...Saint's blood, was she *blushing?*

"Ah. I see. Ah...do you have, perhaps...oh, Ursa's tits." She folded her arms and faced him directly. "I've got no luggage and I own nothing. Have you got any clean rags?"

Istvhan burst out laughing. "Oh, is that all? I may not be married, Domina, but I have many, many sisters. I'll ask Marli and Thorn. One of them's bound to have something."

"That would be a great kindness," said Clara.

Istvhan's smile faded as he let the tent flap drop behind him. He tried to trace the source of the heaviness in his chest, and realized that it was, indeed, disappointment.

Saint help him, he'd actually wanted to think that she was propositioning him. Which meant that he was attracted to a nun.

Bloody hell.

It made no sense. He was not desperate in any sense. His last relationship had ended less than a month ago. Given that Bishop Beartongue, highest ranked of the priests of the Temple of the White Rat in Archenhold, had nearly run him into the ground, he'd been looking forward to a few months of celibacy to recuperate. The bishop was a marvelous woman, but she had a great many aggressions to work out and limited free time to do it in.

He had no regrets about the relationship, nor its end. Istvhan had been a port in a storm and knew it. The bishop understood human hearts too well to play with his. "Much more of this and either you will fall in love out of self-defense or you will begin to think of this as a service to the Temple, like bodyguard duty," she'd said. "And I have no desire to be an object of unrequited love or patient service. Better to call it a pleasant interlude for both of us."

Istvhan had made a token protest, but she was right. Not that he was in any danger of falling in love these days, but all paladins ran on guilt and duty in equal measure. He had taken the assignment to the north with a sense of relief, and not just because he was having a hard time keeping up with her.

Which was why it was so odd that he immediately had such thoughts about a woman he had only just met. Particularly a nun.

The lure of the unobtainable. Which is all your foolishness and none of hers. Istvhan had never yet blamed a woman because he was attracted to her, and he certainly wasn't about to start now.

Truth was, he'd been glad to go for more reasons than love or lack thereof. His people were nomads, and while they often stayed in one place for months at a time, sooner or later, they did move on. He had stayed in Archenhold longer than he had ever stayed in one place, and wanderlust had been nagging at him.

So of course you go haring off to the frozen north and a group of thanes who think outsiders make good sword practice. Excellent plan. He gazed up at the clear sky with its promise of cold and the serrated ranks of pine trees and filled his lungs with the scent.

Marli looked up from where she was scrubbing her mess kit down with a handful of sand. "Captain?"

"Our new arrival has no supplies, and I fear that the phase of the moon has caught her out. Do you or Thorn perhaps...?" He made a vague hand gesture, hoping that she would read whatever she needed to into it.

Marli snorted. "Not a concern of mine," she said, "but Thorn will. Half a moment." She ambled off to a tent and a minute later the other female member of the troop appeared from it and went off in the direction of the command tent. Istvhan decided to leave them to it. He had enough sisters to know what was going on, and he'd also known enough women to know that they didn't all enjoy discussing bodily functions in the presence of strange men. *Or her culture may have something against it. I don't know a damn thing about where she's from. Hopefully she's traveled enough not to hold it against me if I do something egregious on accident.*

Then again, she was enlisting his help to chase down her fellow nuns, so she was likely to put up with a great deal from him in return for that help. *Which means that I must be doubly careful that she is not tolerating things because she feels she must...* He rubbed his forehead. The larger part of power was understanding the power you had over others, even if you would rather not have had that much power in the first place.

He had power over the people under his command as well, so he spent the next few hours on a slow circuit of the camp, checking in with each of his people, trying to identify anything that needed fixing before it became a problem. Most of the problems were very small and could be fixed easily — reactions to the altitude, bits of kit gone missing and needing replaced. The majority could be fixed with a trip to the market, a trip to the medicine kit, or simply with more frequent stops. Brindle delivered a lengthy diatribe about mules, the problem of mules, the attitude of mules, the equipment sent out with the mules, and why oxen were superior to mules in every possible way. Istvhan had listened to this particular diatribe four times already since leaving Archenhold and was resigned to it by now. At the end, Brindle grudgingly confirmed that a gnole had no outstanding issues that a human could fix and Istvhan went away again, feeling as if he had survived a battle.

Galen was last. "Doing well?"

"Well enough."

"Nightmares?"

Galen shrugged. "Nothing bad. Nothing dangerous." He raked a hand through his dark red hair. "I hate to say it, brother, but I think that it's easier out here. Not at the Temple."

Istvhan nodded. There were seven surviving paladins of the Saint of Steel. They lived at the Temple of the White Rat in Archon's Glory, serving as best they could. The Temple had set aside a place for them, a place of calm and quiet, of order and structure. It had been a great kindness and it had helped many of them heal.

The only problem was that when you were in a place of healing, it was hard to forget that you were damaged.

He said as much to Galen, who nodded. "We're all broken," the redhead said. "I don't think any of us are going to forget it. But here..." He stretched his arms out. "I don't know if it's just that the Temple is a reminder of what we've lost or if it's just that I can't be as broken out here, so I'm not. Maybe I'll collapse the first time we get in a real fight.

Maybe the battle tide will come on me and I won't get loose and you'll have to take me out."

Istvhan shrugged. "These things happen."

"But the upshot is that I'm having fewer nightmares here. Whether because I don't feel safe having them or I don't *need* to have them...eh, the Saint only knows." Galen grinned abruptly. "Either way, I'll take it. How's your new friend?"

"The nun? Well enough. Not telling us everything."

"We're not telling her everything, either."

"Yes, which is why I'm not holding it against her." Istvhan shrugged. "It's been, what, a day? We'll get there, or not."

Later that night, when they finally turned in, he thought that it had been a very long day for everyone. Clara had clearly bathed and was combing her hair out. Her teeth were chattering. "Saint's blood," Istvhan said. "Did you wash in a stream? That's pure snow melt. Cold as a nun's ars—"

He heard the words coming out of his mouth too late to stop them and so snapped his teeth shut and nearly choked.

Clara bit her lower lip and made a tiny squeak, utterly incongruous from such a large woman, and began to laugh helplessly. "Well," she managed to say, "mine's certainly that cold now, yes."

Istvhan buried his face in his hands. "Domina," he said weakly. "I am so very sorry. I am a thoughtless boor not fit for polite company."

She snickered. "You've very kindly agreed to take me through the mountains. We'll call it even."

"You're bound to be better company than the barrels, anyway."

She chuckled. "And this is much more comfortable than sleeping in ditches." The last chuckle came out partly as a sigh. "You must think it odd that I am laughing so much when...well..." Her gesture toward the tent flap encompassed the world outside, presumably including the raiders.

"Not in the slightest." Istvhan leaned forward, wanting to touch her arm and offer comfort, but not sure that she'd appreciate it. "I am a warrior, Domina. Those of us who make jokes usually fare better after the battle than those of us who don't." He thought of Galen, who was never at a loss for a joke and who sometimes screamed in the night until he was hoarse. *But he is alive to do it. Most of the Saint of Steel's chosen did not fare so well.*

"When we were in the wagon," said Clara, sounding entirely too calm, "when the raiders were driving us toward Arral country, we sang. And we prayed. And Sister Sigrid told us terrible jokes, and I laughed harder than I have in years."

"Sometimes it's the only way." He didn't like the calm in her voice. Calm like that was usually brittle. But there was nothing brittle about Clara, and he did not know her well enough to say anything more. He stretched himself out on his bedroll, turned on his side, carefully facing away from her side of the tent in case she had to disrobe. *The comb is standard in the kit, but presumably she has no extra clothing either. Damnation, I'm the only one who's got anything that will fit her, and I don't exactly carry a nun's robes as part of my travel gear.* "I've got a spare cloak that should fit you," he said aloud. "It's cold in the mountains this time of year."

"That would be a kindness. Thank you, Captain."

"Did the Arral not clothe you?"

He heard the rustle of fabric and the sounds of movement. "Bastian's mother nursed me back to health when I was half-dead of fever. That took weeks of time and food, and she had little else to spare." More sounds of movement. He gazed at the small travel lamp, watching the flame. "It was complicated, and though I wish Bastian had not died, I am glad that you came along before the issue of my captivity became too pressing. It would have become...awkward."

He snorted. "That's one way to put it. Settled, Domina?"

"I am, thank you."

Istvhan snuffed the light and let the darkness take them.

CHAPTER 5

The mercenaries approached the market the next day with their hands on their weapons and their mouths watering. The smell of cooked meat and spices filled the air. Galen made a sound like a man in the throes of exquisite pain.

Lacking money, clad in Istvhan's cloak, Clara ambled around the market until she discovered a knot of women sitting together behind one of the buildings. Several were smoking pipes, and most of them had drop spindles whirling in one hand while they talked. They looked up at her with interest, but no hostility.

"May I join you?" she asked.

"Sit, sit," said the oldest, a tiny woman with a wrinkle-lined face. "You are the one who Keela took in, yes?"

Keela. Bastian's mother. "I am," said Clara. "Though I was given as blood price to the mercenaries." She jerked her chin in the general direction of the men.

"Ah," said one of the others. "Their leader's a fine big one, isn't he?"

Two of the women cackled. Another gave Clara a worried look. "They have not mistreated you, have they, youngest sister?"

"No, no," said Clara. "Their leader has been very courteous. Though he is worried."

Having dropped that bait, she sat back. The oldest woman raised an eyebrow and gave her an incisive look, but went along. "And what worries him is...?"

"Rumors," she said. "The lands he traveled through before were plagued with a killer who cut off people's heads. He does not know if he has left the killer behind or not."

Looks were exchanged between the Arral women. Several spoke to each other, but their accents were thick and they spoke too quickly for Clara's limited skill to follow. The oldest woman sucked on her pipe stem and then blew a cloud of smoke into the air over her head.

Finally, one of the women turned back to Clara. "We know of what you speak, perhaps." She was middle-aged, with gray hair and a silver-gray shawl with glints of metallic embroidery. She glanced to the oldest as if for approval.

Clara kept her eyes and her voice low. "I would be glad to have something to tell him. It would perhaps gain his favor."

The oldest studied her for a moment, then nodded to the woman in the silver shawl.

"My thane holds the south," said the woman with the shawl. "A month ago, my sister's cousin went missing. Two days later, hunters found his head. Cut off. And a body. But." She leaned forward and tapped Clara's knee, her face intent. "It was not *his* body."

Clara inhaled sharply. "Whose was it?"

The woman shook her head. "A woman. Not a woman of the Arral. But her head was gone as well."

This was much stranger and much more alarming than Clara had expected. No wonder Istvhan had been asking questions. "How terrible!"

"Devil work," said the oldest, blowing another cloud of smoke.

"Any others?" asked Clara.

Murmured denials. The woman in the shawl spread her hands. "The river is running high now," she said. "If there were more, they would float away. No one I know has been lost, but there are thanes we do not speak to."

More nods. "I thank you, older sister," Clara said. "This is not good news, but he will be glad of it."

The Arral women nodded. They understood the importance of proving one's value to the men.

Clara spent a few more minutes with them. She accepted a puff on a pipe from one woman and duly admired another's toothless grandchild. The conversation drifted to other things. Nothing else attracted her attention, mostly complaints about the weather and the harvest, a well that was inexplicably not filling with the recent rains, a child down with spots. It reminded Clara of being back in the convent, surrounded by the small sounds of practical things, the motions of drop spindles, the sound of women's voices.

She was not prone to homesickness by nature. She had chosen the life of a trader for the convent because she could leave for weeks and not feel the weight of time passing. But suddenly the weight of what she had lost — what might be lost forever — rose up and took her by the throat.

Not now. This is not the time. She pinched the bridge of her nose to keep back tears. She had not cried behind the iron bars of the raider's wagons. She had not cried in Bastian's house. She would not cry now. It was not safe, no matter how much the Arral women reminded her of home.

Blessed St. Ursa, give me your peace a little longer. She pushed the tears down. The sisters of St. Ursa learned to let strong emotions pass through them, to remain calm even when their hearts were roiling. The beast inside her must not wake. She waited for the burning behind her eyelids to fade.

When she opened her eyes again, the oldest woman had taken her pipe from her mouth and was looking at her intently. Though the blue of her eyes had faded, her stare was no less fierce. Clara was reminded of a wolf's eyes.

"You say he does not mistreat you," said the Arral elder.

"He does not," said Clara. It was much easier to think of Istvhan than the convent. From what she had seen so far, it was hard to imagine him mistreating anyone. Courtesy could (and often did) hide cruelty, but he was too comfortable with his power. Only the weak needed to lord it over others in that fashion.

"And yet...?"

Clara wiped at her eyes, not bothering to hide it. "I think of what I have lost," she said. "You remind me, all of you." Which was true, so far as it went.

"Ah." Heads nodded around the circle. Yes. This was also understood. Arral women left their families and went to their husbands, sometimes in separate thanedoms, and did not return.

"We all lose much," said the oldest, tapping the ashes from her pipe. "But you are our forever youngest sister. Do not forget."

"I won't," said Clara. They had nursed her back to health, even if she had ultimately been somewhere between a prisoner and a slave. By their reckoning, to be even the lowest rank of Arral was a gift, compared to being thaneless.

She rose to her feet. "I must return," she said. "Thank you all."

The oldest woman went with her, somewhat to Clara's surprise. She ambled up to Istvhan and planted herself in his path, hands folded on her cane.

Istvhan's eyebrows went up, but he bowed very deeply to her. "Honored elder," he said.

She snorted, looking him up and down with her ancient blue eyes, and then spoke, slowly and carefully. "Do you understand my words?"

"Yes, ma'am."

"Hmm." She looked him up and down again. "You are big, outsider."

Istvhan's lips twitched, but he said, very gravely, "Yes, ma'am."

She lifted her cane and poked him in the midsection. "You have our forever youngest sister with you."

"I...ah..." Istvhan glanced at Clara. Clara pointed to herself and nodded vigorously. "Oh. Yes, ma'am," he said.

"You will treat her well."

"Yes, ma'am."

"You will not beat her."

"No! Certainly not!"

"You will not make her carry things that are too heavy."

"Ah...no, ma'am."

Another poke with the cane. "You will let her sleep afterward!"

"Ma'am, I...ah..." Istvhan looked helplessly over at Clara. They were attracting quite a crowd. Apparently the prohibition against outsider men approaching women did not apply to tiny elderly ladies scolding men three times their size. "I...that is..."

"You will!" A determined poke with the cane.

"Yes, ma'am," whispered Istvhan, looking, for all his size, like a very small boy caught with his hand in the sweet jar.

The muffled gasps of laughter behind her were definitely Galen. Clara wasn't sure whether to laugh with him or turn scarlet and sink into the ground with mortification.

"Hmmph." The old Arral woman's scowl lightened. She poked him one last time with her cane, then nodded to Clara. "You will tell us if you have anything to complain of, youngest sister."

Clara bowed very deeply, not trusting herself to speak. Galen was losing his battle with hilarity behind her.

Istvhan watched the old woman totter away on her cane. His expression resembled nothing so much as a poleaxed steer. "What... just...happened?" he asked.

Clara coughed a few times until she had herself under control. "Ah...I'll explain later?"

"Will you?"

"...maybe?"

Galen let out one loud, explosive laugh and immediately tried to look as if it had been someone else.

Istvhan's eyes narrowed. "Something funny, Galen?"

"Yes, Boss."

The two of them glared at each other for a few seconds, and then Istvhan's face cracked in an enormous grin. "Surprised you lasted that long," he admitted. "Saint's blood, what a woman! I wonder if she's single." Galen snickered.

"Anything more we need here?" asked Clara. "I did learn something you might be interested in."

"Galen, is the food situation handled?"

Galen nodded. "They're overcharging us terribly for food that won't keep through winter. About what I expected."

"No surprise there. All right. Round everyone up — I don't want to leave people to get in trouble, market truce or no market truce."

It took a bit longer to get back to their camp, even with the assistance of the extra mule. Galen, who was acting as quartermaster, had loaded up on potatoes. Brindle grumbled when he saw them.

"You don't like potatoes?"

"A gnole likes potatoes just fine. A mule doesn't like hauling so many of them."

"They're cheap and they last forever. Be grateful I didn't get us fifty squash to go along with them."

"A mule would tell a human where to put his squash..."

Istvhan waved Galen over, leaving Brant and Brindle to rearrange the wagon. "Now then, Domina, can you explain what just happened, other than the bit where I'm being scolded like a depraved monster in the middle of the market?"

"Arral don't keep slaves," said Clara. "They adopt them. I am 'forever youngest sister' to Bastian, meaning that I have the lowest rank of any women in his house. Of course, in a society where women can't hold property and can be sold, it's functionally identical to slavery, but the Arral would get extremely offended if you called it that." She rolled her eyes.

Istvhan gazed up at the sky, as if seeking strength. Either he found it or he gave up, because he looked back down and put his hand over his heart. *"Please* tell me if I am making you carry any loads too heavy for you, Domina."

"Of course," said Clara sweetly. "As long as you let me sleep afterward."

Galen bit the side of his hand and made a noise like an injured goose.

Istvhan thumped him, grinning. "All right, all right. Did you learn anything else?"

"Oh yes. Your killer has been here. A month ago. Left a severed head but no body, and a different body, with no head."

The two men's amusement stopped instantly. They traded looks.

"That doesn't surprise you," said Clara. "Which is interesting, because most people would be *very* surprised by a headless body turning up alongside the wrong head." She folded her arms and leaned back.

Istvhan had a remarkably good poker face. Galen didn't. Green eyes flicked to Istvhan, then to Clara, then to the floor.

"Is there something you'd like to share with me?" The trick was to use the same voice the abbess used. The nun voice. The one that assumed that you had done something wrong and you knew it and everyone knew you knew it and you just had to spit it out and get it over with.

Istvhan was made of stern stuff, she'd give him that. His eyelid twitched, but nothing else. Galen, however, snapped like a twig.

"Ist...Boss...ah...maybe we should tell her." He spoke Harshek, so apparently Istvhan hadn't mentioned the language issue.

Istvhan sighed heavily. "If we're ever being tortured, I'm making you go last."

"Only if they use nuns, boss."

"Also, she understands every word you're saying."

Galen swore. Clara inclined her head and said, "I can read and write it, too."

Istvhan gave up. "We've heard about it," he said. "It's not just the chopping off heads. Something very weird is going on, obviously. Someone is leaving bodies behind, and sometimes heads. Sometimes they carry one from one place to another."

"Do you know who it is?"

Galen stared at the ground. Istvhan shook his head. "Not specifically, no. We think it may be more than one person, perhaps some kind of cult. Whoever they are, we seem to be behind them, and I suspect they could make a great deal of trouble for us. If we get blamed for their crimes...well. I would like to know everything I can about what I may be walking into."

He said it smoothly, evenly, plausibly. He met her eyes. His hands were relaxed and his gaze was direct. And Clara was quite certain that he was lying through his teeth.

"You seem well-traveled for a nun," said Istvhan the next day, as they walked ahead of the mules. The air was crisp and cool and though they had set a brisk pace, the day was mostly downhill and easier going.

"I'm a lay sister, not an anchorite." Clara rolled her eyes at him. "Don't you have nuns where you're from?"

"We have *lots* of nuns," said Istvhan. "That's why I'm scared of you."

Clara laughed. She laughed often, and Istvhan was glad of it. "All right, fair enough. Well, my convent sells truffles, rare herbs, and embroidery. Except that my embroidery is not terribly good, so my primary job was to travel up and down the Slicewater Canal, selling our goods."

Istvhan nodded. "Well, that explains it, then."

"Explains what?"

"How you learned about the Arral so quickly. How you knew a gnole clan." He grinned. "How you took Brant and his acorns in stride."

"I think the acorns are quite touching. I hope his trees grow very strong."

Istvhan thought, privately, that it also might explain why Sister Clara had not aspired to take any more restrictive vows. Depending on her background, the life of a trader might not have been available to her, except through the convent.

"Have you ever traveled this way before?" he asked.

She shook her head, looking at the windswept landscape, cut with narrow, tree-filled pockets. "A lonely place," she said. "The Arral clans are spread out and not particularly interested in truffles. And they do their own embroidery." She rubbed the back of her neck. "I was always telling Sister Narzil that we needed to expand further and sell our wares farther afield than just the canal, but I would have gone south, not east."

"Truffles are not so easy to find," said Galen, coming up alongside them.

"And what do you know about it?" asked Istvhan, amused. Galen was a good man, but not above pretending to far more expertise than he actually possessed.

"Ye of little faith. My grandmother was a healer. But there's no money in healing, so she sold herbs. A truffle was a rare thing when she could find one, and it kept her in firewood and lamp oil for a season."

Istvhan held up his hands. "I yield, I yield. Very well, you are a master of truffles."

"Nothing like it." Galen grinned at Sister Clara, and although Istvhan knew that smile meant absolutely nothing but friendship — Galen had definite tastes and they did not run to women — he felt a twinge of...*concern. Definitely concern. Not jealousy, because that would be foolish. I simply don't want the good sister to be led astray.*

She's a nun. People like Galen do not lead nuns astray.

And what about people like you?

He missed the next sentence or two, but was pulled out of his thoughts when Clara laughed again. "No, we keep no truffle pigs," she said. "Pigs are entirely too intelligent and I do not trust them. The young ones are well enough, but they all seem to go a bit mad when they grow into their balls."

"A common enough affliction," said Istvhan blandly.

"Yes, it seems to be." She gave him a wry look. He gave it right back to her. "Other people can keep them and I will eat ham and bacon with a glad heart. And trade truffles for them."

"So how do you find them, then?" asked Galen. "No hounds, no pigs? Even my grandmother had a truffle hound, though he was half-blind and snored like the end of the world."

"We have our ways," said Clara. "You cannot expect me to give up the secrets of my order so easily."

Galen clapped a hand to his chest. "A nun has found me untrustworthy."

"Lay sister."

"Either way. My life is blighted." He cast a tragic look at Istvhan. "Have you ever heard such a thing?"

"A very wise nun, clearly."

"Lay sister."

"You keep saying that."

"It's true." Her lips twitched. "I am not a nun, not in the sense that you mean."

"You live in a convent and serve your goddess, do you not?"

"Saint, but yes."

"Then I fear, sister, that by his standards you will forever be a nun." Galen leaned over and patted her arm sympathetically. "It's all right. You learn to bear up under our fearless leader's assumptions."

"I haven't taken any of the major vows, beyond serving the convent and..." She waved her hand, presumably indicating whatever other vows came alongside that. "I'm not sworn to poverty or penitence or celibacy. Granted, poverty has mostly found me, but that's more a matter of life than oaths."

The word *celibacy* hit Istvhan square in the chest and settled... somewhat lower.

"And celibacy?" asked Galen, giving her an exaggerated eyebrow wiggle. "Has it found you, too?"

She aimed a mock-swat at him. "I suspect, Ser Galen, that my celibacy or lack thereof is a matter of purely academic interest for you."

He ducked, laughing. "Well, you're not wrong. Though if you know any handsome lay *brothers* of your order, I wouldn't say no to an introduction."

"I fear we're an exclusively female order, but I'll keep an eye out."

Galen gave Istvhan a brief, smug look behind Clara's back. A you-can-thank-me-later look. Istvhan grunted.

"Ignore him," said Galen. "He's from around the southern border of Charlock. They can't grow a truffle to save their lives there."

"Desert country, isn't it?"

"Hills and desert," Istvhan said. "Similar to the Arral in some ways, although we are much more flexible about our women and our honor."

"I thought you came from the south, not the west."

"I did. I left my homeland years ago, when I...when I was twenty. My sisters mostly stayed. They run things now. I go back every few years so that my nieces don't forget my face."

"His people are all bandits," said Galen. "Don't let him convince you otherwise."

"And yours are all madmen who paint themselves blue and fight naked."

Galen looked affronted. "My grandmother would never." He paused, sliding Clara a sly look. "Now, my *great*-grandmother..."

"I am certain she struck terror in the hearts of all who beheld her," said Clara.

"Most definitely. My grandfather didn't stop running until he'd reached the southern coast, and he took my grandmother with him."

Clara laughed. She was not classically beautiful by any stretch, but she had a marvelous laugh and an air of vitality that painted pictures in his head about what that laugh would sound like in his ear.

Stop. A nun is a nun is a nun is still a nun.

A nun not sworn to celibacy is...probably someone's fetish. Istvhan wasn't sure if it was one of his, but part of him seemed very interested in finding out, which made no sense at all. He'd taken this trip north because he needed time to recuperate from the Bishop. He'd been worn to a shadow. Human flesh could only take so much.

Galen said something he didn't quite catch that made Clara laugh so hard she had to stop and put her hands on her knees. Istvhan thought dark thoughts and looked away, over the hills, wondering what was wrong with him.

CHAPTER 6

Days passed, and absolutely nothing bad happened.

Clara did not want to be frustrated by this. It was a good thing. You didn't hope for fights, because fights too often led to someone's death. It was just...well...

Even an awkward standoff! Even a difficult bit of negotiation! Something to prove that I'm useful and don't need to be dropped off at the first safe convent along the way!

But they drove through the territory held by the Arral thanes and everyone was polite and no one attacked. Even the weather was fine. The sky was cloudy every day, but that only served to hold the last of the autumn warmth. The mornings were crisp and bright and there was no scent of snow on the wind. Clara tried not to take it personally.

Why is it so important to me to prove myself to Istvhan and his men? It's not as if I'd stay at a convent anyway. If they decide to leave me, I'll just go back to my first plan.

And yet...and yet. It was important to her, for reasons Clara couldn't quite clarify to herself. She was used to traveling alone. Most of the time, she preferred it. She had taken over the job of selling the convent's wares along the canal precisely because she favored it over life in the convent. She could spend days alone with her thoughts, and then be around people without having to be deeply involved in their lives. Her encounters were necessarily shallow ones, good-natured, friendly without making close friends. She never stayed anywhere long enough to overstay her welcome, never long enough to become anyone's confidant or anyone's lover for more than a night or two. At most, she might spend a week on a barge, navigating through the long, lonely stretch two-thirds down the canal. There were one or two barge families that she was always glad to see, and they were glad to see her, and they would travel together for that week, and then part ways for another two or three seasons without a pang.

Days with Istvhan and Galen and Brindle and the others were different. She tried all of her usual methods for being a pleasant travel companion. She laughed at jokes and shared gossip, she did her share of digging latrines and assisting with mules — the mules didn't care for her, but the mules didn't care for anyone, so no one remarked on it — she cooked when it was her turn, and she kept up the pace even when exhausted. She helped Galen haggle and got the prices down to something that was merely egregious rather than obscene. And yet some part of her brain kept whispering that these seasoned warriors must hold her in, at best, good-natured contempt. That all their kindness was because she was a nun in distress, not because she was worthy in her own right.

Stranger yet, she *cared.*

It is easier to travel together in hard country. That's all. That must be all. And I was lonely because I felt so alone and helpless without my sisters, even in Bastian's house. It is only hope and camaraderie that makes me feel less lonely with these people. That's the only reason I am reluctant to part ways, and why I keep hoping something will happen to prove that I am useful.

But nothing did.

The most interesting thing to happen for nearly a week was a mouse getting into the sacks of grain kept for the mules. Brant was extremely upset by this, fearing that his barrels would be violated in some fashion, whether by gnawing or little puddles of mouse pee, Clara wasn't quite clear.

Istvhan listened diplomatically for nearly a quarter of an hour, delaying their start, before he finally said, "Master Brant, I do not know what I can do about this. I do not have a cat or a terrier stashed in my tent. I could put their little heads on pikes as a warning to others, but this is beyond me. Tell me what you need."

Brant wanted every piece of food and gear checked immediately for mice. This would have taken hours and Istvhan had a set look on his face, when Brindle leaned in and said, "Don't smell mouse anywhere else."

"You can smell them?" asked Brant, startled.

"A human can't?"

Istvhan and Brant both shook their heads.

"God's stripes. Humans can't smell. Smells strong. Smells *mousy*." Confronted with their apparent ignorance, he grabbed handfuls of whiskers in apparent despair. "A gnole sniffs the food, lets a human know if mouse smells, eh?"

"Will that work for you?" asked Istvhan.

Brant nodded. "I should like to at least inspect the barrels," he said.

"As you wish, Master Distiller."

Clara, seeing an opportunity to be useful, stepped in. "Tell me what you need lifted," she said. Istvhan cast her a grateful look and fled the scene.

There was no damage. Her tea went cold while she was helping Brant restack the barrels, and he saw her grimace when she picked up the mug.

"Here," the little man said. "My fault. Let me fix it." He laid a finger on the side of the mug and a moment later, warmth began to seep through the metal and into Clara's fingers.

"What did you do?" she asked, astonished, as steam rose from the tea.

"Nothing much." Brant glanced around as if embarrassed. "It's a fairly useless talent. I can heat up liquids. Small amounts, anyway. It would take me an hour to boil a tea kettle."

He seemed anxious about how she'd react. The world was full of minor wonderworkers, most of them with very minor talents, but Clara knew that they still made people nervous sometimes. She smiled at him. "As the one with cold tea, it seems pretty useful to *me*."

Brant sighed. "Better I should be able to sprout acorns."

"Few of us have such blessed talents. Thank you."

"My pleasure, Sister."

She walked away, sipping her newly warmed tea. Did Istvhan know about the man's talent? Did the others? Perhaps he kept it quiet. She could understand that very well. People often became very panicky about things they didn't understand. She went out of her way to talk to Brant a few more times that day, just so that he didn't think she was troubled by his gift.

In truth, she was far more unsettled by something far more mundane. The locals kept watching the wagon. It wasn't anything as overt as being followed. It was just that they would come around a hill and someone would be at the top of the hill, looking over. They would pass between rocks and someone would be on the far side, watching them pass. Never anything you could put your finger on. Never anything warlike or dangerous. Just watching.

"I'd watch us too," said Galen. "We're armed and warlike and in their territory."

"Yeeeees..." said Clara. She eyed the top of a ridge, where someone had stopped to observe them. A hunter, by the bow and quiver of arrows on his back. "I know. It's all quite plausible. I just don't like it."

She half-expected Istvhan to be dismissive of her concerns, but he said, from the other side, "I don't like it either. And I don't have any more to go on."

But day followed day, and nothing continued to happen. They would camp for a day or two in the territory of each thane and buy overpriced food and ask questions. Istvhan's question received the same answer for one or two markets — rumors of a headless body in the south — and then fell away and no one had heard anything.

Clara's answers were always the same. The barred wagons full of nuns had passed through nearly a month before. They had paid their tolls. The Arral had an arrangement enough like slavery that they admitted to seeing the wagons, and enough different that women's eyes slid away from hers when she asked. Clara suspected that they knew that the other nuns would be no one's forever younger sister.

Pushing her anger down was a matter of habit. She did not weep again. She recited catechisms inside her head and smiled and smiled and made jokes in her clumsy Arral, and the beast inside her snarled and she told it, *No. Not yet.*

Fire was in the walls and the convent was burning.

Clara moved too slowly through the building, every step dragging. Priceless tapestries caught fire and she watched the threads burning, one by one, lines of black and orange crawling over the images. She could not reach them in time.

The altarcloth, she thought. *I must save the altarcloth.*

She was in the chapel. The air still felt like glue. The roof burned, the walls burned. Was the roaring in her ears fire or the voice of the beast? She could not tell.

I must save the altarcloth.

"Domina, you are dreaming."

She reached for the fabric with her hands, despite the flames. She had to save it. She had to save...something.

"Hush, Domina. I'm here. You are dreaming."

Her hands were on fire. She held the burning cloth and the flames swept down her arms. Soon it would be in her hair and then everything would burn...

"Domina Clara, wake up."

Clara woke.

She did not have a moment of disorientation, as one might

expect. She jerked immediately into awareness. Istvhan sat cross-legged beside her, not touching, his hands resting on his knees.

"I am here," she said. "Yes?"

"You are here." He was a dim figure in the tent, lit only by the orange glow of the banked fire, but she recognized his voice and the scent of clove and ginger. "You were having a dream."

"Yes." She sat up. "Yes, of course." She took a deep breath. *I am fine. Nothing happened. I am awake. It was not real.*

It still felt real. She reached for calm. *I will not scream. I will not weep. I will not huddle in the corner of this man's tent and shake. The peace of St. Ursa is on me. I am calm.*

"Can you be touched, when you dream?"

She frowned at him, puzzled by the question. "I don't turn to mist, if that's what you mean."

He shook his head. "Some people can't. They lash out, or it makes the dream worse. Should you find Galen having a nightmare, speak to him but do not touch him. He will attack you, and the fact that he will be ashamed when he wakes up will not heal your wounds."

"Ah," said Clara, grateful for the distraction. "That's why he sleeps alone. Not because of rank."

"Rank makes a convenient excuse." He drew his knees up and draped his arms over them, wrists dangling.

Clara shook her head to clear it. The dream still clung to her like the scent of smoke, as if it would cover her again if she laid back down. Unlike Galen, she would not lash out dangerously in her sleep or at least, no more than the next woman might. That was one of the gifts St. Ursa taught her chosen. *The old novicekeeper taught us all well.* It would all have been far too much to explain, and she still could not trust Istvhan enough to put all her sisters' lives in his hands.

"Are there still coals in the brazier? Maybe I'll make some tea."

He moved out of the way, pausing only to hand her the tin of leaves. She hunched over the brazier, staring at the tiny, tame fire that was so small and controlled and so unlike the one that had devoured the altarcloth and the convent.

The pressure against her throat was not easing. She did not know how long her calm would hold.

Talk. Let some of it out. Talk to this man, who you barely know, who keeps secrets from you while you keep your own secrets. Let a little out, or the secret you are keeping will break free of its own accord.

"Is there anything I can do?" he asked, and his voice was so gentle that she nearly broke. He did not sound like a stranger. He sounded like a brother, like a priest. Like a friend.

"I dreamed about the convent burning," she said out loud.

He made a small noise that invited her to continue.

"So much fire," she said. She tested the temperature of the water with a fingertip. It was still cool. "You wouldn't think that a place with so much stone could burn. But there was plaster and wooden uprights and carpets and tapestries and..." She made a whooshing gesture with both hands. "All of it. It went up so much more quickly than I'd thought it could. The thatched roof part, yes, all right, I understood that. But I think the thatch took longer to catch than the rest. We'd all prepared for that, you see." She tested the water again. Barely warm.

"I'm sorry," said Istvhan, still in that gentle, careful voice.

She had started now and couldn't stop herself. All she could do was try to keep control of what she was saying. "The stable didn't burn at all. All that hay and straw, a stray spark should have sent the whole place up. But it didn't even get touched. The wind was in the wrong direction." She sat back on her heels. "I don't think the raiders expected the whole convent to burn like that. I expect they were trying to set a fire on one side and drive us out, then grab us as we came out. It sort of worked, but...well." She snorted. "They got fewer of us than they'd like, and we were half-dead of smoke when they did."

And three of the sisters went to the beast, and if they hadn't, St. Ursa only knows what would have happened. Sister Mallory had broken open one of the barred doors, which was the only reason that some of them, Clara included, had survived.

A bubble formed at the bottom of the cup.

"The funny thing," she said, watching the bubble, "the funny thing was that I was so dazed from the smoke and trying to keep calm that I didn't know what was happening. I thought people were trying to help. They kept rolling us over — to put out the flames, you know — and then leading us away, and then a man kept telling us to get in the wagon, that it would be okay, we were getting away from the fire." She snorted. "The Sister Cellarer kept saying that there was something wrong, that we were in danger, and I didn't listen. I thought she was just shaken up because of the fire. And then the sun came up and we were in a cage on wheels and she'd been right after all."

Two more bubbles had joined the first. She took the cups off the heat and tossed in leaves to steep. "I'm sorry. I did not mean to ramble."

"You've handled this all remarkably," Istvhan said. "I believe you're allowed to ramble a bit. No one will blame you if you are not always a pillar of calm."

"Well," said Clara. *They teach us to be calm, to always be controlled, to keep the beast quiet. Talk too long and dwell on your ill-treatment and you will work yourself into a state, and then the beast will come...* No, she could not say that. But there were other truths. "I suppose that I could run around sobbing and waving my arms, but it doesn't seem like it would do a great deal of good."

"It might do you some good," said Istvhan. "Instead of bottling it all up."

No, my good captain, you do not know what you are asking. Clara handed him his cup of tea. "I travel. I have always been away from the convent for weeks or months at a time. So I keep trying to think as if I am traveling, as if it is all still there, and I will simply go back when this is done."

The grave look in his eyes deepened.

"I know, I know." She waved her hands. "It's not the best thing. But it keeps me functioning. I don't do any good if I can't function."

Istvhan stirred. "You are not a failure, you know," he said, "simply because you can't endure something unendurable."

His words had the air of something well-worn, a thought he had turned over in his head and repeated until he believed it was true. She wondered what Istvhan had endured, to make such words necessary.

Or Galen. Should you find Galen having a nightmare, speak to him but do not touch him. St. Ursa have mercy, what happened to them?

"It's not just that," she said. He raised an eyebrow. "I don't know who is dead," she said simply. "Some of us weren't there. Some of us must have gotten away. Sister Sara had been called out to deliver a baby. I won't mourn for anyone who might yet be alive. And I do not know about my sisters who were still in the cage when the raiders dumped me."

"Did they think you were dead?"

"Close to it. I had taken a fever. Too much smoke in my lungs. They saw no point in wasting food and water on bad weight, so they rolled me off the wagon and into a ditch."

After I begged them. After I said that I was afraid I would kill everyone in my delirium. After...well. Istvhan did not need to know all the gory details.

She took a sip of tea. It was still good, even if it still tasted of tin.

Istvhan reached out, very carefully, and gripped her shoulder. "Will you mourn when you know, then?"

She almost laughed into her tea at the kindness, and the concern behind it. It was laughter because otherwise it might be tears, and she did not dare open up that door any farther. The pressure in her chest had eased a little, enough for calm to find her. "Yes. Once I know for certain who is living and who is dead, once I have exhausted my ability to find my sisters and bring them back. I promise that I will wail and sob and tear my hair."

"Saint's balls," muttered Istvhan. "Just give me some time to get to a safe distance. I do not know that my heart can take it."

She did laugh that time, and felt as if they had stepped back from the brink of something together. "I'll do my best."

CHAPTER 7

Another day passed. Nothing terrible continued to happen. Clara watched a pair of shepherds on a hillside, who had every reason to be there. *And of course they would watch us pass. We are the most interesting thing for miles. There is nothing strange going on.*

There was nothing strange going on with the hunter on the next ridge, nor with the farmer an hour later. It was all very plausible and it set Clara's teeth on edge.

Something was not quite right. The beast felt it and grumbled in the back of her head. She knew too well that the beast was often wrong, was prickly and reactive and no more trustworthy than human senses, and yet...and yet...

She spent the day in a gruff mood. Istvhan seemed to feel it too. Even Galen, who always had a quip or a joke or an outrageous bit of flirtation, seemed subdued.

When they made camp, Brindle's muttered gnolespeech sounded just as irritated as she felt.

"You don't like mules?" asked Clara, watching him unharness the team.

Brindle grumbled, hunching his shoulders. "A gnole prefers an ox. An ox trusts a gnole to do a gnole's job, gets on with doing an ox's job. A mule doesn't." He held out a hand and clucked his tongue to the mule. The mule considered this, then allowed the gnole to lift her hoof and examine it.

"She looks like she trusts you," said Clara.

Brindle shook his head. "A mule trusts a mule. Always watching a gnole, always deciding if a gnole is right or wrong. And if a mule decides a gnole is wrong..." He slapped the mule's flank, half-affectionate, half-annoyed. "Hard to explain things to a mule. Not good with diagrams." Clara snickered.

For all his grumbling, Brindle was efficient and careful with the mules and the mules seemed happy enough in his care. "Are horses better or worse?" she asked.

"Oh, *horses*," said the gnole. "A horse is just smart enough to make trouble for a horse. A gnole doesn't have time to work with every horse until a horse decides a gnole is trustworthy. A gnole has places to be."

Clara snickered again, she couldn't help it.

"And that is why we're walking," said Istvhan. Clara turned and found him standing just behind her. It was a perfectly polite distance, and yet they were both big enough that the space between them seemed small.

"Too much trouble?" asked Clara.

Istvhan nodded. "We don't need great speed. Or didn't. I'm sorry that we can't move more quickly now, to follow your sisters."

Clara sighed, her good humor dropping away. "It's been a month," she said. "Whatever speed might have gotten me, it's long gone. Now I am simply hoping to find where they have gone, and begin the task of getting them back."

The lines around Istvhan's mouth deepened. "Domina..."

"It's all right," said Clara. "I know some of them must be dead by now. Perhaps all of them. You don't have to spare my feelings."

He shook his head. "No," he said. "No, I don't think they would mostly be dead. To raid so far afield for captives, the raiders must have thought they were valuable. That is the part that puzzles me the most. Did you have skilled illuminators among you? Healers? Something?"

Clara knew perfectly well why the nuns of St. Ursa would be considered valuable to certain parties, but that was a discussion she was not about to have. "Some of each, of course. And archivists, though in very specific fields. It has been my suspicion for a long time that we were attacked on the orders of a very specific client, perhaps who had already arranged to buy my sisters and me."

Istvhan nodded. "I'm sorry," he said, after a moment. "But that does bode well for their continued life."

Not quite as well as you think, thought Clara, *but I must continue to have faith...* She gave him as good a smile as she could muster, and went to go help Brindle with the mules.

Istvhan would have staked his life that she still wasn't telling him everything, but he could hardly judge. He, too, had thoughts he would not speak aloud, about why someone might raid a convent and take the nuns away alive.

"I don't want to say it to the Sister," he said to Galen, leaning against a tree and gazing up at the stars. Strictly speaking, they were not both required for watch, but he needed to talk out what he was thinking. "I don't even particularly like thinking it."

He watched the pale oval of Galen's face turn toward him. "Something to do with religion?" said the other man thoughtfully. "Someone who feels the nuns of that order are apostates or heretics or whatever they are? You'd expect them to be killed then, but perhaps they wanted to make an example of them."

Istvhan exhaled slowly through his nose. "Possibly. That's...still a better scenario than what I was thinking."

"Oh?"

"Somebody somewhere is paying for live nuns. Not just women. *Nuns.* If they wanted to kidnap women, there's a great many options in easier reach, but someone crossed Arral territory with slave wagons specifically to get their hands on these nuns. Which means that someone has plans or...desires...that can only be satisfied by women of the cloth."

Galen gave a low whistle. "That's dark, brother."

"You see why I am not speaking of this to Domina Clara."

A late cricket chirped in the fields. The silence between them filled up with all the nightmares that might befall the sisters of St. Ursa, two decent men trying to think like monsters and finding it far, far too easy to imagine.

"You think it's one man?" asked Galen finally.

"No way of knowing. It could be a procurer of some sort, catering to a cartel with extremely specialized tastes. Or I could be inventing monstrous scenarios, and someone just wants a group of scribes and healers." He sighed, rubbing the bridge of his nose. "Perhaps we have seen too many terrible things."

"It was easier, before."

"Everything was easier, before."

"Yes. But we never had to worry about making a mistake. We could just...come in at the end. Everything was clearcut."

Istvhan grunted. He suspected that even before, in the service of the Saint of Steel, things had not been quite so clearcut as that. It was simply that a god made those decisions, not His followers. But that had been another life, another time, and neither he nor Galen lived in that world any longer. Now they muddled through like other mortals and did their best and tried to keep their feet in a rising tide.

"She is very calm about this," said Galen. "Almost too calm."

Istvhan grunted. Galen wasn't wrong exactly, and yet Istvhan remembered waking up from the terrible collapse after the Saint had died. Those first few weeks, they had all been shaky and vague and lost. *Well, our souls had been torn in half, that'll happen.* And then one of the Rat priests, their whiskered god bless them for it, had left a deck of cards, and Istvhan and Stephen and Shane had sat and played cards and Istvhan had made jokes. Terrible, stupid jokes, most of them. And then the other paladins had crept in and even though they didn't play, they sat back and they listened to the conversation and it had *helped.*

There had still been a giant raw wound across all their hearts. Nothing would heal that but time. There was no counting the number of times when someone sat at the card table with tears streaming down their cheeks, or got up and walked away for an hour because everything was too much. But they always came back, because if you were making stupid jokes and paying attention to the cards, for a few seconds at a time there would be a little clear space where you weren't thinking about how broken you were.

One day, Wren sat down and said, "deal me in," and they made room at the table and nobody said anything. Galen sat in the corner for a week and then one evening Istvhan had made another stupid joke and Galen had made a much better one and everyone had chuckled, even Shane, who was always blazingly serious about everything. And then Marcus sat down — Marcus, like Galen, had been at Hallowbind where the paladins had run mad and torn men to pieces with their bare hands — and Stephen had gotten up and fetched another pack of cards and they doubled the deck and for a couple seconds at a time, nobody had to be broken.

When Istvhan watched Clara making jokes with Galen or talking to Brindle or having a calm conversation about faith with Brant, he was reminded of those card games, of snatching moments of normalcy in the face of horror.

But Galen was right too. There was a stillness to Clara sometimes that was worrisome.

"She had a nightmare last night. I was almost glad. You're right, she's too calm. I'm afraid she's bottling everything up and it's going to run her into the ground. I even used the voice on her."

"Ah." Galen knew the paladin's voice well. It was calm and kind and soothing, the voice you used when you and your brothers had just slaughtered a dozen bandits and you were trying to coax their captives to come with you, even though there was still blood running down your sword. It was the voice that spoke directly to people's nerves and made them trust you. "And did it help?"

"Not much. She said that running in circles and waving her arms and crying would not solve anything, so she was refraining. And that she would not mourn the dead until she knew who was still alive."

Galen nodded. "Very sensible," he said. "Very...very *nun*-like."

Istvhan raised an eyebrow. "You say that like you're skeptical."

"Skeptical, no." Galen shook his head. "Not exactly. I just feel like perhaps there's something she isn't telling us."

"There's a great deal we aren't telling her," Istvhan pointed out, even though he'd been thinking the exact same thing.

"I was surprised when you told her to ask about the severed heads."

"It was too good an opportunity to pass up. And it worked."

"Yes. But I don't think she quite believed you that you were just worried about rumors you'd heard."

"Yes, I got that impression too. Well, it was worth it anyway. I suppose we might have to explain about the smooth men to her at some point."

Galen scowled. "I'd like to know what she's hiding first."

"I'd like a lot of things," said Istvhan. He didn't like suspecting Clara. He liked her. He liked the way she carried herself. He'd only met a few women of her size before, and mostly they tried to downplay it, ducking their heads, making themselves small. Clara didn't. Clara walked like she was taller than everyone else and knew it and if anyone cared, be damned to them. As someone else built to a different scale than the rest of the world, he admired that. He hadn't learned to walk like that until he was a warrior.

He pushed away from the tree. "At the moment, I'd like to be out of Arral territory. I'm starting to get jumpy."

"You and me both, brother. Sleep well."

"And you."

CHAPTER 8

"This is the edge of Arral territory," said Clara, pointing. "That marker there is the boundary of the last thane's territory, and there isn't another one."

It was not a particularly dramatic marker. The hills were brown and frosted, the grasses dry. When the wind hissed through them, they rippled, flashing seedheads. The wooden marker was the tallest thing on the hillside. As they watched, a rabbit emerged from the grass and stood on its hind legs, watching them with wide, staring eyes.

"Squares with my maps," said Istvhan. "Do you have a clear direction from here?"

Clara gnawed her lower lip. "Not as clear as I'd like. I suspect north and east, but that's a lot of territory."

"And a couple of different roads," said Galen.

"Pick a road good for a mule, tomato-man," said Brindle.

"...tomato-man?" asked Clara, welcoming the diversion from thoughts of her sisters.

Galen sighed. Brindle pointed at the man's dark red hair. "A man's fur is the color of tomato."

"Can't I be blood-man? Blood-man sounds much more impressive."

"Fur isn't the color of blood. Fur is the color of tomato."

"You see what I put up with, Domina?"

"Indeed."

Istvhan folded his arms, gazing over the hillside. "If we knew what road the raiders took, it would help a great deal. We could get some idea what city they're heading for, at least. But after a month, I doubt there's any tracks that we'd be able to find."

"No," said Clara, watching the hillside. "But we might be able to ask directions."

"The last set of Arral didn't know," Galen said.

"Not the Arral." Clara pointed to the rabbit, which had been joined by two more. "From them."

"Rabbits?" said Galen. He had a half-smile, waiting for the punchline. Another rabbit had come out of the grass. "You can speak to rabbits?"

"Not usually. But I think this is a warrenmind," said Clara, watching the rabbits assemble. They were larger than hares, their ears proportionally smaller, but obviously rabbits nonetheless.

Istvhan nodded slowly. "I've heard of them," he said. "I've never seen one."

"Well, that's what they look like. Let's see if they have a speaker." She held up both hands. "I greet you," she said, in the Arral trading tongue.

The rabbits watched her. More appeared on the edges, all watching her with an eerie, flat gaze. Their heads all moved in unison. Clara had encountered a warrenmind two or three times, and they still made the hair on the back of her neck stand up.

Two of the rabbits stood up and made stilted gestures, lifting their front paws high in the air, then dropping back down.

"Are they...waving?" asked Galen.

"More or less. Definitely a warrenmind. I knew there was one near the Arral border, and I suppose it makes sense it's on the road."

The waving rabbits hopped down the road a few dozen yards, then stood and waved again.

"They want us to follow them, don't they?" said Galen glumly.

"Looks like it, tomato-man." Brindle rubbed his nose. "Smell like rabbits," he added. "Just rabbits."

"Are they dangerous?" asked Istvhan.

"They're rabbits," said Clara. "They can defend themselves a lot better than you'd think, but they don't eat meat and we aren't a threat. They'd probably just go down into their holes and wait for us to leave. They want to talk, so they probably want to trade."

Brindle urged the mules forward at a walking pace. Clara, Istvhan and Galen walked ahead, keeping an eye on the rabbits.

"There are a lot of them on the hillside, boss," murmured Galen.

"I see them."

"This is creepy as fuck, boss."

"No argument there."

On the far side of the hill, they found a dozen more rabbits standing guard over the entrance to a warren. The holes were large and little effort had been made at concealment. Dozens of eyes turned simultaneously to watch them.

"I greet you," Clara called again.

"How many of them do you think you could take, boss? A dozen, maybe?"

"Galen, I've never tested how many rabbits I could fight off at a time. It just hasn't come up."

Something moved in one of the burrows, and two more rabbits emerged. They were dragging a third between them. It had an over-sized head and an overgrown, lumpy neck, like a goiter. Its back half was obviously not well balanced with the front. The ones dragging it were careless of the stones on the ground and their teeth sunk into its nape and one leg. Warrenminds were aware of pain, but not particularly impressed by it.

The goitered rabbit rolled sideways and looked at Clara. Its mouth opened, throat working, and in a high, squealing voice, it shrieked, "Warren greets a humans."

"Nope," said Galen quietly. "That is *not* okay. I am not okay with this."

"A gnole agrees with you, tomato-man."

"It's a warren speaker," murmured Clara. "They have to grow one with a special throat so it can talk."

"Trade?" squealed the speaker. It sounded as if it were in terrible pain. "Trade with a humans?"

"What do they like to trade?" asked Istvhan.

"Information, usually. Sometimes food, although...ah...I don't recommend it unless you're starving. They usually want steel razors and firestarters and hand mirrors, if you've got them."

"I've got an extra razor or two," said Istvhan. He went to the wagon. The warren watched him rummaging through his kit.

"Have you seen people passing this way?" asked Clara.

"A humans, yes. Always a humans is going back and forth. Territory of humans, there." Several of the rabbits pointed back the way they had come.

"The Arral, of course," muttered Clara. "These would be different humans. In an iron cage, on wheels?"

Noses twitched as the warrenmind appeared to consult itself. The speaker, in its high, droning squeal said, "Before the frost. A humans wearing cage. Yes."

"How many?" asked Istvhan.

The entire warren, except for the one lying on the ground, cocked its head sideways simultaneously. Galen made a soft sound of dismay.

"One," said the speaker. "A humans. No?"

"They don't understand individuality quite the way we do," murmured Clara. "They think we're all part of the same multiple creature. They probably understand that we're not the same creature as the ones that went by, but they couldn't tell you how many of us there are." She licked her lips. "Ah...let me try this." Raising her voice, she said "The humans wearing the cage. How big was it?"

The warrenmind twitched noses. "Big," squealed the speaker. "Bigger than you, a humans."

"How much bigger?"

The warren had to think about this for quite a long time. Istvhan unwrapped the thin steel razor and waited.

"A humans and a humans," said the speaker finally. "Maybe?"

Clara nodded. "That's as good as we're going to get. It's bigger than we are, so there were more of them, and there's probably about twice as many, but it's not sure. It doesn't count people, you understand. It thinks counting is for things."

"Which road did the humans take?" called Galen. He still looked very unhappy with the situation.

"Through the carrion trees." The warrenspeaker coughed a few times. "Carrion trees. Carrion. Yes?" Its voice sounded weaker, perhaps from the strain of so much speech.

Istvhan glanced to Clara and she nodded. "As much help as they can give, I think," she murmured. "A razor would be appropriate."

He walked forward. The rabbits were not even as high as the top of his boots, but they still made his skin crawl a little. There was something about the eerie synchronicity of their motions that screamed to his spine that something was terribly, terribly wrong.

He crouched down and set the razor on the ground, then moved back. Two rabbits came up and studied it for a moment, then one picked up the blunt handle in its mouth and the other made a dancing movement to Istvhan. He wasn't sure quite what to make of that, but fortunately Clara came to his rescue.

"Humans thank you," she said, making a sweeping gesture with her arms that vaguely resembled the rabbit's.

"Warren...warren...thanks you." The warrenspeaker coughed again, kicking feebly. Three burly rabbits grabbed it and began to drag it inside the burrow.

"Is it okay?" asked Galen softly.

"The warren doesn't care one way or the other," said Clara. "It'll breed a new one if it has to. They're not like us. An individual to them is like a toenail or a fingernail. They won't mourn the loss because there hasn't been one."

"Let's keep moving," said Istvhan. Most of the warrenmind had turned their back on the humans, but there were still several sentries keeping their eyes open. He didn't want to say anything rude in front of the warren, since he didn't know how good its hearing was, but his skin was threatening to crawl right off his body and run away down the road.

They went on. The line of burrows vanished around a hill. Istvhan slowly got his nerves back, shaking his head.

"Do they bother you?" asked Clara.

"Unnatural beasts," he muttered.

Clara looked at him for a moment too long, then turned her head away sharply. Istvhan frowned. Had he insulted her somehow? Was a warrenmind somewhere her friend?

He would have asked and tried to smooth the moment over, but Galen called out, "Boss, there's a split up ahead. Which way are we going?"

"Hmm. They'll both get us out of the mountains. The north road takes us more quickly to Morstone. But I am more concerned with the Domina's sisters right now."

Clara's brief coolness faded under a smile of acknowledgment. "I thank you, Captain Istvhan."

Now was that formality because she is grateful or because she is still offended? "Don't thank me yet. I still don't know which way we're going."

"Following the warrenmind's directions?" asked Brant, coming from behind the wagon.

"Some directions," grumbled Istvhan. "Carrion trees. Not as helpful as it could be."

"More helpful than you know," said Clara. She nodded ahead to the branching road. "See those trees on the right, with the twisty gray bark? Hawthorn."

Brant nodded furiously. "Carrion tree, of course!" He grinned at Clara.

"We are but simple mercenaries," said Istvhan. "Your fancy tree talk confuses us." Galen elbowed him in the ribs.

"In spring, the hawthorns bloom," Brant explained. "Great clouds of white flowers. And they stink like rotten meat to attract the flies."

"Even a human can smell," added Brindle from the wagon.

The hawthorn trees were on the south branch. Istvhan pointed. "That way, then."

"It's a longer way to Morstone," said Clara.

"A week or two extra is well within our plans," he said. Which was not untrue, so far as it went, though his plans were far more flexible than anyone but Brant and Galen knew. "And if I left nuns in distress, I would fear far more than merely being late."

Clara gave him another of those watching, weighing glances. He gave it right back. She opened her mouth to say something, but whatever it might have been was lost as the first of the bandits attacked.

CHAPTER 9

The bandits yelled when they charged. That was the only reason they didn't take more casualties. The whoops and screams coming down the hillside gave them ample time to draw weapons and form up.

"Saint's balls," muttered Galen. "There's got to be at least twenty of them."

More than that, thought Clara, although a few were hanging back and they had — damn and blast, they had slings. A bullet stone ripped through the canvas of the wagon six inches from Clara's head. Another one found Marli's head and dropped her to the ground. Thorn let out a curse and dragged her back toward the wagon.

Brindle stood on the wagon seat, sighting down a crossbow that looked nearly as big as he was. Clara had always known that gnoles were stronger than they looked, but the recoil on it should have been fantastic and Brindle only grunted.

A bolt sprouted from one of the slingers and they fell. "A gnole does not want a human throwing *rocks,*" said Brindle acidly, lowering his crossbow. "Even at mules."

"Protect the nun!" roared Istvhan, yanking his sword free.

"Protect your own damn self!" Clara roared back. She dashed around the wagon and pulled out the iron sledge that they used to drive tent stakes. Weapons were not entirely necessary for a daughter of St. Ursa, but she would rather use them as long as possible. There were cans of worms and then there were tureens of worms, buckets of worms, entire hogshead-sized barrels of worms. Clara did not wish to open any of them.

The sledge was not a well-balanced weapon, but it had heft and power and it made a very satisfactory dent in the head of the bandit who dodged between two of the warriors and leapt for the mules.

"Unnecessary," growled Clara, as the man fell at her feet, twitching. She knew that attacking the mules was a practical consideration for their attackers — dead mules did not escape or trample their enemies, and anyway, there was good eating on a mule — but she detested the idea. It violated the ancient bargain between humanity and beasts of burden. *If they were warhorses, it might have been one thing...*

These were, very clearly, not warhorses. Brindle had them under control, probably because mules were extremely skeptical of everything. The loud noises and the yelling and the thumping and the men with sharp things in their hands probably had nothing to do with mules, but they were going to bite anyone who got too close, just in case. Clara had to keep one eye behind her and one on the enemy, which left her no time to watch for how the mercenaries were managing. She heard men shouting and at least one scream.

The scream hadn't been Istvhan. She didn't question how she could already identify that, or why she cared about him more than the others. Solid, practical reasons, surely. She'd think of one in a minute.

She bashed another man with the sledge. She missed his head but hit his shoulder, which turned his collarbone to splinters and put him out of action.

An eerie scream rose toward the back of the wagon. It was a man's voice — not a scream of pain but a strange wailing cry that made the hair on the back of her neck stand up. The beast did not like it. The beast did not like being attacked either, and for a moment, Clara felt her control slipping, the world going dim, her sense of self turning inside her skull...

St. Ursa, no!

Her vision cleared. There were more bandits. Of course there were.

She'd been in one or two battles and they were always the same: moments of clarity interspersed with moments of dimness and screaming and loud noises. The world seemed to jump and skitter around her. She reacted to things before her conscious mind had even realized that something was going on. Something smashed into her left arm and it went numb to the elbow, so she hit it with her sledge and she didn't die so that presumably meant she had won. She stepped back and something turned underfoot and it was the arm of one of the mercenaries, one whose name she had forgotten but who had cooked potatoes over the fire and it looked like he was dead and she wanted to feel that, to recognize that a man she had known was dead, but then someone was in front of her and they were trying to kill her so she killed him instead and then it was later and she had gotten shoved back toward the wagon and the mules were plunging and trying to retreat and Istvhan chopped into a bandit in front of her like a man splitting firewood and his back was exposed and another bandit went for the opening and Clara smashed his head open and blood sprayed across them both and then she heard that crisp crossbow noise and looked up and the attacker she hadn't seen fell against her with a bolt in his neck and she staggered backward, lowering him to the ground as if he were merely wounded, even though he was the enemy.

Were they winning? It seemed like they must be winning. She could hear Galen's warcry somewhere off to her left. Brindle dropped his crossbow and grabbed for the reins on the mules, trying to keep them from bolting. The battle was right up against the mules and she tried to force her next opponent farther away, swinging her sledge in heavy arcs. He jumped back once, twice, and then blood came out of his mouth and he fell and Thorn's sword was red as she pulled it free.

For an instant, no one was attacking Clara. She listened. The wagon had stopped rocking. Brindle was making soothing sounds to the mules. Galen was no longer making his strange war cry. Was he dead?

Something slammed into her then, driving the air from her lungs. She tried to swing the hammer, but her assailant had her arm pinned. *Shit.* The beast roared in her head. Her free hand met armor, and then she was being pushed back against the side of the wagon and she smelled ginger and sweat and Istvhan's mouth locked over hers.

...oh.

Oh, I see.

It was the last thing she expected, and even less did she expect her body's immediate response. A pulse beat in her head and between her legs. Her blood roared as if the beast was waking inside her, and she fought it back — *not now, not for this!*

His mouth was very hot. The wagonboard hit at just the right height that he was bending Clara back over it, one mailed arm across her back to hold her body against his. She dropped the hammer and clutched the edges of his tabard.

If I knew fighting bandits would get me this, I'd do it more often.

The kiss deepened. She felt the edge of his teeth against her lips. There was no gentleness to it, only fierceness and need, but that was fine, that was entirely correct. This was a battlefield and they were warriors. Istvhan kissed her as if they were locked in combat and Clara returned it with ferocity of her own. She slid her hand up the back of his neck, which was damp with sweat or blood, and wondered how fast he could get out of his armor.

And then, as suddenly as it had happened, his eyes went wide and he stepped back, pulling his hands away as if he had been burned. "Domina," he rasped. "Did I hurt you?"

She shook her head. He dropped to one knee, his hand covering his heart. His pose was that of a knight offering fealty, but his face looked like a man who had seen his own death. "Domina, *forgive me.* It will not happen again."

"Well, damn," said Clara.

Possibly that was the only response that could have broken the tension. Istvhan's stricken look was still there, but overshadowed with wry amusement. He bit his lower lip.

"Get up," said Clara.

"I should not have done that," he said, rising to his feet. "I am usually slightly less of an ass."

Clara did not know quite what to say. Part of her wanted to shuck his armor off and ride him right there on the road and never mind anything else. The rather more sensible part told her that would be a very foolish thing to do, particularly with everything else going on. *Not now. Not one more complication.*

Besides, men may think they want an animal in their beds, but very few actually want a beast.

"It's fine," she said. "Battles. Yes." She was still breathing hard. She wasn't quite sure it was from the fighting. "Everything gets a little… err…wild afterward. Don't worry about it."

"No," he said, shaking his head. "It does not matter. Battle or no."

She waited for him to say that she was a nun, but he didn't. Instead he gave her another, anguished look, bowed deeply, and retreated as if devils were chasing him.

Istvhan had never been so mortified in his life.

He had done a lot of reasonably mortifying things in his youth, but this was really beyond the pale. He'd practically assaulted a nun. That she'd taken it good-naturedly and even seemed to rather enjoy the kiss was absolutely no excuse.

Istvhan was a very large man. He towered over even the other former paladins of the order. He could loom over someone while sitting down. Plenty of women found that attractive, but he knew, all too well, how easily attraction could turn to alarm. And so he went to great pains to be a courteous, polite lover. When he flirted, he made absolutely sure that the other party was just as interested as he was. He did not ever want to see fear in a woman's eyes.

And he had just thrown all these rules out the window and manhandled a nun.

Saint's blood. I should be doing vigil on my knees on hard ground for this.

Why had he done it? Under the mortification was a good bit of bafflement. It was simply not the sort of thing that he did.

What was I thinking?

Clearly he hadn't been thinking. His faith in his inherent goodness had broken when his god died, but still, Istvhan had thought that not being a terrible human being was at least an ingrained habit by now.

He'd heard movement and he'd come around the side of the wagon, ready to kill, and instead she'd been standing there with blood on her hands and her hair coming loose from its braids and a dead man at her feet and the Saint of Steel help him, he'd suddenly been more aroused than he'd ever been in his life.

Saint's balls, it's a good thing I'm wearing armor or...

Well. He'd have stopped. If she'd said anything, he would have stopped himself. He had to believe that.

Clara hadn't seemed terribly offended. That was something, anyway. *Could I have picked up that she was interested, somehow? Subtle signs?*

His lips twisted. *Ah, yes, how convenient that would be. Gets you off the hook for being an utter shit. How nice. Realistically, she's traveling with mercenaries who are loyal to me and she may think it's safer to play along instead of provoking me.* Women made such calculations all the time. It was simply nauseating to think that one was having to make such a calculation about *him.*

Was it the battle rage? The black tide that afflicted all the former servants of the Saint of Steel? That was a chilling thought. The battle tide made the saint's paladins into killing machines. It did not drive them to assaulting women. That was a different sort of darkness.

Although the Saint would have stopped us, obviously, the same way He stopped us from killing the innocent. Now we are without a guide, so perhaps...

He searched his memory of the fight and could find nothing that would lead him to believe that the battle tide had risen at all. He had been calm. He had kept his head the entire time. There were no gaps in his memory, or at least, no more than normally occurred when fighting for his life.

And at the end of the day, you simply did not go berserk without noticing. It wasn't a subtle thing. You felt it happening. You fought against it tooth and nail or you embraced it, but it definitely didn't sneak up on you.

But he'd still kissed the nun. Hell, if Istvhan was honest, there had been a moment there when he would have been happy to do more than kissing. He had forgotten the others, forgotten their surroundings, forgotten that she was a nun and not for the likes of him. Instead he'd had her in his arms and when he started to push her backward, she'd resisted, just for a moment. Until she'd *chosen* to yield. Weight and power, not small, not fragile, soft flesh and hard muscle, strength meeting strength.

He was half hard just from the memory. He fought it back. *Saint's bones, what is* wrong *with me? It doesn't matter if she decided she liked it, you don't just slam into a woman without asking!*

Vigil, he decided grimly. *Vigil on my knees. I'll take back-to-back watches tonight, and maybe the cold and the pain in my kneecaps will beat some manners back into me.*

It was an easy enough thing to decide to do. They were very short on troops now. Two of his men were dead and of those remaining, only Thorn and Andrel were unhurt. *Which makes any thoughts you're having about Domina Clara doubly perverse. People are dead.*

She'd tasted of sage and salt and blood. The first two, he knew, came from the mixture she used on her teeth. The blood had been from a cracked lip or maybe it had been the enemy's blood or maybe his teeth had done it when he slammed into her but it hadn't stopped him and she pulled him closer and Saint's black and bloody tongue, he was still thinking about it and he wanted more, he wanted to find her and pull her down beside him on the road if that was what it took and—

Galen screamed.

Clara heard that strange, uneasy wail start up again and felt her chest tighten. There was a knot of lust and confusion there, atop the adrenaline and the fear. The beast growled inside her head but she grabbed for the sledge and lurched toward the back of the wagons.

It was Galen. There were four dead men around him, and he was pulling his sword out of the fourth. A straggler, perhaps, or one who had been knocked briefly senseless and then gotten up and attacked again.

He was certainly dead now. Galen had made sure of that. A cut over the redhead's eye sheeted blood down his face, a shade darker than his hair. The mule tied in the back had retreated to the full length of its rope and was hauling frantically on the bridle. Galen turned in place, the war cry slowly fading — and then saw Clara.

He drew himself up and screamed, lifting his sword. His eyes were still green but veiled, as if he could not quite see her.

Something in his scream called the beast closer to the surface. Sudden. Shocking. Clara heard herself roar a response, the beast's voice in her throat, and then Galen swung his sword up and moved toward her, swift and deadly, and she dropped her head between her shoulders, ready to crush this small man who dared to challenge—

Istvhan stepped between the two of them and shouted *"Enough!"* in a voice like a drill sergeant.

Galen jerked backward as if he'd been struck. He dropped his sword and put his hands over his face.

"Domina Clara," said Istvhan, not taking his eyes off Galen, "are you injured?" His voice was calm and cool and penetrating. It did not occur to her not to answer.

It took her a moment to find her voice. Istvhan's shout had been like a bucket of cold water. *Saint's mercy, was I threatening Galen? What is wrong with me?*

"I'm fine," she said. Her tongue felt thick. "Fine. Tend his wounds."

He shot her one brief look over his shoulder and then she felt him dismiss her mentally and turn his attention to his second-in-command. His voice gentled but its authority was absolute. "Galen. Do you know who I am?"

"Brother," rasped Galen. His throat sounded raw. *And no wonder if that sound was coming from it. Is he some kind of berserker?* She'd heard about them, of course. There were legends out of the west of men who went into a battle-fugue, and of course, there were the Saints of Steel, although they had all died along with their god.

Istvhan sheathed his sword, stepped forward, and put his arm around Galen's shoulders. "All right?" he said.

"You did well," said Istvhan, still in that soothing, authoritative voice, leading him out of the range of the panicky mule. "It's over."

Galen's shoulders shook. After a moment he said "You stopped me."

"You stopped yourself." Istvhan shot Clara a glance she couldn't read and dropped his voice. Clara stepped back, giving them room. She would have liked to hear the rest of the conversation, but her curiosity was nothing compared to the sound of Galen's pain.

CHAPTER 10

There were three wounded, which was very good considering how badly they'd been outnumbered. Marli had woken again but couldn't remember the last day and kept trying to get up. They loaded everyone in the wagon, including Galen, who sat with his head down and his wrists draped over his knees. Clara itched to wipe the blood from his face but he so clearly did not want to be touched that he might as well have been carrying a sign.

"Will he be all right?" she asked Istvhan softly.

He gave her a strange, hostile look. His voice was flat and emotionless. "He'll live."

"We need to clean up everyone's wounds..." She made a helpless gesture toward the wagon, knowing they could not stop to light a fire.

"I know, but we can't rest here," said Istvhan. "More may come. Did the rabbits betray us?"

"The warrenmind? No, of course not. They told us that there were humans here, and as far as they're concerned, that was the end of it. No, this was humans. Probably someone gossiped in the market. And the thought of one last prize, so late in the season..." She trailed off delicately.

Istvhan grunted. There was a long, shallow cut along his forearm. He'd wrapped the edge of his cloak around it, but there was a dark stain starting to show through the fabric. "We've got to get away from here. We're sitting ducks. Do you think they'll be back?"

"I don't know."

"I should have expected it," said Istvhan. "I knew there were too many people watching us. But it went on so long and nothing happened…"

Clara sighed. "I felt it too. But I kept thinking that I was being paranoid."

He made a sharp angry gesture. "Later. We can yell at ourselves once we're out of range."

"Can we *get* out of range? With the mules?"

"Mules are good at what mules are good at," said Brindle, who was settling the mule that had panicked earlier. Possibly that was a no. The gnole got onto the wagon seat, glanced around, then slapped the reins and got the team up to a brisk walk. Marli groaned from inside the wagon as the rough road rattled her head.

"Domina," said Istvhan, again in that calm, flat voice, "would you be so kind as to join me in the lead? I wish two sets of eyes scouting, and Galen will be indisposed for some time."

"Of course."

They took point. Clara had kept the sledge. It was in an ugly state, but she was not quite willing to let it go.

Istvhan set a rapid pace that got them well ahead of the wagon. The road ahead was full of twists and places where men could easily hide. It made sense to have an advance scout. *I believe that. But he is not looking at me like another pair of eyes. He is looking at me like a problem.*

He did not speak for some minutes as they walked. Clara's unease grew. Finally he said "Did you shout at Galen as a joke?"

"A *joke?* No! No, I…" *You what? Roared at him because the beast felt challenged and you smelled blood? Care to explain that?*

"You what?" said Istvhan quietly, and Clara finally identified what was lurking under the calm.

It was rage.

Istvhan was furious. The black tide swirled around his feet, which it never did. Of all the broken paladins, he was the one who never lost his head. His berserker fits were rare and easily controlled. When the god died, while his brothers turned into mindless killing machines, he had quietly fainted and woken days later in the Temple of the Rat.

But it roiled around him now, the tide climbing higher. The woman beside him had challenged Galen while he was lost in the battle madness. Roared at him, with a voice that he could hardly believe had come from a human throat. And Galen, who would have gotten loose from the tide on his own, had slid back under and charged her.

If Istvhan had not been there, if he had arrived even a moment later...

And why were you so far away? Why did you not check on him immediately? Because you'd kissed her and were off flagellating yourself for it, and you nearly let them both die because you were too afraid to face her.

"Galen is a berserker. You could have died, Domina. And your death would have broken a man who already spends his nights in hell."

His voice did not shake. He was calm. He was always calm. He would be calm the day that the black tide finally took him, wrenched him off his feet, and he died with a sword in his hand.

She increased the space between them. Was it fear? Could she tell that he was angry?

"I did not taunt him," she said. Her voice was also slow and measured, and he had the sudden sense that she was also angry, that the two of them were standing on a terrible brink and the only thing keeping them from falling was this strange, performative calm. "I did not know he was a berserker. I am sorry if I caused him distress. It had nothing to do with him."

He finally turned his head and looked at her.

She met his eyes squarely. Hers were a shade lighter than his, amber instead of earth. Her stance was deliberately relaxed, the mirror of his. She was still carrying the sledgehammer in one hand, the head dangling beside her leg.

Draw your sword, whispered the tide. *Draw your sword and strike and...and...she will block with the sledge, and if she strikes hard enough, it will drive your arm upward and the blade will break and if she hits your hand instead, it is your fingers that will break. Go for the face with your other hand, sacrifice the sword hand, get the eyes and then the throat.*

He did none of these things. He would do none of those things. Instead he slid his gaze down her arm to her weapon. "You are skilled with a hammer."

"Not particularly," she said. "I use strength and reach to compensate for too many things. A swift opponent with a dagger could come up in my guard easily enough. But in the first shock, hardly anyone tries."

"And because you are large, people think you are slow." He heard his own voice warming, just a little. He understood that all too well. "I thank you for your aid, Domina. I should not have assumed that you could not defend yourself."

She accepted that as it was meant, as a peace offering. "It's all right. I did not exactly explain that I have a history of bashing people over the head."

"Do you?"

"On occasion. I prefer not to. I am not a trained warrior, I have simply learned a few things, working alone." She inclined her head. "There is a certain sort of man who feels that a woman larger than he is a challenge."

"Are the other women of your order warriors?"

"Not in the sense that you mean." Her voice grew cool again. Whatever she was hiding, he was getting too close to it.

"You are not telling me all the truth, Domina."

"No."

The bald admission surprised him, and the Saint help him, twinged his sense of the absurd. The tide receded. He had always been at the mercy of his sense of humor. He huffed a laugh. "Well. At least you are not lying to me outright. What are you not telling me?"

"I am not a spirit or a djinn, Captain Istvhan. Asking me a direct question will not get you answers if I choose not to give them."

He snorted. "And if I decide you are dangerous, and choose to leave you right here at the side of the road?"

"Then you have made your choice." She seemed unconcerned.

"Answer me this honestly, I beg of you, Domina. Are you a danger to me or my men?"

"No." Her response was swift and immediate. "Never."

Strangely, he believed her. He would never step aside from someone asking for aid, particularly not a nun. But now he was starting to think that he could not turn away because of the mystery. What was going on? What secret was she keeping? And why?

The sound she had made toward Galen had been very strange. Not a scream. Not a shout. Something else. His senses had prickled when he heard it and he had come at a dead run, just in time to stop Galen from continuing his attack.

Looking down at the sledgehammer, it occurred to him for the first time that perhaps she might have held her own.

Some secret technique? Could the nuns be skilled in some peculiar magic? You heard about such things sometimes, training grounds that purported to teach secrets both martial and mystical. Istvhan had never encountered one that was anything more than plain military discipline, but merely because he had never encountered it did not mean that it did not exist.

Was what felt like anger coming from her actually something like his own black tide?

He realized that he was staring, and that Sister Clara was meeting his gaze gravely. There was a bloody smear across her cheekbone. He had a sudden urge to lift his hand to her face and wipe it away.

"Let me know when you decide to confide in me," he said quietly.

"Likewise," said Clara. Their eyes met again, and his dropped first.

"Boss," said Galen.

Istvhan started. His second-in-command had climbed out of the wagon. Clara was standing behind him, looking exhausted. Her hair fell into her eyes and she flipped it away impatiently. Saint's teeth, how could he have thought she'd want him? *She can't want anything right now but to collapse.*

Come to think of it, I'm not much better, no matter what my cock is trying to tell me.

"Boss, we can't go any farther. Haller is in a bad way. The mules are completely wrecked. Brindle's walking them, but they're not going to go anywhere in a hurry. Let's make camp here."

Istvhan sighed and looked both ways down the road. "I don't see we've got any choice, do we? Let's get up the big tent and we'll treat the wounded. If there's more of them, we've got no chance."

Clara cleared her throat. "There's a stream just over the rise. Brindle can smell it. If you can spare someone, we'll go get water."

He nodded. "Galen, go with her."

Galen's eyes flicked over him briefly, but he nodded. Both he and the nun loaded themselves up with canteens and went forward, holding weapons free. Istvhan itched to go with them, but his duty was to protect the wounded. *If there's any bandits left, they'll come for the wagon, where our supposed riches are.*

Anyway, Clara would no doubt be glad of the chance to be away from him. Galen might be an unpredictable berserker, but he wasn't inclined to kiss unwilling women. Or willing women, for that matter.

He shoved it all out of his mind and looked in on the wounded. Marli was still patchy and confused from the blow to the head. Colt had a broken arm, which wasn't great but was at least a simple break and could be set and put in a sling. Nils had taken a couple of savage blows to the ribs but would heal. Haller...Haller was dying and there was no point in sugar-coating it. He knew it. Everyone knew it. The blow had taken him in the gut and it was going to be a long, miserable, horrible death. The stench of a gut wound was already starting to fill the wagon.

"I'm giving you something for the pain," Istvhan said. He rifled through the medical chest and took the tiny vials of poppy milk from their hidden box. Haller made a sound, barely a grunt, more of a modulated breath.

He poured two vials of poppy milk down Haller's throat. It was a recklessly high dose, but if Haller died a kinder death because of it then Istvhan would take the stain on his soul. The gods knew, there were enough stains there that one more would hardly be visible.

Outside the wagon, he could hear Thorn and Brant talking. If any of the bandits had been left alive, Thorn had dealt with it. The irony of that was not lost on him.

He rolled a blanket up and slid it under the dying man's head, then went to go assist with the bodies.

CHAPTER 11

"I'm sorry," said Galen.

Clara paused, mid-way through filling the canteens. "Eh? For what?"

"Earlier," said the redhead, his voice clipped. "I threatened you. I'm sorry."

"I'm sorry, too. I shouldn't have reacted as I did."

"No, but your reaction didn't end up with a lot of people dead."

Shows what you know, my lad. "Well. Neither did yours."

"Only because Ist — the boss stopped me."

Clara gazed across the thin band of water. The stream was so small that it went barely twenty yards and then vanished into a mud puddle. *Spring* was entirely too generous a term for its source. *I've seen seeps twice this size. Still, it's water.*

"It's all right," she said. "You did stop. That's the important bit. And you would have stopped yourself if I hadn't shouted at you." *Shouted* was also entirely too generous a term, but there was no point in getting into details. She sank another canteen into the water and watched it slowly fill. "Look, Galen, we've been attacked by bandits and two of your men are dead and one is going to die pretty soon and my sisters are being taken somewhere in cages. I just can't care about this very much." She stoppered the canteen and started the next one.

"Would it be okay with you if we just agree that we're both sorry and then skip to the bit where we've forgiven each other and stopped feeling awkward about it?"

He stared at her while his own canteen overfilled and spilled over and then started to smile. "Yeah. Yeah, I think I would be okay with that."

"Thank St. Ursa." She slung the last canteen over her shoulder where it banged against the others. "Let's get back to camp."

Camp was also a generous term. They found a place with a rock face on one side of the road, and there they stopped. Everyone stood watches, even Clara. Istvhan did not protest. The situation had too much potential for disaster to stand on ceremony.

"Do you think they'll attack again, Captain?" Brant wrung his hands and looked around for a place to plant a soothing acorn.

"I wouldn't," said Istvhan. "On the other hand, I wouldn't have attacked the first time, either." He glanced into the rapidly growing dusk, to where grey-headed vultures were beginning to form a gyre overhead. He was glad they'd gotten away from the bodies. He'd seen scavengers work on men plenty of times, but it was still grim business.

"So they still *might* attack."

"They might do anything. They might grow wings and drop on us from above. You can't expect people to act logically."

He heard a familiar snort. Clara ambled over, arms folded over her generous chest. Istvhan studied the sky. "There's a great truth, Captain. For all we know, they've all gone mad from reindeer mushrooms."

"Reindeer mushrooms?" asked Brant.

"Red ones with white spots. The Arral don't keep reindeer, but they got the name from somewhere."

"I wonder if reindeer eat them."

"Possibly they make you think you're a reindeer," said Istvhan. He looked over at Clara. He'd kissed her and then yelled at her, and it all felt extremely awkward now. *You have to look at her sometime. Don't make it strange. It was your fault, not hers.* She had a faint smile but did not look mortally offended. That was a good sign. "Saint only knows what those men were thinking. We're too heavily armed for a casual attack. They must have thought we were carrying a great treasure. We just don't know."

"We *are* carrying a great treasure," said Brant. "But only to one who knows the worth of Emperor Oak."

"There's your answer. The bandits are being paid by an extremely jealous distiller who plans to destroy the competition before you reach Morstone."

Brant glared at him and Istvhan wondered briefly if the man was taking him seriously. *He does not actually seem to have a sense of humor, or perhaps it's very well hidden...* He glanced at Clara and saw that she, at least, was still smiling.

Haller died that night without waking up again. That was a mercy, although the poppy milk probably had more to do with it. The wagon stank of shit and death. Brant opened the cloth flaps, not caring about possible damage to the barrels. Istvhan took the small camp shovel for latrines and set to digging as soon as it was light enough to see.

The ground was hard and cold and stony. It was slow going but damned if he was leaving one of his men to rot on the ground for the vultures to pick at.

Clara materialized out of the gloom, holding a buckler shield. It was a piece of potmetal taken off the bandits, but whatever its failings as a shield, it worked as a crude shovel. She began dragging dirt out of the hole with it.

"I should probably say something about not expecting nuns to dig graves," said Istvhan, "but I'm grateful for the help." His knees were killing him. He'd done vigil on them, just as he'd vowed, and now it felt like there was a live coal under each kneecap.

"Births and deaths are what the clergy are for," said Clara. "I'm a lay sister, as I'm sure I've mentioned a few times, so they don't usually ask me to shrive people. But I've dug my share of graves."

"And delivered your share of babies?"

"No, that bit scares the crap out of me. I'm the person you send out to boil water so they don't faint."

Istvhan chuckled. "And here I thought you weren't scared of anything. My image of you is forever tarnished, Domina."

He was facing away from her but he could hear the smile in her voice. "Next I'll have you admitting I'm not actually a real nun. But tell me, Captain, how many babies have you seen delivered?"

"Six," said Istvhan.

"Six!"

"Six." They traded places and she began shoveling out the dirt that he had so painstakingly excavated. "I have many sisters and many cousins, as I said. I am no midwife but I am very good at patting a woman's hand and telling her that she is doing marvelously well while she attempts to break my fingers."

"Better you than me."

"Yes, you do seem to have very dainty fingers."

She made a noise somewhere between outrage and amusement. "Dainty! I was hiding behind the door when they passed out daintiness."

"Compared to me, Domina, everyone is dainty."

She turned around to face him and held up a hand. He held his up to meet it and grinned wickedly as her eyes widened. Clara was a woman built to heroic scale, but his hands were still nearly half-again as large as hers. "Well," she muttered. "Be damned."

"Oh, almost certainly." He tackled another section of the pit. "You dig well for such a dainty person, though."

She mock-swung the shield at his head. "Don't think I'm not willing to dig two graves, Captain."

"Just kill me before you start. It hardly seems fair to make me dig my own."

She snorted explosively, excavating more dirt with the edge of the shield. Istvhan absolutely believed that she had dug graves before. Not so much because of the digging, but because she was joking about it.

The first one you dig in horrified awareness of your own mortality. The second one you add in gallows humor. By the third, you're positively hilarious. The only exception he'd ever found to that was children. You couldn't laugh while you dug a child's grave. *Oh, maybe you can, if you've dug too many of them, but the gods prevent me from ever acquiring that particular skill...*

"Did you know him well?" asked Clara. "Haller?"

"No," he said, grateful for the interruption to his thoughts. "He wasn't even supposed to be here. The man he replaced, Potts, came down with a case of werkblight and we had to leave him with the healers."

"Werkblight. Huh." Clara shoved more dirt out of the way. "We don't see many cases up by us. More along the canal."

Istvhan nodded. Werkblight had been a terrifying scourge a dozen years back, popping up seemingly without warning, sometimes spreading, sometimes not. Somebody would break out in hives that rapidly turned into massive skin lesions when exposed to sunlight. A person standing right next to them might walk away unharmed, while a person thirty feet away might be the next victim. The usual rules of plagues did not seem to apply. People had panicked, blaming magic or gnoles or foreigners or bad air, setting buildings on fire, all the usual trappings of human terror in the face of disease. And then one day some priest of the Many Armed God with no healer training had figured out that it wasn't even a plague, it was a severe allergic reaction to something or other, the healers worked up a treatment, and just like that, the fatal plague was relegated to a minor annoyance.

"We carry the meds like everybody else. Got him dosed as soon as the first sore appeared. He was fine, but we left him at the nearest temple just in case, and picked up Haller as a replacement."

Clara sighed. "Isn't that always the way?"

Istvhan straightened up. His lower back grumbled at him. "I think this is as good as we're going to get," he said. "We'll pile some rocks over top, but this ground needs picks, not shovels."

Clara nodded. She finished shoveling the last of the dirt out and let Istvhan help her out of the pit. She looked tired. Her hair had come frizzling out of its braid and there were blue shadows under her eyes. Her robes were streaked with the reddish clay of the grave. Istvhan wanted very much to put his hand against her face and tell her that it would be all right, that they would live through this. He stifled it because that was the sort of intimacy you did not take with nuns. Even nuns who had helped you dig a grave.

Burying Haller was quick and utilitarian. Clara wasn't judging. It had to be, with the possibility of more bandits showing up at any time. Privately, she thought that it was probably unwise to have stopped even this long, but she wasn't going to say it. People needed to bury their dead, even mercenaries.

They wrapped him in his own bedroll and lowered him into the grave. "Does anyone know if Haller worshipped any particular god?" asked Istvhan.

No one did. One of the mercenaries spoke up. "He didn't talk about home much," he said. "None of us had worked with him before." Apparently he thought that sounded too much like a criticism, so he added, "Good man, though. Kept his kit clean and did his share of work. Never tried to get out of it."

"And that's as good a eulogy as you get in this line of work," said Istvhan. He bowed his head. "All right. Gods, if any of you are kindly inclined to our fallen brother Haller, look out for him on the other side." He nodded once, then grabbed the shovel and began filling in the grave.

The other mercenaries murmured their own words and joined in. Brindle took one side of the pile of dirt and set it flying with his strong hind legs. In short order, the earth was moved and stones piled over the top of the final resting place of a mercenary named Haller.

"Are the mules ready?" asked Istvhan, wiping red clay from his face. It had dried and flaked like blood.

"A mule is eager to go," said Brindle. The gnole's stripes were stained orange and his fur had stiffened in short spikes that gave him a particularly fierce expression. "A gnole, also."

"Right. Let's move. There's a town two days from here, and if we make it alive, I intend to sleep for a week."

Clara looked back on that declaration with the weight of a promise. They made it to the town alive, but it took three days and all of them seemed to last a century.

They did not camp. They walked as long as the mules held out and then they stopped until it was light enough for the mules to start walking again. They lit no fires at night. No one even really slept. They sat with their backs to the wagon, shoulder to shoulder, waiting for attacks from the dark.

"You could sleep in the wagon with the wounded, Domina," said Istvhan.

"I could," said Clara, not moving.

"No one will think less of you."

"Mmm." She gave him the best smile she could muster under the circumstances, but she didn't get up. He sat on one side of her, Thorn on the other, all of them half-dozing, half-watchful, waiting.

Clara woke once to find herself slumped against his shoulder. She moved awkwardly, trying to resettle herself, and he only murmured something that might have been "It's all right," but it was clear that he wasn't entirely awake either.

When it was light, they got up again. You could steep tea leaves in cold water and make something that wasn't exactly tea but still had some kind of kick. Galen passed the tea around. It tasted gritty and bitter, but everyone drank it.

They put Marli on the third mule and Thorn led her behind the others. Everyone else watched the woods and the hills for movement. A partridge taking flight set them all jumping, grabbing for sword-hilts, and there were too many partridges and too many geese and everyone made themselves even more tired.

Now? whispered the beast. *Now?*

No. It's only birds. Go back to sleep.

The beast grumbled. It understood watchfulness. It was good at watching. Unfortunately, as groggy as Clara was, she didn't know if she could contain it if something startled it too badly.

Go to sleep. It's cold. You should be napping.

It obeyed.

They rested the mules. They sat on the cold ground and didn't quite sleep. They stood up. They went on again.

By the morning of the third day, Clara had stopped really believing there was a town ahead of them. There was no town. Towns weren't real. What sort of world had towns in it? You just walked along forever, not really sleeping, hoping the wounded didn't die. Maybe they had already died. Maybe everyone had died in the attack, including Clara. They were all ghosts, walking beside the wagon, pulled by the ghosts of mules. Did mules have ghosts? Probably they did, if it would be inconvenient for someone. Mules were like that. There was no town. There was only the road, which was damp clay splotched with stones, like a toad's back. Perhaps it was a toad. Perhaps the whole world was a toad. It was no stupider than anyone else's cosmology. Clara would leave the order of St. Ursa and found the order of St. Toad. They would sleep a lot. Yes. Sleeping seemed like a good commandment for the order. Sleep and hot tea. Yes.

She was working out the various ranks and the secondary rules for St. Toad's worship when Galen said, "There's smoke rising ahead. We're nearly there."

The town probably had a name, but Clara never learned it. It was the Place of Hot Tea and Beds, Sacred Holy Land of St. Toad. There were a half-dozen houses, a blacksmith, and a public house with two stories. Istvhan and Brant went ahead to the public house. The rest of them stood on the edge of town, clutching the wagon sides for support. Brindle got down and patted the mules, telling them that they were good and handsome and patient and almost as good as an ox.

Clara grayed out for a bit, then came to as Istvhan returned. "All right," he said. "Troops, we're in the stable. Brant, Domina, they have rooms for each of you, and we'll put Marli in the third. They've got a doctor who will come out to look at her. Thorn, you stay with her."

As he passed Clara, he leaned over and added "I'm afraid your feet will dangle over the end a bit."

"At this point," said Clara wearily, "so long as my head is on the pillow, I do not think the rest of me has much say in the matter." He chuckled.

The room was the size of a large closet and thus roomy compared to a novice nun's cell, and it was clean. There was a tiny slit of window to let in air and a chamberpot under the bed. Clara peeled off her filthy outer robe and dropped it outside the door, then fell down on the bed. Her legs dangled off. Her arms also dangled off. It did not matter. She slept.

CHAPTER 12

Istvhan wanted sleep more than he wanted air but he could not until his people were settled. The stables were clean and warm by the standards of a mountain in early winter. The woman who ran the public house was definitely used to caravans coming in, but also had not been expecting any this late. She told them plainly that she could provide dinners but not supplies for the road. Istvhan agreed. He would have agreed to just about anything if it included a doctor for the wounded, which it did.

It took an hour for the doctor to get there. He was an older man with shockingly white hair. "I'm nothing fancy," he said. "I treat horses and humans. I was out on a farm when word came."

"It's fine," said Istvhan wearily. "It's been days, another hour won't matter now."

"Mmm."

The word came back about as Istvhan had expected. Colt and Nils would heal on their own. Marli was different. "She needs to not be in a wagon or on a horse," said the doctor bluntly. "Her brain's addled and bouncing around isn't helping. She'll get better...proba-bly...but she needs quiet and rest."

Istvhan nodded. "Right, then," he said, and went to go make arrangements with the innkeeper.

"I'd like to stay with her," said Thorn. "I know the job's not over, Captain, and I know you're short-handed, but..." She trailed off. Thorn was not the type to beg.

Neither was Istvhan the type to be needlessly cruel. "I expected you would. I wouldn't leave one of our people alone with an injury like this. The room's taken care of for a season. I did volunteer you to help chop firewood for our host." He paused. "You'll get snowed in, I expect. Can't be helped. Make for a Temple of the White Rat when Marli's well enough to travel, and they'll make sure everything's square."

"Good of you, Captain. Thank you."

He left Marli's room and went down the hall. Snores emanated from Clara's room. He smiled ruefully. The nun was a trooper, he'd give her that. She'd stayed on her feet for that entire grim forced march, even if she'd been half-asleep and holding onto the wagon toward the end. He checked in on Brindle and the mules, and found the gnole stretched out atop a pile of grain sacks. "They doing well?"

"Eh." The gnole shrugged. "A mule is tough. A mule sometimes pretends otherwise, if a mule thinks it will get out of work, though. A gnole thinks they will be fine." He closed his eyes again, which Istvhan took as a clear dismissal.

At last, with all his charges settled, he spread his cloak and his bedroll over the straw and sank down himself and sleep fell on him as quickly as an enemy.

Clara woke with her back aching and her feet aching and her head aching. She sat up. Everything ached more or less the same amount, so nothing was getting special treatment. She wrapped the blanket around herself. How long had she slept? Was it time for breakfast or dinner?

Apparently, it was dinner. Her robe, newly washed, was waiting outside the door. She shrugged into it. It had been dried over a fire, as was the fashion here, so the fabric smelled strongly of woodsmoke.

Pungent, but not unpleasant, and at least it covered other, more bodily odors. She ran a brush through her hair. She needed a bath badly. Her last splash in the river had been days ago. Still, nobody else was going to be in any better shape.

She came down the stairs and saw that several of the mercenaries, including Captain Istvhan, were standing in the common room of the inn. They waved and Istvhan gestured to a table.

Clara let out an internal groan when she saw the seating arrangements. A long, low table, flanked by long, low benches. The people in this part of the world tended to be short and compact and they built their furniture accordingly.

She sat down. Her knees were higher than the table. She was going to have to bend nearly double to eat. *It's fire and food and you're not being attacked by bandits. Shut up and thank St. Ursa for your blessings.*

Istvhan sat down across from her with a grunt. She looked across the table and saw that his kneecaps were also up around his ears. They shared a long, speaking look across the table, two very large people in a much smaller world, and Clara felt a smile spreading across her face.

"I'm so glad to sit down that I don't even care," said Istvhan. "But it's probably going to take a couple of people and a pulley to get me back up again."

"Oh, Saint Ursa, you and me both."

"Are you doing okay?"

"I feel like you look."

Istvhan glanced down at his scratched hands and rumpled clothes. "I'm so very sorry. You look much better than I feel."

"Is that chivalry I hear talking?"

"Possibly."

The innkeeper provided food. Clara had no idea what it was and didn't care. Some local vegetable that resembled sweet potatoes, with a spicy gravy and unidentifiable meat bits. It was hot and not a tightly packed bar of meat and berries. It was amazing. The entire table put their heads down and ate in steady, business-like fashion, not speaking until they were done.

"Madam innkeeper," said Galen, placing his hand over his heart, "you have saved all our lives. You are a gem among women."

"Ah, get on with you." She waved a dish rag in his general direction. "I know your type. You'd say that to anyone who fed you."

"Yes, but I mean it very sincerely every time."

"And now," said Istvhan, sitting up and then grabbing for his lower back with a pained expression, "may I ask you for the news of the road? Or perhaps share ours?"

"Ah?" The innkeeper pulled up a chair. Clara could practically see ears pricking up among the patrons who lined the bar. It was all innocent enough — travelers were expected to share the news from the road, a payment as real as coin, if less tangible — but she still wasn't sure if she liked it.

What do they know about the ones who raided my convent? The Arral let them pass, even though some of the thanes must have guessed. Are these people complicit as well?

She hated having to be this suspicious. It felt like she was committing some kind of sin against these strangers, if only in her head, by suspecting them of such crimes.

"Bandits," said Istvhan. "Cost me a couple good men and laid out one of my best." He jerked his chin in the direction of Marli's room. "Don't the Arral do anything?"

The innkeeper sighed. "Only if they attack the Arral. And I'm not exactly blaming them for that, because you notice we're not doing anything about them either." She scowled. "Of course, we're mostly farmers and hunters, we don't have the kind of force the Arral do. And I won't swear the nearest thane doesn't get a payoff from the bandits for letting them alone."

"Way of the world, I suppose." Istvhan leaned back. "Anyone I can pass the word to that might be able to do anything about it?"

The innkeeper shook her head. "I've thought about it," she said. "We've got no local lords and we sure as hell don't want anyone's army coming in. Lesser of two evils."

"Paladins?" asked Istvhan. Clara lifted her head, faintly surprised at that suggestion, or at least that it was a mercenary captain who made it.

One of the regulars snorted. "If there was a demon, the Dreaming God's folk would be here already. We've sent word to the Forge God's temples, but they don't much care for fixing problems in the middle of nowhere."

"They should," said Galen, all humor gone from his voice.

There was half a beat of awkward silence and then Istvhan said, "Ah, well," in a hearty voice and held out his mug for a refill. "Way of the world, as I said. But this ale is fine enough it ought to be defended. Another question for you fine people. About a month ago, a pair of wagons might have passed this way." He nodded to Clara to continue.

"Two wagons," said Clara. "With bars. Canvas rolled down over them, though, so you might not see the bars. And I doubt that the drivers would let anyone get close enough to see the contents." She marveled, from a little distance, how calm her voice sounded, relating this information. She had been inside those wagons, watching her sisters, her sisters watching her back. When the canvas came down, things became hot and dim and close. When the canvas came down, you realized how much the fresh air through the bars was keeping you sane. "My sisters. Nuns from my convent. They were kidnapped."

"You can scream," said the man who sat beside the wagon driver. "We are coming to a town. You can scream and shout and there is even a chance that they will hear you." He lifted one hand, which held the ends of a narrow chain threaded through the bars. The middle of the chain passed around the neck of Anais, the youngest novice, holding her tight to the bars. "And if you scream, I pull. She'll definitely choke to death. Her head might even come off, if I pull hard enough." He smiled at them, a flash of teeth in the gloom of the canvas. "So think very carefully before you scream."

Anais looked at them and mouthed, *Do it*. The abbess shook her head. "We will not scream," she said. And they did not, while tears streamed down Anais's face and she breathed in short, panicky gasps and the chain around her throat twisted red lines into her skin.

The innkeeper swore aloud. "A month ago, you say?"

Clara nodded, yanked from the memory and glad to go. Istvhan looked from the woman's face to Clara's.

"The plague wagons," said one of the men at the bar. "Gods be damned."

"They played us for fools," said the innkeeper. Her lips went thin and hard. "They said they had sickness in the wagons and couldn't stop for fear of infection. The leader tossed us coin and we set down bread and meat and wine for him to pick up. Gave the bastards a good damn deal, too, since you don't haggle over rations for the sick." She looked as if she wanted to spit, but didn't. "And they were prisoners, you say?"

"Probably they were sick, too," said Clara. "But I doubt it was anything they could spread. Just ill from being confined and kept in chains."

"I gave them a load of fodder for their horses," said the man at the bar who had spoken. He had turned around to face the table full of travelers. "Only charged them half, because...well. Hells." He looked Clara in the eye, and she saw only regret there. "I'm sorry, Sister. Didn't mean to help them on their way."

"You couldn't have known," said Clara. "It was charity that motivated you. There is nothing to forgive." Absolving the man of his small, misdirected kindness steadied her a little. This was the sort of thing she understood, even if she was a mere lay sister, and not trained in any of the higher mysteries. People wanted to know that they had done their best and that the gods saw them doing it. They didn't need to know that you were a minor member of an exceedingly minor order, they just needed to know that you presumably had some sort of connection to the god you represented.

Which I do, but probably not quite in the way they would expect... Still, St. Ursa had kept her on the trail of her sisters, and that was no small thing. *Thank You. I am still following as best I can.*

"So they did come this way," said Istvhan. "That's useful to know. Thank you."

"I can't believe someone would kidnap nuns," muttered the innkeeper. "Is nothing sacred anymore?"

Galen and Istvhan traded glances, not quite subtly enough for Clara to avoid seeing it. She said nothing. The reasons that the raiders might want these particular nuns was not a topic for general conversation. She folded her hands in her sleeves and looked away, trying not to meet anyone's eyes.

As her gaze traveled over the bar, she caught a glimpse of a man who was staring at her. He was medium height, which might make him tall for this region, medium build. Hair medium brown, skin medium tan. Nothing that would make him stand out, a man designed to fade into backgrounds. If he hadn't been staring at her so intently, she would never have noticed him.

Why is he looking at me like that?

Some men did like larger women, it was true. Clara was aware that she was a striking figure, when she wasn't exhausted and travel-worn. But she didn't get any sense of lust from him, nor awkwardness, merely a kind of chilly appraisal.

You may be imagining things. You were just feeling suspicious a moment ago, and now someone who stares a bit strangely is setting you on edge. Clara examined this thought dispassionately. Could she be imagining things? St. Ursa knew that she'd been through enough in the last few weeks to set anyone's nerves jangling.

No. No, I don't think so. She recognized that little voice, the one that told you to be nice and get along and doubt your own suspicions. It was good at counterfeiting the voice of the convent, the one that told you to be kind and forgive, but it wasn't quite right. She glanced over at the unobtrusive man again. He turned away, face half-hidden behind his mug. *No. Something's going on there. But we're leaving tomorrow, and other people have their own oddities that occasionally intersect with yours. Keep an eye out, but don't panic. Yet.*

The conversation went on around her. Galen described the Arral markets and gave a droll rendition on the current politics. The innkeeper jumped in occasionally with clarifications and questions. With a full stomach and a warm fire, despite the uncomfortable bench and the suspicious fellow at the bar, Clara might almost have fallen asleep.

"Bit of an uproar in the farthest west market," said Galen, waving a hand. "Down south, they said they found the damnedest thing. A dead body who'd had his head cut off — and another head that didn't match!" He waited for the appropriate gasps from the audience.

The innkeeper started. "What?"

"A body with the wrong head," said Galen. "Had you heard this story?"

"No," said the innkeeper. "No, but Farmer Goldeen — out on the south reach — she found one not quite a fortnight ago. Not the wrong head, but a dead body. Her head had been cut off, and it was an awful thing. Goldeen buried her there and described her clothes, but nobody knew who she might be."

Clara sought Istvhan's eyes. He gave her a short, grim nod.

Whatever he's chasing — and he's definitely chasing it — they came this way. Our ways go together a little longer, then. She found that she was glad of that, though she wished the reasons hadn't been so grim. *Severed heads and kidnapped nuns. And a wagonload of barrels and a man obsessed with oak trees. The gods are being more inscrutable than usual.*

"Well," said Galen, leaning back. "Then you're considerably more up to date than I am. Any strangers about? Anything suspicious?"

The innkeeper shook her head. "Though I'm glad to hear that it happened so far away, even if I wish it hadn't happened at all. I hope that means they were moving along. You hate to think of a killer anywhere, but you don't want them holed up nearby."

"No blame on you," said Istvhan easily. "That's not the sort of thing anyone wants. I hope wherever they fetch up, there's someone who can deal with them."

And I am quite sure that was a lie, my fine captain. You want to know where they fetch up because you think you're *the one who can deal with them. What haven't you told me?*

Silly question, of course. Whatever he hadn't told her couldn't possibly equal what *she* hadn't told *him.*

Brant spoke up then, asking if there was a forester who knew about the local trees, and the conversation went off in a different direction entirely. Clara shifted uncomfortably on the bench and decided that she was done. She got to her feet, apologizing her way past the others, and Istvhan rose as well. "A shame to leave such a fine company," he said, "but much more ale and you'll be carrying me to my bed. If you'll excuse me..."

Istvhan made his apologies with only half his mind, while furiously working through the latest news of the smooth men and trying to place the location and time on his mental map of the area. How fast were they moving? He'd despaired of catching up with them, but they did not seem to be moving terribly rapidly either. *Less than a fortnight. We were faster on the road than they were.*

He looked up the steps and discovered that he was eye-level with Clara's backside, which put a brief halt to his mental mathematics. Her robes did their very best to disguise anything resembling curves, but they were clearly outmatched. A man could grab onto hips like that and pull her close and—

"Thank you again, Captain Istvhan," said Clara, when they had reached the top of the stairs.

Ah. Yes. He hauled his mind forcibly out of the gutter. "For what? Dragging you on a forced march through a nest of bandits?"

"Not just for that. For helping me stay on the trail of my sisters." She smiled at him and his heart turned over, which was ridiculous. *She's a* nun.

And you're a paladin, however little you mention it these days. And neither of you are sworn to celibacy.

Vigil on my knees again. And they haven't recovered from the last stretch. Saint have mercy.

The sound from the common room seemed very far away. Her

eyes were warm and he could smell smoke and sage and sweat and he needed to walk away, he needed to walk away now.

"You do not need to thank me, Domina," he said. He seemed a little lightheaded, which was frankly ridiculous, he knew women, he'd grown up with women, even as a callow boy with more balls than sense he'd never had a problem talking to them. Except apparently this one.

"You got me through the mountains," she said. "That's not a small thing."

"You helped to defend my people. And I have made an ass of myself, and I can only beg forgiveness from you again."

She actually looked momentarily puzzled, and then a flash of amusement crossed her face. "The kiss, you mean? I didn't think it was that bad."

"No! No, of course not — but it should never — I should *never* have — not without asking — I am not a man who—"

And I'm babbling. Yep. There I go. Vigil on my knees on gravel. Vigil on—

She kissed him.

She wasn't gentle. Istvhan felt his spine hit the wall and while he was used to letting women take the lead because he didn't want to alarm them, he was not used to having a woman take the lead who was the same size he was and could possibly break him in half. It was both slightly worrisome and terrifyingly erotic. She claimed his mouth like a conquering army and he was entirely willing to surrender.

He slid one arm around her waist, pulling her closer. She made a soft growling sound and leaned into him, her breasts soft against his chest and dear god, he had been celibate for less than a month and he was supposed to be getting some rest and instead he wanted to kick open the nearest door and drag her down onto the bed and bury himself in that softness until dawn.

And then she stepped back.

Istvhan heard himself panting. Her lips were parted and there was a definite wildness in her eyes, but she smiled again and rose onto her toes and kissed his forehead.

"There. Now we're even," she whispered against his skin.

He dragged in a breath and stared at her and then began to laugh.

"Goodnight, Captain Istvhan."

"...Domina."

She turned and strolled down the hallway to her room, leaving him with an aching cock and the definite feeling that the nuns of St. Ursa were not at all what he was used to.

Was that unkind? That may have been unkind.

Clara found that she did not regret it, not one little bit. Istvhan's eyes had gone so wide that he looked like an owl, and for one second she was afraid she really had traumatized the poor man, but then his mouth had opened and his fingers spread across her back, each one hot as a brand. He was all muscle and strength, his hips tight against hers. It had, perhaps, not been as mind-bending as the kiss on the battlefield, but there was no help for it, you could only do so much when people weren't trying to kill you.

And if he went away aroused and frustrated...well, now he knew how she'd felt.

The heat of desire filled her more kindly than all her rage and sorrow had. Clara welcomed the respite. She wondered if he'd knock on her door, and what she would do if he did.

You know damn well what you'd do. Probably not on the bed, because you can barely fit one person on it. On the floor then. Hard and fast, at least the first time. They could take their time later. If there was a later.

Best to do it now, whispered a small, nagging voice. *Do it now before you find your sisters and the truth comes out. There's no chance at all afterward.*

She grimaced as she got ready for bed. No, there never was any chance afterward. It was why Clara had resigned herself to a lifetime of casual relationships. She'd learned that lesson once, learned it hard, and did not need to be taught it a second time.

Istvhan was a handsome man. He made her laugh. He cared for his men. There was depth and warmth and concern behind his good humor. If she was the sort of woman who fell in love, she'd be halfway there already. *And suppose you did go to his bed, and then he learned your secret? Do you really want to see that horror in those big brown eyes?*

She'd seen it once. One lover. A passionate man with a poet's eyes and a way of biting his lower lip that had undoubtedly brought more than one woman to her knees. It had certainly worked on a much younger Clara. He'd talked of traveling together on the canal, selling the convent's wares. A lay sister could not marry, but they were certainly allowed partners. She'd allowed herself to dream.

Well, there was no sense dwelling on it. It was an old pain, long since scabbed over. She'd spent about six months moping and then another six months screwing anything with two legs and a cock, and life went on.

Clara did wish occasionally that she was the sort of woman who could love another woman as more than a sister. It would have made her life a great deal easier. Sister Rose and the Sister Apothecary, for example, had been devoted to each other for over a decade. But it was not in Clara's nature and St. Ursa called only women, so there was nothing much to be done.

He did not knock on her door. She slid between the covers, her body still half-aching with desire, and stared at the ceiling, waiting for sleep to come.

CHAPTER 13

"A gnole suspects we have a problem," said Brindle, reining in the mules.

Istvhan and Clara both looked up. "Oh hell," said Istvhan. "Not more bandits. Not again."

They had left the town behind two days ago, and things had been easy. Easy enough that Clara's back teeth had unclenched and Galen hadn't screamed in his sleep last night. Easy enough that they'd actually made good time and Clara had entertained a brief hope that they might be getting a little closer to the raiders who had taken her sisters. And now this.

There were seven men on the road, all of them on horseback. Clara narrowed her eyes, scanning from face to face, and then stopped on one so unobtrusive that she remembered him immediately.

"I don't think these are ordinary bandits," she said. "Third one on the left was at the inn the other night when we talked about the nuns." Istvhan grunted.

The leader kicked his horse forward. Istvhan rested his hand on his sword hilt. Behind her, Clara could hear Galen quietly giving orders.

"Captain," said the leader. "I have a proposition for you."

"You're not my type," said Istvhan.

The man smiled tolerantly. "We have no quarrel with you, captain, nor your men. The woman with you, however, is of great interest to us."

Clara could feel the sudden weight of eyes on her. Galen. Brant. Brindle. The mercenaries. She could almost hear the thoughts. *Why do they want you? What have you been hiding?* Only Istvhan was not looking at her. Istvhan stood beside her and she heard his breath go out softly, and then the next sound was the scrape of steel as his sword left its sheath.

He took a step forward, getting his shoulder in front of Clara. "I'm afraid that she is not for sale."

"I was not offering to pay." Another tolerant smile. "There is no need for weapons. She will be quite safe, Captain. I have no interest in harming anyone. And I am certain that she is eager to be reunited with her sisters."

Clara felt her breath hiss through her teeth. *He knows where they are.*

In her head, the beast roused. *This one? Now?*

Not yet. Down. There was still a chance they might get out of this. A small, infinitesimal chance, but if she could get information... "Where are my sisters?" she asked.

"Come with me and you will see them."

"Somehow I do not trust your good intentions," said Istvhan.

The man shrugged. "I will take her to her sisters. I give you my word."

"Where are my sisters?" Clara repeated, hearing a growl rattle the edge of her voice. Calm was finally deserting her. *Not yet, dammit. Talk. Talk your way out, get information, and you will not have to wake the beast and Istvhan will never know...*

"They are honored guests."

A second man rode forward, his hands filled with gray rope. Clara recognized a net and felt the rage building in her chest, a rage that no catechism could contain. A net. A heavy net for beasts.

You know where my sisters are.

You know what I am.

It was all slipping away. It would be over soon. Everyone would know.

"Ropes?" asked Istvhan. "Is this how you treat honored guests in Morstone?" Even through her anger, Clara recognized that he was fishing for information.

"For our safety and hers."

"Tell me where they are, and whatever you are being paid, I will double it."

"Oh, I doubt that, highly." The leader gazed at Istvhan, then gave a short, surprised laugh. "You don't know, do you?"

"Know what? Why you kidnap nuns?"

Don't tell him. Don't...oh hell, it doesn't matter. He's going to find out in the next few minutes anyway. Clara felt an unexpected stab of anguish for what she was about to lose. *Should have knocked on the door that night at the inn, Istvhan.*

No, perhaps it was better this way. The shock would not be nearly so great as if he'd bedded her.

"Give us the nun," said the man in the lead. "Give us the nun and we walk away. We have no interest in you."

The beast growled in her head. *Now? Now?*

Seven of them. Some of our people are wounded. All of his are mounted. Saint's teeth, maybe I should let them capture me. They're determined to take me alive and I've got a better chance of learning where they're holding my sisters this way.

"You should probably give me up," she said in an undertone. "They want me alive."

"Domina," said Istvhan, just as quietly, "they will have to go through me first."

"But—"

"Come and take her," Istvhan shouted, and stepped in front of Clara. His sword was held upright and he looked like a knight, doomed and gallant, not like a mercenary. He was going to die.

The leader kicked his horse into a run.

Now? Now? The world was dim, her vision slipping, but she could still see Istvhan standing in front of her, brave and foolish and utterly mad, and he was going to die because of her and there was only one way that she could stop it.

Now?

Shit. Yes. Now. She threw down her sledge, took a deep breath, and turned into a bear.

Istvhan saw something happen in the corner of his vision. A ripple. He jerked back, fearing the enemy had somehow launched an attack from that quarter, and instead of Clara standing next to him, there was a mass of fur and fangs.

He had lived for a good many years and had a number of experiences. He had still never been so close to a live bear.

It was gigantic. It towered over him, a behemoth bigger than a horse. Behind him, he distantly heard the mules screaming.

The bear roared. Its teeth were longer than his fingers. It took two steps forward toward the raiders, and the lead horse, which had been running toward Istvhan, suddenly decided that it would rather be anywhere else at all. It spun on its hind hooves. The rider tried to get his mount under control and sawed on the reins, but the horse was maddened, throwing its head back, until the bear roared again and the animal reared, plunged, and threw its rider clear.

He landed in the road. Istvhan noticed, with the last shreds of his attention, that his neck was not at an angle found in living men. The other horses had broken and run, and their riders, less foolish or more fortunate, were letting them.

And just like that, the road was clear, except for the dead man and the dust and a bear bigger than anything he'd ever seen.

Where the hell is Clara? Did she fall? Did it come down the hillside and attack? What the hell is going on?

She was nowhere to be seen. He looked for her under the bear's feet and saw her robes. *Shit. Shit. Shit.*

The bear dropped to all fours. It was as high at the shoulder as a horse and twice as massive. It turned its head toward him.

It appears I am going to die.

The tide was not rising. He did not look at the bear and think of all the ways to kill it. He had no idea how to kill it. The black tide, which had carried him against men and monsters, was apparently just as flummoxed as he was. The bear had trampled Clara and it was probably going to kill him in very short order and he had no idea what to do.

Of all the ways I could have died, I did not see this one coming.

Perhaps if he wounded it in a way that slowed it down, it would leave the rest of his men alone. Perhaps he could get in one last strike for a woman that, under other circumstances, might have been more than a friend. He commended his soul to the Saint of Steel, lifted his sword, and stabbed the bear as hard as he could in the leg.

The results were not all that he could have hoped for. The shaggy coat threw off his aim and the stab turned into a slash that hit hide and fat and nearly bounced off. *Saint's balls, what are bears made of? The damn thing's practically wearing armor under there!*

The bear swung its head around with a guttural snarl, swatting at the sword. It ripped the blade out of Istvhan's hands and he watched it clatter into the dust. Then the bear roared.

This is it. The last thing I see. He looked straight down the bear's gullet, a red tunnel framed by massive teeth. Black lips curled back and he staggered back a step, not even thinking to run, waiting for those jaws to close over his head.

The bear's breath smelled like salt and sage and one very tiny part of his brain thought that was odd and the roar went on and on and sounded like *"Graaughhharrr....aaa....fuck,"* and that was even odder and then the bear seemed to ripple and got a great deal smaller and Sister Clara was naked on her knees in the dirt, clutching her shoulder while blood poured down her arm.

CHAPTER 14

Istvhan went to his knees in front of her. Had he taken a blow to the head? Had the bear knocked him unconscious? He looked around wildly for the bear and there wasn't one, or rather, there was Clara, and she was kneeling in the wreckage of her robes and bleeding and his sword was still on the ground, and that meant...that must mean...

"You're a *shapechanger?!*"

"You're quick," she said, in a voice that still had quite a lot of growl to it. "With the sword, too."

She was a bear.

She had turned into a bear.

He'd kissed a very large bear with teeth like daggers.

He'd stabbed a woman who had fought beside him.

He had ten thousand different things to say, questions to ask, curses to utter, and could think of none of them. Reflex took over. He swung his cloak off his shoulders and over her body, then grabbed for one of the torn sleeves of her robe to bind the wound.

"I'm sorry," he said. "I didn't know. I thought the bear had trampled you." He spared a glance down the road and saw that the men on horseback were long gone. "I'm so very sorry. I never meant to hurt you, Domina."

She tilted an ironic eyebrow at him. "No, you were all set to die for me, weren't you? I should be more grateful, but this hurts like a stone bitch."

"Yes, Domina." He pried her fingers away from her arm and held the cloth against it. She gnawed on her lower lip while he tried to determine the extent of the wound.

Perhaps the bear's hide had protected her, because it was, if not particularly shallow, at least not deep enough to risk the arm. The edges were ragged and it bled through the first layer of cloth even as he bound it, but he kept wrapping. Her skin was soft but the muscle underneath was rock solid, the kind that could swing a sledge-hammer without even noticing.

"There," he said finally, tucking the ends of the wrapping.

She sat back, testing the motion. His eyes went to her chest involuntarily and Saint's balls, she had magnificent breasts and they were *right there* and he was going to have to do vigil standing on his *head*, he'd stabbed a nun who was also a bear and now he was ogling her while she was bleeding, gods above, was there no end to his personal depravity?

"I'm so sorry," he said again. He couldn't stop apologizing. If he apologized to the end of time, it probably wouldn't be enough. How dare he even think such things? What was wrong with him? "Domina, I am a *worm*."

"Well, I'm a bear, but you probably guessed that already."

He gaped at her. She snorted. "Anything left of my robes?"

Istvhan picked them up and shook them out. The looseness had saved them, but the sleeves were destroyed. He yanked the remaining one off and slid the now-sleeveless robe over her shoulders. Trying to get her injured arm through the ragged hole meant that for a moment her body was pressed against his side and Istvhan told himself very firmly that he had stabbed her in the arm and he was a profound degenerate for thinking of anything else at this moment or possibly ever again and she was very soft with a core of iron under it and then, thank all the living gods and dead saints, Brindle appeared next to him. "A bear-lady is hurt bad?"

"Not bad," she said. "Nothing vital."

"Then a bear-lady should get off the road." The gnole looked very hard at Istvhan. "A gnole thinks a human should go talk to other humans. Before other humans get strange, yeah?"

Istvhan jumped as if he'd been stung. "Yes. Of course." Saint's blood. A shapechanger. Were the others going to become violent? "Brindle..."

"Go, go. A gnole has traveled with a human who lived in a damn sword. Bear-lady is nothing."

"Yes, but..."

The gnole peeled back his lip to show a single canine tooth. It occurred to Istvhan, somewhat belatedly, that perhaps Clara would prefer not to have her attacker standing right in front of her. He jumped back, hands raised. "Yes. Yes, of course. A moment."

"So," said Galen, as Istvhan retrieved his sword and walked back to them. He looked as poleaxed as Istvhan felt. "So that's why they wanted the nuns."

"What?" Istvhan blinked at his second-in-command. "Why they... oh *shit.*" He wiped the sword blade on his sleeve and slammed it back in the sheath. "Oh blistering shit. It's not just her. It's the whole convent. Those raiders weren't kidnapping nuns, they were kidnapping *shapechangers.*"

"Iron cages," said Galen, looking over his shoulder. Brindle had gotten an arm under Clara's good side and was helping her to her feet. "They rounded the lot of them up like animals."

"She's not an animal," said Istvhan. "I mean...she talks."

"So did those rabbits," said one of the mercenaries sourly. He did not look pleased.

For reasons he couldn't even begin to articulate, he bristled. "Shut up, Andrel. She saved our asses just now."

"Which wouldn't have been in danger if she hadn't been with us," the man said. He folded his arms and glared up at Istvhan. "Those men weren't here after money."

It was more words out of the mercenary than Istvhan had heard since the trip started. Possibly the man had been saving them up. "Andrel, enough."

"Sure, you'd say that," said the mercenary, staring up at Istvhan. "How long has that beast been sucking your—"

Andrel was on the ground and Istvhan's knuckles hurt. He gazed thoughtfully at his knuckles, then down at the man. "We do not talk that way about nuns," he said calmly. "Do we?"

Andrel started to get up. Galen shot Istvhan one quick look — *Is this wise?* — and then placed his boot on Andrel's chest. "I'm willing to forget you said that about a nun," he said. "I suggest, however, that you remember exactly why you are on this trip, and who is in charge of it."

The mercenary put his hand to his face and muttered something.

Galen put a little weight on the boot and said, "I didn't quite catch that."

"I...apologize," grated Andrel. "I spoke rashly."

"Good," said Galen, letting him up.

Istvhan rubbed his forehead, feeling the sting in his hand. "All right," he said. "Let's get the hell out of here before they get their horses sorted." He looked over at the other two mercenaries. "Davian, flank the wagon. Colt, you're in the back. I'll take point again. Galen, opposite flank. Brant, if you would be so good as to keep an eye on the wounded? And Andrel, you bring up the rear." He kept his eyes on Colt and Davian, wondering if he was about to have a mutiny on his hands.

Colt saluted. Colt *never* saluted. "Sir." He walked behind Andrel until he passed the wagon. Istvhan felt a stab of gratitude.

He waited by the mules until Brindle returned. The gnole gave him a hard look and flicked his ears sharply, which Istvhan knew meant something, but he had no idea what.

"Andrel..." Galen began, coming up beside him.

Istvhan sighed and rubbed a thumb over his bruised knuckles. "That was ill-done of me," he said. "All it taught him is that I'm bigger than he is, not that he's wrong."

"Mmm. What do you think?"

"About Andrel?"

"About her." Galen jerked his chin toward the distant figure of Clara.

"I don't know what I think. This is not a situation that I have ever had to think about. They did not cover shapechanging nuns in basic training. I have no thoughts whatsoever."

"Well, you'd better cook up a few quick. You're the boss."

He raised his hands, let them drop. "How about I put you in charge and you tell me what you think?"

"Not a chance. I'm crazy, remember?"

"So am I."

"Yes, but you hide it well. Anyway, she likes you better."

Istvhan cleared his throat. "You know that she and I...ah...we haven't done anything. I've treated her as a sister-in-arms." *A sister-in-arms who I kissed. Which was a mistake. Absolutely a mistake. A mistake for which I was attempting to atone. Until she kissed me.*

As if he hadn't relived that kiss a hundred times a day. As if he hadn't spent the last two nights lying awake, knowing that she was right there, only a few feet away. Wondering what would happen if he dragged his blankets next to hers, imagining her body under his, until he was rock hard and aching and not able to do a damn thing about it because, again, she was only a few feet away.

I should definitely atone for something.

Stabbing her was probably not the best form of atonement.

"I know," said Galen.

Istvhan raised an eyebrow. Too late it occurred to him that his statement might have been taken as horror or disgust, but Galen's eyes were level.

"You don't look at her like a woman you're bedding," said Galen. "I've known you for — gods, a decade at least? You get this kind of warm, lazy look. But you look at her like she's a problem and you haven't figured out the solution yet."

Istvhan grunted. "Well, I've certainly figured out that the problem was a lot more complicated than I thought."

"You're telling me. How the hell did they capture a convent full of *werebears?*"

Istvhan grunted again, looking over at Clara, who stood by the mules' heads. She had pulled her robe and his cloak around her shoulders, but her chin was lifted and her back was straight. If her shoulder pained her, she gave no sign.

Perhaps Istvhan had lived too long, but the very confidence of her pose screamed vulnerability to him. *She is frightened. She was not frightened when she sat in front of a stranger's tent with a sword, but she is frightened now. When she is truly calm, she slouches and makes jokes.* He could not shake the feeling that it was all his fault. He wanted to fall to her knees and beg her forgiveness for having attacked her. He wanted to apologize for Andrel. He wanted to apologize for the human men who had hunted her and her sisters.

"We should push on," said Galen. "Find a defensible spot."

That was a command decision and Istvhan should have been the one to make it, but he appreciated Galen's tact. "Yes." He nodded to Brindle. "Are the mules calm?"

"A mule is a mule," said the gnole. Brindle jerked his muzzle toward Clara. "A mule was just startled."

"Weren't we all," muttered Galen.

Istvhan walked ahead, meeting Clara. She eyed him warily.

"Don't worry," he said. "I'm not planning on stabbing you again."

"Don't think I'm not grateful."

"I'm sorry."

"I know."

They looked at each other. Then they very carefully did not look at each other.

"So their leader looks pretty dead," said Istvhan, who was at the point where a corpse was a welcome break in the tension.

"He does, yes."

"Shall we search the body?"

"That seems wise."

They walked to the fallen rider, not quite together. Their bodies didn't seem to know how far apart to stand. Istvhan's nerves screamed that Clara was upset and in pain and needed comfort and his guilt screamed that the only reason she needed comfort was because some idiot with more steel than sense had stabbed her. His cock offered that she still had really impressive breasts and was summarily shouted down by the other body parts.

Istvhan knelt down. The only thing of interest was the leader's belt pouch, which had a few coins. He glanced up at Clara. "I'll be honest, I don't know whether to offer you the money or not. Would that be insulting?"

"Probably, but as I'm currently penniless, I'll take it." He handed it over.

"Do humans know where a mule is going?" called Brindle. "Because a gnole would like to know too."

"They'll be back," said Clara. "Probably not with horses, though. Istvhan—"

He swallowed hard. He could hear anguish in her voice where he had never heard it before, and guilt gnawed at his gut. But he was a paladin, or had been, and that meant facing things head on. He got to his feet and met her eyes.

She squared her shoulders. "I want you to know that I couldn't have saved your men."

He blinked at her. "What?"

"Haller and the others. If I'd turned into a bear."

"I don't understand."

"If I'd gone to the beast during the fight, I'd just have spooked the mules, and your men would have possibly tried to attack me. Close quarters aren't great for that. So I didn't change. But if I thought I could have, I would have saved them. Even if it meant…"

The speech was disjointed, but Istvhan followed well enough. "I never thought you could have. And Haller was on the other side of the wagon from you, anyway."

She stared at the ground. It occurred to Istvhan that possibly she was feeling as awkward about the whole situation as he was.

He hauled the dead man out of the road. Another one for the vultures. At this point, he was surprised they didn't just camp out on top of the wagon. He gestured to Brindle to walk the mules forward and rejoined Clara in the middle of the road. "We need a defensible position. Again."

"Indeed."

CHAPTER 15

It was a little easier once they were moving. If Istvhan was scanning the road for attackers, he wasn't looking at her. If he wasn't looking at her, she didn't have to look in his eyes and see horror and fear and all the other things that normal people carried in their eyes when someone changed into a bear in front of them.

Brindle had been the easiest. The gnole had looked up at her, very serious, and said "Don't worry. A mule was only startled, bear-lady. A mule is fine now." Clara longed for a world where the emotional state of the mules was the most important consideration. It seemed like it would be kinder. (She had a sneaking suspicion that Brindle was doing his best to reassure her that a certain gnole had also only been startled and was fine now, and was touched despite herself.)

He had also dressed her wound. "A gnole would lick it, but some humans strange about that," he said. "Not because of bear-lady. Because of some humans." Which was also touching in its way, although Clara was secretly just as glad to have the cut cleaned with water and not gnole spit.

"If they can't use horses, they'll be slower," said Istvhan, dragging her attention back. "That's something."

Clara nodded. "And they won't use arrows. They won't risk hitting me. Too valuable." Her lips twisted bitterly. "They'll come with nets."

"The nuns of Saint Ursa," said Istvhan.

It wasn't a question but she answered it like one anyway. "All of us. Yes. It's why we join. We don't have a lot of choice."

He looked at her and Clara braced herself for disgust. He had not recoiled from touching her, which gave her a shred of hope. *Probably he is too busy thanking the good star of his birth that he did not bed a monster that night at the inn.*

She looked away. She did not want to see it. There was a reason everyone went to the convent in the end. It wasn't just that your parents dragged you, horrified and at their wits' end, although that was some of it. It was simply that it was easier to be among other women who understood. Who never looked at you with horror or disgust or simply the knowledge of *otherness* in their eyes.

"Ha!" said Galen, with sudden explosive force. She jerked her head around, startled, and registered Istvhan doing the same.

The red-haired man was grinning for the first time since the bandit attack. Grinning and looking at her the same way that he had before, the same mixture of glee and sardonic amusement. "Ha! I see now!" He leveled a finger at her. "*That's* how you find the truffles without pigs!"

Clara blinked.

"It is, isn't it?"

"Galen..." Istvhan began.

"It's true," said Clara. "One of us wakes the beast and sniffs them out." As a bear, the smell of truffles underground was abundantly obvious, like a cloud of earthy smoke hovering over the forest floor. She found herself beginning to smile despite herself. "It's easier than keeping a pig. Pigs are the worst."

The silence that followed was not quite as fraught as it had been. Istvhan cleared his throat. "So you are born like...?" He made a slight gesture with one hand, meaningless enough but Clara didn't need an explanation.

"Yes. We aren't bitten by bears or anything. If I bite you, nothing will happen."

"I saw the size of those teeth, Domina," said Istvhan. "I wouldn't call that nothing."

"Well, no." She coughed. "But nothing *unusual*." They were all speaking with a sort of desperate lightness. *If we can just get over this bit, if we can pretend this is all normal, we can figure out where to go from here.*

Having been here once or twice before, Clara was no stranger to this sort of conversation. She was simply a little surprised that Galen had been the one to get them there.

He surprised her again a moment later. "Relax, Sister," he said. "I go screaming berserk at the drop of a hat. You turn into a bear. Honestly, I'm a little relieved that I'm not the strangest one in the room anymore."

"You're always the strangest one in the room," said Istvhan, "no matter what anyone else can turn into."

"Pfff." Galen grinned up at Clara. "So how did they catch you?"

"Fire," said Clara. "The fire makes the beast crazy. They don't understand it. One of the first lessons that gets drilled into us is to never let the bear out when there is fire." She swallowed at the memory of flames licking the altarcloth. "When we're frightened, the instinct is to go to the beast. But if you do that during a fire, you die and sometimes you take a lot of people with you. So we are trained not to do that, over and over. And once we had escaped..." She lifted her shoulders in a shrug. "They had crossbows and reinforced cages. They knew what they were doing, and what manner of beasts they were capturing. The food and water they gave us was drugged, but we had no choice. You do not let the beast get hungry." She shuddered at the memory of the iron cages on wheels, rattling over the road, bouncing and sliding sideways whenever the wheels jumped the ruts. All the sisters sitting inside, groggy and half-stunned, trying desperately to keep the beasts down.

None of them wanted to be the one who broke. As soon as one went to the beast, it would go badly for all of them. There was a great deal of human intelligence inside the bear, at least at first, but drugged and trapped, the animal would overpower that intelligence quickly. Then the bear would lash out and everyone's control would break and the cage would be too small and full of blood and rage and dying.

"Let me die," Clara had whispered to her captors. "Let me die outside. Kill me if you must. Don't let me kill the others."

They had been reluctant, but her sickness offended their sensibilities. She had soiled herself when she could no longer drag herself to the hole in the wagon floor. They pulled her from the cell and threw her into the ditch. She lay unmoving while one prodded her with a spear.

"Dead already?" asked one.

"Close enough," said the second one, and spat. Clara heard the wagon rattling away, the sound of voices fading into the distance. Then she had lost consciousness.

"And you woke in the house of the Arral?" said Istvhan, as she relayed as much of this as she felt like recounting.

Clara nodded. "I was found property. But they treated me as kindly as they would treat any outsider. They had no idea, of course."

"And your sisters are being taken to Morstone."

"So he said." Clara grimaced. "But they've taken the southern route, which is longer. It might simply be that there are more towns to buy food, or better roads, or something like that."

"There's also a chance they'll be keeping them somewhere to recover," said Galen. "You want to give the crowd a good show. You don't just dump half-dead captives out into the amphitheater."

Clara felt the word *amphitheater* enter her gut like a knife. *It's what you suspected would happen. You always knew.* But hearing someone else say it made it real and likely and terrible.

"Thank you, Galen, for that cheerful thought," said Istvhan acidly.

"Sorry, Boss."

"I don't know much about Morstone," she said, looking straight ahead. "But I suspected that it was probably going to be something like that. It could not have been for...parts...or they would have killed us where we stood. There must have been some reason to take us alive. We would be a dramatic spectacle in a gladiator pit, would we not? Nuns and novices about to be torn apart by beasts, and then... then..." *Amphitheater.* The word had barbs. She could almost feel it twisting.

Her voice cracked. Istvhan caught her arm, pulled her halfway into a hug, then recoiled. "Sorry," he said. "Sorry."

"It's all right." *You kissed me once, Captain. Are you thinking better of that now?*

"No, it isn't. I already stabbed you, I should know better than to grab you."

She managed a laugh around the pain of the word in her guts. It sounded like a normal laugh, which was a relief. Going to the beast had left her feeling hollowed out, as if she had been struggling to contain something too large. But the change and its aftermath had shredded her calm, and the emotions she had been struggling to contain for weeks were threatening to well up in the hollow left behind.

No. Tears later. Not now. You don't mourn until you know they're dead. Which was all well and good and practical, but when was she allowed to mourn for the friendships she had cut down in the roadway, as surely as if she had used her claws?

It occurred to her that Galen, who was a little mad, might actually still be interested in friendship with a beast. Istvhan...

Don't be a fool. By the grace of St. Ursa, you haven't gotten any of his men killed. You've actually done him some good. He's done you some good as well. The ledger's balanced. But if you don't get far away from him and his men, the next time those raiders come, they'll leave dead men behind. The best thing you can do — the thing a friend would do — is get as far away from Istvhan and his men as you can.

She took a deep breath, let it out again. The tears went away, but the word *amphitheater* stayed stuck in her belly, throbbing, for a while longer.

It took the better part of an hour to find a place to pull the wagon off the road safely. The hills came together there in a little stone shoulder, providing cover on two sides. Clara was so jumpy that she almost offered to turn back into a bear in hopes of getting scent of the enemy. She didn't, mostly because one of the mercenaries was staring at her with eyes like holes in his face. That one was worrisome. She'd seen Istvhan punch him, and that was more worrisome, because Istvhan was not a leader who ruled by fear.

You know perfectly well what happened. Istvhan's standing by you, even after you didn't tell him all the truth. Even after he learned what you are.

Still, Clara was used to men like Andrel. The few people outside the convent who knew mostly struggled, but they came around. But every now and again you found one who could not cope, who hated you for being what you were, as if somehow you were changing shape at them, personally. People like that were dangerous. It was best to get away from them quickly.

It would be best if you got away quickly, no matter what.

She kept her eye on Andrel while she helped drag the wagon into position. The bulk of the wagon barricaded off the gap, but the mules had to be unharnessed so that it could fit in place. "A mule will back up," said Brindle, "but a mule doesn't enjoy it."

Clara nodded. She would miss Brindle, if not the mules. *Perhaps when all this is over...*

The odds of anything ever being over seemed so remote that she abandoned that line of thought at once. She wolfed down a bar of the pressed meat rations and dusted off her hands. Her bear-self could and would eat things that her human-self found disgusting, but St. Ursa only knew when she would stumble across anything like that. *And time is of the essence. I have to get away. I can't afford to keep stopping for a snack.*

And then there was nothing else to do. She could carry nothing, so she did not pack. She'd just have to leave the coin and her robes here. It wasn't the first time.

She took a deep breath, stepped away from the rocky wall, and went to find Istvhan to tell him that she was leaving.

"I'm going," said Clara. She tugged Istvhan's cloak off her shoulders and offered it to him, one-handed. "I'm sorry to have caused your people trouble."

Istvhan blinked at her. "Going where?" His brain was moving slow for some reason, possibly because a person he'd quite liked had turned into a bear next to him and he still wasn't quite recovered. Was she going to use the privy? *Oh, she probably needs an escort, we're in hostile territory.*

"Away. I'll draw them off. It's me they want. Once they know I'm gone, they'll leave you alone."

Away? Away by herself?

"Don't be ridiculous," he said, more harshly than he intended. "You're injured. They'll kill you."

"That's exactly what they won't do," she said calmly. "I'm worth a great deal alive and nothing dead." She rolled her head from side to side and stretched her good shoulder. "And first they'll have to catch me."

"No. Absolutely not."

Clara drew herself up to her full height. "I am not asking your permission, Captain Istvhan. I am not under your command. I am very grateful for your escort this far, but our ways part now."

She took half a step forward and Istvhan wanted to laugh with recognition. She would have loomed over a smaller man, and if he took a step back, even involuntarily, he would lose the battle before it had begun. He'd done it himself any number of times.

Oh no. You cannot physically intimidate me, Domina. Not as a human, at any rate. I know this dance too well. He took a half-step forward instead.

Something flickered in her eyes. Acknowledgement? Something else? He did not know. He realized too late that he was too close. He could have leaned forward and kissed her. She could have reached out and choked the life out of him. *And if we combine the two, things will get extremely strange.*

"You can't go," he said. "You haven't got any boots."

Whatever she was expecting, it wasn't that. She looked down at her bare feet, which were already bruised and muddy from the walk. Breaking their gaze let him shift back a half-step without seemed to give ground. "I don't need boots," she said. "I don't plan to have human feet for most of it."

"You're still not going alone," he said.

"You cannot stop me."

"From going? No. So I'll go with you."

She hadn't expected that. Her eyes flickered again and there was an edge of uncertainty to her voice. "You're a mercenary, Captain Istvhan. And I am not paying you."

He sighed. "I'm not a mercenary," he said. "I'm a paladin."

"A paladin? A holy warrior?!" Clara put her hands on her hips. "And you've been giving me crap about being a nun when I'm only a lay sister?"

"Is this really the time?" asked Istvhan.

"Yes, it's the time!"

"It's only that men who would like to put you in a zoo are probably going to come back soon."

"Then they can wait! I am not done yelling!"

"Yes'm," said Istvhan, and stared contritely at his toes.

"You're a paladin!"

"More or less. Less these days."

"But a paladin!"

"I feel very bad about it."

Clara waved her hands in the air and had to catch her robe before it fled for the ground. She didn't know why it was so aggravating, except that it was. Over a week and he'd never mentioned it and she'd been acting like he was a particularly noble mercenary instead of a particularly ignoble holy warrior and...and...dammit, it wasn't *fair*.

"Have you been sitting there smugly judging me this whole time, then? Because if you have, I remind you that I'm a lay sister! And I told you up front!"

"You didn't actually mention the bear thing, though," said Galen from the sidelines. Both Istvhan and Clara turned wide, furious glares on him. "Right, I'll just go...stand watch...over there..."

Istvhan turned back to her. "I promise that all my judgments have been positive?"

That wrung a laugh from her, even if it was an exasperated one. This wasn't important. Not really. She was just very angry and the beast was still just under the surface, which didn't calm her at all. "Fine. But you're not coming with me. I'll go as a bear and move much faster. You'd only slow me down."

"Domina, a question."

"Yes?"

"Can bears read maps?"

Her breath hissed through her teeth. "You know we can't."

"I know nothing of the sort. I've never talked to a werebear before. But if you can't read maps, then may I point out that you won't know where you're going?"

"I'll go north over the mountain," she said. "Pick up the road to Morstone over there."

"The road curves north as well. If you aren't careful, you'll miss it and wind up a long way out of your way. And if you have to backtrack, you'll very likely run into these raiders again."

He was right. She hated that he was right, but he was. She didn't know the area and the bear...well, the bear's sense of direction wasn't good. It would be all too easy to drift to one side or the other and not notice until she was staring at an impassable cliff. *Damnation.* And the raiders had nets and nets were very hard to work with if you didn't have hands, and...oh hang it all, she had to get away so she didn't put everyone else in danger, but he was a goddamn paladin and there was no getting traction with people like that.

She glared at him. He folded his arms and waited.

"Fine," she growled, turning away. "Be ready in ten minutes."

"Is this a good idea, Boss?"

"Almost certainly not. What else can I do?"

Galen considered this, while Istvhan hastily shoved supplies into his pack. "Let her go off by herself?"

"And have her end up in some bastard's menagerie? No."

"Tie her down?"

"I really don't want to fight her," said Istvhan. "I feel weird fighting women."

"You stabbed her once today already. With a sword."

"Yes, but she was a *giant goddamn bear* at the time."

Galen looked unconvinced. Istvhan wasn't entirely convinced himself. He rubbed his temples. "Look, it's...different."

"Uh-huh. Also if she's a giant goddamn bear, she can eat you for lunch."

"Thanks for the vote of confidence."

"Am I wrong, boss?"

"...no." Istvhan was reasonably sure that he could take on Clara-as-human in a fight, and also quite certain that Clara-as-bear could turn him into minced paladin.

"Then I guess you're stuck." Galen looked over at her, then started to laugh.

"What so funny?" Istvhan swept more food into the pack. How much did a bear eat? Was she going to kill deer or something? Should he help?

"I was just thinking, first you're with Beartongue and now you're chasing after someone with an actual bear's—"

"*Galen.*"

"Look, I'm just saying you have a type. A weirdly specific type."

"If you ever make that joke again, I will end you."

"Sure, sure. I'll see you in Morstone, shall I?"

"Yes. Get everyone there, and I'll meet you at the Temple of the Rat." He swung his pack on his back. "And say a prayer for me, while you're at it."

"To which god?" asked Galen.

Istvhan searched the other man's face. Their god was dead, and the shared wound of that would bind him to Galen and the other lost paladins until the day they died. "I suppose to the Rat," he said. "But perhaps it might be worth offering a prayer to the ghost of steel."

Galen nodded, short and sharp, and turned away.

Clara pulled her robe more tightly around herself. She could see that Istvhan was packing her kit alongside his own, and she did not know whether to be touched or annoyed. Bears had little use for silverware. *But when you are a human again, you will appreciate it. And you will have to ask him to carry your clothes as well. Showing up somewhere stark naked to ask if they have a spare blanket you can borrow is only funny once.*

She ground her teeth. It was so frustrating to rely on another person. Many of the Sisters traveled in pairs for just such reasons, but she had always done well enough alone, taking orders up and down the waterway, coming back on a hired barge to fill the orders later. She stashed a sack of clothing outside of large towns as a matter of safety, but she'd only had to use that a handful of times in a decade. In life, if you were careful, there were simply not that many times when you absolutely, positively, had to turn into a bear.

Someone cleared their throat behind her. Clara turned and saw Brant standing there. The distiller's face was transparent with some emotion, but she couldn't quite put her finger on which one. *Please, Saint Ursa, don't let it be religious awe.* You got that sometimes. It was better than abject horror, but it was still exhausting.

"You're leaving us here," said Brant. "You and the Captain?"

Clara nodded.

He held out his hand. "Please take these. In case we don't meet again."

Puzzled, Clara held out her own hand, and he dropped three

acorns into it. They were smooth and glossy, the shells tapering to a fine point.

"Plant these somewhere," he said. "Wherever you feel an oak might be happy. I hope to see you in Morstone regardless." He bobbed his head in a quick approximation of a bow and then hurried away. Clara was left gazing down at a handful of acorns and found that her eyes were prickling with tears for no apparent reason.

"I'm ready," said Istvhan behind her. She shoved the acorns hastily into her pocket and turned to meet him. If she focused on her irritation, she would not start crying over acorns or acceptance or anything else.

"Took you long enough," she grumbled, swiping surreptitiously at her eyes. "Let's go."

Brindle nodded to her, whiskers forward, and said "A bear-lady travels safe, eh?" Galen lifted his hand. Clara and Istvhan walked down the road and did not look back.

CHAPTER 16

When they could no longer see the camp, Clara nodded to the hills to the north side of the road. "That way. Going rough this time." She would have turned into a bear at this point if she were alone, but it seemed awkward to do in front of Istvhan. What was she supposed to say? "Hold my clothes?" "Avert your eyes?" She gritted her teeth and stayed human, stepping off the road. The forest here was mostly pine and the ground was a carpet of dry needles, crunchy and not completely unpleasant to walk on, except when it wasn't. Her feet were already bruised from the long walk down the stony road. Dammit, she'd been looking forward to having leathery pawpads again for a bit, just to give her feet a rest.

She made about a hundred yards into the forest, with Istvhan walking upslope behind her, and then she stepped on a particularly sharp chunk of forest floor. Stone. Bark. Pointy twig. It didn't matter. She grunted, balanced on one foot, rubbed the red mark on her sole, and decided that this was stupid. *It's not like he's going to forget that you're a bear if you don't turn into one again.*

"Hold my clothes," she said, shrugging out of her robe. She didn't dare look at him, just thrust the bundle of cloth in his direction, stiff-armed. He took it from her hands.

"Um," he said.

"Stand back," she said, and then before he even had time to do that, she lost her nerve and told the beast to come forward. *Now. Yes. Wake up.*

The world spun and crystalized around her. There. Yes. Like that. Bears could see as well as humans so that was no change, but the *smells!* They painted the landscape in whorls and eddies of sensation. A background layer of pine, sharp and acidic. A trail of musk where a deer had passed. Istvhan's breath, steaming out in clouds, and the scent of ginger muscle rub that followed him everywhere. As a human, she found that scent oddly comforting. As a bear, she had no particular opinion. It was just what he smelled like, an anchor point to his identity.

She dropped to all fours. There. Yes. That was better. Her back feet were still a little sore from where she had bruised them, but nothing was getting through the thick black leather of her paws.

She took a deep breath and her skin shivered around her, everything settling into place. It had been too long. Her last transformation had only lasted a few seconds and then she'd had to shove the beast down violently. This was better. This was what it was supposed to be like, senses awakening and muscles moving and that sudden implacable confidence that came of knowing that you were the most powerful thing in the forest.

"Ah," said Istvhan. "Hello?"

She grunted at him, then nodded. It wasn't a gesture that came easily to bears. She had to wag her head up and down, which would have been threatening to another bear, but it seemed to make Istvhan relax.

"Right," he said. He took a deep breath and seemed to steady himself. "You doing all right? Shoulder not bothering you?"

She shrugged. Shrugging was easier for the beast, although it did set a twinge off again. The wound was mostly in the shield fat, which had few nerves to speak of. Humans didn't have shield fat. This was clearly a gross oversight on the part of the gods and someone should rectify it immediately.

"Ah...okay. Let me know if there's anything...right." He stuffed her robes into the top of his pack and shouldered it again. "Lead the way."

They traveled uphill at a brisk pace. Clara tried to steer the bear toward the routes that a horse could not take easily. They would not come at her on horseback again, but she suspected they would ride a little way, dismount and fan out to search, then mount up again. It's what she would have done, under the circumstances. No sense making it easy for them.

Mostly, though, she reveled in the sudden peace inside her skin. Bears understood fear and anger and lust, but those were short-lived emotions and once they were gone, they were gone. They did not angst. The bear did not worry that she would not find her sisters, or fret about what Istvhan thought of her true nature, or fear for the rest of the mercenaries left behind. The bear simply walked forward and existed and Clara sank into the peace of that existence and thought of nothing.

They traveled for an hour, then two. Clara tried to remember to stop occasionally for Istvhan to rest. Perhaps three hours later, Istvhan cleared his throat. To the bear, it sounded like just a noise, but there was enough of Clara to recognize that he needed to say something. She rose from the half-submerged parts of the bear's mind and turned back toward him.

"It's starting to snow," he said.

"Hrrwuff," she said. The air tasted sharp and cold, and even if only a few flakes were drifting down, the scent of snow overlaid the scent of pines like a sheet of translucent paper.

Eventually, they emerged from the treeline. Wind spat snow in their face. Istvhan cursed, pulling his hood down tight, arms wrapped around his body. The bear, protected by fur and fat, felt nothing but the prickle of the cold on her nose. She dropped her head and went forward.

Above the treeline, the slope was all loose scree. Terrible leg-breaking surface for horses. She approved of that. If they circled the top of the mountain above the treeline, it would be difficult to follow, and they could head downslope again on the north side.

The small, submerged part of her mind that was still entirely human brooded, even as the beast part picked her way up the slope. Scree moved under her paws and the air smelled sharp and clear and clean. What was Istvhan thinking right now?

She looked back and thought that probably what he was thinking was that he was cold.

The snow was not accumulating, but the wind was brutal. Istvhan moved well enough, for a human, his breath frosting the air, but it was only a matter of time before he began to flag. Heat was easy to lose and hard to replace.

She aimed toward the lowest part of the slope but it didn't do much good. The wind was whipping along the treeline, flinging snowflakes with malicious glee. Istvhan had his head down between his shoulders and he was beginning to stumble. She kept having to stop and wait for him to catch up and it took longer and longer each time.

Well, there was no help for it. They could go back into the trees or...

"Hrrwufff!" Clara stopped and turned sideways to Istvhan, crouching down as best she could.

"What?" Istvhan's teeth chattered and he clenched his jaw to stop it. "What is it?"

"Hrrwuff!" Her joints weren't set up to gesture to her back. She tried to sink down farther.

Fortunately Istvhan was quick on the uptake. "Um. You...uh... want me to ride you?"

"Wufff!" She nodded.

He looked at her. Blessed St. Ursa, what was he waiting for?

"It's just...uh..."

"Wuff."

"This feels like some kind of weird sex thing," muttered Istvhan.

Clara growled.

"I'm not saying it is! I'm just saying that you don't usually ride other people unless they have very specialized interests." Clara rolled her eyes. She could feel him tugging at her fur, trying awkwardly to mount. "Sorry. I'm trying not to pull your hair."

"Hwuf."

Even if they had not been massive killing machines, it was unlikely that bears would ever be domesticated as riding animals. The bones and muscles were all in the wrong places. *No more comfortable for him than for me, I suspect.* His weight was significant, but her bear-self was capable of dragging a full-grown elk for a mile without breaking a sweat. The important thing was that she was a roaring furnace of heat. Istvhan threaded his hands in her fur and gradually his shivering eased.

Despite his weight, she made better time, and she stopped worrying about staying out of the wind. He kept trying to shift his weight as if he were riding a horse, which didn't do any good and was rather annoying. Human-Clara was aware that he meant well and therefore prevented Bear-Clara from sitting down and scratching vigorously to dislodge the weird bur that had fastened onto her back.

She reached the far side of the mountain they were circling — mountain was probably an exaggeration, but the hills in this land had ambitions — and plunged back into the trees. Istvhan sat up and back, like you would on a horse going downhill. She wished bears could sigh. The man actually had a backside. Clara had checked surreptitiously several times on the road. It wasn't a bad looking one either. So why the hell did it feel like his pelvic bones were resting directly on her spine?

Well, there go my plans for making extra money by renting myself out as a riding animal for children's parties, she thought, and hrwuffed with laughter.

This hillside rubbed shoulders with the next one, and they did not need to go down as far to begin going back up. A tree leapt out at her, where another bear, presumably a real one, had set their claws. The smell was a magenta smear of dominance. A smaller male, by the height. The bear wanted to stand on hind legs and leave her mark as well, prove she was taller and not to be trifled with. Clara squelched this urge. The bear grumbled but obeyed.

It began to grow dark as they reached the treeline again. The air smelled like more snow coming. The bear had excellent vision in the dark, but Istvhan's weight was beginning to tire her. More than that, the effort of keeping human thoughts inside a skull that wanted to think other thoughts was exhausting. She could feel them welling up around her, wordless and primal, so rich they were almost bitter, leaving a gamey taste on her tongue.

No. Keep thinking. Keep going.

More, whispered the bear without words. *More.*

Not now. Keep going. And then, quietly, *Please.*

The cave wasn't much, more of a depression in the rock with a large boulder blocking half the entrance. It was at the top of the ridgeline and had a good view of the approach, and more importantly, it was out of the wind. Istvhan rolled off the bear's back and entered the cave on his knees. It immediately seemed a great deal warmer than the surrounding air.

The bear — he didn't know whether to think of her as Clara or as just *the bear* — shoved her way in after him. The small cave got even smaller. She curled herself up, head toward the entrance, and collapsed like a dog on a hearthrug.

"Staying a bear?" he said.

"Hwuf."

"Right. Okay." Istvhan was exhausted. He pulled a piece of journey bread out of his pack and tore it in half. "Food?"

The bear took the bread politely from his fingers. Neither the bread nor his hand would have made more than a mouthful. Istvhan took two bites of his and found that even chewing made him tired. *But hey, you have a woman eating out of your hand. That's something, right?*

He spread out his cloak. There was not a great deal of room. He ended up with his back against the bear, which was certainly warmer than the stone wall. "Just don't roll over in your sleep."

"Hrruf-ruf." Was that a laugh? It might have been. He hadn't known that bears could laugh, but presumably if bears turned into women, they might learn. His thoughts began to drift, to bears and women and men chasing them across the hills, and then he slept.

CHAPTER 17

Istvhan woke with his head pillowed in someone's cleavage.

He was lying on a cold, hard surface and his shoulder was sore and he had a crick in his neck and he couldn't quite remember how he'd gotten there, but none of this seemed particularly important. What was important was that his face was buried in soft, warm female flesh. A great deal of female flesh. Whoever's breasts these were, they were spectacular.

I'm dead and in heaven. I always knew I'd die, but I thought my sins would catch up with me. This is wonderful.

Admittedly, he couldn't remember the name of his partner, but she seemed to be naked so that presumably meant they had been introduced and had gotten through all of the preliminary stages. He slid one hand over her hip and confirmed that yes, she was definitely naked and also that the rest of her was as generously made as her breasts. *I was clearly far more virtuous while I was alive than I realized.*

"Ahem," said the owner of the breasts.

"...wub..." said Istvhan, who was wondering how much he could fit in his mouth before it got weird.

The woman inhaled, which did amazing things. Istvhan gave himself up to bliss.

"Ahem."

Something clicked in the back of his brain. Clara. Sister Clara. *Domina* Clara. Werebear.

Nun.

"I've never seen a man in armor move that fast," said Clara dryly. "Are you all right?"

"You turned human in your sleep," squeaked Istvhan. He had flung himself across the floor of the cave so quickly that he'd scraped his ear on the stone, but this was a minor consideration. He was stiff with horror, except for the part of his anatomy that had been stiff with something else.

"It happens sometimes." Clara folded her arms across her chest in an attempt at modesty. Breasts like hers had not been designed to be contained by mere forearms. Istvhan stared at the ceiling of the cave. *Nice cave. Good cave. None of the sticky up or hangy down bits, but of course that's limestone, you don't get that in this area. Right. Okay. You face-planted in a nun's breasts and made wub noises. A nun who you stabbed with a sword about twelve hours ago. Is there any coming back from this? No? Okay, that's what I thought.*

"We are trained not to change into the beast in our sleep," said Clara, who was fortunately not privy to his thoughts. "But changing into human...it rarely matters and it's hard to train out."

"How do you train not to turn into one?" asked Istvhan, still staring fixedly at the ceiling.

"Same way you'd teach a child not to wet the bed, if a bit more dramatic. The novices sleep in a dormitory and the minute someone starts to show signs of changing, the keeper of novices dumps a glass of water on their head. Not harmful, but you wake up instantly and it breaks you out of the dream."

Istvhan raised his eyebrows and looked down in spite of himself. "I'd think if you were already upset, having water dumped on your head wouldn't help."

She shrugged, which did tectonic things to her anatomy. Istvhan returned hastily to perusing the ceiling. "I can't say it's enjoyable, but it works. And bears dislike water a great deal less than humans do."

Istvhan pictured water running down Clara's shoulders, over her skin, tracing the path down from her collarbone and dripping off... other bits...

The ceiling was definitely not cutting it. He gazed out over the ledge at the gritty gray light of early dawn. *Trees. Snowy trees. Yes. Excellent. Evergreens, by the look of them. Yes.* There was nothing particularly erotic about evergreens. In fact, if Istvhan had to pick the least erotic tree he knew, it would definitely be an evergreen. Something with pointy needles and a bad attitude. One of those trees. You couldn't cut boughs and lay them down and spread your cloak over them and make passionate love to anyone with trees like that. You'd get jabbed in places. Lots of places. You'd be better off with the stone floor, no matter what it did to your knees when you were kneeling over her and...goddamn sexy evergreens, leading innocent paladins into temptation.

"Perhaps you might hand me my clothes?" asked Clara.

"Ah. Yes. That is a thing I can do." He hastily dug her clothing out of his pack and held it out to her. "Are you going to go as a...ah...not as a...hmm."

"Bear," said Clara. "You can say the word, it's all right. I'm not sensitive about it."

The hell you're not, thought Istvhan, but wasn't about to say it aloud.

"At the moment, neither of us are going anywhere." She gestured out the cave mouth, at the evergreens that he'd been looking at. He followed her gaze, puzzled, then looked down.

The shale slope that they had come up the evening before was covered in a fresh blanket of snow. It was utterly pristine, blindingly white, and if they walked on it, they were going to leave a trail of footprints as clear as signposts. Istvhan grunted in dismay. "Damnation. Can we climb up, do you think?"

"I won't swear that we can't," said Clara. "That boulder there, if we could get onto it, we could maybe go over the top of the ridge. But we'll still leave some kind of track."

Istvhan rubbed his chin. His beard itched. "Well, it's covered our trail so that's useful, I suppose." He watched as the wind blew across the snow, sending white flakes skittering along the surface. "The wind should scour it clear soon enough, but I don't know if we're far enough ahead of pursuit to trust it to clear our footprints that quickly."

"That's my thinking," Clara agreed. "If we stay here for a few hours, we may be able to go on without leaving as much of a trail."

Istvhan contemplated a few hours alone in an isolated cave with a...*a nun, dammit, she's a* nun...*a nun with really fantastic breasts, absolutely top quality, you just didn't see breasts like that every day...will you shut up, you lecherous doorknob? You already had your face mashed against her not twenty minutes ago and she can't get out of this cave without you, so act like a damn gentleman already.*

Also, you stabbed her. Stabbed. Pointy metal jammed into flesh. Women do not forgive you for that in a hurry. Men either, generally. He drew his knees up and rested his wrists across them. It was cold inside the cave, but the blanket of snow had warmed the landscape a little. Now he just had to figure out how to spend a few hours in Clara's company without acting like a complete ass.

He closed his eyes and leaned his head back against the stone wall. *Easier said than done...*

Bears sigh for ursine reasons of their own, not from frustration or sorrow. Clara had human reasons to sigh, but squelched the urge.

When Istvhan realized who — or what — he was cuddling up to, he moved like he was touching something unclean. *He tried to hide it, but that just shows he's polite, not that he wasn't disgusted.*

The snow had laid a blanket of quiet across the world. She strained her ears but could hear nothing but birdsong. She wondered which one of them was going to be first to break the silence.

"So what's it like being a werebear?"

Apparently it was going to be Istvhan.

"Dunno," said Clara. "What's it like *not* being a werebear? I've never not been one."

Istvhan grunted. After a minute he said "Well, there's less turning into a bear, for one thing."

Clara laughed in spite of herself. "Yes, I imagine. Ah...hmm. It's a bit like having another set of thoughts in your head, I suppose. Like when you talk to yourself, there's the you doing the talking and the you getting talked to, although they're all the same you. Does that make any sense?"

"It does, actually. Like when I think 'Istvhan, you're a fool,' I'm both the fool and the person thinking I'm a fool."

"Does that happen often?"

"Constantly. Particularly around beautiful women."

Clara didn't quite know what to do with that. *Does he mean...no, it's probably just reflex. You're a bear.* "Right. Except the bear doesn't think in words the same way, and it doesn't feel the need to keep a running commentary on my life. Half the time I don't know it's there unless something happens to wake it up."

"Like what?"

"Strong smells. Hunger. Danger." She scratched the back of her neck. "Whenever I get in a fight, the beast wakes up and starts wanting to know if it needs to take over." Istvhan made an odd sound, almost like recognition. "But I'm not in fights very often. It's mostly smells. Smoke, blood, sickness — those will wake it up every time."

"And truffles?"

"Definitely truffles."

"And once it's woken up?"

"Most of the time I tell it to go back to sleep. There are really not very many circumstances where turning into a large bear is helpful. Mostly it listens. Sometimes it doesn't, and I'm pushing it down while I try to do something else."

"I understand that more than you know."

Clara glanced at him, surprised. He couldn't possibly, and yet the way he said it...

They sat in silence for a little while, gazing down the valley. Birds chirped in the trees and from the ground. Clara heard an alarm call and looked around in case it was signaling the presence of men on horses. A very harassed-looking copper jay broke from cover, mobbed by the smaller birds, and a few minutes later, everything settled back into peaceful melody.

"Do you feel the presence of the goddess when you change?" asked Istvhan abruptly.

Clara blinked at him. *What an odd question. No, what a* paladin *question.* "You mean Ursa? She's a saint, not a goddess. She was a real person, about three hundred years ago, or that's what the records say."

"Still. Is she present when you change?"

"Now *that's* a complicated theological question." Clara leaned back against the rock wall. "Some of the sisters say that it's Her direct blessing that lets us change at all, of course, but it doesn't feel much like a blessing sometimes. When you're feverish in a cage and all of you praying not to be the one who goes to the beast...no, I'm pretty sure St. Ursa isn't overseeing us directly, because that would be monstrously cruel, making us change like that." She spread her hands. "Sister Mallory always says that if St. Ursa didn't exist, we'd be obligated to invent Her, just to have an explanation. Or maybe just so we had someone to watch over us."

"But you have not felt her presence directly?"

Clara shrugged. "Again, how would I know? Perhaps I feel it all the time, and have nothing to compare it to. That's why it's faith." She snorted. "I talk to Her in my head. I pray. If I didn't have Her, I suspect I'd pray to someone else. Perhaps She's just the name I put on that which I pray to, and it's easier to picture the divine as a saint who understands the beast."

"Interesting theology for a nun."

She glanced over at him. Blue stubble shadowed his cheeks and his eyes were dark. Even after bandit attacks and long days on the run, he was obnoxiously handsome. She remembered the warmth of his lips against her skin that morning, before he realized what he was kissing, and her gut clenched, but she was determined not to show it. *This is why you don't get entangled. This is why you don't fall in love.*

"We're not an evangelical order," she said lightly. "But you're a paladin. You're genuinely god-touched, aren't you?"

Istvhan made a small noise of pain. "I was," he said. "Once."

Clara frowned. "What? How does that...wait..." A half-remembered memory clicked into place. The Saint of Steel. The god who had died. She'd almost forgotten. It had been years ago and she had never met one of their paladins. "Your god...?"

"Dead," said Istvhan bleakly. The blue shadows on his face deepened. "Died or was murdered, if a god can be murdered. We still don't know. Just that He was a golden light in our hearts, and then He was gone."

"I'm sorry." She reached out and took his hand before it occurred to her that the touch of a werebear might disgust him. He did not recoil. He gazed down at their hands as if they belonged to two other people, his eyes distant.

"It was almost four years ago now," he said. "I don't know how much you know about the order."

"Virtually nothing. I didn't know any of you survived."

He nodded. "We didn't have a temple up here. Mostly around Archenhold. The Saint was a warrior god. We were — are — berserkers." One corner of his mouth twisted up slightly. "The priests think — or thought — that His paladins were born berserkers, that in another time and place we would have been the sort of madmen who gnaw their shields and are consumed with battle. Much like your order, now that I think of it." He glanced up at her and smiled, less with humor and more with recognition. "We were born a certain way, and the god took it and made it holy."

Maybe he does understand. Can *he understand?*

No. That's too much to ask for from someone who is human all the time. Even if he gnaws his shield in battle, it's still with human teeth.

"So it's not just Galen," she said.

"No. He is my brother-in-arms." Istvhan slowly opened his fingers until her hand lay flat in his palm. It struck Clara again, looking down, that his hands were larger than hers and that was strange. She could not remember the last man that she had known who was built to the same scale. "Once the god died, we no longer had control of the battle madness. The black tide, we call it now. We're all afraid of it. We're waiting for the day it pulls us under and doesn't let us go. But there was a time, Domina, when we were the holiest of killers. We would go into a place and kill those that the god commanded and spare everyone else. The god would literally stop our blades from falling on the innocent. It was…" He let out a long breath. "We were righteous and holy and unstoppable. And it was good, Domina. It was so damn good."

The longing in his voice was terrible to hear. Clara moved her hand, only a little, and he caught it, thumb lying like a bar across her knuckles. "I will tell you something else," he said softly, looking up, "paladin to nun, that I dare not tell my brothers."

I'm only a lay sister, Clara wanted to say. *I can't give you absolution. You've felt more of your god than I ever have of mine.* But she said none of these things, only tilted her head and waited. Even the very lowest of lay sisters knew when someone needed to give confession.

"I think sometimes now, about the guilty and the innocent. Our god was judge and jury and we were His executioners. I never questioned His judgment. I couldn't have. But the longer I spend around the Temple of the Rat, with all their priests and lawyers, as they try to sort out guilt and punishment and expiation, the more I think that it was all far too simple." He shook his head slowly, almost incredulous. "When the god died, we ran mad. The priests lit the temples on fire and burned each other alive. There was a place called Hallowbind, and the paladins there tore men apart with their bare hands."

"I'm sorry," said Clara.

Istvhan shrugged. "Are these the actions of good men, Domina? Even the mad don't do this to each other. Perhaps we were always on the edge of this terrible violence, and the Saint was no better than we were. I do not know." He lifted her hand and Clara felt his breath wash across her fingers. "So you see, Domina," he whispered, "you are not the only one with a beast inside them."

The air between them changed instantly, charged and crackling. Clara met his dark eyes and thought *we have been talking of gods and murder, this is not the time, you must be mistaken, what is wrong with you...?*

The look in Istvhan's eyes did not make her think she was mistaken.

Her mouth felt suddenly dry. She licked her lips and his eyes locked on her mouth. *No, don't be ridiculous, you're barely human, he knows that, he recoiled from you this morning, he can't possibly mean...*

He leaned forward. His lips parted slightly. Dark eyes bored into hers and she could not seem to get enough air. She had been kissed before of course, even by this same man, but never by a man who knew what she was, never by one who had seen her change and wanted her anyway.

You are mistaken. You must be. That cannot be what he means. He cannot want you. You should not want him.

What did *she* want? She wanted...she wanted...to tear each other's clothes off and drag him down right there, never mind the stone floor or anything else. *Right.*

Istvhan was very close. She could feel his breath across her skin.

Outside the cave, birds suddenly started up, shrieking alarm calls. A pebble fell down from the entrance. Istvhan jerked back and both of them looked up, just as a human voice said "Don't bother, Thom, she's miles away by now."

CHAPTER 18

Istvhan cursed the saints, the gods, the world, humanity in general and the men on the ridge above them in particular. He did it internally, however, because neither of them dared to make a sound.

Keep walking, he thought. *Keep walking and don't make me kill you.*

His gaze dropped to Clara and he amended that to, *Don't make us kill you.*

Her head was cocked to one side, eyes fixed on the entrance to the cave. Istvhan could not even hear her breathing.

He'd heard it just a moment ago. Her lips had been parted, almost panting, and somehow everything had shifted around them. Perhaps it was her explanation that she did not feel her saint. It finally settled inside his head that she was with the convent because of what she was, not because she was dedicated to holiness.

And Istvhan, who could no longer touch holiness, might be able to touch her.

Footsteps scraped on the rock. The voice said, "Look, there's no tracks. We'd see footprints if she'd come this way."

Yes. Excellent. Keep thinking that. Good man.

Someone — Thom, presumably — said, "I want to check anyway. This place is all full of holes. She could be hiding in one."

The voice was practically over their heads. The men were walking along the ridgeline, and if one found a way down, Istvhan and Clara would be trapped in a cave, trying to fight on their knees.

"Yeah, and so could a snow lion. It'll take your damn face off."

"Worth the risk. You know what one of those things is worth in Morstone?"

Those things. Istvhan watched Clara's face go hard as her jaw clenched.

More footsteps. Istvhan heard the sound of loose rock sliding and stifled a sigh. No hope for it. The man was *right there* and in another minute, he was going to come around the side of the rock blocking the entrance and things were going to start happening very fast. Istvhan settled his hand on the hilt of his sword.

"Look, there's a cave right—"

Istvhan exploded out of the cave, swinging.

The man named Thom was shorter than Istvhan, but that didn't much matter, since he was standing and Istvhan was still half-crouched. He had a net draped over one shoulder but certainly wasn't expecting to use it. Istvhan's sword whistled through the air.

Thom's reflexes were good but his balance was not. He managed to jump back, only to lose his footing on the rock and slide down the hillside on his back.

His companion shouted from the ridge. Istvhan turned to meet the second man, jammed his sword upward and took the man in the gut. He nearly lost his own footing as the shock traveled through his arm.

Someone else shouted. Saint's balls, there had been a third man who hadn't spoken. Istvhan tried to haul his sword out of the dead man without falling down the slope himself.

A bear roared practically in his ear.

Istvhan skidded downhill a few feet, regained his balance, and looked up just in time to see the bear bite the third man's face off.

The bear who was also Clara.

The man had been shouting. He stopped. The crunch of massive teeth into bone was horribly loud. The bear shook her head and the man dropped down the slope, a red ruin where his face had been.

All right, Istvhan thought. *All right, that was...that was a lot. Okay.*

Small black eyes turned toward him. Blood ringed the bear's muzzle and stained her chest. She growled.

"Easy," said Istvhan. "Easy. Nice bear?" The bear had seemed friendly enough the day before, but blood lust was something else again. Clara spoke of the bear as if it were another person inside her. *Instead of lusting after her and interrogating her about comparative theology, maybe you could have asked a useful question like, "Does the bear always remember who your friends are?"*

The bear made a low grumbling sound and pawed at her muzzle, turning away. Istvhan thought she looked almost embarrassed, although how a bear could look embarrassed, the Saint only knew. Either saint.

He looked downslope and discovered Thom was gone. "Oh hell," he said aloud. "I think one of them got away. We'd better get moving before he brings reinforcements."

"Hrrwwuff." The bear nodded and started over the ridge.

"Wait for me!" He scrambled into the cliff and grabbed his pack. The bear waited. Her long pink tongue came out of her mouth and licked at the blood, which was...yes, it was a lot to take in. Everything was a lot right now.

They started down the far side, slipping and sliding on the loose scree. The dead man had fallen over the ridge and rolled a few yards downhill. Istvhan wiped his sword on the dead man's tunic, then took his money. The bear snorted approvingly.

The bear who had bitten a man's face off.

It's not like you haven't seen worse. Istvhan came from a berserker order. He had seen every possible variation of what swords could do to human flesh. Frequently his brothers and sisters in arms had been the ones doing it. It was just...well...

The crunch replayed in his head. The bear had fangs as long as his thumbs.

Right. Okay. Woman with sledgehammer surrounded by dead bodies, weirdly sexy. Woman turned into giant bear, biting faces off, deeply not sexy. Please make a note of it.

He immediately resented himself for being an idiot. *What, did you expect her to stand around and get murdered just so you could keep your cock hard?*

No, obviously not. That was just...a lot.

Clara stomped downhill, feeling the scree slide under her paws. She could hear Istvhan on the slope, though he was starting to fall behind. She didn't know whether to slow down so that he could catch up or to start running and never stop.

Clara's eyesight wasn't capable of the fine close focus of a human, but it didn't need to be. She'd been able to see Istvhan's expression just fine. *Shock. Horror. Something like that. Well, what did you expect? You bit a man's head in half right in front of him.* However close they'd come for a moment in the cave, it was definitely over now.

It's for the best. This is why you never sleep with anyone who knows what you are. Men say they want an animal in bed, but they don't mean one that weighs seven hundred pounds and eats elk.

"Bear — Clara — wait for me..."

Bears do not grit their teeth normally. Clara could feel the puzzlement of the beast, wondering why it was keeping its jaw tight. She grimly relaxed and paused at the bottom of the slope, waiting. It would do no good to get separated. He'd just try to find her, because he was a paladin and no matter how disgusted he was, his sense of duty would keep him going. If only he'd truly been a mercenary, he would probably have decided to cut his losses. *Damn, damn, damn.*

At least this side of the ridge was warmer. The trees started much closer to the ridgeline and the snow only clung in the deep shadows. The wind was not nearly so fierce. She did not feel obligated to give Istvhan a ride on her back, and thus could not be hurt when he recoiled in horror at the thought.

Hours passed, while Clara brooded and Istvhan crunched through the pine needles. She thought they must be getting close to the road now. If they were being followed, she had heard no sign yet.

How long would it take for the man who had escaped to bring back his fellows? *I suppose it depends on how badly he was hurt, falling down the slope.* Clara hated to hope for a man's injuries, but it would certainly make her life easier.

She lifted her head, sniffing for the scent of horses, and smelled something unusual.

Burning? A fire? No, it wasn't quite right for that. It smelled burnt the way that a skunk did, a choking scorched-hair smell, but there were undertones like rotten milk and something else. It smeared the scent landscape in the bear's head. She sneezed twice, then turned in place, trying to place where it was coming from.

"Problem?" asked Istvhan.

"Hrrrffff..." She didn't like the smell. More importantly, the beast didn't like the smell. That was unusual. The beast was agnostic about most odors. Food smells were good, fire was bad, all other smells just existed without any particular emotional context.

The heavy smell seemed to be concentrated on a spot between their position and the road. Clara debated the possible ramifications, then decided that it was too important to make the decision alone. *Go to sleep,* she told the bear. *Go back down for a little while.*

The excitement of the fight had worn off. The beast did not resist. She shook herself and stood up. Istvhan hurried to put the cloak around her shoulders. *Just like a paladin.*

"Pursuit?" he asked.

"No, not close by. I smell something else. It's very odd. Burnt and sort of rotten. I don't know what it is, but we should probably go around it. That'll be a bit out of our way, though."

Istvhan went very still. "Burnt," he said slowly. "Like burnt hair? A thick smell?"

Clara blinked at him. "Yes. Exactly. Do you know what it is?"

"Unfortunately I might." He sighed. "I'm sorry, but I need to see it. If it's what I think it is..."

Clara raised her eyebrows. "More secrets?"

He laughed, although not with a great deal of humor. "Yes, I suppose. I should have told you, but...would you believe that I'd forgotten this one completely, what with the last few days?" He waved a hand vaguely over his shoulder in the direction of their pursuers.

"I suppose I would," Clara admitted. "Very well." She started to turn into the bear again and...

...found herself on her knees, the woods spinning around her.

"Domina!"

"It's all right," she muttered, trying not to faceplant in the pine needles. "It's fine."

"It's clearly not." He went to his knees next to her. "Are you ill? Injured?"

"No. Too many changes too fast, that's all." She mustered a smile. "It's like running. It's not hard to do once or twice, if you're used to it, but too many on top of each other and you start to get winded. Give me a minute."

"Stay human," he suggested. "If it's what I think it is, the smell will be strong enough for our noses to pick up once we get close."

"What do you think it is?"

"Severed heads." He handed her her clothes, and helped her to her feet while she considered this.

"Your wandering killer?"

"Yes. At this point, trying to keep any more secrets feels extremely silly. If you're a spy for an unknown cult, you're hiding it well."

"Well, St. Ursa's real. I might be a spy for a known cult."

"Yes, but are you really a spy at that point?" They started down the slope together. Istvhan stayed within arm's reach, probably in case she fainted again. Clara did not know whether to be grateful or to wish he'd go farther away. The bear hadn't cared that he smelled like ginger. The human cared very much indeed.

"Galen and I work for the Temple of the White Rat," Istvhan explained. "There's been a series of murders in Archon's Glory. One of my brothers found out what was doing it. We call them the smooth men. They're a...well, we aren't sure what the hell they are. The best guess is some kind of golem. They make heads in a kiln and then stab the heads into decapitated corpses to control them. The bodies eventually decay away and they have to kill another one. When one was caught in Archon's Glory, the rest fled. Reports started to come from the north, so Galen and I came to follow them."

"Ah," said Clara. "And Brant's barrels?"

"Oh, very real. But they're our cover story. I really did want many fewer guards, too." He grimaced, and she suspected that he was thinking of Haller. "We've been trying to keep it secret because we literally do not know who or what is behind these things. Rogue wonderworker? Cult? A golem-maker?"

"I thought the secret of making golems had been lost centuries ago."

"So did everyone else."

"Hmm." Clara gnawed on her lower lip. "Interesting. You think they're going to Morstone?"

"No idea. We had planned to follow the trail. Brant knew that we might be taking detours. Now it looks like we might still be behind them." He rubbed the back of his neck. "Morstone would be a good place for them to set up shop again, anyway. Big city, huge slums, lots of people who can vanish without anyone kicking up a fuss. Even the White Rat hasn't made much of a dent there."

And my sisters are likely headed for the fighting pits there. The shudder that went through her was not from the exhaustion of too many changes. She breathed in, and caught another whiff of the burnt smell.

"Ahead, I think."

It was farther away than she expected. The smell was so strong that it carried. She was glad, by the time they reached the source, that she wasn't the bear. Her human nose was running and her eyes were burning. To a more sensitive nose, it would have been nearly intolerable.

"Dammit," said Istvhan softly, looking down at the headless corpse. "Sometimes I hate being right."

CHAPTER 19

The body looked the way that all the smooth men's victim's looked —
headless, half-rotted, with a deep hole running from the stump of the
neck into the body. The smooth men had a tapered spike in place of a
neck. The amount of both force and precision it took to jam that
spike into the body was astonishing. Doctor Piper, the surgeon to the
dead in Archon's Glory, had had a lot to say about that. "Could a
human do it? Sure. Humans can do all kinds of things, particularly
when they aren't held back by moral compunctions. Could they do it
consistently and well, on the first try, every time? Definitely not."

"Hmm." Clara studied the body dispassionately. "Rotten, but the
scavengers haven't done much."

"They don't, as far as we can tell. They don't like the smell. Not
even vultures will touch them. Useful for us, insomuch as we're more
likely to find the heads, but I don't like what that says about the
smooth men themselves." He coughed.

"So there's a severed head around here as well?"

"Probably."

In fact there were two, a man and a woman. Istvhan looked down
at them and groaned.

The necks were ragged, the eyes staring sightlessly at the sky.
Neither matched the body and they were a great deal fresher.

Clara crouched down, her sleeve over her mouth, and studied the heads. "That's a ragged stump. If they used an axe, they didn't use it well."

"It's not an axe." Istvhan. "They open their jaws somehow and bite the heads off. It's pretty horrible."

"...ah."

Her voice was absolutely inflectionless. Istvhan cursed himself. "Not like that," he said. "I mean, not like you do. Like you did. Oh, hell."

Making a bit of a mess of things, he observed internally. *Keep talking, though. I'm sure you can make it worse.*

"I know it shouldn't matter," he said hopelessly. "About you and the — the — with the teeth—"

Clara gazed at him in silence. Istvhan talked to fill it, which was the worst possible thing he could do and he knew it was the worst thing he could do and yet he seemed to be doing it anyway. "He'd be just as dead if I ran him through with a sword. It doesn't matter to him. I'm trying not to let it matter to me."

"No," said Clara, "biting people's heads off *should* matter, I think. You don't want to start doing it for fun."

"Well, no, of course not. But..." He rubbed both hands over his face, mostly to shut himself up. After a moment he dropped his hands and said "I'm going to stop talking now."

"That would probably be for the best, yes." She stood up, dusting off her hands. "I suspect that lump over there is our second body."

Istvhan turned and followed her gaze to a crumpled shape under a low pine tree. It might have been a log or a rock, except that it appeared to be wearing ragged clothes.

"Do we do something with these bodies?" asked Clara. "Burn them or put a stake through their heart or something?"

"If we had time and tools, I'd want to bury them. But as it is..." He shrugged. "We've got our own problems right now, and I don't believe in any god that would punish two souls for not getting a proper burial when they were murdered."

Clara smiled. It was a genuine smile, which surprised him, given that he'd just made a spectacular ass of himself. *Not a nun, but she takes faith seriously nonetheless.*

"What else have you learned about them?"

"We know there's at least two of them. They can't replace themselves, it takes two. They seem to go inert once they're pulled out." He stared down at the second head. "I suspect they caught two people traveling together and took both their bodies." He tried not to imagine what it must have been like for the second of the two, seeing their partner slaughtered in front of them and knowing what was coming next.

"Convenient for them. Will they be able to pass as human?"

Istvhan frowned. "No, but also yes? They're clearly wrong if you look at them up close. No one has skin like clay. No pores, nothing. And they don't have hair, so they wear hats or hoods. But how many people really say anything? You're not going to point at someone in the street and yell, "That person isn't right!" In small towns, no, they'd stand out, but in a big city, all they have to do is walk away. Civility and not wanting to get involved does the rest."

"So why keep it a secret, then? Why not spread the word as far as you can?"

Istvhan scowled. It was a point of contention between himself and the Bishop. She was right, and he knew she was right, but it galled him to let people carry on in ignorance when knowledge might have saved them. "We spread word about the smell, and told people there was a new type of creature out there. A perfumer mixed us up vials that replicate it, and the Temple of the Rat had them out to every town large enough to field a constabulary so that they'd know if they found signs. That's how we picked up the trail here in the first place — you can get slewhounds on it. But we were vague about the description beyond the smell. Bishop Beartongue is of the opinion that if you tell people that someone who looks different is possibly a supernatural murderer, it will lead to a bloodbath."

Clara inhaled sharply, then coughed and covered her face with her sleeve again. "Arrgh. Let's move away from these poor people before I get sick." They tromped down the hillside together. Istvhan wasn't sure how close to stand to her. Did she want him to stand farther away? Would she think that he was disgusted by her if he did? *Dammit.* This wasn't the sort of thing a person should have to worry about when there were decapitating monsters running about. He gave up and just followed her downslope. She was better in the woods than he was. He wondered if the bear part helped, or if she'd simply spent a lot more time in the countryside. He'd started life that way, but his country was drier and full of chaparral, not hundred-foot pines.

When they were far enough away that the smell had faded to a lingering unpleasantness in the back of the throat, Clara said, "I don't let it eat them."

"What?"

"When the bear kills someone. It doesn't usually want to fight. It would much rather run away. If that man hadn't been blocking the way from the den, so that it felt cornered..." She shrugged, looking uncomfortable. "But if it does bite someone's head off, I don't let it eat them afterward. You don't want the beast to get a taste for flesh."

"Oh," said Istvhan, which seemed woefully inadequate.

"It doesn't happen often. I've only had to do it twice before."

"Ah."

"Your bishop is right," she added, which seemed like an abrupt change. "It would be a bloodbath. People are already...not kind to difference. If you sent out messengers saying that there were murderers and all you could say was that they looked a bit strange? It wouldn't end well."

"You're not wrong," Istvhan said. "But it galls me. We know that they'll keep killing, and this way maybe we could get ahead of them somehow. I keep thinking if we could get the description right..."

Clara snorted. "There is no description so perfect that a mob will step back and say, 'Oh, sorry, wrong person.' Trust me."

It occurred to Istvhan that maybe she hadn't changed the conversation at all. Clara might have a pretty good idea of how people reacted to frightening differences. Maybe, once again, he should just shut up and listen.

However willing he was to listen, she did not add anything else. Nor did she turn back into a beast. Instead they slipped and slid down the slope, the pine needles crunching and sliding underfoot. The snow thinned out as they descended, first into gritty drifts, then into white shadows under the trees, then gone completely.

"I miss shoes," muttered Clara, stopping to rub her feet. "It's the worst of the change. You always end up somewhere without shoes."

"And clothes."

"Oh, well." Was that an actual grin? Yes it was, however quickly she tried to hide it. "It turns out that if you walk up to someone, look them in the eye, and say, 'Pardon, I've just been robbed. May I borrow your coat?' they almost always oblige. The trick is to not look even remotely ashamed. Then you ask them to direct you to the local constable's office, then the constables panic and get you a blanket, you give them an entirely fictitious description of the thieves, and they escort you back to your barge, or to an inn, or whatever. As long as you're indignant, everyone else falls in line. But no one ever has the shoes."

Istvhan laughed. "Or socks, I should imagine. One of my fellow paladins knits socks at an alarming rate. He says it soothes him. Keeps us all in socks, anyway, although sometimes his choice of yarn is...idiosyncratic."

"Useful friend to have, though."

"Oh, very." Istvhan wished Stephen were here now. Stephen took the weight of the world on his shoulders and never complained, which could occasionally be annoying but was also useful when things were spiraling out of control. On the other hand, he was terribly bad at talking to women. Fortunately, he had fallen passionately in love with an odd little perfumer, the same one who had mixed up the scent vials to help track the smooth men. Istvhan quite liked her. She wanted to spend the majority of her days locked in her workshop and then come out and be with Stephen, and then go back to her workshop. Right before he'd left the city, Stephen told him that she had moved a second chair into the workshop so that he could knit *in the same room with her,* which, judging by

Stephen's reaction, was a declaration of affection unmatched in modern times.

Clara stopped moving suddenly and put up a hand. "Do you hear that?"

Istvhan cocked his head and listened. After a moment, a thin thread of human voices came through the muffling trees. "Someone talking," he murmured. "No, someone yelling. Up ahead?"

"Downslope," said Clara.

"Did they get ahead of us?"

"I don't know. Maybe. It's also possible we've reached the road."

"I'll scout ahead. They'll be looking for you, not me."

"Pretty sure they got a good look at you when you drew a sword at them," said Clara, a bit dryly. "I'll come with you, but I'll stay in the trees until we're sure."

Istvhan nodded. They moved toward the voices, as quietly as possible. A dry pine forest was the very worst thing for stealth. Everything crunched and snapped underfoot. Nevertheless, the trees began to thin and Istvhan caught a glimpse of packed mud and gravel. He felt weak-kneed with relief. Roads he understood. People, for the most part, he could deal with. Forests were difficult. It was very hard to negotiate with pine trees; they didn't want to come to the table at all.

He gestured to Clara to wait and crept up the last lines of trees. The voices were louder now.

"Da," said a woman's voice wearily, "it's stuck up to the axle. You can't pull it out and you're going to kill yourself trying."

"It just needs a little wiggling," said a querulous male voice.

"And if you throw your back out, I'll be trying to lift both you and the wagon, and how will that help?"

Istvhan reached the road and looked out onto a wagon. The side was painted with the words, "Doctor Mason's Genuine Herbal Medicines," all lettered in a riot of colors that practically glowed in the afternoon sun. The wagon was tilted at an angle and one of the front wheels had sunk deeply into the mud. Two surly-looking mules stood at the front, their ears half-back and expressions of deep annoyance on their faces. An old man was trying to dig the wheel out, and a young woman stood over him, her hands on her hips, wearing an expression not unlike the mules.

"Da, I swear by the Lady of Grass that if you throw your back out, I will leave you here and run away to start a new life as a dancing girl."

"You'll never do it, girl, you've got bad ankles. So did your mother, the gods keep her. Whole family, really. Faces like angels, but bad ankles."

"Think it's a trap?" murmured Clara in Istvhan's ear. Her breath was warm against the side of his face, and Istvhan wished that he was in a position to appreciate that more.

"If it is, it's a very strange one."

"My ankles will hold out longer than your back."

"Don't sass me. Do we have a board we can fit under the wheel?"

"Only if I start tearing open crates."

"Don't you touch those crates. That medicine can't be jostled or exposed to light."

"It's getting jostled plenty with all that heaving you're doing."

"That's fine, as long as they're in the crates. I'm going to try again."

"Da..."

The old man set his back to the wheel and began to strain. His face turned an alarming shade of violet. Istvhan decided that this had gone on long enough and emerged from the trees. "Pardon, gentlefolk," he said, "but perhaps I can be of some assistance?"

CHAPTER 20

"Sir!" The old man straightened. His mouth stretched into a broad smile and his eyes positively twinkled. Istvhan recognized the effect immediately. *This is the face he shows to strangers. Interesting.*

"You *are* a strapping young fellow, aren't you?" said the old man. His voice had rounded out and become positively theatrical. "And I fear that you find me temporarily embarrassed by the condition of my wagon. But I gaze upon your muscles, my good sir, and it comes to me that perhaps you might be the answers to my prayers. Yes, truly the gods have shined upon the hour of our meeting!"

"You need me to get your wagon unstuck," said Istvhan, amused.

"In a word, yes. In a word. I could not have put it better myself, and I have, if you will allow me to boast, a vocabulary the breadth of which has never been fully plumbed."

The young woman put her hand over her eyes.

"You see before you the illustrious Doctor Mason," he continued, "purveyor of the finest herbal treatments for all manner of ailments. If you will but aid me in freeing my wagon, I would be delighted to offer you a free bottle — no, two free bottles! — in gratitude."

Istvhan was reasonably familiar with such medicines and wondered if the bottles would prove fatal or only make his hair fall out. "No need," he said. "Let me take a look at your wagon."

"Of course, of course! But what is your name, young sir?"

"Istvhan."

"Tolly," said the young woman, nodding toward Istvhan. She had a wary but appreciative look. Istvhan was used to seeing women look at him that way, and took no offense at either the wariness or the appreciation.

"My beloved granddaughter, light of my life, joy of my heart, comfort to my old age. And you may call me Doc Mason, as I feel we shall all be great friends. Particularly once the wagon is unstuck."

The comfort to his old age gazed at the sky as if contemplating braining him with a bottle of his own medicine.

Istvhan inspected the situation. The wagon was well and truly stuck. The wheel had gotten jammed deeply into mud, and no amount of forward momentum by the mules was going to help if it didn't also get some lift upwards. He grabbed the wheel and hauled. It budged, but only enough to let him know that it was theoretically possible. The mud was nearly at the axle. *Perhaps if the weight was off on the wagon side...hmm...and I had a lever...*

A familiar voice said, "Let me get that for you." Clara stepped up beside him, hooked her hands under the back of the wagon, and threw her weight into it as well.

It moved a little more, but not enough. "Levers," said Istvhan. "Also, you were supposed to wait in the woods."

"Was I?" She rubbed her hands across her thighs. "Can't imagine why you'd think that."

"No, neither can I."

"Madam!" said Doctor Mason. "My goodness!" His eyes swept over her torn robes, much the worse for wear for having had a bear erupt out of them twice in as many days. "Has some ill befallen you? May we offer our assistance?"

"Set upon by bandits," she said smoothly. "My bodyguard here stood them off."

Demoted from captain to bodyguard. Ah, well. "Yes, indeed. How many did I stand off, do you remember?"

"Five," she said promptly, giving him a severe look. "One of which had a necklace of human ears."

"Great gods!" said Doc Mason. "The barbarism! The sartorial degeneracy! What has the world come to?"

"Sister Clara," said Clara, extending her hand.

"She is being far too modest," said Istvhan, cutting in. "You see before you the Mother Superior of the Order of Saint...Galen."

"Mother Superior!" Doc Mason dropped to one knee in the mud and kissed the hem of Clara's robe. It took him a moment to find a sufficiently unmuddied portion, during which Clara glared daggers at Istvhan.

"Please, no," said Clara. She and Tolly had to help the old man to his feet. "I am — err — not traveling in the open. It is hardly safe, as you have seen."

"You may call her Domina Clara," said Istvhan, and pretended not to see Clara's expression.

"Are you going to Morstone?" asked Tolly.

"That was our plan, before we were set upon," said Clara.

"Then you must accompany us upon the road! At least as far as the next inn!" said Doc Mason. He waved his arms. "My wagon is at your service, Domina. My medicines. My life."

"I don't think that will be necessary," said Clara.

"Nevertheless. A wise man serves the gods and the servants of the gods, and in doing so, serves himself better than—"

"Let's see if we can get your wagon unstuck," said Istvhan. "Domina, would you care to help me find a lever?"

"A good tree branch ought to do it," she said. They headed back toward the woods. "Mother Superior," she said under her breath. "Really?"

"Bodyguard? Really? Anyway, probably not wise to keep introducing yourself as a nun, given that there are people on the lookout for them right now."

She looked chagrined. "I know. I realized it as soon as it came out of my mouth, but it's reflex. I've been a Sister for over twenty years."

"Indeed. We'll have to think of another cover story, though."

"Did you want me to introduce you as a mercenary captain and claim to be your troop?"

Istvhan grinned. "You could serve in any troop that I ever commanded, Domina. Or command it, most likely."

She gave him an odd look. He got the impression that she was flattered, if wary. "Me, or the bear?"

"I was under the impression that you came as a package. However, you are to be preferred. You are good company, you work well in a group, you fight competently and clear-headedly, and you do not smell."

"I had no idea the bar was so low."

"You'd be amazed how many competent fighters cannot work with others."

"I meant the smell."

"You'd be amazed by that, too." He scanned the woods for likely looking branches. "My kingdom for an axe."

"Do you think they're on the up-and-up?" She jerked her chin back toward the wagon.

"I think he's a snake oil salesman. That said, it's definitely safer to travel in a group, and I am fairly certain that I can take him in a fight."

"I suspect a damp towel can take him in a fight. Still, I feel like this is a strangely elaborate set-up for a trap."

"Same. And they're acting about like I'd expect, inviting us to the next inn with them, but not actually telling us their destination. They have more to fear from us than we do from them at the moment."

Clara pointed to a young tree. "That one work?"

"Yes, if we can get it out of the ground." The roots were sunk deep. "Or chop it down."

"You could use your sword."

"I will pretend you did not say that."

"Why do men get so defensive about their swords?"

"They're remarkably fragile when they're not in use."

Clara gave him a look. He gave it right back to her. "What?"

She very obviously decided to let that one go. "Perhaps the good doctor has an axe."

They returned to the wagon. "Do you have an axe?" asked Clara.

"Tolly, fetch the Domina the finest axe at our disposal!"

Tolly scurried into the wagon and returned a moment later with a small hatchet. "It's the only axe at our disposal," she said.

"It will do very well," said Istvhan.

"All right," said Istvhan, once the lever was acquired and in place. "On my mark...mark."

Clara heaved. The mules pulled. Istvhan threw his weight against the lever. With a loud squelch, a plop, and a spray of mud that coated him to the neck, the wheel came free.

"You did it! You did it! The gods be praised! Though I am not sure that they would approve of a Mother Superior lowering herself to unstick a wagon, but in this case, surely the divine has showered blessings upon us!"

"Well, something's been showered on them," said Tolly, stopping the mules and coming back to look at the mud-splattered pair. "Domina, Mister Istvhan, would you like to stay in the wagon for a few hours while I wash your clothes and dry them on the roof? It's the least we can do after you've helped us."

"I would be grateful beyond words," said Clara.

Tolly sized her up. The woman came barely to Clara's collarbone. "If you'd like, I'm a dab hand with a needle as well. Nothing of mine will fit you, I fear, but I could at least sew up some of the damage in your robe."

"You are a saint among women," said Clara, "and I am something of an authority on the matter."

Tolly smiled. A little of the wariness crept out of her eyes. *She isn't sure if she really thinks Clara's a nun, but a woman in ruined clothes is apparently universal.*

"Yes, yes," said Doc Mason. "Into the wagon with you! And we'll have you put to rights quicker than the great hero Mardok cleaned the legendary cesspits of Atieum!"

"What was so legendary about them?" asked Clara.

"Best not to inquire, my dear Domina. Best not to inquire."

Clara was uneasy in the wagon. She hadn't given it any thought climbing in, but as soon as the door closed, her pulse jumped. She went hastily to the door and opened it again, just to make sure it wasn't locked. She sat back down and closed her eyes, breathing deeply through her nose.

Istvhan looked at her quizzically.

"The wagons. Before. We climbed in and then..." She waved her hand. "It's fine. I didn't think, that's all. Your wagon was open-sided, so it never took me the same way."

"Do you need to go back outside?"

Clara glanced down at what she was wearing, which was a blanket. "I suspect I might give the good doctor a heart attack."

"He might have a medicine for that."

Clara snorted. The inside of the wagon was hung with sheets of canvas and packed to the rafters with boxes of bottles that clinked whenever either of them moved. Instead of beds, which might have taken up valuable box space, there were hammocks slung from the ceiling. Presumably one or two of the boxes was actually food, but the majority had DOC MASON'S MEDICINE stamped on the side in block letters.

"He's got enough medicines to cure an army. Or kill it, depending on what he's selling."

Istvhan found a half-full bottle, uncorked it, and sniffed gingerly. "Whew! I imagine it's popular, whatever it is!"

Clara took a tentative sniff, and laughed out loud. "Well, there's enough booze in there that I suppose you'll die happy, anyway." She sniffed again. "Herbs, definitely. Sweet woodruff, probably. Ginger. Something citrusy. Bergamot, maybe. That'd be expensive, though, so it might just be lemon balm."

"I've heard of worse tonics." Istvhan sniffed, too. "That perfumer friend of mine could probably smell this and tell you every ingredient, right down to what wood they burned to distill the alcohol with. All I'm getting is ginger and alcohol, though."

He re-corked the bottle and turned to set it back down. The blanket slid off his shoulders and down around his waist. He had dark hair across his chest, thickening in a line downwards. Clara found that her thoughts suddenly had very little to do with herbs.

No, dammit. Stop. He made it clear that he's not getting past the thing where you bit a man's face off. And he was probably only interested in you because you were the only woman traveling with him that might possibly be interested back.

Also he's a goddamn paladin. Paladins are always trouble.

They were. St. Ursa did not call paladins — not that there was any need, when all of Her Chosen could turn into gigantic beasts more or less on a whim — but the orders that had paladins also had problems. When you had a whole group of people dedicated to killing people for your god, even if they had the very best of intentions, they got...strange.

Istvhan said as much earlier. Righteous violence is one hell of a drug. They may be vital, but they aren't something that you want to get involved with. Even if...

He pulled the blanket across his lap, grumbling, and tried to adjust the ends. It was not a sexy motion, or even a particularly suggestive one, but she caught a glimpse of lean hips and appreciated all over again just how broad his shoulders actually were and how much they tapered downward.

...what was I thinking about, again?

Istvhan reached over and gripped her good shoulder. Clara blinked at him, but his eyes were warm and concerned, nothing more. "Feeling any better?" he asked.

"I...oh, yes." She glanced reflexively at the small door. "It's not so bad. I don't know if I'd want to sleep in here, but this isn't anything like the...other wagons."

He nodded and gave her upper arm a comforting squeeze. He had very large hands.

The door opened. They both jumped back hurriedly, as if they'd been doing something illicit. Tolly came in, holding a small kettle. "Everything's washed and drying on the roof," she said. "We'll get underway here shortly, but I thought I'd bring you some tea."

"Did I say that you were a saint already?" asked Clara. "It is true. Possibly truer than it was."

Tolly smiled. "It's no trouble. I had to heat the washing water anyway." She squeezed past the two of them, found mugs, and poured tea. Her smile widened a little when she handed Istvhan his mug, and it occurred to Clara that she was quite a lovely young woman.

That's the sort of person that Istvhan should be chasing after, she thought, staring down into the tea. *Someone kind and entirely human. Where you don't have to worry if they're going to suddenly break out in fur and fangs because there's a truffle somewhere in the vicinity.*

"These were in your pocket. I'm not sure if you wanted to keep them...?" Tolly handed Clara the acorns from the emperor oak.

"Oh! Yes, thank you." Clara took them gratefully. It had been a small but meaningful kindness and she meant to plant them.

Tolly left again, and the wagon began to move a few minutes later. Clara leaned back somewhat gingerly, not sure what was loadbearing and what might contain herbal tonic. Bottles rattled around them. When she glanced over, Istvhan was watching her.

He's just trying to make sure you're not going to panic and bolt. Don't get excited. In the cave, earlier, you either misunderstood or he was just talking or...oh, it doesn't matter now. Get to Morstone. There's no time for stupid complications.

The stupid complication in question leaned back on his elbows, which did things to his chest that were unfair to witness. Clara closed her eyes and wished for a rosary. *Blessed Saint Ursa, giver of strength, protector of women, be with us now and in our darkest hours. Keep us from those who would do us harm, and lend us Your strength to protect those who cannot protect themselves. Saint Ursa, Your hand is upon—*

"The hinges aren't reinforced," said Istvhan.

Clara's eyes snapped open, got an eyeful of semi-naked paladin, and lost her place in the catechism. "Ah...the what now?"

"The hinges on the door," said Istvhan. "I took a look when you were opening it up. They're on the outside, of course, but there's no lip and they're basic metal. If it's a trap, between the two of us, we can bash our way out."

"Good to know." Privately, Clara suspected that if it was a trap, the bear could take the entire wagon apart, unless there were steel bars hiding behind the sheets of canvas.

"They might still be planning to turn us over to our little friends on the road, but I don't know if there's any way to guard against that." Istvhan scratched his cheek. He hadn't shaved since they had fled into the mountains, and the skin above his beard had gone from blue stubble to short dark hair. Clara guessed that it must itch like the devil.

"If we stay with the wagon, they'd need horses to catch up with us," said Clara. "And even assuming the one who got away got back to his people to report in, they can't take horses across the mountains any faster than we could walk. We're probably in the clear for a day or two, and if they're fool enough to bring horses near the bear..." She shrugged.

"Unless they've got more parties between here and there," said Istvhan.

"We're valuable," said Clara, "but I can't imagine we're *that* valuable."

"At a guess, the men we encountered are general procurers. Somewhere between a bandit and a trader and a bounty hunter. They likely have a network of buyers and bring in anything they can turn a profit on — people, furs, rare beasts. I doubt they were looking for you specifically, particularly since the raiders believed you were dead, until we were too interested in the fake plague wagons."

Clara nodded. "Makes sense. I saw the one that first night in the inn. He had plenty of time to find the rest of his network and inform them that there was a nun asking questions. They may believe I was another member of the convent who was not present when the raiders came." She groaned. "Of course, if word got out to look for sisters of St. Ursa asking questions about those wagons, I'll be fighting these types off every time I ask if anyone's seen them."

"I'll ask," said Istvhan. "Nobody thinks I'm a nun."

Clara snorted. "No, you're a paladin, which is worse."

"Hardly. Paladins are afraid of nuns. Show me a nun who's afraid of a paladin. We melt if you look at us harshly and tell us the god will be very disappointed."

She had to laugh. "You've foolishly revealed your greatest weakness. I shall have the upper hand from now on."

He smiled. His dark brown eyes were nearly black in the dimness of the wagon. "You've always had the upper hand, Domina."

CHAPTER 21

"Your clothes are dry," said Tolly, at the next stop. "And if you want to hop out and...ah..." She blushed.

"Thank you," said Istvhan. He could use his clothes. Being stuck in the wagon half-naked next to a much-too attractive nun was not easy. It had been bad enough when he had clothes himself. Somehow, when she'd been naked, it had been easier to remember that she was capable of turning into a bear. Women just didn't wander around the woods in the nude, in Istvhan's experience. There were too many mosquitoes and unpleasantly placed twigs. His brain knew that something wasn't right.

But plenty of women sat with a blanket wrapped around them, and when he was also wearing just a blanket, his brain stopped looking for a trap and started noticing things like the smooth lines of muscle over her arms and shoulders, the round curve of her belly and thighs. Her thighs were heavy with muscle as well. If she locked them around Istvhan's hips...*no, no, don't think about that, think about something else.*

She tore a man's head apart about ten hours ago. With her teeth.

This took the edge off, a little.

He'd be just as dead if you stabbed him. And you've killed enough warriors in front of civilians to know that half the time, they scream and wet themselves and try to get away from you. It's not less monstrous just because you have a piece of metal to do it with. Would you rather she'd let him come up behind you and hit you over the head?

Obviously not. And the Saint knew, he'd found her terribly attractive after that first battle, spattered with blood. Attractive enough that he'd lost his head completely and pushed her back against the wagon and taken a kiss she hadn't offered. *Which is proof enough that you are far more of a brute beast than she is, and you should shut up and put on your damn clothes and stop trying to sneak looks at her.*

He turned his back as Clara climbed into her robes, which were wrinkled and much the worse for wear, but at least slightly mended. He was very glad to see, when he turned back around, that Tolly had managed to repair the rents so that they did not keep gaping open and threatening glimpses of female flesh. Paladins were famous for resisting temptation, but life was a lot easier when temptation kept at least ten feet away and only offered easy things, like wealth and vengeance and earthly dominion.

When he was dressed himself and had emerged from the wagon, Doc Mason waved to him. "Ah, my boy! We were stuck longer than I hoped, but the inn is just around the next hill," said Doc Mason, waving grandly as if he owned both inn and hill.

"No, it isn't, Da," said Tolly. She kept her eyes on the mules. "You're confusing this road with the one near Friddle."

"Hush, impertinent child! My mind is still as sharp as it ever was! We shall come around this bend and it shall be laid out before us, the...Sign of the Wild Rooster, I think? Wet Rooster? No matter." He waved again.

"You said that about the last three hills."

"I am quite certain about this one."

Clara and Istvhan traded brief bemused looks. Tolly clucked her tongue at the mules and urged them into a walk. The wagon rounded the low hillside and on the far side, stretching out before them, was... more road. Scrubby brushland. There was a broken down fence to one side, and a farmhouse, far in the distance, with the roof fallen in.

"Ah...hmm," said Doc Mason. "Friddle, you say?"

"Sign of the White Rooster is by Friddle. The next inn on this road is another half day, after we join the main road, and it's the Three-Legged Horse."

Doc Mason sucked on his teeth. After a moment, he turned back to Clara and Istvhan, a trace of sheepishness on his face. "Well, my friends, I see we will need to make camp for the night. I will offer you the hospitality of the wagon, Domina Clara, and..."

"No," said Clara hastily. Istvhan wasn't sure if it was the fear of being closed in a wagon again, or simple desire not to kick an elderly man out of his own bed. "I am quite used to sleeping on the ground. If we may borrow the underside of your wagon, to keep the damp off..."

Doc Mason sighed. "My chivalry is injured, but my sciatica thanks you, my dear. Yes, of course. It is a poor repayment for getting us on our way, but I will do better when we arrive at the Three-Legged Horse."

The Three-Legged Horse was at the intersection of the minor road past the mountains and a far larger one, where the southern trade road curved north toward Morstone. "We've lopped about a week off our travel time," said Istvhan, "though I can't say I enjoyed the mountain route much."

"I hope that means we're a week closer to the raiders," said Clara, watching Doc Mason haggle with the innkeeper.

"It should. The smooth men apparently took the same route we did, so I'm not sure how far behind them we are now."

"Those bodies weren't two weeks old."

"Definitely not. I wonder if they had to go to ground for a bit and wait for a new set of hosts to come by."

"Those poor people." Clara frowned. "What do you think they do if they can't find a new person?"

"We don't actually know. We don't know much of anything. It

takes two of them to transfer between hosts, and if they get separated, they're vulnerable."

"So there could be...what? Random clay heads out there in the woods, whose bodies rotted away under them?"

"Very possibly." Istvhan gave her a wry look. "Delightful thought, isn't it?"

"You have an odd definition of delight."

"Mmm."

Tolly came back from tending the mules. "Granddad got you two rooms," she said. "Err — is two right?" She looked from one to the other.

"Yes!" said Clara, a little too quickly.

Tolly smiled. Her eyes crinkled up at the corners. In a few years, she'd probably get laugh lines there. "All right. We weren't certain."

"One never quite knows with bodyguards," said Doc Mason, having finished his haggling. "Whether or not they want to sleep on the floor in front of the door or something equally dramatic. Barricading the doors and the like. Which I'm happy to accommodate! Just tell me so that I can stop this scoundrel of an innkeeper from trying to fleece me, like the tenderest of lambs."

Clara was of the opinion that if Doc Mason was a sheep, he was the sort of mutton so tough that wolves would break teeth on him, but she wasn't sure if he would take that as a compliment.

"I think I can avoid building any barricades," said Istvhan. He grinned at Clara over Mason's head.

The trip to the Three-Legged Horse had been easy. They walked alongside the mules when the mules walked, and rode on the wagon when the mules trotted. There was space enough for four, if someone sat behind the drivers, although both Clara and Istvhan found the leg room a trifle lacking. Mostly they walked.

Doc Mason was a charming travel companion, full of questionable information and stories that Clara did not believe for an instant. Tolly was much quieter, probably in self-defense, but she laughed often and she reined in her grandfather as easily as she did the mules.

It was not as cold as it had been in the mountains. Sleeping under the wagon at night was no different than it had been with Istvhan's company, if you didn't count the sexual frustration. Still, Clara had to admit that a real bed would be nice, even if it was almost certainly going to be too short.

She opened the door to her room. Yep. Exceedingly short, and tucked into an alcove so that her feet hit the wall. She sighed.

"Mine's the same way," said Istvhan, leaning out his door. "Still, they've got a bath house. I'll take it."

"You and me both." She hadn't had more than a splash in a ditch since being the bear, and the change always left her feeling vaguely oily. "I think I brought half the mountain with me. Mostly between my toes."

The tub, as it turned out, was also rather small. Nevertheless, Clara dumped hot water over all the bits she could fit into it at one time and scrubbed with the sand that the innkeeper provided until her skin was pink and smarting with the feeling of clean, clean, clean.

Being able to bite through a man's head and walk through a snow-storm was very useful. Clara just wished that it didn't come with the sense of being oily.

Or with horrifying one's travel companions. He's been very polite, though. I should be grateful.

She was pulling on the loose belted robe that the innkeeper also offered to travelers — not completely clean, but a lot cleaner than her own clothes, which were currently being smoked over a fire to kill the smell and any bugs — when someone banged on the door to the tiny bathhouse.

"A moment!" Clara pushed her feet into the much-too-small sandals. *Still, so very civilized, supplying sandals. I approve.* She hobbled to the door and opened it.

"I let you go first because I'm a paladin and chivalry is not dead," said Istvhan, "but if you don't hurry up, I'm going to remember that I'm a very lapsed paladin and that you can easily beat my ass in a fight."

"Is chivalry only for people you can beat up, then?"

"Generally." He held the door open for her anyway. "Also there's a lot about horses, and I don't fight on horseback."

"Oh? Why not?"

"Horses hate berserkers. Absolutely hate them. They'll throw themselves over to get rid of us. And...ah...at that point they become a threat." He looked oddly embarrassed.

"And if they're a threat...?"

"Let's say that it doesn't always end well for the horse. The battle tide spares the innocent, but not if they're trying to kill us. May I have a bath now?"

"Good to know," Clara said. "Yes, of course." She stepped out of the way. *Interesting. I wonder what the beast will think of a berserker?* She remembered roaring back at Galen. That had been a challenge, one large predator to another. *Perhaps I already know.*

A more pressing thought struck her, and she called back over her shoulder "The tub's too small."

"Of *course* it is."

"I've been thinking," said Doc Mason over dinner. "Well, we've been thinking." He put his arm around Tolly. "You two are headed Morstone way, aren't you?"

Istvhan and Clara exchanged glances. They had folded themselves into the small chairs and were devouring food as fast as it was put in front of them. The local delicacy was a thick wheat noodle with an equally thick sauce and a great deal of late-season squash smothered in butter. Istvhan could not remember the last time he'd had butter on something and was fully prepared to eat the entire harvest on his own.

Clara, at his elbow, was putting a similar amount of damage on the food. *Well, she was supporting quite a large body for a while...and carrying you...hmm, I wonder how food carries over for shapechangers.* He also wondered if Doc Mason had expected the bill for dinner to be quite so high.

"Normally, as we start to approach Morstone, I'd hire a couple of men as guards," said Doc Mason, who did not seem particularly troubled.

Clara paused, fork held aloft. "This is an extremely well-traveled road," she said. "We've seen two guard posts. Is there still a problem with bandits?"

"Oh no, not bandits." He waved his hands. "No, it's for the show. Selling Doc Mason's Herbal Medicines!" The words rolled off his tongue as if he were singing them. Tolly shook her head silently and gazed at the ceiling.

"Is tonic selling dangerous?" asked Istvhan.

"It can be. The shows are an event! A performance! And I fear that not everyone enjoys a performance." His voice dropped and became somewhat less theatrical. "Also, there's usually a few drunks and they often think it would be delightful to get up on stage with me."

"Ahhh."

"Ohhh."

Both Clara and Istvhan made nearly identical noises of comprehension. "You need a bouncer," said Istvhan.

"Ideally, yes. And as the two of you are also heading in the direction of Morstone, if you do not mind a day or two out of your way..." He spread his hands. "We don't stay at many inns at night, I fear, but I can offer you hot food whenever we pass one."

Given the speed at which he and Clara were tucking in, Istvhan suspected the good doctor might lose money on that bargain. He glanced over at Clara and raised an eyebrow.

"Our companions are a ways behind us, and won't catch up for at least a week," he said. "But I must yield the final decision to the Mother Superior."

Clara kicked him under the table. Istvhan smiled serenely, glad that she was still barefoot.

"It sounds like an excellent deal for us," said Clara. "But what do you get out of it? We might be dangerous fugitives."

Doc Mason chuckled. "I am counting on the dangerous part," he said. "Though I'd prefer the gentleman leave his sword in the wagon during the show. It is all fun and games until someone loses their head."

Istvhan stiffened involuntarily. So did Clara. Mason looked from one to the other. "Did I say something wrong?"

"It's a long story," said Istvhan. "We'll tell you on the road, maybe." He reached for another slice of squash.

"Then it's agreed!" Doc Mason beamed at them. So did Tolly.

When they had finally finished making up for days of trail rations, Clara and Istvhan made their excuses and headed upstairs. Istvhan cleared his throat once they were in the upper hallway. "Do you still think this is on the up-and-up?"

Clara paused outside her door. "I do." She worried at her lower lip with her teeth and Istvhan found his eyes riveted on the motion.

The last time they had been in an inn hallway together, she'd kissed him until his back hit the wall. Istvhan suspected that wasn't going to happen again. *You've stabbed her, insulted her, and compared her to the smooth men. You're lucky she doesn't slap you every time you look at her.*

He realized it was his turn to talk and managed, "Oh, ah?"

"Even if we assume that they're going to drug us once we're near Morstone and drop our neatly bound bodies at the gate of the amphitheater...there's just no way they could find out that I was still alive in time, and then happen to be waiting at the exact right place." She folded her arms and leaned against her door. "Doc Mason's a tough old bird and he might be able to hide what he's thinking, but I don't think for a second that Tolly knows what I am."

That caught Istvhan's attention. "Really? You can tell?"

"Usually." Her smile held a bitter trace. "They give me a little too much space and they watch me constantly when they think I'm not looking."

Am I doing that? Istvhan wondered. He felt an immediate urge to take a step closer to her, just to prove he didn't care. *Except I might care? But I* shouldn't *care, unless I should care very much, since that's part of what she is. But...* He cleared his throat and told himself to stop babbling. "So Tolly isn't watching you all the time."

"Not at all." Clara's smile grew, and lost the edge. "Actually, she's watching *you.*"

CHAPTER 22

Tolly *was* watching him. Istvhan realized it the next day. It wasn't in any way sinister, and he would be lying if he said he wasn't a bit flattered, though. It was the sort of look he was used to getting from women who were interested in men, and particularly interested in big, well-muscled men who cleaned up reasonably well.

It was just a trifle inconvenient, because while Tolly was quite attractive, she was also at least fifteen years younger than he was, not to mention their host's granddaughter.

Also, Clara found the whole thing *hilarious.*

"Well, you're a paladin. This must happen to you all the time," she said, as they collected firewood for the campfire that night. "Lovely young women swooning after men in armor, committed to the cause of justice, off to the next battle with demonic forces..."

"That's the paladins of the Dreaming God," said Istvhan, trying not to grit his teeth. He shouldn't be annoyed. He'd given his brother paladin Shane crap about this for years. Shane was so handsome that he almost *had* been a servant of the Dreaming God. Women looked at him and lost the power of speech. "I was Saint of Steel. We're not the pretty ones."

"Oh, I don't know..." His heart rose. "Galen's a good-looking man, even if he doesn't want anything I've got." His heart sank again.

He grunted. Clara picked up most of a log under one arm. *"Have you ever fought demons?"*

"A couple times. They mostly get into farm animals."

"We had that happen to a rooster once." She headed back toward the wagon, carrying her log. "Hard to tell at first because plenty of roosters are bastards, but when the novicekeeper went to wring its neck, it started speaking in tongues."

"Saint's balls. What did you do?" Rogue demons were dangerous and could jump to humans if they could get a foothold.

"The Abbess and Sister Sigrid drowned it in holy water. I'm not sure if it couldn't jump out of the rooster or if it just decided we weren't worth the trouble and went back to hell. Sigrid said it was a young, stupid one, though."

Istvhan suspected that even a young, stupid demon would think twice about bothering a nun again. He was flesh and blood and had had his soul purified by divine fire on a regular basis, and even he was routinely frightened by nuns.

Am I frightened of Sister Clara, though?

He grimaced and answered his own internal question. *No, I'm bloody goddamn terrified. And not just because she can turn into a bear.*

"The last one I helped with was in a feral sow," he said. "We had two paladins of the Dreaming God with us. They took the demon that was in the sow and the rest of us tackled the sounder of pigs she had with her."

"Now *that* sounds unpleasant."

Tolly turned to stare at them as they entered the circle of firelight. "Did I just hear that right? You fought a demon?"

"And he was incredibly brave, too," said Clara. Tolly's eyes shone with hero-worship. Istvhan gazed across the fire at Clara and thought dark thoughts.

Traffic picked up even further as they traveled north. There was rarely a stretch of road where Istvhan couldn't see a farm cart in the distance or another merchant passing by. Troops wearing the wave-and-sword insignia of Morstone passed by at least once a day. No one offered them violence, and Istvhan stopped reaching for his sword hilt every time he saw someone in a field or cutting through a distant copse.

"How do you think the others are doing?" asked Clara one night, as they lay side-by-side under the wagon.

"I am trying not to worry. Galen's a perfectly skilled commander, even though he hates it. Brindle could keep the mules going if they had four good legs between the three of them. But the mountains are treacherous nonetheless."

"I worry that the raiders will come for them, thinking I'm still there," Clara admitted.

"Galen will tell them you've left. Probably invite them to search the wagon if they'd like. He's...an original thinker."

She chuckled. "He gets it from his boss, I imagine."

"I'm not really his boss." Istvhan rolled on his side to face her. It seemed very intimate, even though they were outdoors. Banked firelight left orange splashes across her skin, and the shadows of the wheels were edged with purple. "We don't have much rank left among the Saint of Steel's chosen. Only seven of us made it out alive. There didn't seem to be much point."

"So few of you."

Istvhan nodded. He braced himself for the follow-up — *what happened? How did it feel? What is it like to feel your god die?*

Clara surprised him. "How long did you serve Him?"

"Not as long as some of the others. I was in my mid-twenties when the madness came on me. Which is, perhaps, why it holds me more lightly than some of the others." He decided to turn the question back. "But you went to the convent when you were young?"

"Mmm. Yes. When I had the change. I was...eight? Nine? Everyone in the valley knows that if a child isn't...right...you talk to the Sister of St. Ursa."

"Isn't right?" He felt a flicker of anger for nine-year-old Clara. "I don't know that I'd call turning into a perfectly good bear 'not right.'"

Clara laughed once, loudly, then put her hand over her mouth. "Well," she said, her eyes dancing, "I appreciate that I am a perfectly good bear. But it was rather shocking for my parents. And not the sort of thing you expect a normal family to deal with. They weren't bad people, but they were out of their depth. It's much easier if the convent takes us." She sobered, rolling back to stare up at the underside of the wagon. "There are stories of families chaining up their daughters out of fear of the beast. And since the bear comes out particularly when you are frightened or angry...well. A self-fulfilling prophecy. There was one when our former abbess was a novice. She broke out of the cellar they kept her in, killed her family, and ran to the hills. But she had no idea how to hunt as a bear, so she would descend on farms and kill livestock. The convent had to deal with her."

"Deal with her?" Istvhan was fairly certain he knew what that meant.

She nodded. "If she had been content to live wild in the woods, we would have kept an eye on her, but let her be. But she put us all at risk. The convent is not an open secret, but enough people have sent daughters there..." She trailed off, shaking her head. "You cannot let them think that we are wild beasts. If that is allowed to fester, we all die, and what becomes of the next generation of St. Ursa's daughters?"

"Is it St. Ursa then? Was this a god's work?"

Clara shrugged. "I don't know. St. Ursa's blessing is what we call it, when we're being formal and ecclesiastical."

"Ah. Yes." He understood that. "We called the battle madness the Saint of Steel's gift. But that was courtesy, really. I think we were likely all berserkers, like the old stories, and the Saint of Steel merely gathered us up and put us to use."

Clara pointed a finger at him. "Exactly. Yes. If I had to guess, I would say that St. Ursa did not cause this, but was rather the patron of those who have the beast. But it's different with a saint than a god. Gods you can actually get to, if you have a priest with a true calling. Saints, you just have to hope they know what they're doing."

"Not mine," said Istvhan. "Not anymore."

She met his eyes squarely, taking the blame. "You're right. I apologize. That was ill-spoken of me."

Istvhan shook his head. "Don't worry. I still forget myself sometimes. Although mine actually was a god, not a saint. A mistranslation, they think, and of course it stuck. Although I won't swear that the Forge God did not prefer that." He smiled. "A god of blacksmiths would never be quite easy with a battle god calling themselves the God of Steel."

"Mmm. Where did He come from, originally? Do you know?"

"Up north and west somewhere. One of the little countries with a lot of coastline and too many umlauts. They grew a lot of berserkers up there, if you believe the old stories, and it makes sense that when they spread, the blood went with them. When the ice moved in and those countries became uninhabitable, they came south." He shrugged. "It's mostly died out over time, I suspect. The center of the Saint's power was around Anuket City and Archenhold, and a few scattered temples up as far as the south reaches of Charlock. If someone had the battle tide come on them, they usually found their way to us."

Clara nodded. "St. Ursa was only ever in our valley, as far as we can tell. If there's others like us — and I suspect there must be — they've made their own peace. We'd get sisters from, oh, maybe two weeks' ride away, but not much more. Part of my job as a trader was to listen for anything that might be a sister of St. Ursa who needed our help, but it rarely happened. Once there was a daughter along the canal, but her mother had been from the valley. It's something in the blood, I think, though it skips many generations." Her lips twitched. "It has to, of necessity. We don't have children."

"Oath?" She wasn't sworn to celibacy, a fact that he contemplated four or five times a day.

"Biology. The beast wakes up before puberty, and while we bleed like ordinary human women, we're not fertile." She scowled. "Which seems extremely unfair. All the mess when we're never going to do anything with it."

He laughed. "My sisters would definitely agree with you there. Is it only women?"

"One of us lived as a brother, but he was very old when I was a novice, and he had the same parts as the rest of us."

"Did you have a choice, if you didn't want to live at the convent?"

"Did you, if you didn't want to go berserk?"

He shook his head. "No, but I think...few of us wanted to. When the god took you, it was pure divinity, slammed directly into your veins." He swallowed, wondering how to explain. "It was like nothing else on earth. You were the instrument of justice. You could fight an army by yourself. The world was outlined in golden fire. We went willingly, even knowing that afterward, our bodies would be absolutely wracked with pain."

"Mmm. You'd go back to that if you could, I take it?"

Istvhan stared at nothing. "My brothers would, I think. Almost all of them."

"And you?"

He was tempted to make a joke and deflect it, but this was Clara. He owed her the truth. Of all the people he had met, she was the one outside his order that came closest to understanding what it had been like. "I don't know. Sometimes it seems obvious. Other times, I think perhaps it was like a drug. We were all addicted to righteousness and glory. Perhaps it's best, after all, to leave it behind." He raised an eyebrow. "Is being a bear...err...?"

"Not like that," said Clara. "It's frightening if you aren't used to it. Most of us were glad to have someone who understood what was happening. But of course, convent life isn't for everyone. If you were not used to the discipline or the work, it would seem cruel."

"So what became of those who did not wish to stay?"

Firelight left her eyes in deep shadow. "There are many bears in the woods around our valley," she said. "They are taught how to hunt, and they know that to come too near to humans means death. But the ones who go into the beast that way do not come out again."

CHAPTER 23

"Time for our next performance!" said Doc Mason cheerfully. They had pulled off the main road an hour earlier and onto a smaller byway, lined with hedgerows. Farm buildings stood off in the distance, but the road itself was often in shadow. A few red and orange leaves still clung to the trees. Birds sang and scuffled through the fallen leaves.

Clara had not seen the village until they were nearly on top of it. Tolly handled the reins, driving the mules into a large field beside the town's largest inn, and stopped the wagon. Doc Mason went into the building to announce that he would be selling that evening, and emerged with bread stuffed with cooked peppers to share around.

"Do we need to do anything?" asked Istvhan, as they finished the meal. It wasn't quite noon yet, and he wasn't sure how long it took for Doc Mason to prepare for his 'little show.'

"Only watch and be amazed," said Doc Mason. He lowered his voice. "Also, once the crowd gets here, play along."

"What?" said Istvhan, but the peddler was already past him, undoing bolts on the sides of the wagon, flipping up levers, and then, quite astonishingly, the wagon unfolded.

The bulk of the wagon remained in one place, a narrow stage with one back wall and stacked boxes of questionable medicines. The other wall broke in half down the middle, folded outward, and became a frame for the stage. The sheets of canvas that Clara had noted earlier were unfurled. Inside the wagon, she had only seen the backs. The front sides were painted in extraordinary colors, proclaiming the wonders of Doc Mason's Medicines. On the left side, a deathly sick patient who appeared to have boils, buboes, and some kind of lightning attacking his head lay dying in vivid shades of bilious green. On the right, the same patient had leapt to his feet, waving a familiar bottle. Tolly unrolled one more canvas, covering the back of the stage (and, conveniently, their hammocks and small living quarters.) This canvas had enormous renderings of medicinal herbs, sparkling with colors that Clara had certainly never seen any of them show in nature.

"Does mint even come in that shade of blue?" asked Istvhan under his breath.

"I'm not sure anything actually comes in that shade of blue."

Doc Mason bustled up to them. "Domina Clara, I could not ask you to put yourself out in the service of mere commerce. Would you be willing to keep an eye on the crowd?"

"Do you expect trouble?" asked Clara, amused. "Previous customers, perhaps?"

"Domina!" Doc Mason looked indignant. "I have never left an unsatisfied customer behind! No, if anything the customers may be too satisfied. In areas where, perhaps, the local flow of libations has run dry, I fear that occasionally customers have been known to...ah... rush the stage in their enthusiasm to sample."

"Fair enough." Clara raised an eyebrow at him, wondering if she was about to make an enemy. Still, she had to be sure. "But doctor, if your intent, as I think, is to sell this medicine to people for coin, I have to ask you what is in it. And don't say herbs. Herbs can kill or cure, and I could not stand by and watch you hand out dangerous concoctions in the guise of a miracle cure."

Istvhan shifted beside her, just enough to free his sword hand, and Clara felt a rush of comfort. *He has my back. That's good.*

She had expected Doctor Mason to become theatrical and florid in his defense, but he surprised her. Instead, he said, "I'll drink a bottle in front of you, if you like. Though after the show, by preference, because that much alcohol's more than I can handle right now." He met her eyes gravely. "I don't promise cures," he said. "They want a show and I give them one, but if someone comes up and says their grandmother is dying, I tell them to take her to a priest or a healer. This is a fine tonic and I drink it myself — in small quantities! — but the most I'll swear to you, Domina, is that the ginger will settle your stomach and there's enough willow to sort out a headache. The rest are general healing herbs, no more than you'd get from an apprentice healer. No foxglove, no wormwood, nothing that'll lay you out or cause you any real harm, unless you're fool enough to guzzle a whole case and pass out."

"I can't hold you accountable for that," said Clara warmly. "Thank you."

The theatrical mask slid back down over his face as smoothly as oil. "Then we are agreed, good Mother Superior? You will watch an old mountebank go through his tricks and whistle a warning in case of nefarious doings?"

"Never fear, Doctor. I'll watch from the back and make sure that no one is plotting anything."

"Excellent, excellent. And should you see any rotten vegetables going by, please catch my eye."

"Is that a concern?"

"My dear Domina, there are those in this world with absolutely no appreciation for the finer nuances of showmanship."

Doc Mason was as good as his word. The crowd gathered, in much greater numbers than she had expected, all of them hanging on his every word. He went from warming them up with tales of his travels to the sales pitch almost seamlessly, but Clara listened to his patter and found nothing terribly objectionable. He somehow managed to be as self-deprecating as he was grandiose, which was quite a trick.

"And this stout fellow!" cried Doc Mason, waving Istvhan onto the stage. "My dear sister's boy! You would never know it to look at him, my friends, but he was a sickly child, and many were the nights we thought that he would turn his face to the wall and expire. But we raised him on a spoonful of Doctor Mason's Astonishing Herbal Medicine at every meal, and now look at him! Can you credit it? And as sound of wind as he is strong of build!"

Istvhan, with a broad grin, spread his arms and flexed a few times for the audience. Cries of female appreciation (and a few male ones, as well) rose from the crowd.

"You see? You would scarcely credit that he is the same fellow! And all of it, thanks to Doctor Mason's Astonishing Herbal Medicine!" He paused dramatically, then added "Well, and fresh outdoor air and good hard labor on the farm. But I like to think that my medicine had something to do with it!"

The crowd laughed appreciatively. Doc Mason waved Istvhan offstage. He flexed a few times for good measure, to more laughter.

"The truth of it is, my friends, that every man's fate lies in the hands of the gods. It is they who determine the hour of our death, not any potion that anyone may sell you. Now, there are those, as I'm certain you know, who would claim that they could work miracles! Claim to sell you recipes from the ancients, which they simply found lying around somewhere, in the middle of a field perhaps. They would take your money and promise that their medicines could stay the hand of death itself. I don't need to tell you fine people that this is a ploy to separate the foolish from their coin, do I? Charlatans!"

The crowd booed appreciatively. Clara raised an eyebrow, wondering where the man was going with this.

"So I promise you no such thing, my wise friends. We are all in the hands of the gods." He leaned forward, lowering his voice, and the crowd leaned toward him, straining to hear his every word. "But who among us would not wish to spend those allotted hours in better health? To soothe their aches and their upsets, to put a little fire back into their bellies? Hmm? I'm an old man, my friends — no, no, I won't deny it! — and I won't pretend that the cold doesn't get into my joints during winter. And that, my friends, is why I take the finest tonic known to man or beast, Doc Mason's Herbal Medicine!"

He swirled his cloak theatrically and drank from the bottle. The crowd cheered. Doc Mason wiped his mouth. "Made from only the finest herbs, grown under a kind sun, and rare forest plants picked in the full moon, this recipe came down through my family for generations, but it was I who put the finishing touches upon it, who decided that we could no longer keep it to ourselves, but that it was my duty — nay, my privilege! — to bring Doc Mason's Herbal Medicine to you, my friends..."

"Very clever," murmured Istvhan in Clara's ear. She jumped. She'd been just as caught up in Doc Mason's spiel as the crowd. His breath was warm and she hadn't expected it. Apparently, the herbal medicine wasn't the only thing putting heat in people's bellies tonight.

"Hmm?" she said, trying to cover her reaction. *Blessed St. Ursa, I thought I'd been getting over this.*

Apparently not. Istvhan kept his face close to hers so that the crowd couldn't hear him. He was close enough to kiss, which seemed like quite an interesting idea. *Don't be absurd. Not in the middle of a crowd and a sales pitch.*

"Telling them they're too smart to fall for a sales pitch. It's a particularly elegant sales pitch, if you can hold the crowd." He nodded. A stray lock of dark, wavy hair fell across his face. Clara wanted to reach out and push it aside. She curled her fingers into her palm.

"He certainly seems able to."

"Mmm-hmm. Good for repeat business, too. He's not promising a cure, just that they'll feel a bit better. People remember when cures fail them. If he comes back by in a year, though, plenty of them will swear up and down that they felt better when they were downing his potions."

"He would have made an impressive priest," said Clara, amused. "Can you imagine that voice, all fire and brimstone?"

Istvhan winced. "All too easily. We cleared out a few nests of cultists run by priests who could whip up a crowd. They're not my favorites."

"Ah, well. There's that."

"You fought cultists?" whispered Tolly. Clara hadn't seen the other woman slip through the crowd.

"Long ago, in another life. It's less interesting than it sounds. Mostly blood and mud and yelling and falling down and getting back up again. And more mud. Being the musclebound tonic-drinker is a lot more fun." He grinned down at her. "When does he start taking money?"

"In about ten minutes," said Tolly, cocking her head to listen. "He'll talk about the ingredients some more, do a brief bit on the patron gods of each herb, and then offer them the low, low price of a silver thaler a bottle. Once he gets to balm-of-ages, it's my cue to go to the wagon and start selling."

They watched Doc Mason rattle through ingredients, with a brief segue into the tragic love story of the nymph who inhabited the willow tree and fell in love with the son of the moon. "And let that be a lesson, my fine young ladies, to never give your heart to a pretty lad who cannot see past his own reflection!" Women in the crowd chuckled knowingly.

"He's very good at this," said Clara to Tolly. "I assume he's been doing it a while?"

"My whole life." Tolly gazed at the distant figure on the stage with fondness. "I was born in that wagon. He traveled with my mum and my grandmum for years before that."

"What an adventurous life you must have led," said Istvhan.

Tolly blushed rather more than the praise warranted. "Not nearly as much as fighting cultists and protecting nuns."

"The nuns are occasionally an adventure," said Istvhan, side-eyeing Clara.

"Ahem." She gave him an amused glare. "Are you going to take over the family business someday, then? Change it to Doc Tolly's Herbal Tonic?"

"Gods, no." Tolly made a warding gesture. "I don't even like the stuff. I thought that maybe when Grandda retires from the road, I'd take up being a traveling merchant. Odds and ends, from one place to another."

"That's what I do," said Clara absently, thinking of the canal. "It's not a bad life." Istvhan's eyes widened and she hastily amended, "Used to do. Before I joined the, uh, Order."

"Of course being a Mother Superior must be much different," said Tolly.

"Much. Yes." Clara prayed there would be no follow-up questions. Tolly was a sweet young woman but she was no fool.

Fortunately, Tolly had other concerns. "You must let me pick your brain sometime, about your routes and what you sold. I've been keeping track of lightweight goods that would be worth transporting, but I've only been able to cover the towns we stop at and the travelers' rests." She frowned. "I've also thought about purchasing one of those instead, but it's a gamble. You have to find one that's inexpensive enough to buy, but which gets enough wagon traffic to be worthwhile. Still, it would mean I could stay with Grandda, since he'll never admit he's getting too old to travel."

"Certainly safer for a young woman than traveling alone," said Istvhan.

Tolly gave him a saucy look over her shoulder. "Who says I'll be alone?"

Clara laughed. From the stage, Doc Mason announced the powers of balm-of-ages to soothe colicky babies and toothache.

"That's my cue," said Tolly. She started toward the wagon.

She got about five steps and then her path was blocked by an enormous man with shoulders like a blacksmith. Tolly sidestepped smoothly around him and he wobbled a bit. "Eh? Hey!"

Both Istvhan and Clara tensed up, but Tolly was clearly no stranger to this sort of thing. She was already moving into the crowd. The man swung around, saw Istvhan, and his eyes focused. "You!"

"Who, me?" said Istvhan.

"You were the one up on stage." He advanced.

"I was, yes."

"Think you're strong, do you?" said the man. Clara guessed he was probably drunk. He was talking just a hair too loudly, though he hadn't begun to slur any of his words. *Drunk enough to be brave, not drunk enough to be slow. Dammit.* She began to drift toward the pair. Perhaps she could invent an errand for Istvhan and get him out of the way before the drunk got belligerent.

"No more so than any other man," said Istvhan, which was both a lie and probably too many words all in a row for the other man to follow.

"Yeah?" There was a young woman with him, patting his arm furiously and murmuring that they should go. He ignored her. "Yeah?" he said again.

"*You* know how it is," said Istvhan heartily. "Look at you, my friend, you're clearly strong as an ox yourself."

She thought for a minute that he might have managed to deflect the other man's ire, but it wasn't enough.

"That's right," said the man, "I'm the big man around here. And don't forget it." He swung.

Clara started forward, ready to grab the fellow by the collar and drag him back, but Istvhan was faster. He caught the man's wrist and pulled forward, one foot tucking neatly around the man's shin, and dropped him facedown into the dirt. His female companion squeaked in horror.

"Careful, man," said Istvhan, in a loud, hearty voice. "The footing here makes fools of us all, eh?" He reached down and pulled the stunned man to his feet, slapping him on the back. "Nearly fell myself. I think the mules have been leaving calling cards."

The man blinked at Istvhan. Clara could almost see the words trying to penetrate through his drink-addled brain.

"That's the problem when you're as big as we are," said Istvhan. Sympathy dripped off his words and he enunciated *we* so clearly that they could probably hear it clear to the wagon. "A lot farther for men like us to fall, eh?" *Us* got the same treatment.

"Oh, aye," said the man, clearly confused as to what was going on.

"Are you his lady? Lucky man, yes." Istvhan smoothly handed the drunk off to the young woman who had gone bright crimson with embarrassment. "No, no, sir, give the young lady a chance to look you over." He nudged the drunk in the ribs in a friendly fashion. "I know it'd take a lot more to put a man like you down, but the ladies do love to fuss."

And just like that, it was over. The man was tugged into the crowd, muddy and mumbling. Istvhan beamed and waved, while Doc Mason carried on his stream of patter. Tolly caught Istvhan's arm. "Are you hurt?" she whispered.

"Not in the slightest."

"He was huge! I was afraid he was going to murder you!"

"Now that hurts me," said Istvhan, putting a hand over his heart. "So little faith."

"No — no — of course I knew you could deal with him, but—"

"*Balm-of-Ages*," said Doc Mason from the stage, with great emphasis, "yes, truly the most amazing and *timely* of herbs for so many conditions..."

"Oh no!" Tolly hiked her skirts and ran for the wagon.

"That was very well done," said Clara softly, coming up beside Istvhan. "I was going to make up an excuse to drag you away."

"The day I cannot handle one drunken lout, Domina, is the day that my brothers put me on my pyre."

"Some drunken louts handle easier than others."

"That sounds like a euphemism and I like it." He wiggled his eyebrows at her. She elbowed him.

"You talk that way to your Mother Superior?"

"I hear the order of St. Galen doesn't stand on ceremony."

Tolly began closing up the wagon, which folded together with remarkable speed. Doc Mason stood on the back step, still selling tonic and keeping up a steady stream of patter. Clara wanted to help, but Tolly clearly knew exactly what she was doing. She kept an eye on the crowd as well, which was not dissipating, even as the line of customers grew shorter.

"How do you suppose he ends this?" Clara asked.

"No idea, but I'm guessing he's got a plan. He's far too polished to leave it to chance."

Istvhan was correct. "And now we must take leave of you all," said

Doc Mason to the crowd, as the last customer stepped back, clutching their bottle. "It pains me to leave you, but other towns must learn of Doc Mason's Herbal Tonic! Lad! Lass! Step up, if you will!"

"Did he just call me a lass?" asked Clara in an undertone.

"You're more of a lass than I'm a lad. I'm forty."

"I'm thirty-six."

"See, I win." Istvhan stepped up on the back of the wagon and stretched down a hand for Clara. She stepped up beside him, taking the outrider's position at the back. Tolly cracked the whip smartly and the mules leapt forward at a good trot, despite the gloom. They must have been used to this kind of late evening journey.

Doc Mason, on the driving block beside Tolly, waved extravagantly to the crowd. "Be well, my friends! Be well and healthy! Tell your friends!" He continued waving until they rounded a corner and were out of sight.

CHAPTER 24

Tolly dropped the mules to a plodding walk after about ten minutes, and Istvhan and Clara climbed down to walk beside them. "Do you always make such a dramatic exit?" asked Clara.

"I must, Domina, or else they will be at our doorstep all evening. I am an old man and need my sleep."

"Mm-hmm."

"There's a travelers' rest up ahead," said Tolly. "We never go too far after a show. It's not as good as an inn, but it's cheaper."

The rest was substantially better than many places that Clara had camped. It clearly served as a frequent stop on the road for traders. For a few coins, there was firewood and fodder for the mules. Doc Mason haggled with the attendant in a desultory fashion, and then pulled his wagon into position.

"Not much custom right now," he said, climbing off the wagon, "or I'd have tried to get him down farther. The off-season's always hard."

Istvhan set to work building up a fire while Clara pulled their blankets out of the wagon. Doc Mason ate a few bites of food, but waved off Tolly's offer of more. "No, my dear, I'm fine. It's the very small crowds and the very large ones that take it out of me. That was a fine size, and reasonably well-behaved."

"Reasonably," said Istvhan, a bit dryly.

"No fruit, anyway. And you put a stop to that one fellow, my boy. I'm glad of it. Bad for business when fights break out. That man had clearly taken a bit more drink than was good for him."

"He was huge!" said Tolly. "I only saw him out of the corner of my eye — and you actually fought him?"

"No, I tried very hard not to fight him. It was my fault to begin with," said Istvhan. "Big men get used to being the biggest, and they see anyone larger as a threat."

"Fault's a strong word," said Clara.

He grinned at her. "Yes, Domina, but notice he didn't swing at *you.*"

She snorted. Tolly's eyes went round. "Who would try to hit a nun?"

"More people than I'd like," said Clara. "Also, I doubt he could focus on a holy symbol at that point."

"Which is why you have a bodyguard," said Istvhan easily. He grimaced down at his tabard. "Unfortunately I was telling the truth about the mule droppings. I think he wiped about half of them off on me."

"I'll wash it for you," volunteered Tolly.

"Never fear, I'll wash my own," said Istvhan. "I'm capable of it, when I'm not head to toe mud."

"I don't mind."

"I would feel guilty asking you to do it again." Istvhan picked up his stained tunic and rummaged in his pack for soap. "Shout if you need me for anything." He headed toward a long line of willows and the sound of running water. Tolly watched him go, then climbed inside the wagon.

"We rarely have any problems at travelers' rests," said Doc Mason. "Particularly not at this season." It wasn't freezing, but there was a definite bite to the air. Clara was glad that they had extra blankets.

"And now," said Doc Mason, picking up one of the remaining bottles, "I shall do as I promised, and down a bottle in front of you. Would you care to join me, Domina? I hate to drink alone."

She laughed. "So long as you drink first."

He pulled the cork and drank down a long draft, then smacked his lips.

"You're good at that," said Clara.

"Drinking? Mastered it in my youth."

"No, at selling tonic to strangers."

"You flatter me, Domina."

"I do nothing of the sort. There's as much skill in holding a crowd rapt as in mixing herbs, and you know it."

Doc Mason chuckled, then sobered. "I was an herbalist's apprentice once," he said. "But I couldn't handle all the death and the wounds and seeing people at their lowest ebb. Took the heart out of me. I prefer to leave them laughing and happy. Then I drive away, and in my head, they are always just as I left them. It's a coward's way, perhaps, but it's what I can do." He passed the bottle to Clara and she took a sip, wiping her mouth. It tasted herbal and sweet on the tongue, and burned all the way down.

"Gah," she said, wiping her mouth. "You're not undercharging for the alcohol, anyway."

Doc Mason laughed. "It's dreadful stuff," he agreed. "You won't go blind, that's all I can promise. I work with four or five distillers and they're all good quality, but whenever a batch comes out wrong, they set it aside for me." He took another slug of it himself. "I won't say it grows on you, but throw in enough honey and herbs and you won't care. And if it tasted good, no one would believe it was medicinal."

Clara snorted. "You're not wrong there."

"And what about you?" asked Doc Mason. He turned a thoughtful eye on her. "You aren't really a mother superior, are you?"

Clara froze, bottle halfway to her lips.

"I've no doubt you're really a nun," he hastened to assure her. "You pray when no one's looking and you bless your food and the first drink of water. More than that, you carry yourself like you expect that a god would listen to you."

"I didn't think I was *that* arrogant," muttered Clara, downing a rather larger sip of herbal medicine than was wise. She coughed.

"No, and that's the trick. You don't carry yourself like you expect to be obeyed. An abbess would. You don't expect other people to listen to you, just a god, and you'd do the god the favor of listening in return."

"Just a nun, I'm afraid," she admitted. "Though we were truly attacked by bandits on the road. Mother Superior was Istvhan's idea, so that no one questioned why I'd have a personal guard."

"Is he really your bodyguard, then?"

She grimaced. "He seems to think he is."

"Ah..." Doc Mason sat back, looking both regretful and amused. "More's the pity, I suppose."

"Eh?"

"If I don't miss my guess, that's my granddaughter going down to the stream, probably with lust in her heart." He nodded toward the line of willows, and Clara caught a glimpse of Tolly vanishing into the trees. "A genuine bodyguard, she might have a chance. But a man who follows you and takes your safety to his heart...no, I'm afraid she's going to be disappointed."

Clara cocked an eyebrow. "You don't seem particularly concerned about your granddaughter...ah..."

"Canoodling?" Doc Mason grinned. "She's a grown woman and she knows her own mind. And Istvhan's a good man and would break her heart as gently as possible. That's all you can hope for with youngsters."

"There might still be canoodling," said Clara. "He can't have me."

"Because you're a nun?"

"What? No, I — ah—" *Oh goddammit, why didn't I just say we were a celibate order?* She wiped her mouth. *Too much herbal medicine, that's probably it.* "It wouldn't work out," she muttered.

"I highly doubt he knows that," said Doc Mason.

"Well, he ought to," said Clara crossly. "And Tolly's a fine woman. He ought to be honored to have a chance at canoodling with her."

Doc Mason coughed, took another slug off the bottle, then corked it. "Ah. Yes. Well, I'm going to bed. Those shows are rough at my age, and my voice will take a day to recover at least."

"I'm sorry we didn't tell you the whole truth," said Clara. *And still aren't, for that matter. Though at least this wasn't a lie. Nobody ever asks if you're all the way human.*

"I know. The lie's been twitching at you like a fly on a mule. I could see it every time I said the words, 'Mother Superior.'" He patted Clara's arm. "I figured I'd chase off the fly. Sleep well, *Domina.*"

"You as well, Doctor." She poked the fire until it was safe to leave, then rolled herself into her blankets under the wagon. Neither Tolly nor Istvhan had returned from the river.

Some dark emotion gnawed at her gut and she dragged it up ruthlessly into the light. *Jealousy? Is that it? You have no right to be jealous and you know it. He isn't yours. You have no claim.*

No, it wasn't jealousy. It was...envy.

She exhaled and stared at the underside of the wagon. Axles. Boards. Iron mechanisms that probably did something important. All of them quite innocuous, painted orange by the dim light from the coals. Not a particularly useful thing to stare at, when you were trying not to think about the fact that you envied a girl half your size and only a little more than half your age.

I had a good life, until the raiders took it. I had sisters and a home. I traveled and my work interested me. I was healthy and my body did what I asked. I had lovers when I wanted them. I had no cause to envy anyone. Even if those lovers would not remain if they knew the truth. Even if the only time one had learned the truth, the man had recoiled in horror and fled her as if she were a devil. The young man with the poet's eyes, the one who'd talked about building a life together.

Four months of ridiculous youthful passion, pursued mostly in winter, while she waited for the canal to unfreeze. They'd found every sheltered place within a mile's walk of the convent, and made love there at least twice. She'd been young enough and fool enough to believe that maybe she could simply never go to the beast again, just abandon half herself for love.

And then one day they'd run afoul of a wild hog and her half-grown brood and she'd had to choose between letting them both die and waking the beast, which was no choice at all. Even a bear might balk at fighting off a family of angry boars, but the sow respected teeth and claws and mass and fled into the woods.

A moment later, so had he. "What *are* you?" he gasped, and she hadn't known how to answer, so she didn't say anything, just stood there in the ruin of her clothes, while he tore off as if the hounds of hell were after him.

Oof, I am clearly maudlin tonight. Too much herbal tonic.

She didn't usually dwell on him. It had been half her lifetime ago, and while time didn't necessarily heal all wounds, it certainly blunted the pain enough to get on with things. *What the hell was his last name? Started with a K, didn't it? Or a D?*

You learned better and you got on with things. You learned that you were what you were, and tried to be the best version of that person, because you were never going to be anybody else. And you stopped envying other people because everyone had problems you didn't know about.

Except apparently tonight, when she was envying Tolly, because she could have a tall, good-natured paladin and Clara couldn't.

But I would not be other than as I am. I like being who I am. It's the rest of the world that I would like to change.

The stream was not quite as cold as snow melt, but it had its origin in the mountains and it certainly wasn't warm. Fortunately, it was also shallow. Istvhan found a convenient rock and set to work scrubbing and smacking his tunic against it, while keeping a wary eye out for unexpected sinkholes.

He enjoyed hot water enormously, but deep water, particularly deep *cold* water, made him very uneasy. If he couldn't put his feet on the bottom and breathe comfortably, there was too damn much of it. It came of being raised in a desert, most likely. *Although I was never afraid of it until that one river crossing...*

The battle tide that rose in the Saint of Steel's chosen made them supernaturally skilled fighters, but it had its blind spots. It was not omniscient — witness its total bafflement in the face of Clara's shapeshift. And during one particular battle, it had driven him forward, he and his comrades, in pursuit of enemies crossing a ford. *Clever bastards knew exactly what they were doing, too. That was their plan all along, pull us across where they knew the terrain and we didn't.*

The gravel crossing was carefully constructed. Half the paladins were charging across it when the trapped side gave way, dropping them into fast water. A few managed to get their footing, or were grabbed by their comrades, but four were swept away.

The other three drowned. Istvhan, through pure luck, smashed into a boulder small enough to grab. He broke two ribs and cracked another one, but he clung to that rock for nearly an hour, until Stephen came out of the battle tide long enough to look for survivors. Probably the god had helped.

In that hour, Istvhan had gotten so cold that he was almost warm again. To breathe, he had to haul himself upward, out of the water, long enough to get his face clear, then sink back down. The stone was too slick to stay upright and his ribs ached when he breathed, but the god in his head ordered him to hold on and so he held fast. *And they very nearly had to break my arms to get me to let go of that damn rock, too. If I could have, I'd have named it and carried it around with me.*

He smacked his tunic against a rock to which he felt far less emotional attachment, then paused. Someone was coming through the trees. They were not moving like they were trying to be stealthy.

Tolly called, "How is it going?"

He relaxed. Tolly was unlikely to try to drown him. "It's mostly out," he said, picking up the soap and scrubbing again. "Fortunately, I don't wear white."

"You might look good in white."

"Like a knight in shining armor?" He snorted. "I was never knighted. Not landed, not rich. And the pal...people I know who wear white usually have access to a laundry staff." Paladins of the Dreaming God wore white tabards. You could really start to resent them, if they didn't go around radiating goodness and decency like some kind of furnace.

Tolly was silent for a moment. He could hear her moving closer, hear the sounds of small stones turning under her feet.

"Grandda likes you," she said, quite close now.

"I like him, too," said Istvhan, who had a pretty good idea where this was going and was hoping that he was wrong. *If that wasn't a stand-in for 'I like you,' I'll eat this tunic.* "Mind you, I was a little uncertain at first, since the world's full of charlatans and snake oil peddlers, but I'm glad I was wrong."

Tolly nodded. In the moonlight, she looked young and graceful, beautiful and...young. *Saint's teeth, everyone gets younger every year, I think. Except me.*

"It must be lonely, being a bodyguard," she said, turning toward him.

Istvhan, who was capable of recognizing a hint when it bashed him in the head, bent over his tunic on the rock and scrubbed harder. "Not really," he said, careful not to look at her. "You're never alone. You're always around someone else. By definition, really."

"Not being alone isn't the same as not being lonely," Tolly said.

He risked a glance up. She'd taken a step closer. She was slim and dark-eyed and reminded him of a gazelle. *Just as long as she doesn't suddenly turn into one. I don't think my heart can take any more were-women this week. Not without some warning.*

She smiled at him and drew her fingertip down the line of her throat.

Saint's blood, I suppose this is about to be awkward. He had absolutely no desire to offend Tolly. He liked her. He just wasn't the least bit interested. She wasn't quite young enough to be his daughter, but he definitely had nieces her age, and while there were plenty of men who wanted young women in their beds, he wasn't one of them. *It goes along fine for a bit and then, just when you're feeling like a particularly virile stallion of a man, they say something about what year they were born or mention some ancient history that you actually lived through and suddenly you feel your bones turn to dust and your hip spontaneously breaks in three places.*

Istvhan had had a fling with a much younger woman once. A

week later he'd found a stark white hair on his groin and had never been able to shake the feeling that the Saint had been punishing him.

Tolly unbound her hair and let it fall over her shoulders. Had Istvhan not just been thinking about stray white hairs, the thought of all that blonde hair draped across his chest — which had been decidedly salt-and-pepper since he turned forty last year — would not have been quite so unsettling.

"Tolly..." he began. *There is never any easy way out of this situation. You reject her before she's committed to seducing you, and you look like an arrogant ass. She comes out and propositions you, and she feels rejected. Damn, damn, damn.*

Well, he was a paladin, which meant erring on the side of being an arrogant ass in most circumstances. *And at least this way she feels like you're a fool, not that she's not worthy.* "You are a lovely young woman," he said, "and if I were not bound to someone else's service, I suspect that I would be thinking very ignoble thoughts right now."

"How ignoble?"

"Oh, fairly ignoble. But alas, it can't be. I'm sorry. There's an oath."

She frowned. "You took an oath?"

"Yes. The men of my order don't...ah...act on ignoble thoughts."

"What order?"

"The Order of St. Galen." He apologized to his friend in his head. Galen had acted on any number of ignoble thoughts, as Istvhan knew from years of living down the hall from him.

She took a step closer, chewing on her lower lip. Istvhan lowered his head and beat the hell out of his tunic on the rock. "What, never?"

"No." He thought about trying to make up some complicated theological reasons, but the simple lies were best. *Of course, there goes any chance of trying to seduce Clara before we get to Morstone. Great. Well done, sir.*

It was probably for the best. You certainly couldn't do your best work in the bedchamber when the bedchamber consisted of the space under a wagon, with occasional mule sounds. It was just that when they slept so close and he could feel the heat of her skin and thought about sliding a little closer and warming his hands against that heat...

"I'm sorry to hear that," said Tolly.

Istvhan heaved a sigh. "Yeah," he said. "Me, too."

Clara had just about convinced herself that the reason she was still awake was because the ground was hard when she heard footsteps. A moment later, Istvhan dropped down beside her and began pulling his blankets into position.

"What are you doing here?" she said, startled. There hadn't been enough time for Istvhan and Tolly to do anything — well, not anything worth doing, anyway. She had thought better of Istvhan.

"I'm going to sleep," he said. He sounded puzzled. "Do you want me to take the other side?"

"Why aren't you with Tolly?"

She could only see the bottom half of his face. The wagon wheels cast spokes of shadow across the rest. "I managed to convince her that the Sacred Bodyguards of St. Galen are sworn to celibacy. Don't laugh."

"You *what?*"

"Look, it was the best I could come up with on the spur of the moment. It was that or 'Look behind you! A rabid unicorn!' and running away."

Relief warred with...was it anger? It certainly felt like anger. *Why would she be angry?*

I'm angry because I wanted him to go off with Tolly so that I could prove that I was okay and it didn't mean anything to me. That I wasn't jealous. That I was happy that Istvhan had found a nice human woman to dally with. And instead the damnable noble bastard went and was damnably noble.

"Why didn't you...just...just..." For some reason, the only word that she could think of was *canoodling* and it didn't seem at all like the right word. "She's very nice!"

"She could be my daughter," said Istvhan, stretching out next to her.

"She could *not.*"

"I'd have had to be fairly precocious, but it's theoretically possible."

"Yes, but..." This was not the conversation she'd meant to have. "She's a lovely girl!"

"Oh, very."

"You don't have to not...err..." *Hell with it.* "You don't have to not canoodle because of me."

"Canoodle?" He sat up so fast he nearly cracked his skull on an axle and ducked down, swearing. *"Canoodle!? I have never canoodled in my life."*

"You don't expect me to believe that."

"You had better. When I do it, it is *not* canoodling."

"Same thing."

"Madam," said Istvhan, his voice dropping nearly an octave, "I have made love. I have had sex. I have bedded, rutted, fucked, and on one occasion, with enthusiastic consent and a great deal of oil, I have sodomized, but I have never, not once, *canoodled.*"

Clara's mouth hung open but she did not seem to have anything useful to say.

"Now," said Istvhan, still in a deep, savage whisper, "if you are done trying to whore me out to our host's granddaughter, I am going to sleep. Virtuously alone."

Clara was not sure it counted as alone when she was less than two feet away, but this did not seem like the time to bring it up. "Well. Good night, then," she said, mostly so that he wouldn't realize he'd struck her speechless.

"And to you, Domina," he said, all smooth politeness.

She rolled over. So did he. They both stared into the dark, but neither one of them were sleeping.

CHAPTER 25

Istvhan spent the morning feeling alternately surly and guilty. Surly because Clara had been throwing him at Tolly, and what did she think he was, anyway? He had standards. Tolly was a sweet girl, but Istvhan was old enough to be her father, allowing for the precociousness and so forth. *And it's not like I just jump on any woman that comes down the road, dammit.*

Then Guilt kicked in. *Of course she'd think that. You went from being pleasant to a nun to bending her over the wagon and putting your tongue halfway down her throat, out of nowhere.*

Surliness jumped in immediately — *did she think that didn't mean anything? Was it that lousy? She kissed back, dammit...*

And then Guilt was back — *sure, and then you stabbed her, so why are you surprised she's trying to throw you at any other woman in the vicinity to keep you at arm's length?*

A third thought tried to intrude. *She also turned into a bear and bit a man's head in half?* Surly and Guilty turned on the newcomer and pummeled it into nonexistence.

This did not make for a pleasant morning. He grunted a lot.

"Sore head?" asked Doc Mason. "I've got a tonic that helps with that."

Istvhan snorted, which was as close as he could get to a laugh at the moment. "Does it cure that, as well?"

"Oh yes. Amazing the number of things it cures. Hangovers, scurvy, broken hearts..."

Istvhan side-eyed him over that last one. Doc Mason side-eyed him right back. Since Tolly was sitting on the wagon seat, driving the mules, he couldn't very well ask the doctor what he meant by that.

"Another two days to Morstone," said Doc Mason, waving his arm at the road ahead. "Unless I've mixed the road up again." Istvhan grunted again.

"No, you're right," said Tolly. She sounded subdued this morning, which put Guilt back into ascendency.

They paused at an inn to water the mules and pick up a midday meal. Istvhan went to find Clara and handed her one of the heavily spiced sausages that constituted a local delicacy.

"Thank you," she said, in the carefully neutral tone of someone who doesn't know who, if anyone, is angry, and whether or not they deserve to be.

"Another show tomorrow evening," Doc Mason said, gesticulating with his sausage. "A town called — oh blast..."

"Boriss."

"Right, right. We came through three or four years ago. Lovely place. Then we'll go down the road a bit more and stop for the night, and we'll be at Morstone by noon the next day." He tapped his nose. "I'd love to have you on stage again, young man, if you're willing. The story about your sickly youth sells tonic hand over fist."

"Yes, of course," said Istvhan, determined not to grunt any more. *Act civilized. They've been very kind to you and it'd make the trip a lot easier.*

Then Clara tapped him on the shoulder and he heard himself grunt again. *Dammit.*

She drew him back toward the stables, well out of earshot. "Captain Istvhan," she said, all cool formality, "I wish to apologize."

Captain. They were back to *captain* again. Fine. "Domina Clara," he said, matching her coolness, "no apology is necessary."

She inclined her head a fraction, acknowledging either his words or his tone, he wasn't sure which. "I feel that it is," she said. "Your private life is none of my affair, and it was wrong of me to act as if it was." She was meeting his eyes and he could not read a damn thing in hers, as unreadable as amber. "I apologize for having acted as if you owed me an explanation in any way."

The words sank into Istvhan's gut and he looked away. *Your private life is none of my affair.* No, of course it wasn't, because she wasn't involved, was she? And she'd made damn clear that she didn't want to be involved, either. *What did you expect? You stab her, you force her to drag you along with her, you grab for her like an untried boy with his first woman and then recoil like that boy at his first battle when she kills a man, and now you have the gall to feel rejected? Saint's balls. She's been friendly because she's a decent woman, that's all, and maybe you could have been friends, if you didn't keep making a hash of things.*

Surliness pointed out that she'd also made a bit of a hash of things. Guilt countered that she'd apologized for it like an adult. Istvhan tried to seize control of the mental situation. "Domina."

Clara raised her eyebrows.

"I should apologize to you as well," he said. "I have not handled any of...anything...as well as I should have."

"Well," she said, thawing a bit, "it's been a pretty long week for both of us."

"Not as long as the month you had before that."

"And that wasn't as long as...well, however long ago your god died. We really don't need to play 'who's more miserable?' do we?"

"No, no." He rubbed his forehead. "Domin...*Clara*...I'm pretty sure we were well on our way to being friends. Weren't we? Was I wrong?"

The edge of a smile touched her face. "I thought we were, yeah."

"Do you think we can still manage that? If I avoid stabbing you again?"

The smile grew. "I honestly don't care about the stabbing."

"I care! You can't just go around stabbing people and expecting them to get over it!"

"But I *did* get over it."

"But you shouldn't have! I mean, I'm glad you did, but you shouldn't just forgive people for stabbing you just like that."

She rolled her eyes. "Do you want me to stab *you*? Would that make you feel less guilty?"

"It might, yes!"

Clara sighed. "No stabbing," she said. "I've a philosophical objection."

"Nuns are sadists," he muttered. "I always knew it."

"And paladins are martyrs. What would you do if you accidentally stabbed one of your brothers?"

"Oh, it's less of a problem. I choked one into unconsciousness once when the tide rose and he didn't snap out of it. He broke Galen's arm, Galen smashed up his ribs, we're all good friends and would die for each other."

Clara stared at him for a long moment, then gazed up at heaven as if seeking strength. "Do you see what I'm up against, St. Ursa?" she asked the sky. "Are you hearing this?"

"It's different," muttered Istvhan.

"Because you're men?"

"No, of course not. I'd choke Wren or Judith, too. We're comrades-in-arms. It doesn't count."

She folded her arms and looked down her nose at him. "Because I'm a nun?"

Istvhan felt suddenly pinned to the roadway. "Mmmrhrf," he said, staring at his feet.

"Sorry, I don't believe I caught that."

"I said, *maybe a little.*" He held up his hands defensively. "But not really! Mostly because — well — we spar all the time! We're always hitting each other with sticks! You don't keep track!"

Clara rubbed her hands over her face and turned away. "Wait here," she said over her shoulder.

Istvhan waited, unsure what was happening next but quite sure that he had put his foot in it, yet again. *I used to be good with women. I really did. I remember it distinctly.*

A young stableboy came out of the stables and cocked an eye at Istvhan. "You waitin' on a horse, sir?"

"No, a nun," said Istvhan.

The boy looked at him as if he'd lost his mind and retreated into the stables. Istvhan contemplated the life choices that had brought him to this moment and whether he could have turned aside at any point.

He had just concluded that everything had started to go wrong about the time when he learned to walk when Clara reappeared. She was carrying two long staves, the sort that usually had a hoe or a pitchfork attached to the end. She tossed him one. "We're getting ready to leave," she said. "Carry this."

Istvhan swung it experimentally. "Is there some reason you're giving me a large stick?"

"Yes. I'm going to hit you with the one I'm carrying, and you're going to try to stop me."

"...I see."

He followed Clara to the wagon. Doc Mason climbed up on the seat and waved grandly to the few people in the street. "Doc Mason's Herbal Medicine!" he called. "Tell your friends!"

Once they were well away, Clara fell back behind the wagon. The mules were not putting on any particular turn of speed this afternoon, which meant they could keep up easily. "All right. You want to spar? Let's do it."

"Um," said Istvhan. There did not seem to be a polite way to say that, whatever his flaws, Istvhan was a trained warrior who had spent much of his life dedicated to combat, and Clara, whatever her virtues, was not. "I...ah...don't want to hurt you?"

She whacked him in the shins. He yelped.

"I didn't mean—" She went for his shins again, and this time he danced backward out of the way. Clara followed, jabbing her stave at his feet, and he had to either retreat into the ditch or block. He blocked.

Clara's style was all strength and no finesse. *I suppose when you're a bear, you don't really need to learn finesse.* She was ungodly strong, though. He had to set his feet to keep from being shoved backward by her blows. *And when was the last time that happened? Probably scrapping with one of the Dreaming God's people, they're all overmuscled like that.*

The stave was too short to use as a proper quarterstaff and too long to serve as a practice sword. His old sword-master would have groaned to see how he was gripping it, but she would also have been the first to admit that you worked with what you had. He made a tentative jab in Clara's direction and she smacked it aside with enough force to make his palms sting.

It is possible the lady has some aggressions to work out. The black tide whispered to him that all he had to do was wait for her to lunge, step aside, and crack her across the back of the skull and it would all be over. He ignored it.

Clara spent about five minutes chasing him back and forth across the road and blocking his occasional swings. "You're toying with me," she said, panting. "Don't think I don't realize that."

"Not as much as I thought I would be," he said. He was also panting. He could have ended it at any time, but blocking those hammer-like blows was taking a toll. He could see how she'd cut such a swath through the bandits. "If you ever felt like dedicating your life to the blade, I could make a terrifying warrior of you."

"Not much point, is there?" She managed a grin, albeit with a lot of teeth. "Can just...change..."

He swung at her and she blocked, but this time he pressed the advantage, throwing her relentlessly backward. He knew far more about leverage than she did, and step by step, she backpedaled, until she was driven against the back of the wagon.

Istvhan saw the moment when she realized what was happening, but it was too late. Her back was already against the wagon's back step. He forced both staves up until their faces were only inches apart. "What if you were inside the wagon?" he said. "Or in a tight space? Could you change then?"

"No." Her face was flushed and there was sweat slicking her forehead. The rise and fall of her chest was driving him mad. Was this what she would look like if he bedded her? The same fierce grin of physical exertion, the flushed skin, the gasp of her breath in his ear? Would she moan or would she growl when he thrust into her? It occurred to him that the wagon had stopped moving but he couldn't think why that was significant, not when Clara was looking at him with her eyes full of fire and frustration and her body was so close that he could feel the heat rolling off her skin.

Her lips parted and his eyes locked on the movement. "I guess," she whispered, "I'd have to...*improvise.*"

She dropped her shoulder and let one end of her stave fall. Suddenly deprived of resistance, he stumbled forward against her. For one glorious moment, his body was pressed full length against hers, his leg between her thighs, and then she half-turned and dropped the stave completely and slammed her fist into his face.

"*Gnrrfff!*" He stumbled backward.

Through his fingers, he could see that she looked appalled. "I really expected you to block that!"

"I didn't."

"I noticed. Fine! We've both hit each other! Are you happy *now?*" she yelled, putting her hands on her hips.

"I kind of am, actually!" he yelled back, rubbing his jaw.

Doc Mason cleared his throat. The two of them spun around, drawing together instinctively, like children caught misbehaving.

"Obviously this is none of my business," said the doctor, looking from one to the other, "but if this is some kind of, ah, *sophisticated* canoodling, I'd appreciate it if you could do it out of earshot? I'm uncomfortable witnessing other people's love lives."

"*No one* is canoodling," said Clara, with great emphasis.

"Not my business," said Doc Mason hastily.

"No, no. We were just...ah...sparring?" *Is that a reasonable explanation? Because we were. At least until I started thinking about other things we could be doing instead.*

Doc Mason hooked his thumbs in his belt and rocked back on his heels. "Looks like you got the worst of it, lad."

"Yes, well...nuns, you know how they are..."

"Oh aye, I do indeed."

Clara threw her hands in the air and stalked back to the wagon, which had stopped a few yards ahead. Tolly asked something in a low voice that Istvhan couldn't quite make out. Clara's response, however — the word *"Men!"* delivered at the top of her lungs — was clearly audible. As was the sound of Tolly's heartfelt agreement.

Istvhan ran a hand through his hair and sighed.

"First question," said Doc Mason. "You all right? She cracked you a good one."

He touched his jaw. It was sore but didn't feel like it was going to swell too badly. Either she'd pulled the punch at the last minute or she simply hadn't had a very good angle to begin with. "I've had much worse sparring against other warriors, but don't tell her that."

"Still, you all right? This isn't a regular thing? I don't need to hide you in the wagon and spirit you away?"

Istvhan looked at him blankly, then finally put two and two together. "Oh! No. Certainly not."

"In that case...word of advice, young man," said Doc Mason.

Istvhan gave him a look. "I'm forty. I haven't been young for quite some time."

"Stuff it, youngster, I'd kill to be forty again. Forty is barely out of the cradle when you're my age." The doctor poked Istvhan in the chest with one gnarled finger. "And I've been married three times, so I know a little something about women."

"I was married once," said Istvhan defensively.

Doc Mason raised an eyebrow.

The problem with being a paladin was that you were fundamentally honest. "For about six weeks. It was more of a fling with extra paperwork."

"Well, two of mine lasted until death did us part. And the other one was a fine woman who couldn't handle life on the road. We parted friends. So you'll take my advice and you'll like it, youngster."

Istvhan bowed his head and waited for whatever folksy wisdom was about to land on him.

Doc Mason cleared his throat. "Don't assume she knows what you're thinking."

Istvhan waited politely.

"That's it, youngster. That's the whole advice."

"Really?"

"What were you expecting?"

"I think I was expecting more charming country metaphors. About how I was twisting myself around like an eel on a griddle or something similar."

"Nah, I save that stuff for the shows." Another poke in the chest. It didn't do much because Istvhan was wearing his chain hauberk, but presumably it was the thought that counted. "Unless I miss my guess, you think she knows exactly how you feel and isn't interested. But she doesn't. So quit talking yourself out of your feelings, go find her, say, "I'm hopelessly in love with you, thought you should know," and then let her decide how she feels about it."

"But I'm *not* hopelessly in love with her," said Istvhan.

"You sure about that?"

Istvhan blinked at the doctor. "I'm not really the sort who falls in love," he admitted. "Never got in the habit of it. I enjoy women's company, and I enjoy the...ah..."

"Canoodling?"

"...I really wish we weren't calling it that, but yes. And then when it's over, we both move on."

"And you never wanted more?"

Istvhan spread his hands. "I have my brothers-in-arms. I don't need more."

Doc Mason shook his head. "Well, then tell her you want to canoodle."

Istvhan stifled a sigh. It was difficult to explain to someone who came up to your collarbone that when you were very large, it was much safer to be subtle. Good-natured lust became something frightening if she felt like you were looming over her.

The thought came, unbidden, that he had to work very hard to loom over Clara, and that if she wasn't interested in his advances, she could make her displeasure known with three-inch fangs.

"I do appreciate your advice, sir," said Istvhan. Politely.

"No, you don't," said Doc Mason. "The young never do. Now help me back onto the wagon. My sciatica is killing me."

CHAPTER 26

Clara spent the rest of the trip to the next village talking to Tolly about trade routes. Istvhan tried to eavesdrop but rapidly decided that it was too specialized for him to make sense of half of it. Tolly, however, ate it up, and the pair were soon lost in conversation about weight-to-profit ratios and currency conversions.

Finally, they reached the field where they would perform the next show. Doc Mason went off to stir up interest from the locals and Tolly set to work on the wagon. Clara ambled over to a tree and sat down.

Istvhan weighed how mad she was likely to be against the fact that the staves had been stowed in the wagon. *Was* she still mad? He couldn't tell. She hid everything too well and it was part of what frustrated him. *Not that I think she'd be nursing a grudge, so much as I'm not sure she'd let herself be angry if she deserved to be...*

Right. Paladin. Stoic warrior, charging boldly into danger, so on and so forth. He walked up to the tree, trying to look harmless and good-natured and also sexy, which was a complicated thing to convey. He wasn't sure what to do with his hips. "May I join you?"

She raised one eyebrow and then said, "Yeah, go ahead."

He sat down beside her, back against the tree trunk, in the band of shade offered by the branches. "Don't worry. Doc Mason thinks we're both mad as the mist and snow, but he doesn't hold it against us."

"He's probably right. I don't know whether to apologize for hitting you or hit you again."

"I think we're even."

They *were* even. That was what was killing him. She was as big as he was and as strong as he was and he couldn't intimidate her. His black tide was no match for her beast.

Saint's teeth, but she was magnificent.

And he still wanted her. It didn't matter that she could turn into a bear, except that turning into a bear seemed pretty damn cool, particularly in somebody you trusted to watch your back.

Don't assume she knows what you're thinking.

Could she really not know that I want her? Is it possible?

He tilted his head to look at her and smiled. "Domina?"

"Captain?"

"You hit like a nun."

"No, I hit like a lay sister. If I hit like a nun, you'd have been laid out on the road."

Istvhan laughed. "Fair enough. How's your hand?"

She grimaced. "You've got a skull like a bull elk," she said. "Only without the magnificent rack."

It was one of his great weaknesses. He had never been able to resist a straight line. "I think you've got that covered."

A long, long pause, during which Istvhan thought, *oh hell, much too soon,* and then she snorted, which wasn't quite a laugh but was close enough. "Thanks."

He reached over and took her hand in his, turning it to look at her knuckles. They were red and swollen, as one might expect. He ran his thumb down the side of her hand, under the little finger. "Does it hurt when I do this?"

"No."

"That's where it usually breaks on a punch." He stroked down the back of her hand next to it. "Sometimes here. Anything?"

"No." Her eyes were riveted on the motion of his hand.

"Good." He lifted her hand to his lips. She raised her eyes to his face, clearly startled, but did not pull away.

He kissed each one of her injured knuckles, and then lowered her hand. "Domina," he said, and rose and went away to the other side of the wagon, wondering if that counted as subtle or if he'd just made a fool of himself again.

The show was a repeat of the first, though fortunately without the drunk. This time, Istvhan was born one of sickly triplets and his two fictional brothers were even larger and lived back on the farm. Doc Mason sold another two cases of tonic and they retired to a campsite back on the main road.

"A question for you, Doc," said Istvhan.

"Hmm?" Doc Mason looked up from the fire. He had settled in with a mug of tonic and Tolly kept pushing food on him, with minimal success.

"While we were traveling before we encountered the bandits, we heard some alarming tales. Stories of severed heads, or bodies appearing with heads that didn't belong to them."

"Gah." Tolly's eyes went very wide and she nearly dropped her spoon. Her grandfather, however, showed no sign of shock. His eyes narrowed and he gave Istvhan a long, thoughtful look.

"You *have* heard of it, then," said Istvhan quietly.

Doc Mason glanced around, as if someone might be listening beyond the circle of firelight. "I have," he said, just as quietly. "And you are a very good liar, my young friend, but you have not just 'heard stories' about this, have you?"

Istvhan made a noncommittal sound, but Doc Mason's eyes were resting on Clara. Her expression was carefully blank, but that, in and of itself, was a confession. *She may have been a merchant, but she must have been one of the scrupulously honest ones. I knew she was hiding something practically since we met.*

Mind you, it wasn't the sort of thing that one could easily have guessed.

Finally Doc Mason turned back to him. "Very well, keep your cards close to your chest if you wish, my young friends. Yes, I've heard. It was some years ago now."

Istvhan raised his eyebrows. "That long ago?"

"Seven or eight years, yes." He poked at the fire. "Started north of Morstone. Only one or two at first. Then more. For a whole season or two, no one in the small villages would go anywhere alone if they could help it. Then it stopped, or seemed to."

"Why didn't you tell me?" Tolly demanded.

"Oh, you already knew," said Doc Mason. "The Beast of the Leeward, remember?"

Tolly looked startled. "That? That was this? But I didn't hear anything about severed heads!"

Doc Mason snorted. "Oh, they were in there. And also that the Beast was a giant wolf, a monstrous bear, a man who was half-bat, a werewolf, a feral child raised by dogs, a man who could fly, a wonder-worker who drank blood but could not touch virgins, a demon possessing any and all of the above, and probably a few dozen other stories I'm forgetting. Oh, and a cult. Did I mention the cult?"

Clara had gone tense when he had begun talking about were-wolves and monstrous bears, but she thawed now. Tolly said, "No, you didn't mention the cult."

"Definitely a cult. Nobody knew what it was a cult of, mind you, except murdering people."

"But the heads?" asked Istvhan.

"Mmm." Doc gave him another thoughtful look. "Yes. I spoke to a few people who had actually been there, and who weren't prone to histrionics. They all said that there were headless bodies found."

"Did any of them get a look at the perpetrators?"

"Not reliably. One said he saw a man fleeing the scene. Said he looked ordinary enough, and wondered if he was responsible or just someone who didn't want to be caught near a dead body for reasons of his own."

"Wait," said Tolly. "Wait, the husband of the first victim said he saw something, didn't he? Said it was some kind of beast on four legs, but it crawled sideways?"

Doc Mason rolled his eyes. "That's how the story traveled, anyhow. I wouldn't put much stock in it. But tell me, friend Istvhan, what do you know about the Beast of the Leeward that we do not?"

Istvhan took a deep breath. "It's not precisely a secret," he said. "But you travel to many villages and you know what people are like about strangers, so please use discretion in who you tell. I don't want a mob on my conscience."

"I'd prefer not to have one either," said Doc Mason.

Istvhan recounted the story of the smooth men and their depredations in Archenhold, though he heavily downplayed the Temple of the White Rat and implied that the entirely fictional order of St. Galen had been responsible. "And so we came north looking for them," he said. "Following the trail of bodies. But we got separated from our main group and hope to reunite in Morstone."

"Interesting," said Doc Mason, after the paladin had stopped speaking and a little silence had fallen over the party. "Terrible. But interesting."

"You say these things have come back here?" said Tolly. "Now?"

"I don't know that they ever left," Istvhan admitted. "Perhaps they just got better about hiding the bodies. We don't know how many there are. They seem to make more of themselves, given the chance." He held his hands out to the fire. "Be wary of strangers with very smooth faces, I suppose."

"I can see why your bishop was cagey about informing people," said Doc Mason. "Perhaps she doesn't give people enough credit, but if the story spread and the details were lost..." He shook his head. "No, I can see it going badly as well. How often do these things change bodies?"

Istvhan shook his head. "We don't know for certain. However long it takes for one's body to decay. The doctor who examined them said that they seem to secrete some kind of gunk that seals the wound a bit, so they last longer than you would expect from a dead body, but they're still finite. Eventually, they're ready to fall apart, and they need to find a new host. I doubt they can go more than a few weeks."

Doc Mason nodded. "I'll keep an ear to the ground," he said. "Did you say the Temple of the White Rat knows?" And at Istvhan's nod, he snorted. "Of course they do. They have their scaly tails in everyone's pies, don't they?"

"Generally for the good of humanity," said Istvhan mildly.

"Ah, well. True enough, and that's more than you can say for the vast majority of people who claim to be doing things for people's own good. They meddle, but at least they clean up afterwards." He leaned back, looking from Istvhan to Clara and back again. "I'd be lying if I said that I hadn't been wondering what brought you along this road in the first place. Now I know." He shook his head. "And I can't say that I'm happier knowing it, either. Forewarned may be forearmed, but I doubt I'll sleep any sounder at night, knowing these things are out there." He looked over at Tolly and his face softened. "But at least I know there's a paladin and a nun trying to stop them, and that's got to count for something."

"From your lips to the gods' ears," said Istvhan. "And by Their grace, we'll put a stop to this yet."

Clara lay beside Istvhan for what might be the last time and wondered what to say, or if she should say anything at all.

She was still reeling from that moment when he had kissed her hand earlier. Yesterday, she would have said that kissing someone's hand generally made you look like a blithering idiot. Then he'd taken her hand and lifted it to his lips and it had been less of a kiss and more like a caress. She'd stopped breathing. She'd stopped thinking. Her entire consciousness had narrowed down to the strip of skin across her knuckles and the warmth of his mouth against it. She'd had actual sex that was less arousing.

Then Istvhan had released her and smiled and sauntered away and left Clara ready to scream.

Calm, she thought. *Calm. Blessed St. Ursa, grant me your peace...*

It hadn't felt much like peace lately. The fear and the frustration had felt like she was swallowing bile and it was hot and roiling under her breastbone. Lust warmed her more kindly than the fear did, but she still felt too full of emotions she didn't dare let out. She'd slipped a little when fighting him. It had felt too good to strike out and she knew better than to go too far down that road. You got in the habit of releasing your anger with your fists and things went bad quickly. Thank St. Ursa it had been Istvhan, who was big enough and tough enough to take it, and to keep himself safe in the process.

Maybe berserkers understood these things better than other people.

She would have liked to be the bear for a little while. The bear was easy. The bear didn't feel these things. But she couldn't very well sneak away in the dark without Istvhan noticing, and what was she going to say? He'd probably insist on guarding her in case someone in this well-settled land happened to wander past and saw a giant bear and ran screaming for hunters to come and deal with it. It wasn't even a bad idea to do so. If one of her sisters had planned to do it, she'd have insisted on coming along in human shape to make sure nothing went wrong.

It just wasn't fair. He was lying beside her and...and breathing. *Well, of course he's breathing, what do you expect him to do?* It was just that every breath reminded her that he was right there and alive and she could roll over and grab him by the hips and drag him on top of her and say...well, probably not "Take me now" although that had a certain straightforward appeal to it.

No. No, it'll just be more feelings. More emotions. You're nearly in Morstone. You can't afford more of this. Your sisters need you to be strong and calm.

Clara thought fixedly of her sisters and mostly what came to mind was Sister Sigrid whacking her across the back of the head and yelling, "You've got a good-looking man *right there* and you're not doing anything about it?"

Yes, Sigrid, that's exactly what I'm doing. Or not doing, in this case.

She'd genuinely thought he wasn't interested. All those moments of closeness where she was suddenly very aware of the width of his shoulders and the thickness of his thighs, the way his eyes were as dark as fine chocolate...she'd thought those were all one-sided. Men didn't want to bed the beast. The fact that she still wanted him and he couldn't possibly want her had joined the other emotions stewing in her chest, being shoved down as far as they could go.

And then he'd kissed her hand and breathed against her fingers and saints have mercy, you didn't do it like that if you weren't interested in someone. Which meant that he still wanted her. Even knowing about the bear.

He'd kissed her up after the battle and it had been good — much, much better than anything she'd felt in a long time — but he hadn't known then. Which was probably why she was still reliving the sensation of his lips moving over each knuckle because it was more than any man had ever done, knowing the truth of what she was.

A man who could see past the beast was a man that she could fall in love with far too easily.

The thought stabbed her like a knife. She could not be falling in love. Not right now. Not with her sisters in peril. Gods and saints alive and dead, how could she even think such a thing when her fellow nuns had been dragged to Morstone in chains and were probably being driven into a gladiatorial pit to fight to the death? *What kind of... of...utterly self-centered, irredeemable ass would pick this moment to go mooning after a man?*

Another stab inside her chest. She wanted to scream or weep or howl or explode. None of those things would help.

The beast sensed her torment and half-roused, but saw no enemy. *Hurt? Where?*

No, she told it. *Not hurt. Hush. Not now.*

It settled, and she fixed her mind firmly on meditations, wishing for prayer beads. She counted catechisms on her fingers instead, until the beast slept and her tension eased.

We reach Morstone tomorrow. And then I need to put this man aside and focus on my task, because saint help me, I think I may already be falling in love.

CHAPTER 27

At first glance, Morstone looked like a junk heap built on a dock.

Water slapped against immense pilings and gulls swirled through the air overhead. The city itself was almost impossible to take in at first glance, a jumble of architectural styles and materials built on top of each other in layers that looked more like debris washed up on a water grate than like deliberate building.

"I don't see much stone," said Clara.

"You won't," said Doc Mason. "Morstone is a corruption of *moristone*, from *mori*, meaning salt. Salt is their biggest export. They had to import the actual stones from a quarry. The high-rent districts are all on islands in the river."

"There's a river?" said Istvhan doubtfully. Clara could understand his doubts. It looked more like a lake.

"It's high tide," Tolly said. "Be grateful, at low tide the smell will knock your socks off. Coming in like this, you get a little time to get used to it before you get the full experience."

Clara wiped her nose. She could smell the mudflat smell of rotten fish and seaweed from here. She couldn't imagine how much worse the smell was at low tide.

Particularly since they're probably using the river as a sewer, too.

"It's a river delta," said Doc Mason. "Very fertile soil, I'm told, if you like that sort of thing." He waved his arm upriver, and Clara could just barely make out the distant squares of fields, already harvested for winter.

"It would have to be, to sustain a city this size," said Istvhan. "I suppose they control the trade down the river, though. Archon's Glory does that as well, where we are, and Anuket City, across the river. They have a fine old rivalry about it, too."

"No rivals here. It's the only navigable river for miles. And they don't allow anyone else along the coast to sell salt, either."

Clara raised her eyebrows. "Don't allow?"

"Morstone's fortune is built on salt," said Doc Mason. "You're allowed to dry salt. And you are graciously allowed to sell it to Morstone, at any price they choose to give you. If you do not wish to accept that price, you are allowed to watch them take it anyway, and burn your town in the bargain."

He sounded tired, and Clara suspected that he knew a little more about burning towns than he might wish to. What had he said earlier? *I drive away, and in my head, they are always just as I left them.' Except at least once they didn't stay that way, did they? Morstone came after them.*

"And no one can stop them," said Clara thoughtfully. "Can they?"

"A great navy might," said Doc Mason. "But there are no great navies volunteering to do the job. One of the great merchant consortiums might be able to challenge them, but they dare not risk being cut off from the salt trade. I suspect that if change comes to Morstone, it will come from inside." He slapped the reins across the necks of the mules and they picked up the pace.

"The world runs on salt," said Istvhan, nodding. "Where I am from, there are two city-states who control a tributary each of the great river between them. Both of them well-located, both of them wealthy, but one has a salt mine upriver and the other one does not. So Anuket City is by far the more powerful of the two now, and I suspect the mine has something to do with it, even if the ruler that actually controls the salt charges Anuket City a criminal amount for their wares."

Traffic increased as they approached. At first it had only been occasional farm wagons coming back from early morning deliveries, but now there were carriages and oxcarts and rickshaws. Clara had never seen so many different kinds of carts. There were large trade towns on the canal and sometimes they had two or three different styles of transport, but nothing like this. She counted eight different designs of horse cart alone before she gave up.

"No walls," said Istvhan, gazing ahead. "No fear of invaders, I take it?"

"If an enemy got close enough on land, they would fire the bridges," said Doc Mason. "You note how the road starts going up ahead of us? It becomes a causeway at high tide. If an army tries to invade, they will be up to their armpits soon enough, and then the archers could stand on the ring road and rain arrows down on them. And most of their food comes from the sea, so burning the farm fields won't starve them out."

"Navy or nothing then."

"Indeed."

"I hate boats," muttered Istvhan, to no one in particular.

"Do you get seasick?"

"No. I just hate them." He avoided Clara's eye. "They're on the water."

"That is what makes them boats, yes."

"You can't *deal* with water."

Clara raised her eyebrows. Doc Mason put his chin in his hand and leaned forward. "Whatever do you mean, my boy?"

Istvhan looked over, clearly saw that all three of them were looking at him, and hunched his shoulders. "You can't fight it. You can't talk to it. You can't bribe it or negotiate with it. You can't even run away from it. It's like an earthquake, except all the time."

Clara smothered a laugh. It was hard to imagine gallant Istvhan, who had faced a wedge of men on horseback with only his sword, being afraid of the sea. *Then again, you've seen him talk his way or fight his way out of everything. He is very confident in his ability to do those things. Perhaps it would be unsettling to have a foe that responds to neither, and doesn't even know it's your foe.*

Which was interesting. And perhaps said a lot about what someone like Istvhan feared most of all.

The causeway split into three parts as they approached the city. Two fanned out in a broad circle around the outside of the pilings, and the center one went straight up a bridge and into Morstone. There was an enormous open space here, full of wagons being turned, wagons being unloaded, horses being watered, and money changing hands. A forest of stalls sprung up around the edges, some of them built out over the water on pilings of their own. Tolly pulled the mules up near the edge.

"Here we must part ways, my friends." Doc Mason helped Clara down from the wagon, which she didn't need but pretended to anyway. "Our business is not in the city proper, but on the ring road."

Istvhan pulled his pack from the back of the wagon and shouldered it. Clara, with no possessions to worry about, settled for fending off the hawkers who descended on the wagon, trying to sell trinkets, cure-alls, and dried cheese on a string. "We don't want any," she said, folding her arms. "We're in the business ourselves. That one's a fake. So's that one, but it's a better fake. No. Go fleece someone else, gents." The crowd retreated reluctantly, but fortunately a mail coach appeared and spilled its occupants and the hawkers abandoned Clara and Istvhan for new marks.

"It has been a pleasure," said Doc Mason, shaking hands with both of them. "Istvhan, should you ever decide to quit the ecclesiastical lifestyle, I would be happy to have you accompany me again. Domina Clara, I hope that you find what you are looking for."

She smiled at him. "I hope that you sell an extraordinary amount of tonic. And Tolly, if you find yourself on the far side of the Arrals, give my name to the merchants along the canal. They won't cheat you."

Tolly kissed Istvhan on the cheek and hugged Clara, then scrambled up on the wagon seat. She clucked her tongue at the mules and they ambled off along the outer road, leaving the two standing in front of the gates.

"Well," said Clara. "I suppose that's that, then." She turned to Istvhan and took a deep breath. "Thank you, too, Captain Istvhan, for all your help. I hope your men arrive safely."

"I hope they do too," said Istvhan, "but I imagine you'll find out when I do. If you think I'm leaving you to rattle around in this city alone, you're out of your mind, Domina."

"I do not recall asking you," said Clara. She squared her shoulders. "You've been an extraordinary help, but I can no longer impose upon your time."

"You're not imposing," said Istvhan. "And we're not discussing this here where everyone and their god can hear us." He caught her forearm and felt the muscles tighten under his hand, but she let him pull her aside, out of the street, and into an alley.

She shook him off once they were out of the street and settled back against the wall, arms folded across her chest. "Captain, I appreciate that you wish to help, but—"

"Domina, for god's sake. Drop this captain nonsense. You've called me Istvhan for weeks now."

She glared at him. "If we're doing that, then my name isn't Domina either."

He gritted his teeth. She was right, dammit. "Fine. Clara...what on earth do you plan to do alone in this city? Do you even know where to start making inquiries? You're going to bring the raiders and their bosses straight down on your head."

"And I suppose you have a better plan? You've never been here before either."

Istvhan put one hand on the wall next to her head and leaned forward. He couldn't loom much, but he did his best with what he had to work with. "I have contacts at the Temple of the White Rat. The Rat gets everywhere. They will help us. They'll know who to ask, or at least where to start asking, and how to do it without getting people's backs up."

Clara seized her lower lip in her teeth and worried at it until it seemed it might bleed. Istvhan reached out without thinking and ran his thumb across her chin. "Don't," he said. "You're hurting yourself." His voice was still too angry and he tried to gentle it, but...just... *dammit. What do I have to do? What am I doing that's wrong?*

Stop thinking with your cock, he told himself, *and start thinking like a paladin. You were one once, if you haven't completely forgotten.*

Her eyes were full of shadows. He shoved down lust like he shoved down the battle tide and focused on his voice. Careful. Soothing. Kind. A brother's voice, although he was not feeling the least bit brotherly. "Clara," he said. That was better. That came out correctly. "Clara, you don't have to do this alone. Let me help."

She swallowed hard. In another woman, he would have expected tears in her eyes, but she was fighting them back, he was sure of it. She would not show weakness, no matter how much it cost her.

One of her hands moved. She rubbed her knuckles against her sternum as if it pained her, then winced almost imperceptibly and stopped. Her injured hand, of course. Istvhan laid his hand in the center of her chest, his palm between her breasts. A great intimacy, but for once he had nothing carnal in mind, only comfort.

She inhaled sharply. He searched her face, not looking down, and then her hand crept up and covered his. He could feel her breath catching, as if there was something in her chest that strangled her.

"You keep trying to leave me behind. Have I offended you so badly?" He felt himself smiling, because it hurt when he said it, and sometimes you smiled so that no one would know how much you hated the pain.

She took another halting breath and her fingers laced tightly with his. "No," she said.

"No?"

"I try to leave because I can't think straight when I'm with you." She smiled a little too, and Istvhan suspected it was for the same reason. He could feel her heart beating against his fingers. "You see? I forget that I don't know who to ask or where to go. I think only that if you're not here, maybe I'll start thinking clearly again."

"It seems like neither of us are thinking clearly," he said. And then, because there was really only one way to follow that sentence, Istvhan kissed her.

It was far more hesitant than the first time or the second. He only brushed his lips across hers, like a question — *Do you feel this too? Is it only me?*

Against his palm, her heart began to pound. He rubbed his hand in the tiniest of circles, as if soothing an ache, and her lips parted under his. Another brush and another, soft and careful, and it felt like the answer to his question was right there, but he would have had to deepen the kiss to learn it.

No. Let her decide what she wants, because she wants it, and not because you're kissing her senseless.

He pulled back, searching her face. "If you truly cannot bear my company, then let me take you to the Temple of the Rat." It would kill him to walk away, but he would if he must. If he was overwhelming her, it was safer for her and her sisters for him to be elsewhere. "I will speak to the priests on your behalf and then, if it is what you wish, I'll leave you to them."

A shudder went through her. He felt it, though he could not see it. He stepped away, letting his hand drop. "Come along. Let's find the temple."

It was never hard to find the Temple of the White Rat. Everyone in the poorer parts of any city knew where it was. You went there for food or healing or simply because you had a problem and there would be someone who could either help you, or point you in the right direction. Of all the gods that Clara had encountered in her travels, the White Rat's people came the closest to genuinely making the world a better place.

Istvhan asked for directions twice from beggars and dropped

coins in their palms afterward, and that was enough to set them in the right direction. Clara followed close behind him, keeping an eye on his back. She had never been in a city this size before and the smells and the sounds formed a multi-layered din that left her squinting, despite it being an overcast day.

Istvhan seemed to have no trouble with it. That surprised her. Somehow he seemed like a creature too large to live in cities, as if he would constantly be ducking doorways and turning sideways through alleys. She kept catching herself hunching her shoulders, even when she was in no immediate danger of running into anything.

"Big place," she said, when they paused at the corner of an intersection.

"Very," said Istvhan. "Not quite as large as Anuket City, but that's the only one I know that's any larger. And it's much more..." He fumbled for a word, and finally settled on "Organized."

Clara nodded. *And now we have retreated to completely safe topics, like street layouts, because otherwise we will have to talk about that kiss and if it meant anything and if I will send you away.*

She swallowed. The hard place in her chest still ached, but there had been a moment, as his palm lay across it, when it had loosened. It had hurt, like a muscle drawn so tight that any lessening was agony, and yet her whole body cried out for more. Cried out so strongly, in fact, that the beast heard it and rumbled under her conscious mind. *Now? Now?*

No. Hush. We're safe.

She followed Istvhan through another winding alley. The thought of leaving him behind was crushing. *You've left it too long,* she thought bleakly. *You left it too long and dammit, you're in love, aren't you? Now what's worse — loving him or losing him? Which one lets you function for the next few days, until you get your sisters back?*

You don't have to decide right now, she told herself. *Not until after you've visited the Temple and sorted all this out. You don't have to choose yet. You won't lose him today.*

The intense relief that followed that thought told Clara that, rightly or wrongly, she'd already made her choice.

CHAPTER 28

Istvhan had visited several temples of the Rat in his day. They all tended to be rather similar, though adapted to the architectural style of the area. You had the sprawling compound, the buzzing hive of activity, the line of people seeking food, the healer's quarters and then the quiet, somewhat austere buildings that housed the organizers and the problem solvers and the lawyers. In Anuket City, there were mechanical devices to streamline the system. In Charlock, the central hub of buildings was surrounded by a maze of colorful tents that were moved in various positions depending on the weather and favorable astrology.

In Morstone, however, for the first time, Istvhan saw a temple that was overwhelmed.

Space was at a premium because of the docks, so the Morstone Temple was less sprawling and more warren-like. It folded around the dock it was on, spiraling upward, and underneath were slung dozens of the large hammocks they favored here, the enclosed kind that resembled a pupating caterpillar.

It was jammed to capacity. People lined up to wait for the healer, some of them holding obviously broken limbs or coughing miserably. Children much too young to be here were waiting in line too, with the too-adult expression of children who were running errands for adults too ill or too busy to go themselves. The legal offices — or at least, what Istvhan assumed were the legal offices — were also over-whelmed. A woman leaned against the wall, waiting her turn, while tears slid down her face. An older woman beside her was trying to coax her into drinking a sip of water and saying the meaningless things you say to strangers in distress: "Honey, I don't know what's wrong, but I promise, you'll get over this, it will be all right, I prom-ise..." Acolytes wearing the Rat's sigil darted through the crowd with expressions ranging from enthusiasm to panic.

"Saint's teeth," muttered Istvhan. "We need to talk to someone in authority, but I hate to pile even more work onto these people."

Clara looked around, shaking her head. "Do you want me to be a nun for a bit?"

"Will it help?"

"Oh, yes." Her smile had a faintly malicious edge to it. She took a deep breath, put her shoulders back, folded her hands into her sleeves, and suddenly she was every inch the woman who had come into a stranger's tent and informed him that he would be escorting her across the mountains. Istvhan took a step back involuntarily and wondered how he'd ever had the balls to kiss her.

She planted herself in the path of an acolyte, and said, "Bless you, child, I have need of your assistance."

The acolyte stopped as if he had run into a brick wall. "Muh...I... ah....ma'am?"

"Sister Clara." Her lips curved just slightly and she inclined her head. Terror spread across his face.

"I'm sorry, sister, I didn't mean — I — disrespect—"

"You are forgiven," said Clara kindly. "You have not sinned against me. I am here with important news that must be delivered to someone well-placed within the hierarchy. Who is it convenient for me to speak with?"

The acolyte's eyes darted back and forth, indicating to Istvhan that it was not convenient to speak to anyone at the moment and also that the young man felt it was probably not worth his soul to say this out loud. "If you'll follow me, sister?"

"How the hell did you do that?" Istvhan murmured in her ear as they were led out of the main compound and through a door by the legal offices.

"When bears are threatened, they stand up on their hind legs and fluff their fur to look big," she replied, just as softly. "This is just the ecclesiastical equivalent."

They were eventually handed off to Faizen, a lean black man with closely cropped hair. His upper lip had clearly been cleft and sewn together, either as an infant or later as a result of some injury, and had left him with a permanent sardonic expression, but his voice held nothing but genuine concern.

"From Archenhold?" he said, after Istvhan had introduced both himself and Clara. "Welcome to the madhouse. I wish I could say that we can help you, but..." He spread his hands.

"Did something happen here?" asked Istvhan. "Some recent catastrophe?"

Faizen gave a brief choking laugh. "No, paladin. This is actually quite a good day, by our standards. No one is giving birth on the floor and hardly anyone is screaming."

Istvhan stared at him in frank disbelief.

"I know, I know." The Rat-priest raised both hands as if to ward off Istvhan's gaze. "I know. This is shocking if you come in from somewhere else. I trained in the temple in Anuket City and...I know."

"Do you need more money? More people?" Istvhan honestly could not imagine the Temple of the White Rat leaving the Morstone arm of the faith to struggle like this. Bishop Beartongue would be up in arms.

"No, we need a different *city*," said Faizen. "This place has failed on every possible level a state can fail, except that it's got an army under control of the Sealords. There's no government, no courts, no services. If your neighborhood's dock supports fall down, tough shit. You move or you get a bunch of people together and figure out how to jam enough trash into place to hold the neighborhood together. We've got the Rat's support, which is why we can do this much, but not even the Rat's coffers can fund running the entire city, and even if

235

they could, the Sealords would see that as a direct threat and we'd be out. And then who would take care of these people?" He spread his arms wide.

"You're stuck," said Clara sympathetically. "Trying to do the greatest good for the greatest number without getting shut down."

"You have plucked the pearl from the meat, yes. The first thing the temple does when we expand to a new area is bring in healers and set up a soup kitchen," said Faizen. "Once we're getting people fed, we worry about housing. At that point, it seems like you always need lawyers to represent people. Then we start worrying about general problem solving, and we keep adding the ranks of solicitors sacrosanct." He passed a hand over his tightly cropped hair. "We've been stuck at the housing stage for about a hundred years now. Short of raising an army and overthrowing the Sealords, I don't see us getting past that any time soon."

"And the Rat doesn't do that sort of thing," said Clara.

Istvhan grunted. The White Rat did not overthrow governments, although Istvhan was fairly certain that Bishop Beartongue had more knowledge of the occasional targeted assassination than was entirely ethical. Not that she'd ever do it herself, of course. But it was something of an open secret among the upper ranks of the solicitors sacrosanct that people who called themselves Sin Eaters came and went from the temple sometimes and you didn't ask where they were going or what they were going to do when they got there.

Still, it was entirely possible that whatever was going on here, simply offing a couple of these Sealords would only make it worse for a great many people. *Or they're busy elsewhere, or they don't operate in this area. You can fit what I know about those people into a thimble, really.*

"I feel guilty for adding to your burdens," said Istvhan.

"Of course you do. You're a paladin." Faizen shook his head while Clara muffled a snort. "The Rat provides as best He can. He provided us a god-touched builder the other day, if you can believe it. This poor kid shows up fresh from the Forge God's temple, where his god actually handed him off to the Rat somehow, and then it turns out he can do things with cantilevers and...I don't know, I don't understand

how any of this works. I didn't know gods could actually trade staff."
He rubbed his eyes. "Sorry, I'm babbling. I'm very tired. You're here,
Paladin Istvhan, and I must believe that you will be the solution to a
problem, or we will be the solution to yours. Tell me what I can do for
you."

Istvhan outlined his trip's mission quickly, and waited as Faizen
digested it. "Huh," the man said finally. "I don't know of any headless
corpses about, but that doesn't mean anything. I'm an organizer, not
an intelligence gatherer, and half the things people tell me, I forget.
But we have people who can look into it."

"Rather more pressingly," said Istvhan, "there is Domina Clara's
problem." He gestured to her and she recited her story. She seemed
more absent than usual as she did it, or perhaps saying the same
words, over and over, had worn the edges off them and made them an
emotionless repetition of facts.

Or perhaps, as always, she is too calm. Though she had not seemed
so calm when he kissed her, and whether that was a good thing or a
bad thing, he did not know.

"That seems a long way to go," said Faizen. "A very long way. Is
there some reason, do you know, why someone would wish to kidnap
your sisters...?"

Not a stupid man, thought Istvhan. Not that he'd expect someone
highly ranked in the Rat priest hierarchy to be anything less.

Clara glanced at Istvhan. She had been fairly quiet since their
kiss, and he did not know if it was because of that, or the city, or...*well,
take your pick, really, it's not like we don't have enough things going for a
dozen people to brood over.*

"You had best tell him the truth," said Istvhan. "All of it." He held
her eyes. "Better yet, show him. The Rat works best if their hands are
not tied."

"Are you sure?" said Clara.

*I am sure that he'll think we're completely mad if you don't transform
and prove it, but I don't think that's what you're really asking.* "Your secret
will be safe with him, or I will stand the reckoning."

Faizen put up an eyebrow at the threat. Clara nodded and rose, unfastening her robes. Istvhan rose as well and put his back to the door. This was not the time when you wanted someone to come barging in.

She dropped her robes to the floor in a puddle of fabric. "Uh," said Faizen.

"You get used to it," said Istvhan. Saint's teeth, but the woman's ass was as majestic as her breasts. He wanted to grab her rounded hips in his hands and...

Her skin rippled and he stopped thinking about that, and started worrying about whether or not the cramped office was big enough for the transformation.

It was, but only just. Two chairs were knocked over and the desk groaned under the sudden weight of paws.

"Hrrrwwwff," said the bear in Faizen's face.

The rather nice Rat-priest looked like he was about to scream, so Clara told the bear to go back down inside her skull. The bear did not much like the dark, enclosed room and the smell of tallow candles, so it obeyed.

Faizen said "*Aiiihh...*hhhhhh...hh...h...*huh?*" or words to that effect.

"You get used to it," said Istvhan, who was guarding the door.

Faizen's mouth worked and he blinked a few times. "Was that real?" he said finally. "Not an illusion?"

Clara picked up her robes and began shrugging into them. "Quite real," she said. Her heart was thumping, partly from the physical strain of transformation, partly because you never knew when someone was going to react extremely badly.

Fortunately, the Rat chose his priests of sterner stuff. Faizen sat back in his chair and began to laugh. "Incredible," he said. "I've heard stories of werewolves, but never...I didn't actually believe them."

"In fairness, I've never met a werewolf," said Clara. "They might just be stories. But the nuns of my order are werebears." She wiped her nose. The scent of tallow and human and wood was still ringing in her head like a sound, mixed with the background cacophony of dead fish and salt water that characterized Morstone. "We think they may have been kidnapped for a menagerie, or perhaps use in gladiatorial pits."

Faizen groaned. "The games. Yes, of course. Sealord Antony has been touting his drowgos legion for months. It would be quite a coup if one of the other Sealords could find something to match them."

Clara felt his words like knives, the way the word *amphitheater* had felt weeks ago.

"Right," said Faizen. "Right. Okay. Above my paygrade. Way above. Let's take you to the Bishop."

Bishop Raulann was a tall, leggy woman, as dark as Faizen, but with pale hair pulled back in many narrow locks and secured with a metal comb. She looked up inquisitively at Faizen as he entered.

"You're not going to believe this," said Faizen.

"I'm not?"

"Not in a million years." He sounded rather pleased about it.

At least this office was a bit bigger, Clara thought. She waited while Istvhan and Faizen explained things between them, and then called the bear up again.

Raulann was much calmer than Faizen. She didn't scream or yelp or even stammer. Her brown eyes went very wide, and then she, too, began to laugh. "Oh my. Rat have mercy. How are you doing that?"

It took Clara a moment to put the bear down again. It was displeased with all this coming and going. She got a mental image of a bird popping in and out of a hole in a tree, the closest the bear could manage to a dramatic monologue.

She staggered a bit as she came out of the transformation. Istvhan grabbed her arm to steady her. "Sorry," she said. "Too many changes close together. Give me a moment."

"Yes, of course," said Bishop Raulann, as Istvhan guided her to the chair. "Yes. My goodness. That was real, then?"

Clara nodded.

"It's not an illusion," said Istvhan. "Or if it is, it covers all the senses and also she gets about eight feet tall."

"That is one hell of a thing." She paused. "Ah...are you under a curse? Do you need it broken? Because I'll be honest, I've never seen anything like it, but we could send you to our healers..."

"No, no." Clara managed a chuckle. "No, I was born like this. That's not the problem." She laid out her story yet again. Raulann listened intently. Her questions were few and mostly to clarify timelines and the extent of the transformation. When Clara had finished, she leaned back in her chair again, balancing on the back two legs, and rocked back and forth for a moment, thinking.

"All right," said the Bishop. "I can't keep you here. It's nothing personal, we just don't have space. And...well...if people are going to come hunting for a nun matching your description, I'd rather they didn't go through a bunch of sick and hungry people to get to them."

"Completely fair," said Clara. "More than fair. I'd be devastated if I brought trouble to your temple."

"We don't actually have the ability to protect you anyway," said Bishop Raulann. "The Rat doesn't call warriors, and it's hard to hire anybody when the army pays so much better. We've got a few retired fighters and bouncers in case of emergencies, but I doubt they can do half so much as you can on your own."

"She's not alone," said Istvhan.

"Yes, of course."

So much for your offer to leave me with the Rat, Captain. Though if Clara was being fair, she couldn't fault him. She had only encountered smaller outposts of the White Rat's faith in her travels, but they had not been anything like this. It was clear that they were barely keeping their heads above water. It would have been cruel to simply dump her problem in their laps and expect protection as well as aid.

"I'm sorry we can do so little. I know if you came from the south, you had reason to expect that the Rat had a great many more resources to put at your disposal. As you've seen, though, Morstone is...different."

"I'm sorry," said Istvhan. "I had no idea. I don't know if our bishop in Archenhold has any idea."

Raulann shook her head. "Oh, they all know. That's not a complaint, incidentally. They've got their own flocks to maintain, and the Rat sends a great deal of material support and manpower. We can only operate at such a level that will not get us shut us down, and you're looking at it." She smiled faintly. "And more lawyers won't help anyway. You need actual laws for that to work, beyond, 'Whatever the Sealords say.' So we get by. And while we cannot defend you, we do have a spy network, albeit a somewhat specialized one. We can put that at your disposal."

Clara inclined her head. "I'd be very grateful for anything they can turn up."

"In addition," said the Bishop, "we maintain a number of safe houses. And one of our priests is...ah...well...eccentric but trustworthy. Of necessity, I fear, you will have to tell him the truth, but he will find it all fascinating and will not be in the least alarmed." Her lips quirked. "I apologize for that. I imagine it is probably very tiresome to be fascinating."

"It's better than being stoned in the streets," said Clara.

"Yes, but one prefers to have more options available." She drummed her fingers on the desk. "Our information network, as I mentioned, is extensive but erratic. However, I can definitely put word out looking for any nuns arriving in barred wagons, or unusual prisoners slated for the gladiatorial pits. The Sealords introduce new challengers on the first new moon every month, so it will be at least a week. We have a little time." She paused, then leaned forward and touched Clara's hand without any apparent hesitation. "And I can promise you that the word would be everywhere about a group of nuns turning into bears in the pit, so we can be certain they have not yet been presented."

Clara sat back in her chair and let out a long, shaky breath. Something in her chest loosened a little. "Thank you," she said. "That means more than you know."

Raulann nodded. "They may not be slated for the pit at all," she said. "We will make inquiries as we can, but this is not easy. The Sealords pay well to keep their amusements a surprise. One-upping one another is how they display their power." Clara nodded.

"If that is all..."

"Oh no," said Faizen, clearly amused. "There's more!"

"More than an ecclesiastical shapechanger?" said Bishop Raulann. "Good heavens. When I asked the Rat to bring us something interesting, I should probably have been more specific."

Istvhan snorted. "Mine may not be urgent, though I fear it's just as unpleasant." He outlined the situation with the smooth men.

"And you think they've come to Morstone?" asked Raulann.

Istvhan spread his hands. "I think they're in the area. It's worth alerting the city watch if you can."

"There isn't one," said the Bishop.

Clara had rarely seen Istvhan taken aback. "There isn't?"

"Ironically, one of the few good things the Sealords did in recent memory. They were a corrupt pack of bullies, extorting money from impoverished neighborhoods. Though I can't say that the Sealords did it out of altruism — the former Watch got too ambitious and their commander wanted to be made a Sealord himself. The army...dealt with the problem." She grimaced. "It actually got a lot safer around here once they did. At least we've only got one Sealord per district sweeping through and extorting people."

"I have yet to hear anything about the Sealords that I like," muttered Clara.

Raulann shrugged. "The three Dovekies are the least awful of the lot, and the best you can say about them is that they treat the lower classes like cattle, which means they think they should have food, water, and a decent place to sleep in order to maximize profits. We work primarily in Dovekie districts. The other four...well...if you're thinking of going to the Sealords directly to ask about these clay men, I'd get that idea out of your head right now."

"How do we get word out, then?" asked Istvhan. "Are there paladins?"

"No real tradition of paladins up here. They have a lot of gods of the sea, but if one of them calls a paladin, you get a god-touched privateer. Haven't heard of one recently, though. In the little villages, they have the Benandanti, the Good Walkers, who banish demons and lay spirits to rest, but they're much more loosely knit, and a lot less martial. We'll send word to community leaders, but..." Raulann steepled her fingers. "I see why Archenhold's Bishop was reluctant to put word out. Start going after people with the wrong sort of expressions and you're declaring open season on many vulnerable souls. And if you start warning people about severed heads and corpses, god knows what we'll get. Gah. What a *mess.*"

"Walking corpses sound a bit like Sealord Antony's drowgos," said Faizen.

"You mentioned those before," said Istvhan. "What are they? And do they have eerily identical heads?"

"No, their heads are all different. As different as corpses, anyway. Supposedly he's got a tame necromancer who raises the drowned dead," said Faizen. "They're a great favorite in the arena, because it's hard to kill the dead."

"A *necromancer?!*" Istvhan looked more appalled by this than he had been by any of the other myriad tyrannies of Morstone. "In public? Working for a government official?"

"I know," said Raulann, "I know." She closed her eyes wearily. "In any decent society, we'd have paladins crawling out of the woodwork to put a stop to it. But the Rat doesn't call paladins and the Forge God's temple says they'll handle it just as soon as we can identify the necromancer *and* we've got an army available as backup. The Sealords are like one of those families that all hate each other, but god forbid an outsider threaten any one of them. They'll band together in a heartbeat. And Morstone, Rat help us all, isn't an easily conquered city."

Istvhan grunted. Clara didn't blame him. Necromancy was like demons or rabies. In most of the world, it transcended notions of right and wrong and blame and guilt. You just dealt with it as quickly and thoroughly as possible and hoped like hell it didn't happen often. Fortunately it was much rarer than either.

"What about the Dreaming God's people?"

Raulann sighed. "Two death or glory charges. They didn't end in glory. We stopped asking. They're good people, but even for paladins, they're dim. No offense intended, Paladin Istvhan."

"None taken. It's the sort of thing the Saint of Steel's chosen were for, before..." He trailed off, and no one moved to fill the gap. "And no one else is appalled by the necromancer? No one with power? No one who can stop things?"

The Bishop's smile was humorless. "Welcome to Morstone, Paladin Istvhan. We hope that you survive your stay."

CHAPTER 29

It was early evening by the time they left the temple. The Bishop took them to a man with heavy jowls and a massive gut and nimble, ink-stained fingers. He took down the names and descriptions of the raiders, and of Clara's sisters, asking questions about each of them. Clara was embarrassed to realize that she could not remember what Sigrid's eye color was or the Abbess's height. "She always seems taller than she is," she said cautiously. "But she has a personality like that. I think perhaps she's actually rather short, but that's not how I remember her. And she walks slowly, as if she was thinking about each step in advance, because her hips hurt her."

Ironically, she could have recognized each of their scents, but that wasn't much use either. How did you explain the differences in sweat and skin and breath, when the convent all used the same kind of soap and wore the same kind of robes? And how did you put that into words that would mean anything to someone looking for them?

Faizen explained about the bears. "And how much you choose to tell your people is up to you," he said. "I realize it sounds quite mad, but treat it as if it were written in the Rat's own hand."

The man's gaze flicked from Faizen to Istvhan to Clara, then back. He gave a single, explosive grunt and began to write furiously. Clara had originally guessed that the man was a scribe, but changed her

opinion to de facto spymaster as soon as Faizen said "your people."
But he did not ask for proof, or offer any comment. He simply took
notes and then nodded to Faizen. "I'll get them out to people in the
next day," he said. "Though it won't be quick. We'll focus on things
related to the gladiatorial pit, but we only ever get to speak to some of
the workers on their days off." He glanced over at Clara and gave her
a small nod. "Your descriptions are good though, Sister. I believe we
can work with these."

"Please," she said, resisting the urge to throw herself at his feet
and beg him to find her sisters. "It's been too long, and I'm afraid for
what might happen."

He nodded, and Faizen ushered them away, into the dim streets of
Morstone.

"Proctor Ethan is a little odd," warned Faizen. "A good man...the
best...discreet!...but...odd." His delivery was rapid-fire, as if he
couldn't quite decide whether to warn them off or beg them to give
the proctor a chance.

Istvhan shrugged. "I've met many odd people," he said. "Arguably,
I'm one of them."

Faizen did not look encouraged by this. "Ah...yes. Well.
Somewhat."

"What does he do?" asked Clara. "For the Rat, I mean. Is he a
lawyer?"

"Oh no. No, no. He cares for people's animals." Faizen must have
caught their puzzled looks because he ran a hand over his hair. "Morstone's full of animals. There's a dovecote on every roof or a chicken
coop. People have cats or terriers for the rats. Most inns keep a slop
pig. Hell, a few of the old families even fish with cormorants still. So
that's where Ethan comes in."

"He heals animals?" hazarded Istvhan.

"Nothing so grandiose. But this is one of the problems the Rat has
to solve." Faizen shook his head. "You'll get people who won't leave a

house that's literally halfway in the river because they're afraid they won't be able to take their dog, or who won't go to the healer, even if they're half-dead, because they're afraid their chickens will starve with no one to feed them. If we can find them somewhere to go where they can take the dog or the cat or the chickens, that's the easiest, but a lot of times..." He lifted his hands, let them drop. "We have a couple people who handle relocation. We've actually got a few farms outside the city who will temporarily house poultry or doves or dogs, and thankfully, there's a strong local belief that if you harm a cat, the ship's cats will learn of it and refuse to work, so the sailor temples step up there."

Istvhan had a fairly good idea how the Rat worked by now. "And if there should be excess eggs or young cockerels or squab, and if people should be grateful for the Rat's help and wish to donate that excess to the hungry?"

Faizen grinned. "We solve each other's problems, Paladin Istvhan. It is all part of the Rat's ministry. Ethan goes all over the city for people who need help but are afraid no one will care for their animals. So he's always out feeding the chickens so someone can actually visit the healer, or whatever. And he helps take in some of the...odder...creatures, too." He paused. "Ah...do you like animals?"

Istvhan very carefully did not look at Clara as he answered. She was wearing a heavy hooded cloak provided by the Rat, but he could practically feel her eyes on him. "Mostly, yes. I can't say I have much luck with horses or mules. Dogs like me."

"They don't like me," said Clara. "Not at first, anyway." She smiled faintly. "If their human acts as if I'm normal, they usually come around."

"Is it the scent?" asked Istvhan, interested.

"I imagine so." She shrugged. "Though cats don't seem to mind. As far as cats are concerned, my scent is in very poor taste, but most humans are in very poor taste, so they don't hold it against me."

"Well, that's cats for you." Faizen nodded.

They arrived at last at a very strange house. It had been built up in a gap between two much larger buildings, but even by the standards of Morstone's somewhat eccentric architecture, this one was odd. The planks were enormous and curved outward in places, and if there was a straight angle in the place, Istvhan couldn't see it. It looked like a weaver nest built in wood instead of straw.

"...huh," said Clara.

Faizen hammered on the door, then stepped back and waited. After a minute, he hammered again. "Sorry," he said apologetically. "He gets into the middle of something and you have to keep reminding him you're here."

After the fourth round of hammering, the door opened. The man in the doorway was short, slim, and wore the robes of a minor functionary of the White Rat. He had tied the long sleeves back, but the lower hem was dripping wet.

"Faizen!" he said. "It's you! Oh, I'm sorry, I didn't mean to keep you waiting, I was just transferring the banded salamanders. They've laid eggs, you know, and you have to get them out of the jar before the eggs hatch or they tend to go to cannibalism, and no one wants *that*."

"Certainly we must avoid cannibalism," said Istvhan, in his most diplomatic voice. Clara elbowed him in the ribs. "What? Cannibalism is a real problem!"

"Especially in salamanders," said Proctor Ethan. He was the sort of man who looked as if he should wear thick spectacles, but apparently nature had blessed him with decent vision. He grinned up at Istvhan and thrust out a hand. Istvhan shook. The man's hand was extremely damp, not in a sweaty fashion, but in a "only recently extracted from a jar of salamanders" fashion.

They stepped inside. Faizen performed introductions all around. Clara pushed her hood back and shook Ethan's hand, and received the same soggy benediction.

Ethan's home was an odd concoction of cabinets, nooks, and niches, each of them jammed with glass jars and enormous ceramic bowls. "It was an old ship," their host explained. "Most of one, anyway. A seer told the captain that as long as he stayed close to his ship, he'd never be ill in his life. When he retired, he had the ship dismantled and built his house out of the wood. There wasn't a lot of space, though, so he built up and around another building that was already here — it's a bakery now, keeps everything warm even in winter — and then he still had wood left over and he was afraid to lose any of it, so he had cabinets and shelves and stair-cases built all over. It's such a weird shape that hardly anyone wanted to live here for long, particularly since the doorways are all so low..."

"I'd noticed," said Istvhan dryly, trading a glance with Clara. Both of them had almost bent double entering the room.

"I'm sorry," said Ethan. "I'll put you in the tall galley. Err, you'll have to share with Maude."

"Maude?" said Clara.

"She's a Northern Great Toad. You'll love her. Everyone loves her. Except mice, of course. It's a bit cold, that's the only thing. Maude likes cold. Most amphibians don't, of course." He re-tied the strings on one sleeve. "Anyway, I love the house because there's so many places to store my jars."

"Did it work?" asked Istvhan.

"Did what work?"

"Keeping the wood from the ship. Did the captain ever get ill?"

"Oh no." Ethan grinned. "He lived to be nearly a hundred, and then he was stabbed. By a jealous husband, if the stories are to be believed."

Istvhan felt a strong urge to remove his hat. He wasn't wearing one, so he settled for putting a hand over his heart.

Faizen had waited patiently through all of this, and now cleared his throat. "There's a reason we need them to stay with you," he said. "And it requires utmost discretion."

Ethan blinked. "Oh," he said, sounding rather more focused. "Yes, of course. Is someone after them?"

"Someone would be, if they knew who they were." Faizen glanced over at Clara. "Do they know Sister Clara by sight?"

"The original raiders would, but it seems unlikely that they are looking," said Clara, thinking. "I am fairly distinctive, I grant you, but the people who know that I am still alive were mostly killed in the attack." She paused. "I won't swear that one or two might not have survived and ridden hell for leather here, though."

"Oh dear. May I know why?"

Clara glanced at Faizen. He nodded.

"Is it wise, so soon?" asked Istvhan worriedly. He didn't like how pale she got when she stacked transformations so close together.

"I'll be ravenous afterward," she said. "But no one ever believes you unless you show them." She stripped off her cloak and then her robes. Istvhan took them. Ethan's mouth fell open. Faizen gazed at the ceiling. Istvhan kept his gaze firmly above her collarbone, because if he looked any lower, naked lust was going to cross his face and make everyone uncomfortable.

She dropped down to her hands and knees, surprising him. *Then again, with the low ceilings...oh gods, the things we could do with her in that position...* He looked at Ethan instead, who had turned scarlet and was starting to back away.

The pressure in the room changed. The jars rattled softly on the shelves. The room was suddenly a great deal more crowded and Ethan's jaw, already hanging open, looked in danger of imminent dislocation.

"Oh my," he said softly. "Oh my heavens. Oh by the Rat's tail and toes. What *are* you?"

"A person," said Istvhan, hearing the harshness in his voice and trying to pull it back. "A sister of the Order of Saint Ursa. This is the gift their saint gives them."

"Oh my, yes. And you're real, ma'am?"

"Hrrwufff." If a bear could roll its eyes, Clara did.

"And you can do this voluntarily? At will? Not under the full moon?"

"Hrrwuf."

"May I touch you?"

Istvhan was astonished at the strength of his reaction to this. *Am I jealous? Of this reedy little man with his salamanders?*

He had absolutely no right to be jealous. He didn't. He had no claim on Clara, except that he had kissed her a few times and stabbed her once. Stabbing someone did not count as an exclusive relationship.

The bear sighed and stepped forward. Ethan sank to his knees and buried his hands in the bear's fur, then began a quick physical examination. "Can you open your mouth? Thank you..." He peered into the bear's jaws, clearly unconcerned by the massive canines. Over his shoulder, the bear gave Istvhan a do-you-see-what-I-have-to-put-up-with look.

"Incredible. And do you eat raw meat in this form?"

"Haauuughghh," the bear said, which Istvhan assumed was as close as it could get to *Hrwuff* with its mouth open.

"And it doesn't upset your digestion? What if you turn into a human with a stomach full of raw meat?"

"Haaauugh."

"I didn't quite catch that?"

"I believe she is saying, 'I cannot answer with my mouth open,'" said Istvhan. The bear shot him a look that he chose to believe was gratitude. It was not an expression that came easily to ursine features.

"Oh! Yes, of course, I'm so sorry. Please, turn back if you like."

Clara materialized on her hands and knees. Istvhan hurriedly dropped the robe over her shoulders, even though he was quite sure that Ethan's interest was purely academic.

"Thanks," she said. He offered her a hand up and she took it, which worried him a bit. Was she woozy?

"Forgive me, but do you have something to eat?" she asked, looking over at Ethan. "A lot of changes today, and I'm starving."

"Of course. I'm sorry, I should have offered...oh dear...what would you like?"

"Anything," she said, "provided there's a lot of it."

Ethan vanished into the back room and emerged with a loaf of bread and some dried fish. Clara's eyes lit up. They settled at a small table and Clara proceeded to tear the bread apart with her hands and devour it like a starving wolf.

"Sorry," she mumbled, through a mouthful of crust. "Normally not a barbariammf..."

"This is incredible." Ethan patted down his robes until he extracted a small, grubby notebook and a stub of pencil. "You're an actual bear? Do you breed true in bear form?"

Clara paused, bread halfway to her lips. "I haven't tried."

The proctor blinked at her. "Oh. Oh, I'm sorry, no, of course, that was a very personal question. Do you have any children? Are they human?"

Faizen cleared his throat. "Perhaps we could discuss this later," he said. "Ethan, may they stay with you?"

"Yes, of course." Privately, Istvhan suspected that Ethan would try to stop them from leaving, at least until his questions were answered. "Oh dear. Do you also need bear food?"

"Most human food is perfectly good bear food," said Clara.

"Yes, but does it go the other way? That's what I was trying to ask earlier. If you eat raw meat or carrion as a bear, does it disagree with you as a human?"

"...I try to avoid eating carrion."

"Yes, of course." Ethan made a note. "What about the size of the meal? If you eat as a human, are you full as a bear? If you eat a large meal as a bear and turn back into a human, what happens to the extra food? And the waste products from the food, how do they scale—"

Faizen caught Istvhan's eye. "We'll be in touch," he murmured, moving toward the door. "Contact us if you need anything. And try not to go out in the city too much."

"All right," said Ethan, as the door closed behind him. "Let's talk about your mass."

"Uh..." Clara glanced at Istvhan. "I can just pray the rosary for the saint. She doesn't get upset if there aren't regular services for Her."

Ethan blinked a few times, looking a bit like a frog himself. "Oh! No! Your mass. Your personal mass. Your weight. You're much larger as a bear. Where does it go, when you're a human? Where does it come from, when you're a bear?"

"It's part of Saint Ursa's blessing."

"So a miracle, then..." He wrote this down. "Do you have any sensation of getting lighter or heavier when you change?"

"No," said Clara, finishing off the last of the bread and starting on the strips of dried fish. "I have the sensation of the bear coming forward or going back in my head. It eclipses everything else."

"Oh, fascinating! So the bear is a separate entity?"

"It feels separate." Clara glanced at Istvhan again.

He shrugged helplessly. "I'm just a paladin, Domina. I've never been a bear."

"Right. Well, I can't tell you if it's actually separate or if we're just trained to think of it as a separate being. It feels like...err..." She waved her hands, clearly searching for a word. "Are you familiar with intrusive thoughts?"

"Oh yes. You don't want to think them but then they get thought anyway."

"More or less. I don't have intrusive thoughts. I have an occasional intrusive bear."

That was interesting. Istvhan rested his chin on his hand. *I suppose we who follow the Saint of Steel think of the battle tide as something separate from us as well. Perhaps if we were bears instead of berserkers, we would treat it the same way.*

Ethan continued to pepper Clara with questions while she systematically worked her way through the fish. "And the change comes on when?...uh-huh...fascinating. And the full moon...nothing. So much for the stories...Do you heal faster? Oh, that's interesting..."

Istvhan waited until she had finished eating before he felt obliged to intervene. "Proctor Ethan," he said. "I thank you for your hospitality. It is very kind. And I am certain that Domina Clara will answer any questions you have over the course of our stay. But we have had a very long day that began very early, and she had been changing form more times in rapid succession than is healthy."

"Oh!" Ethan set down his notepad. "Yes, of course. I'm so sorry. You're just very fascinating, Domina."

"So I'm told," muttered Clara.

"Please, come this way."

He led them down a set of steps, under a low lintel — both Istvhan and Clara ducked — and down a hallway lined with even more jars.

"So you keep salamanders," said Istvhan.

"Not just salamanders. Amphibians are my great love, but I've kept a great many animals over the years. When people pass away with a pet no one else knows how to take care of. And in a city like this..." He waved a hand. "Lots of sailors get very unusual pets. Parrots are the least of it. Snakes, lizards, monkeys...gods, do not even *talk* to me about monkeys. The Rat wants us to live peacefully alongside our fellow creatures, but I do *not* think He meant monkeys."

A noise came from behind Istvhan that sounded very much like a lay sister strangling a laugh.

The tall galley was much cooler than the rest of the house. It was long and narrow, but fortunately as tall as the name implied. Istvhan straightened up with a sigh of relief and felt the vertebrae in his neck crackle.

There were no beds as such, but one wall sported a wide built-in bench that ran the length of the galley. The bench was padded and heaped with pillows and folded blankets. The other wall had a fireplace, though no fire had been built, and stacks of firewood lining the wall on either side.

Ethan knelt in front of the hearth. "It still won't be terribly warm," he said apologetically. "This bit is actually below street level, so the wind off the river hits it and the heat from the bakery doesn't reach this far. But we'll warm it up a bit, and there's tons of blankets."

"We've been sleeping under a wagon," said Istvhan, "mostly to keep the rain and the frost off. We're used to being cold at night."

Ethan looked appalled. "Good heavens, we can certainly do better than that."

"A fire would be heavenly," said Clara, sitting down on the bench. There were dark circles under her eyes. She kicked off her sandals and slumped against a stack of blankets. "I could fall asleep right here."

"Feel free," said Istvhan. "I don't think we need to save the world or climb any mountains tonight.

"Thank St. Ursa." She stretched out on the bench, leaning back against the stack of blankets. "Wake me when it's time for dinner. Or breakfast. Or...you know, never mind, maybe I'll just sleep."

Istvhan had planned to watch over her sleep, like a good paladin would in a strange house, but his eyes struggled to stay open. After Ethan padded out, wishing them a good evening, he draped a blanket over Clara, pulled one over himself, and became instantly dead to the world.

CHAPTER 30

Istvhan woke early, not out of any particular virtue but because he had slept in his chain hauberk, which was a generally terrible idea. He was stiff in muscles that he had forgotten existed. He stared at the ceiling, waiting to see if the gods loved him enough to send a masseuse, preferably a little old woman with a bent back and hands like the claws of death. (In Istvhan's experience, such women were just this side of divinity.) The gods ignored him. Istvhan sighed and got up.

He spent most of an hour in the courtyard, stretching and doing sword drills, until at least everything hurt more or less equally, then slung his swordbelt back around his hips and went inside.

He paused in the doorway of the tall galley, partly to make sure that his head cleared the low lintel, partly because Clara was sitting on the bench inside, her head tilted back against the wall, her eyes closed. She had a knotted string in front of her and her lips moved silently as she drew another knot tight.

Of course, she has no rosary beads. Istvhan wondered if he could find her a set, if that was a gift she could accept from him. *Mind you, if you're trying to seduce her, a rosary is not the sort of gift that makes one think of bed sports.*

Yes, but it would mean something to her. More than just a silly lover's gift. Something that matters to her like she matters to me.

Distant warning bells went off in his head at the thought. He straightened, banged his head on the lintel anyway, and Clara's eyes flew open. She smiled sympathetically as Istvhan rubbed the top of his skull. "I've done it twice this morning already."

He lowered himself to the bench next to her and stretched his legs out. "Doing well otherwise?"

"Mmm." She looked away.

"Let me see, how is my Domina dictionary coming along..." He raised his hands as if flipping through invisible pages. "Was that 'I am not doing well, but I don't wish to complain'?"

She snorted.

"Ah! That's 'Yes, but how dare you call me out like that.' I know that one."

Clara gave him a reluctant laugh and he felt as if he'd won a prize. "Do you have a dictionary like that for everyone you know?"

"Only the ones that I care about," he said.

She inhaled. He waited, not willing to push any farther.

"This is going to drive me mad," she said finally, gesturing around her. Istvhan took it to mean the city, not the room itself, which was inoffensive as rooms went, low doorways aside.

"The waiting is always hard," he offered.

"It's not just that," said Clara. "The waiting is miserable, yes, but it's the fact that I'm not doing anything. I know the Rat's people will be better at this than I would be. There's a lot more of them and they're in positions to know who to ask and how to ask without raising suspicion. I know I'd blunder through like a bull in a cathedral and cause more problems. It's just..." She let her hands drop into her lap. "It's hard for me to trust that things are really happening, if I'm not the one doing them."

"Ah," said Istvhan. "You have never had to learn to delegate."

"No. There's only the one of me, traveling."

"It's a useful skill to learn." He reached out and took her hand, very aware that it in was in her lap and that meant that his fingers were mere inches from somewhere dangerous. He rubbed his thumb across her fingertips, feeling the rasp of calluses, hoping that he was moving slowly enough. *Maddeningly seductive is good. Maddeningly pushy is bad. Though it is beginning to seem that I must remind her every day that I am interested, or she finds a way to talk herself out of it, or convince herself that I've changed my mind.* He wondered if she thought he was fickle, or if she thought so little of herself that she expected men to lose interest after five minutes.

Clara raised an eyebrow at him. "I don't have any underlings to delegate things to."

"It doesn't require underlings. Just people you trust."

"I don't have many of those, either."

"Ah." He smiled. "That's a different matter. You should always have someone you can trust."

"I trust my sisters with my life," she said, looking away.

"And I trust my brothers. Though many of my brothers are very broken people, so trust becomes a combination of my faith in them and my understanding of what they can and cannot do."

She twisted her lips sideways, clearly thinking this through. "I suppose that you're right. I trust my sisters with my life, but I would not ask the Abbess to pull me up a cliff. She would absolutely wish to, but she's physically unable. At least as a human."

"There, you see? Trust is one part faith and one part predictability."

"It seems very cold, when you put it that way."

Istvhan raised his eyebrows. "Perhaps. But it also means that we love our friends enough not to put them in situations where they will be called upon to do things that they cannot do." He lifted their clasped hands a little, let them fall. "Galen, for example. He is my brother-in-arms and I would die for him, but I do not put him in situations where he has to share sleeping quarters with another person."

"Mmm. The nightmares?"

"Not entirely. If you wake him from a nightmare, it can trigger the battle-tide. He's gotten better — now he is sometimes violent, but he has not gone berserk for some years — but he is very afraid of what he might do, unknowing."

Clara shook her head. "All that from the death of a god..."

"We all paid a price," he said quietly. "Mine, I think, was very light compared to the others. Stephen lost his will to live for anything but duty, Shane lost his certainty, and Galen lost control. The others..."

"And what did you lose?"

He had known that those mild brown eyes could become sharp, but it still unsettled him. Usually he would have deflected such a question, but it seemed like they were past a time for secrets. "I think, perhaps, my ability to let anyone closer than arm's length. I am amusing and rather too clever for my own good and so it is easy for me to be liked. But once you have had a god inside your soul and lost it, anything more..."

She nodded.

"Perhaps that's why I'm doing this so badly," he said. "I care for you. We are friends, I think, and perhaps more."

Her eyes were shadowed. He did not know whether to say more or scramble to take back what little he had said.

He could have let it go. A sensible man would have. But he was a paladin, and they were prone to self-flagellation, if not literally, at least metaphorically. "Do you want me to leave you here? I promised that I would." He paused, and then, Doc Mason's advice ringing in his head, he added, "I am hoping very much that you will say no."

Clara took a deep breath and let it out again. "I must stay calm," she said. She lifted her free hand and rubbed her sternum. *When she is driving herself mad trying to shove all her feelings down, that is where she feels it instead.* "I must. It's not just my life in the balance. But at this point, I think, being alone in a strange city would be just as hard. And the waiting. And who knows that I won't snap and do something completely mad, like trying to single-handedly raid this colosseum on my own?"

Relief surged through him with an intensity he hadn't expected. "Well," he said. "At least this way, there'd be two of us."

She laughed, though she didn't meet his eyes.

"It will be all right," he said. "I know what it's like to have a feeling so strong it overwhelms you. I'm here."

"For how long?" she asked, covering his hand with hers.

"For as long as you need me," he said, and there was absolutely no choice after a statement like that but to kiss her.

His lips were half an inch from hers and then the door to the galley slammed open.

"Sorry to bother you, I just need to check on Maude," said Ethan. "Ah, Ser Istvhan! Would you mind holding a toad?"

Istvhan looked at Clara. Clara looked at Istvhan. She choked back a laugh because the alternative was to scream.

"I suppose we are all called to serve in our own ways," said Istvhan, rising to his feet. "Will I get warts?"

"*That,*" said Ethan with more venom than Clara had ever heard him express, "is a slanderous myth." He fumbled around in the space behind the woodpile. "She's usually down here, let me just...ah, there you are, sweetheart." He emerged with the largest toad that Clara had ever seen. It was nearly the size of a cat, with enormous golden eyes and a baleful expression.

"She doesn't live in a jar, I take it?"

"Nope. I got her a very nice jar, but she hated it. Prefers to lurk about down here. Let me get a look at you, Maude...yes, good, weight is fine..."

"The jars are impressive," said Clara, "but those tubs upstairs amaze me. You must have very fine potters here."

"Oh yes," said Ethan. "The Leeward has the best potters around. Enormous clay banks along the river, you see." He handed Maude over to Istvhan. She looked disgruntled, but every toad that Clara had ever encountered looked disgruntled, so it probably didn't signify. "Fortunately, rich people demand perfection and poor people can afford the stuff that doesn't quite pass muster."

The Beast of the Leeward. Clay banks. Istvhan met Clara's eyes over

Ethan's head. It was the most tenuous of links, barely even circumstantial evidence, and yet...and yet...

She lost the next few words of their conversation, trying to map the area in her head. The Leeward was across the river and upstream, partly sheltered from the wind off the ocean by a quirk of topography. Many more trees along there than on this side, which received the full brunt. Something could hide there, certainly, but what?

"Necromancer?" said Ethan, bringing her back to the conversation. "No, I don't know anything about that. They're bad, I hear. Very bad. Sorry, here, if you could just hold her here — don't drop her, they're not good at being dropped—"

Two things came clear to Clara simultaneously.

The first was that if she did not find something to occupy him, Istvhan was going to try to hunt down the rumored necromancer.

The second was that, god help her, she might go with him.

I've got to get him out of here, she thought. *Or distracted, or something. We've got days until the Rat's people come back with information. If he sits here brooding over it, he'll work himself up to...what was it the Bishop said? A death or glory charge?*

If he did, Clara couldn't very well let him go alone. One paladin would have no chance. One paladin and a bear still had no chance, but they'd take a lot more of the enemy down when they went.

If I thought we might succeed... Necromancers were anathema. To die removing one was a trade that any paladin would gladly make. Any nun of St. Ursa as well.

We can't. We can't. We need to help my sisters. And that means I need to get Istvhan's mind off necromancers.

The obvious thing to do would be to screw his brains out, which would have been enjoyable, but had its own perils. Clara knew she was on the brink of falling in love. *Oh be honest, you've slid over the brink and are trying to catch yourself before hitting the bottom. And if he's in your bed, in your arms...no, you'll hit so hard you leave a crater.*

She braced herself for the inevitable panicky tightness in her chest at the thought. It didn't come. Instead she found herself vaguely annoyed with herself. *Still angsting about this? Really? It's inevitable. You know it is.* She gazed at him across the room. He was turned away from her, holding the large, rather annoyed looking toad, while Ethan expounded on its magnificence. She already knew what his expression would be, the good-natured bemusement of a man reflecting on the choices that had brought him here. *Such a glorious inevitability, too.* He was not wearing armor and the long, sinewy line of his arms would have set a far more chaste woman than Clara salivating. She traced the curve of shoulder down into bicep with her eyes and wished she could trace it with her fingers, or possibly her tongue.

But if she did succumb, what if he regretted it? What if he woke in the morning thinking that he'd just engaged in some kind of bestiality? And even if she dodged that pitfall, what about the far more prosaic possibility that Istvhan simply wanted to bed her and then move on? *My ability to let anyone closer than arm's length.* Men — even paladins — were not always known for their constancy. Hell, the paladins of the Dreaming God were notoriously randy. She'd never heard that about the Saint of Steel, but that probably didn't signify, since Istvhan was the first one she'd ever met.

And let's not kid ourselves. You may give as good as you get in bed, but do you really think that you're enough to distract a paladin from taking down an abomination? Particularly for days on end?

No. Making a paladin — or a priest, or a nun, or even a lay sister — choose between a human and their god was almost always a losing proposition. Fortunately, she had another idea.

"Istvhan?"

He turned toward her, still brandishing the toad. The toad glared between his fingers. "Domina?"

"Since we've got a few days to wait..." She rose to her feet. He smiled at her, eyebrows lifting. "What say you we investigate this Leeward Beast of yours?"

"Domina," he said, his eyes dark with pleasure and something else, something almost feral, a hunter hard on the scent of prey, "I thought you'd never ask."

CHAPTER 31

"So how do you plan to do this?" asked Clara the next morning, as they left Morstone behind, on the far side of the river this time. "It seems like grabbing strangers at random and demanding that they tell you about monsters would be a tad conspicuous."

"Pshaw!" He actually *said* 'Pshaw,' too, which Clara had never actually heard pronounced by anyone who was not at least eighty years old, usually with muttonchop whiskers. She gazed at him in mild astonishment. "Far too conspicuous, Domina. We shall be as subtle as serpents."

"Oh, we shall? How exactly?"

"I," said Istvhan, "am going to buy people drinks."

Three bars later, Clara had to admit that Istvhan's technique had a great deal to recommend it. He would enter an inn and buy a beer. Then he would tell the bartender that he was traveling through, but he'd heard about the so-called Beast of the Leeward. Since Istvhan had a loud, carrying voice, he could generally expect someone to come up to the bar and claim to have seen the Beast, whereupon Istvhan would buy them a drink. Someone else would show up to say the first person was lying or drunk, because *they* had seen the Beast themselves.

Clara, who came in a few minutes after Istvhan, would find someone, preferably female, sitting quietly in the corner. As the conversation at the bar got louder, she would roll her eyes, look over to the quiet woman, and say, "There was a terrible murder in my hometown about a decade ago. There were no witnesses at the time, but it's amazing how many people apparently saw what happened. I'm surprised the murderer had room to swing the axe for the crowd that must have been there."

Her chosen mark would usually snort acknowledgement, glance at the bar, roll her eyes as well, and then tell Clara how the only person she believed was her cousin (or brother or aunt or friend) who had said something totally different. When they were done talking, Clara would exit the bar, and a few minutes to an hour later, Istvhan would disentangle himself and report what he'd learned.

Most of it squared with what Doc Mason had told them. There had been *something*. It had scared people senseless. It had left mutilated corpses in its wake, both of people and animals. Some of the bodies were headless, yes, but a lot more seemed to have been ripped up by some kind of animal, particularly around the head and torso.

"I don't know if it's the smooth men," said Istvhan. "Sure, a decapitation could have grown in the telling to this, but it could also have simply *been* an animal."

Clara nodded. "Maybe it's all a wild goose chase," she said.

"Maybe. Still, someone has to check." Istvhan groaned as they approached the fourth inn. They had been working their way west along the river, which was fairly well settled, though the little towns bled into each other after a while. "Oh gods, I don't know if I can handle another beer."

"You're hardly touching them," said Clara, amused. "I've been watching, and you never take more than a sip or two."

"A sip or two too many. It's all rice beer. And they flavor it with beach plum. I never could stand fruit beers."

"Order something else?"

"Something else is wine. Beach plum wine. Or brandy. Three guesses what it's made out of."

"Clearly you are on the horns of a dilemma."

"I hate horny dilemmas, Domina."

Clara was still trying to think of a response when Istvhan swept through the door to suffer another round of beach plum.

In the end, it took six inns before they got a lead of any interest. Clara ended up talking to a barmaid who said that her brother had nearly been taken by two men, not a monster, and if you asked her, it was a couple of killers working together. "All that stuff about a beast is just a bag of moonshine. People don't want to think regular people are capable of that kind of thing."

"I imagine, working here, you've seen a lot of what people are capable of," said Clara.

"Have I *ever*." Her voice was heavy with disillusionment. Clara put her age at about twenty and felt positively antediluvian.

"Two men could be the smooth men," said Istvhan afterward. "Or just a regular pair of killers, naturally."

"Naturally."

Istvhan rubbed his forehead. "Let's get dinner at this next one," he suggested. "It's getting late enough that people are coming in for the evening and that's a lot of beach plum to suffer through on an empty stomach."

The seventh inn served rice, crayfish, and pickled beach plums. Clara smothered a laugh. The crayfish, at least, was excellent. "Shall we call it a night?" she asked, stealing the beach plums off Istvhan's plate. "Or one more?"

"One more," said Istvhan.

Clara suspected that left to his own devices, Istvhan would keep saying "one more," until dawn or beach plum poisoning, whichever came first. *Oh well, if he keeps going too long, I'll tell him I'm tired and need a break. And better plums than necromancers...*

"One more," said Istvhan, two hours later.

"This is the third 'one more' we've done," said Clara. She sounded amused more than annoyed. "Do I have to hit you over the head to make you call it a night?"

"Possibly." Istvhan didn't want to add that if they stopped at an inn, they'd have to get either a room or two rooms, and he didn't know which it was going to be and was a little afraid to find out. *If it's two rooms, then I have to worry that she'll decide I decided I wasn't interested after all, and if it's one room, then...well...either it would go very very well or very very awkwardly.*

He had never particularly minded making a fool of himself, but Clara...well, Clara *mattered*.

He glanced over at her as she walked beside him. Twilight was already spreading in the shadows of the buildings and starting to creep into the street. Her skin seemed luminous in the dim light and the cloak added bulk to her shoulders, making her the same size as Istvhan. In a world that was often too small for him, where chairs and beds were never quite large enough, Clara seemed like an expatriate from a shared homeland, from some country he could not remember but very much wanted to visit.

She turned her face toward him, a questioning smile on her lips. Probably she was about to ask where the next inn was. Probably he should kiss her and keep on kissing her until there was never any question of his interest.

Her eyes met his and she must have read something there, because something flickered in her gaze. Her smile grew more puzzled and a line deepened between her eyes.

"Hey, young man! Wait!"

An old man came hobbling after them. He had a seamed face and walked with a cane.

"Can I help you?" asked Istvhan politely, sensing that the moment had passed.

The man shrugged. "Not a question of help," he said, gesturing back towards the inn they had come from. "Heard some of the stories that those fools were feeding you about the Beast. Wasn't that way at all."

"You saw the Beast yourself?" asked Clara.

He looked over at her. "Aye, but no one listens to me. Saw it the night before that first girl was taken. Didn't know what it was. Everybody tells stories after it got famous, but me, I saw it long before then. And got laughed at for my pains." He spat on the ground.

"No laughing here," said Istvhan. "I'd rather hear from someone who saw it before they had an idea in their head what they were supposed to be seeing."

The old man pointed his cane at Istvhan. "Yes. Exactly! And it was a Beast. Anyone who says they saw a man didn't see what I saw. Nor was it a wolf, either. That was just foolishness."

"A bear?" said Clara, in a voice so neutral that Istvhan could feel his ears turning beige.

"Pff. A bear'd do no such thing. Maybe if it had the hydrophobia, but it wouldn't last more than a week. No, the thing I saw..." His voice dropped and he looked around. "I lived in the next town over then. My daughter's man, he hauled pottery for a living back then. Was coming back with him one night late and I saw a thing I've never seen afore or since."

Clara and Istvhan both leaned forward. The old man's eyes sparkled appreciatively. Istvhan wondered how long it had been since he'd had such a rapt audience.

"It went on all fours but it didn't move right. Had a limp, not like mine here, but like all its legs were wrong. Like a spider that got half-swatted, still crawling around. Thin legs, and a thick body, like that. Maybe the size of a sheep, nothing like a bear. And there was something coming out of its back, and you'll say I was drunk but I wasn't. I was helping my daughter's man, and you don't drink when you got fragile cargo." He studied their faces, and must have decided that they weren't going to claim he was drunk. "Sounds mad, but I swear by the River Giant, it had some kind of face on its back. That was its head, the thing on its back, not where you'd expect an animal to have a head."

"A face?" Istvhan and Clara glanced at each other. "Can you tell us more?"

"Aye. It was the next town over, though on the far side of it.

Picking up a delivery at the old porcelain works, we were. The road wound around, away from the river, because there's a mucky spot there, an oxbow lake filled in with trees. Can't take a wagon through it. My daughter's man, Sing, stopped to repack some dishes, said they were clinking too much and were near to breaking. I stepped into the trees to tend to some personal business, begging your pardon, young lady—"

Clara grinned. "I've occasionally had to attend to such business myself, sir."

"—well, you know, then. It was in a patch of trees that I saw it. Moving like a crushed spider, one leg at a time and dragging some of the others sideways. I saw it and it saw me and it came rushing at me as fast as it could, and then it was a race, because I had a bum leg then too." He slapped the side of his thigh. "I got to the wagon yelling at Sing to forget the damn dishes and he looked up and saw it coming. Then he let out a yell too and jumped in the wagon, and a damn good thing, because the donkey wasn't having any of it. Took off faster than I'd ever seen that animal move, and I'd known her from a foal." He shuddered. "I looked back and saw it standing there in the road, one side of it kind of slumped over, and that face on its back staring at me. Donkey didn't slow down until we were nearly at the river. Only lost one set of dishes, though."

Istvhan exhaled, mind whirling. The old man looked back and forth between them. "It's true," he said. "I know how it sounds. My son-in-law saw it too, although he's three years in the grave and can't tell you himself."

"No, no," said Clara hurriedly, "we believe you. We...uh..."

"Saw something like that once ourselves," said Istvhan, coming to the rescue. "Not here. A long way away, on the other side of the mountains."

It was the old man's turn to lean in. "Never say so! When?"

"Five years ago," said Istvhan, pulling the number out of thin air. "After the Beast left here."

The old man exhaled through his nose. "Did it kill anyone there?" he asked bleakly.

It was that bleakness, as much as the story of a head on a creature's back, that inclined Istvhan to believe the man's tale. Most of
what he'd been told had been from people vying to describe how
huge and horrible the Beast was, and every death added weight to
their story. The more deaths, the better the story, as long as the
deaths were far away in time or distance.

Clara looked at him, waiting for him to answer.

"A few people," said Istvhan. "A...a man I knew killed it. The body
was already dead, you see, but the head was a magic thing riding it.
He smashed it." Which was the truth, or close enough, and no sense
saying that it had only been one of the saint-knew-how-many others.

Their informant let out a long, long breath. "Thank the gods," he
said. "Thank the River Giant. I tell you, young man, I haven't slept
that well since that night, thinking it was still out there."

"We're trying to find out where it came from," said Clara. "Can
you tell us anything more about where you saw it?"

The old man considered. "The delivery was from the old porcelain works, like I said. They're out of business now — one fell to the
Beast and his husband couldn't go on after that. Took the heart out of
him. A couple little houses, though I don't know if anybody's still in
them. The only other thing on that road is Stachys's pottery." He
rubbed the side of his nose. "Odd one, Stachys. Some people know
more than they let on, but him...I think he knows less than he actually knows, if you understand me."

"Slow?" asked Istvhan, wondering what the local euphemisms
were and how to navigate them.

"Not exactly. Not so you'd call him simple, like. You could tell him
you were sick and he'd say he was sorry to hear it, and then you'd
have to tell him that meant you weren't coming to pick up a load
because he wouldn't connect the two. He wasn't mean, he just
couldn't put two and two together. Knew his way around clay,
though."

"You think he might have seen the Beast, though?"

The old man shrugged helplessly. "Maybe. It was in that area.
Whether he's still alive, or if he'd think to connect whatever he saw to

the Beast, though, your guess is as good as mine." He shook his head. "There's not much left out that way anymore. I hear tell of odd people coming and going sometimes, though, so be careful if you do wander that direction. Could be no more than a drifter or two down on their luck, but it wouldn't be the first time a band of thieves made use of one of the old potteries as a base of operations. I'd be on your guard."

"Always," said Istvhan, and meant it.

CHAPTER 32

"What do you think?" asked Clara softly, as they took the road around the oxbow lake. It was just as the old man had described, although in even worse repair. It was well and truly dark now, and although Clara went through life with the understanding that she was easily the most dangerous thing in the woods, there was still something here that made her want to whisper.

"Matches up with what Doc Mason told us," said Istvhan. "And the face in the creature's back, that screams smooth man to me. If one's body fell apart and the only thing left for it was to put it on an animal, I could see it. But then again, who knows? It's been nearly a decade. And we know they can work anywhere with a big enough kiln, so they may have left."

"And after a decade, there may not be anything left to find." Clara frowned. "Though nobody would have made the connection to clay and potteries back then, so possibly we could turn something up. The old porcelain works, perhaps? Or this Stachys person?"

"Porcelain works first, I think."

Armed with the old man's directions, they continued along the curve of the road. Dead leaves rustled in the copse of trees, and Clara heard a twig snap. Even knowing that it wasn't nearly loud enough for anything human-sized, it made her nerves tingle. *Don't be absurd. What, do you think they're putting clay heads on squirrels now?*

The mental image should have been funny, but wasn't. She wished she hadn't thought of it.

Istvhan looked over his shoulder at the woods.

"I could change," she suggested. "If you're worried about something there."

"Mmm. Realistically, there can't really be any predator big enough to require that, is there? I'm just twitchy. Too many ambushes in the last month."

Clara chuckled. Istvhan smiled, but looked back over his shoulder again. "That said...do you have the energy to change and then change back? I'm wondering about the smells."

"I should be okay." Clara handed him her pack and slid her cloak off her shoulders. He averted his eyes as she undressed, which she found somewhat amusing. "You always look away when I do this," she said. "Is the change that unsettling?"

"I've never gotten a good look," he said, surprising her. "It seems like I should be able to see it happen but somehow I don't. You stand up a bit and then there's a shadow and then you're a bear."

She paused, holding her robe up to her chest. "That's what it looks like when my sisters change too. I've seen it hundreds of times, and I miss it every time. I can usually feel it coming on before someone else does it, and I still never catch it."

"Oh?" He met her eyes, keeping his gaze on her face. "What does it feel like?"

"The beast wakes a little. As if it senses someone coming. It's how we teach the novices not to change in their sleep. As soon as your beast starts to mutter, you dump a glass of water on whatever girl is about to go over."

"What if someone doesn't plan to change? Can you do it spontaneously?"

"Yes, although usually I have to be panicked or angry. And then you don't get any warning, which is dangerous, because the beast doesn't like surprises, and another bear suddenly appearing is very surprising. Right, I'm getting cold. One moment." She tossed the robe to him and asked the beast to come forward.

The world got brighter and then the smells covered everything — river, swamp, mud, tree, small animal, dry grass. The mud here had a thick algal scent, a gray-brown taste of clay. And Istvhan, of course, a beacon of metal and leather and sweat and ginger muscle rub and a trace of plum. (The bear didn't understand humor, but Clara laughed internally.)

Nothing like the burnt carrion scent of the clay men. She changed back, shaking her head. Istvhan held out her robe and she stepped into it.

"If it isn't the change that bothers you," she said, as he dropped the robe lightly around her shoulders, "why do you never look?"

His breath touched the back of her neck like a caress. "I would like to very much," he murmured, "but you've never given me permission."

What the hell is wrong with me? thought Clara, pulling on the cloak. *Love or not, I should have been riding this man until we both walked funny.* But not in the middle of the woods. Certainly not in the middle of swampy woods, while they hunted monsters.

Still.

She caught his eye briefly, and the hunger there was so raw that she felt as if she'd drunk cheap whiskey, something that burned all the way down to her toes. "Right," she said, clearing her throat. "Probably another hour to moonrise. Where's this porcelain place? I'd rather not be out here fumbling around all night."

The porcelain works was overgrown with weeds, the main building in disrepair. It looked as if someone had carefully tidied up, sold all the fixtures, and then simply walked away and let time and weather take its toll. Possibly that was exactly what had happened. There was nothing to indicate that anything strange had ever taken place there. There was a large brick kiln, now home to bats, and a wasp nest had grown over the door to the little house beside it.

"Not promising," said Istvhan.

"No. I can't imagine the bats staying too close to anything that smelled like those corpses we found." She rubbed the back of her neck. "On the other hand, I doubt the smooth men are hanging out close to the main roads, either. Let's go back into the trees a little way and I'll try smelling again."

Istvhan nodded. He let her lead the way, scanning the darkness, and reached out reflexively to take her robe when she stopped. Clara held on to it for a moment and he looked toward her, surprised.

I'm probably mad, she thought, feeling giddy and absurdly euphoric. *I'm much too old to feel this way.* "Istvhan," she said, letting her end drop, "you have permission to look."

He inhaled sharply. She saw his nostrils flare and his eyes go wide. And then he *did* look at her, drinking in the sight that he'd been studiously avoiding so long. His gaze lingered over her breasts, dropped lower, and Clara could actually feel a blush starting. *Blessed St. Ursa, it's as bad as losing my virginity, except I'm sagging in a lot more places.*

"Seen enough?" she asked.

"Not nearly," he said. His voice was rough with desire. "I could look at you all night. But you should probably change before I'm not able to stop at just looking."

The bear came forward, grumbling that mating season was in spring, not fall. Clara stifled an internal sigh and told it to sniff.

The world smelled of mud and water and trees and Istvhan. She was about to tell the bear to go back again when the breeze carried something to her nose, something that smelled of rot and burning.

There! That! Follow that smell!

The bear was unconvinced. It was a bad smell. Why would anyone go toward it? Clara exerted her will over the matter and the bear, grumbling under its breath, went forward.

"Do you have something?" asked Istvhan.

"Hrwuf."

"One of these days," said the paladin, following her, "we shall have to work out a system. One hrwuff for yes, two for no, that sort of thing."

"Grrrrr..."

"That sounded like a no."

"Hrwuf."

"See, now I have no idea what you're saying...wait, you're panting? Are you laughing? Do bears laugh?"

"Hrwuf!"

"This is all very complicated."

The smell got stronger. There was no path here now, which did not particularly bother the bear. The undergrowth was mostly tall, reedy grasses, which bent easily as the bear passed. Clara knew from experience that she was leaving a trail as wide as an ox, but there was nothing much to be done about it. The smell grew stronger and the bear dropped its head, pulling its lips back in disgust.

She came out of the bear shape easily, even though the world spun around her and she had to take a minute before she could climb to her feet. "Are you all right?" asked Istvhan.

"Too many changes. I'll be fine. I should probably eat something, but that smell..."

"I can just make it out myself, but I can't tell where it's coming from."

Clara nodded. Istvhan held her robe up and she shoved her arms through the sleeves. His fingers brushed the tops of her shoulders and it occurred to her suddenly how very careful he had been to drop the fabric onto her before, rather than touch her skin. This time, his fingertips lingered just a little, sliding up her collarbone before he released her.

I'm just woozy from the changes, she told herself firmly, which was absolutely a lie. She scrubbed at her nose with the side of her hand, which was one of the least sexy gestures a human was capable of making. "It's ahead of us. I think this is older than the one we found in the woods, though." Istvhan nodded.

The reeds were much more annoying as a human. The leaves had sharp edges that dragged at her skin and promised her the mother of all papercuts. Istvhan took point, shoving the leaves aside. "I can still do that," she said. "It's just grass."

"I'm wearing armor."

"Fine, be logical about it."

They emerged from the grass into a clearing, surrounding a large building. It resembled the pottery works they had seen before, with a large chimney and piles of broken crockery. Weeds grew up wherever the earth had not been packed hard, and the chimney was cold and quiet, but there was a light on inside.

"Somebody's home," murmured Istvhan.

"The smooth men have been here," said Clara. "But I can't tell you how long ago, or if they're here now."

"They might be here, but haven't made a new one for a while. The smell, whatever it is, seems very strong when they switch hosts."

"Do they need lights?"

"We're not entirely sure. Piper, the one doctor who examined one, said that he thinks the eyes are the same clay as the rest and they see with their whole head somehow."

"...I dislike that immensely."

"Yes, we all do." He gestured to the door. "Shall we see who's home?"

"Let me eat something first. If I need to change again, I'm going to want something more substantial in my stomach."

"The beach plums aren't cutting it?"

"I could *murder* a beach plum about now."

Istvhan dug through his pack and pulled out one of the ration bars. "This is the last one I've got. Remind me to stock up in town."

Clara wolfed it down and felt the hollowness in her gut ease a bit. "That's better. Normally I'd carry some, but then again, normally I'm not changing four or five times a night."

Istvhan nodded. He waited until she was done, put his hand on his sword, and went up and knocked on the door.

The man who answered did not say "Hello?" or "Excuse me?" or "What are you doing here at this ungodly hour of the night?" or any of the things that one might expect a person to say when a nun and a paladin knocked on his door after moonrise. Instead, he stared at them with a puzzled air, as if he knew them from somewhere and couldn't quite place them.

"I'm sorry to disturb you," Istvhan began.

"Oh," said the man in the doorway. "Oh, you're...people, aren't you?"

Clara did not like the implications of that at all. She eyed the man's face but he was certainly not one of the smooth men. No sculptor could have ever recreated the looseness of his skin in clay, the way that it hung like wet parchment from his face and gathered in folds at his neck. He looked desperately sick, and yet his arm, braced against the door frame, was corded with muscle that rivaled Istvhan's. Clara's eyes traveled down the heavy line of tendon and sinew to the middle of his forearms, which were wrapped in rags. The rags were spattered with dry clay. The man's pants were also covered in dry clay, in long splashing lines up the insides of his thighs.

Istvhan was a trifle quicker on the uptake than Clara. "You're a potter, aren't you?" he said.

"For my sins." The man took a step back. "You...you're not from the..." He paused, made a vague back-and-forth gesture above his eyes. "I'm sorry," he said after a moment. "I'm not as good with words as I used to be. Come in, I think. If you're safe." He stepped back from the door.

"*Are* we safe?" asked Clara in an undertone.

"From him, probably. *For* him, probably not." Istvhan put his hand on the hilt of his sword and stepped inside the doorway.

Nothing immediately jumped at him. Clara watched as the lines of his back relaxed fractionally. He stepped aside and gestured to her. "Clear."

The room beyond was covered in gray-brown dust. Shelves lined every wall, covered in pots and bowls, stacks of parchment, discarded clothes and withered plants that had not been watered for a long time. There was a table with a single chair, and a low bed by the hearth. A door in the far wall, if Clara was not completely turned around, led to the large studio they'd seen from outside.

The potter was moving around the room, trying to set out mugs and find chairs for them, but he was clearly having a difficult time. He would pick up a mug, put it down, and then seem to forget what he had been doing. "Guests," he muttered. "Guests. I'm sorry. I haven't had real guests in a long time. *They* don't drink, you know. Not water, not wine. Although sometimes if it's very dry, they have to dip their heads in water. They get disconnected if they dry out. Like a plant's roots, I think. It needs a little water where it presses against the soil." He paused, a mug forgotten in his hands. "Unless they changed that, too. They keep making improvements. But he doesn't tell me anything, he just brings me the design. Once I make it, he takes it away, and then they cast the molds themselves. Or that's how it used to work. I don't know now."

Clara and Istvhan traded looks again. "He?" asked Clara, trying to keep her voice pleasant and not accusing.

"Him. You know. You must know, you're here." The potter looked down at his hands, saw the mug, and smiled. "There, that's three. We'll have some wine."

He took a stoneware jug from a shelf by the door. Those shelves looked marginally cleaner, and Clara saw a few glass jars among the ceramics. Sardines in oil. Pickled eggs. *Someone is bringing him food,* she thought, *or perhaps he is going to the market.*

"Are you Stachys?" asked Istvhan.

"Yes. Yes, of course. Didn't I tell you? No, I might not have. I'm sorry, my mind's not what it was." He smiled up at them.

Istvhan found a low bench without anything on it and carefully moved it to the table. "May we sit?"

"Yes. Yes, I should have offered." Stachys took the chair. "What brings you visiting?"

Clara sat down on the bench next to Istvhan. Given their heights and the size of the table, it was not as uncomfortable as it might have been. She rested her elbows comfortably on the tabletop. "We were hoping that you could tell us more about...ah...*Him.*"

CHAPTER 33

"I sculpted a bust at first," said Stachys. "I mostly make...I made... bowls and cups and things. I wanted to sculpt but you can't make a living as a sculptor, not unless you have a patron. I didn't have one. I'm not very good at talking to people. I wasn't then, either. Better than I am now, of course." He paused, looking guilty. "I'm not blaming him, you understand. He didn't mean to do it."

"Didn't mean to do what?" asked Istvhan, in a voice so gentle that Clara could hardly believe it was coming from a man that she had personally seen gut an enemy on his sword like a rabbit.

"He didn't know how people worked." Stachys looked embarrassed, then turned his head and lifted up the side of his hair. Clara caught a glimpse of a red scar, long healed, and a place where the skull bent inward in a manner that human skulls were not meant to do. She inhaled sharply.

"He didn't mean it," said Stachys, letting his hair fall back into place. "He just got frustrated. He thought I was clay, like him, and I could just fix the spot. He didn't know that humans didn't work the same way."

"No, of course not," said Istvhan, still in that gentle, inexorable voice, like snow falling. "He learned, though."

"Yes. He learns so fast. Faster than I do, now." Stachys laughed, a little too loudly, and took another drink of wine.

"So he was a bust," said Clara, trying to hold up her end. She suspected her voice wasn't as gentle as Istvhan's. Maybe it was a paladin thing. "At first."

Stachys nodded enthusiastically. "Yes. I made him." He wiped his hand across his mouth. "I was lonely. I didn't mind making bowls, but I was tired of not making anything else. So I made a bust and I talked to him. And I thought...oh, I can't really remember now. The old story, though, you remember? The sculptor makes a statue of a woman, and he loves her, and she comes to life because he loves her?"

"I love that story," said Istvhan.

"Me too." Stachys sighed, focusing on the mug in front of him, tapping the rim over and over. "Oh, me too."

"So then did he come to life?"

"Not at first. I did something. I think I did something. Or maybe someone else came and offered to do something?" His face screwed up, and he rubbed the side of his head. "There was a man, I think. Unless that happened later. I'm sorry. It was a long time ago, I think?"

"It's all right," said Istvhan. "I'm just curious. He is very impressive, isn't he?"

Stachys beamed. "I think so," he said. "Although..." His brow knotted with sudden worry, every emotion passing across his face as clearly as a child's. "I worry sometimes. I know he's smarter than me, since then. But I don't know what he does when he's not here." He stood up, consumed with sudden, jittery energy, and began prowling among the shelves, looking for something. "Did you tell me your names? I can't remember now."

"Yes," said Istvhan, before Clara could speak. "But it doesn't matter. We can tell you again if you forget. But tell me, what happened after he came to life?"

Stachys groaned. "I did it," he said. "I loved a statue and it came to life. I was proud. I was so proud of him. But I hadn't thought. You can't just make a bust. If you make a bust, they're stuck. Just a head. He wanted a body. A whole body. I tried to make him one. I really did, but..." He dropped back in his chair, abandoning whatever he'd been searching for. "I couldn't make it work. I could make a body, but it didn't do anything. I tried to put him in it, but the clay was just other clay. It wouldn't come alive. Then he got frustrated and he bit me." Stachys shook his head, seemingly less angry than bemused. "I hadn't even sculpted teeth. But he had them." He rubbed the side of his head again, and Clara pictured one of the smooth men, sitting on a pedestal, unhinging its jaw and taking a chunk out of the side of someone's skull. She shuddered.

"I'm amazed you survived," she said.

"Oh, me too. I nearly didn't. I was on the floor for hours. I think he called for help, but of course he couldn't talk to the neighbors. They wouldn't have understood at all. But one of my neighbors, the sweet woman who brought us goat milk, she found me and she patched me up. And when I came back, he was still waiting for me, just like he had been. And he was so kind. He felt terrible."

"Of course," said Istvhan. "He didn't understand about the bodies." He squeezed Clara's arm under the table and she took the hint to let him take the lead. "But you did manage to give him a body, didn't you?"

Stachys hung his head. "It wasn't good," he said. "It wasn't sculpting. He said he was done with that. He thought flesh would work. After he'd had mine, he said he could bring it to life. It was still hanging off his lips when I came back. Just a chunk of bone and hair by then, but he could make the skin flex like it was alive. So he asked me to kill someone and bring him the body, but I wouldn't. I wouldn't!" His throat worked as if there was more he wanted to say, but the words wouldn't come.

"I know you wouldn't," said Istvhan, in the soft paladin's voice.

"I bought a goat carcass at the market. I had to sew the bust into it, the base, and it was top-heavy, but it worked. He made it walk back and forth. It was dead, but it wasn't dead. He made it run away, and I didn't see him for days. I thought he was gone."

Clara had a sudden sense of what had to be coming next and reached for the wine to dull it.

"He came back, though."

"He came back," said Stachys. "He was excited. He said he had found a better body." He stared into his mug. "She used to bring me goat milk," he added dully.

Istvhan squeezed her hand again, perhaps feeling the way that her skin had crawled with sudden gooseflesh.

"So then he had a human body," said Istvhan. "But it didn't end there, did it?"

Stachys shook his head. "He wanted more like him. He was lonely. I should have been enough for him. He was enough for me. But he said I didn't love him after he killed her, and he needed someone of his own. Someone like him. He said I owed him, since I made him. You can't just make one of something, like some kind of fool god."

"And you made more of the clay heads."

"I made him promise not to kill anyone else," said Stachys. "I did. He swore. But he got a body from the graveyard, and I made the second head for it." An old, familiar bafflement seemed to cross his face. "I didn't love that one," he admitted, as if admitting to a great sin. "I know I was supposed to. But he kissed it and then it was alive too. Then he wanted another one, then another..." He put his face in his hands.

"You had to start making molds," said Istvhan.

"Once I'd done the first one, they figured it out. How to pour the slip and fire it. They got another body from the graveyard. Her body had worn out by then, but he came back with a new one. He said it was a criminal who'd been hanged. He *said.*"

"I'm sure he did," said Istvhan, hearing his voice roughen just a little as horror fought to get through. *Don't think about it. Just keep talking.*

"I had to make the molds. It didn't work if they did it."

"Because you had the talent."

"No, no." He shook his head, so wildly that his hair struck him in the face. "No, no. Because of love. You can't bring anything alive unless you love it. That's what the story is about, you know?"

"Yes, of course," said Istvhan. "That's what the story is about."

"You said you didn't love the second one," said Clara gently. She couldn't do the voice, but she could come close. "Did you love the molds?"

"No." Stachys hung his head. "No, I didn't. But I loved him. I loved him, so I could make things that made him happy, and it was like love. I didn't want to kill anyone, that's all. I just wanted to make things." He frowned. "He was angry that none of them could talk. I couldn't make them talk. I tried, but I couldn't. One of the molds, though, those could laugh. It wasn't good. I stopped doing that." He took a large swallow of wine and stared at the table. "Did you tell me your names?"

"Yes," said Istvhan. "And you're Stachys."

"Yes...yes of course..." The man's mild blue eyes were clouded. "He lied about the other bodies being from a graveyard, didn't he?" he said quietly.

"I'm afraid he did," said Istvhan.

"People think it would be amazing to create a living thing," Stachys mused. "But then they do things and it's your fault because you made them..." The potter shook his head. "I don't know how people have children. How they don't go mad from it."

"You gave him life," said Istvhan. "Can you take it away again?"

"Oh no," said Stachys. "I tried once. Didn't I?" He frowned at Istvhan. "I'm sorry...I forgot your name."

"It's all right." The paladin's voice was achingly trustworthy, and the line across Stachys's forehead eased. "I'll remind you later. What happened when you tried to take the life away?"

"Oh," said the potter. He darted a quick, embarrassed look downward, then lifted his rag-wrapped wrists. "That's when they took my hands."

Istvhan stared at the potter's hands and for a moment, he could not speak. He had been so busy thinking of the smooth men as clay heads that he had never considered anything else.

But there they were. Hands the same pale stoneware color as the smooth men's faces, flexing in the same impossible fashion. Someone had carved tendons in the back, made perfect renderings of the nails. An incredible sculptor, or...

"Those were molded from your real hands, weren't they?" said Clara softly.

Stachys nodded. "I made them years ago, for a set of sculptures. He found the mold. He thought maybe if he had my hands, he could sculpt. He couldn't, though. They can't. They can make heads from the molds, but they can't design a new one. It never comes alive." He gave a short, bleak laugh. "Faces are hard."

"So he took them and gave you the copies." It was hard for Istvhan to say that in the paladin's voice, in the soothing, gentle tones that they all learned. It was the voice you used when you were trying to calm someone who had just watched their village be slaughtered before their eyes, the voice you used on survivors, the voice you used to try and talk someone down before anyone else was hurt.

You learned to do it early, until it was second nature. The Saint of Steel's chosen were good at it. Not as good as the paladins of the Dreaming God, who could use it in imperative mode and drive demons to their knees, but good enough for most things.

He had never had to use it to talk to a man who had unleashed a wave of murderous golems across a continent, and who was looking at him with such pained, cloudy eyes.

"Yes," said Stachys. He rubbed one of the alien hands across the back of the other, and the sound was a soft clink of fired pottery. "He was so angry. He wanted not to need me anymore. But now no one can make the molds. So they just keep making the same faces, over and over again."

"How long does a mold last?" asked Istvhan.

"My molds? Many dozens of casts," said Stachys proudly. "The outsides aren't pretty, but as long as you wet them occasionally, they'll last years. The only time they break is if somebody drops one." His smile faded. "The last one I made...that one's not good. The plaster's fine, but I was angry. It was wrong to make it. After that, he started trying to make his own." He stared down at the clay hands, the fingers moving smooth and knuckleless as he tapped on the table.

All this time, he could have been making hands for people who lost them, thought Istvhan wearily. *Probably legs or arms, too. Instead we get a murderous set of statuary, and now he can't work the clay at all.*

Clara was looking at him, eyes intent. Waiting for him to make a decision? Waiting for him to kill this poor fool where he stood?

Instead Istvhan rose and bowed to Stachys. "It has been good to meet you," he said. "Thank you so much for your hospitality."

"Yes, of course," said the potter, rising as well. He bobbed his head. "Come back any time. I get so few visitors. Would you like to buy a statue?"

"Perhaps next time," said Istvhan, who would have gnawed off his own hands before having one of Stachys's works in his home. "I'm sure we'll see you again."

CHAPTER 34

"Well," said Clara. "Well." She looked over at Istvhan. "Do you believe him?"

"Oh yes," said Istvhan. "I believe him. At best guess, he's a powerful wonderworker. Or was. Might still be, though if he can no longer sculpt, perhaps his ability to channel it is gone."

"What a bizarre talent to have," said Clara, staring into the darkness. "Though I suppose you could go your whole life without realizing you had it."

Istvhan smiled painfully. "Much like being a berserker. That doctor I know has a theory that we're all wonderworkers, but circumstances never conspire to reveal our talent to most of us." Doctor Piper was an odd person, but he knew more about the smooth men than Istvhan himself.

Clara shook her head slowly. "Well. What do we do, then? Kill him?"

Istvhan winced. "That would probably be safest," he admitted. "There's a chance his constructs might fall apart if we did. Most wonderworkers can't create things that outlast their death."

"But you don't want to."

The paladin couldn't meet her eyes. "It used to be so easy," he said, half to himself. "I knew who was innocent and who was guilty at a glance. My god turned my blade aside from the innocent. Now... now I don't know at all. I've killed plenty of men who were trying to kill me, but this would be murder." He pictured the blade sliding into flesh, the confused eyes clouding over even further. *You're a paladin. You do what needs to be done so that others may live. That's what you're for. You're a weapon in the hand of the gods, that's all.*

Most weapons didn't have a conscience. Istvhan's sword wouldn't wake up at night, sweating, remembering what he'd had to do. Wondering if he had, in truth, been a servant of justice at all or if the god's vision had been as clouded as a mortal's.

"I can do it," said Clara.

"Can you?" He was surprised at how he sounded, mildly curious, as if she'd just informed him that she could wiggle her ears.

"I won't enjoy it," she said. "And I don't know that I could use the bear to do it. The bear won't think he's a threat. But if it comes to that, I can probably beat his head in to save hundreds of innocent people."

Nuns were always more practical than paladins. *And would you let her do it, because you were too weak? Could you stand out here and be shamed and grateful while she kills some poor fool too damaged to remember your name?*

"What did you used to do with complicated cases?" asked Clara.

"We turned them over to more complicated people."

"Paladins aren't complicated?"

"Paladins can't afford to be complicated. We're born to do a job and not think too much about it. Gods don't choose us for our emotional complexity." And that, suddenly, sparked the solution that he should have seen already. "We can take him to the Rat."

"Can they kill him?"

"They solve problems," said Istvhan. "However those problems must be solved." He thought of Bishop Beartongue, imagined her calmly and regretfully murdering Stachys. It was surprisingly easy to do. If she'd thought it was the only way, she'd have wielded the knife herself. "It's the best solution. We've talked to him for ten minutes, and you saw what he's like. What if there's some key to defeating the smooth men that we just didn't ask about?"

"Do you think anyone will try to stop us?" asked Clara. "I don't know if he'll come willingly. We might need a wagon and a sack."

"Honestly, I'm a bit surprised the smooth men haven't tried to stop us," admitted Istvhan. "You'd think they'd keep a guard on him, just in case of—"

And the rest of what he was saying was lost, because Clara knocked him down.

The air went out of his lungs in a woosh as he hit the ground. Clara was on top of him and then she was a great deal larger and a great deal hairier. Claws dug into the earth on either side of his head. He had a sudden shocking sense of mass balanced precariously over him, and then he was looking at the underside of the bear as it launched itself at something that had been coming up behind him.

The tide rose. Istvhan fought it back reflexively, and then he saw movement. A man coming up from the opposite direction as the first, axe held high, about to bury it in the bear's back.

No! Istvhan launched himself upward and grabbed the man's leg, trying to pull him off balance.

There was a horrible moment where he registered that whatever was in his hand felt much too pulpy and soft, and then, with a wet gristly noise, he tore the man's leg clear off.

Clara saw the man coming for Istvhan only an instant before he struck. The blade was already poised and about to fall. She flung herself at Istvhan and managed to slam him down to the ground, already in mid-change as they fell. *Now!* she yelled to the beast. *Now, come forward, help!*

The beast roared through her. Changing this fast hurt, as if whatever force usually deadened the sensation lagged too slow to help. Her skin burned as hair forced through it and if she had not already been in mid-leap, she might have staggered and crushed Istvhan and saved their enemies the trouble.

The beast smashed into the figure in front of it and it exploded like an overripe fruit.

Oh god, thought Clara, gagging internally as the smell hit her. Then the beast was gagging externally as well. Bears were not above eating carrion, but this was horrific, rotten like a pumpkin left in the field until December. The stench of decayed meat mixed with the thick, burnt scent of the smooth men.

It was too much for the bear. The bear didn't like fighting and it hated that smell. It ran over the top of the fallen corpse and just kept going, down the path that the smooth man had come from, trying to get away from the stink and the horror of a dead thing that had moved like a not-dead thing and whatever it was, the bear wanted none of it.

Wait! yelled Clara inside the beast's head. *Wait, stop! We have to go back, Istvhan's in trouble! There's another one, I can hear it!*

The bear did not care. Istvhan was not a cub and the bear did not feel any need to defend him, assuming that it even registered that there was a friend there at all. If he had been another bear, then presumably he would do the sensible thing and run away as well. The bear was *done.*

Stop! Dammit, stop! Oh shit oh shit! Clara was panicking and she knew she was panicking and that meant she was losing control. She hadn't done that since she was fourteen. The abbess had turned into a gray-furred grizzly, knocked her down, and sat on her. There was no one to stop her now and the bear was running and the panic only fed into that and now the bear wanted nothing but to run, as far and as fast as its paws could carry it, and the stink was on its fur but if it ran faster, maybe it could get away from that as well—

Stop! Stop!

Her panic only fed the bear's alarm. It reached the road and swung its heavy head toward the river. The river, which would have boats, and people on boats, and all it would take was one to be awake and raise the alarm about a monstrous bear in the place where the Beast of the Leeward was once seen.

Stop! Shit!

Her internal cries went unheard. Her panic melded with the bear's fear, and for the first time in decades, Sister Clara lost control of the beast.

Istvhan had been in many battles in his life, enough that many of them had blurred together, but he had never, so far as he knew, torn anyone's limbs off before. Chopped, yes, any number of times, but ripped off bare-handed, no. Admittedly, he was a berserker and things often got very dim and confused when the black tide rose over his head, but still, you'd remember a thing like that, wouldn't you?

He certainly was never, ever going to forget the muffled *pop* as the femur came out of the socket, and the way the smooth man's leg suddenly dropped six inches. The realization that it was now being held on only by the fabric of the man's ragged trousers made his gorge rise.

The smooth man toppled sideways and backwards. Istvhan shoved down his nausea and lunged forward, still on his knees, grabbing for the axe. His hand came down on the man's wrist and he pulled and there was another set of wet popping noises, this time all the small bones of the hand and wrist coming loose — *Saint's black and bloody tongue, I'm going to be berserk* and *puking if this keeps up* — and Istvhan got the axe and most of the fingers with it.

The fingers went immediately dead as soon as they were separated from the body. Istvhan buried the axe in the smooth man's head. Pottery shards flew and the rest of the body went limp.

"Right," said Istvhan. "Right." His stomach roiled but did not rebel yet. The smell was truly extraordinary, though, and it made him no promises of further good behavior. He flung the axe aside and drew his sword, turning back to Clara.

Or, in this case, the large and notable absence of Clara. There was a smooth man who had been comprehensively dismembered and nothing else.

"Clara?" he called. "Clara, where are you?" Surely he couldn't just be overlooking a bear the size of a horse.

He saw movement in the trees behind the studio and stepped toward it. "Clara...?"

Three more smooth men emerged. Istvhan's heart sank. Had they encountered the bear already? *Don't be ridiculous, of course they haven't. They'd be deader than they already are. And they can't possibly have killed her, because you wouldn't miss a body that size.*

The thought flashed through his head of a clay head riding the bear's flesh and he stomped it down immediately. *She probably just got the hell out of the way. Or is chasing down another one.*

He lifted his sword, waiting for the clay men to come to him. The black tide was rising inside his skull, swirling around him, and he was no longer sure if he should fight it down. *Three more that I can see, and how many after that? They must have been watching the main road, not expecting us to come from the direction of the porcelain works. How many guards would I put on a man, if I suspected that his death meant that I and all my kind would die as well?*

Pain blossomed in his ankle before he could mentally answer that question. He let out an undignified yelp and kicked sideways, feeling a weight dragging at it.

It was the smooth man that had been torn apart by the bear. All that was left to it was the head and a chunk of shoulder and collarbone. It was somehow hitching itself along using the shoulder, and its mouth was wide open. And apparently it had bitten him in the ankle.

His stomach informed him that every moment it spent not vomiting was now a personal favor from the divine.

He stomped down hard on the head and felt it crunch under his heel. The crunching seemed to go on for far too long and he risked a glance over his shoulder, only to see two more smooth men behind him. *Five against one. Still no sign of Clara.*

The black tide rose higher, and this time, Istvhan let it come.

The river was a silver snake through the trees and a smell of muddy water. The bear's paws pounded on the ground, no longer even remotely under Clara's direction. *Well, this is typical,* she thought, somewhere behind the bear's eyes. *I spend weeks fretting that falling in love with Istvhan will send me over the edge, and what actually does it? A goddamn bad smell.*

She laughed. She couldn't help it. It was just so ridiculous.

And with the laughter came a resigned calm, and the calm spread to the bear. The headlong flight became a ground-eating lope, and while Clara could not stop the beast, she thought perhaps that she could steer it.

"The key," the abbess had said, decades ago, "the key is to use the beast's instincts to your advantage."

Right. She spotted a likely looking target and aimed the bear's mind at it. *There.* That *will be safe.*

It is a common myth that grizzly bears cannot climb trees. They can. Their claws and sheer mass make it difficult, but given a big enough tree and a determined enough bear, they can get surprisingly far into the branches.

The tree in this case was a squat, sturdy oak, gnarled by the wind off the river, with a massive trunk and a rather short crown. The bear went up it, tearing off great slabs of bark, and finally settled about fifteen feet off the ground.

Clara waited.

The bear groomed itself like an ungainly cat, raking its claws through its fur, trying to get the horrible smell off. The burnt stuff tasted even worse than it smelled. The bear snorted, shaking its head.

Clara continued to wait.

Perhaps half an hour later, when the bear's sides had stopped heaving and its heart had slowed, Clara sent an experimental tendril of thought. *Back?* she suggested. *Human?*

The bear was wary of this. Being human had gotten it a face full of rotten meat and bad smells. Not even *good* rotten, but so rotten that not even a wolverine would touch it.

Clara pointed out that her human nose was numb and stupid and would not smell the rot nearly as strongly. The bear allowed that this was the case and began to slowly inch down the tree, backwards.

Clara pulled her mind back to allow the bear to handle the descent. Its claws might make it clumsy, but it was still infinitely better at it than Clara-the-human would be. Instead, she thought of the smooth man and the speed at which it had moved. For some reason, she had thought that they would be slow. They must be slow, because the flesh was rotting and so surely they could not be fast or particularly strong. She had not expected it to move as swiftly as a human, nor to wield its weapon as if it weighed nothing.

There had been at least one more there, and Istvhan had been prone on the ground. Had she tried to save his life, and by doing so, doomed him?

Her fear bled over and the bear stopped, claws deep in the bark.

Calm, she told herself. *Calm.* And to the bear, *Keep going.* Whatever had happened, it was long past and fear would not help anyone. She recited a catechism in her head and the bear, comforted by familiarity, resumed its descent.

CHAPTER 35

Istvhan was in a foul mood. He'd come out of the berserker fit when there was nothing left to kill, and then had to check each of the corpses to make sure they were genuinely dead. His ankle still throbbed where the head had bitten him. *It's better than checking the corpses to make sure there aren't innocent bystanders, at least.* Stachys hadn't come out to see what the commotion was, thankfully, and god only knew where Clara was. *Probably far away from this stench, if she's got any sense.* These smooth men had been *rank.*

His body ached. When the black tide rose, you forgot that you were middle-aged, forgot that your muscles and tendons had limits, forgot that pain was anything but a goad to spur you on to greater carnage. Then the tide receded and you were left in your body with all the strained ligaments and screaming muscles. The Saint had buffered his paladins from the worst effects when He was alive, but there wasn't a damn thing for Istvhan to do about it now, except slather on muscle rub and hope that he'd be somewhere safe enough to take a dose of poppy milk when he had to sleep.

Clara's absence worried him more than he wanted to admit, even though it was a damn good thing that she'd gotten out of range. But if there had been other smooth men about...no, the bear was clearly more than capable of handling one, it was just that it had been nearly an hour and she wasn't back. Was she expecting him to meet her at an inn? He cursed himself for not having set up a meeting point with her in case they got separated. That was basic planning and he hadn't done it because...because...well, because he was walking on eggshells trying not to demand anything from her, trying not to sound as if he had a right to dictate her behavior. *And this is what thinking with your cock gets you. You're so hopeful of getting laid that you forget things that a raw recruit would remember.* He grumbled to himself, annoyed at his own foolishness.

"Istvhan?"

He turned, his grumbling and soreness forgotten in a wave of relief. Clara stood on the path, looking none the worse for wear, although she was wearing a coating of mud and gore and not much else.

"Clara!" He ran toward her and swept her up in his arms, or tried. Given their respective sizes, it became more of a very enthusiastic hug. "You're alive," he said, not even caring that his nose was mashed against the side of her head.

"So are you!" They clung together in the middle of the path and eventually it reoccurred to Istvhan that she was naked, although that was, admittedly, somewhat eclipsed by the fact that she stank.

She released him with a shaky laugh. "I'm covered in horrible gunk."

"So am I," he said. "Stachys has to have a pump or a well or something. Let's see if we can find it."

"How is he?"

"Didn't come out at all. It's for the best."

She sobered. "Istvhan — I'm so sorry."

"Sorry? For what?"

"For running and leaving you behind. I tried to stop the bear, but it really prefers not to fight most of the time, and having that one just...come apart like that...was too much for it." The moon was bright enough for him to see her flush, and to note that it began somewhere around her neck and spread out in both directions. He would have liked to consider how far down it went, but the smell on both of them hit him again and he grimaced.

"It's for the best," he said. "The battle madness came on me, and it doesn't always subside merely because I'm out of enemies." He spotted an aged pump handle and pointed. "Look, water."

There was a look in her eye that made him think that the conversation was not quite over yet, but the promise of getting clean overrode any other concern. They took turns working the pump while the other one sluiced the worst of the muck off themselves.

A beautiful woman bathing by moonlight should have been extremely erotic, but the fact was that it was very cold and he ached and also there was nothing sexy about the contortions that either of them had to make to get properly clean. Even if he had maintained any sort of arousal, the frigid water from the pump would have put it to flight.

"I fear my robe is a loss, again," Clara said, holding up the offending piece of clothing. "It tried its best, but there's only so much mending to be done."

"You'd think your order would have designed breakaway robes by now."

"Believe it or not, we often go for years at a time without having to suddenly turn into a large animal. It rarely comes up in day-to-day life." She reached into the pocket and fished out the acorns that Brant had given her.

"Half a moment," said Istvhan. He shook wet hair out of his face and dug through his pack. There was a large, lumpy package at the bottom, taking up space that had previously been occupied by field rations. "It's not much, but you won't cause a scandal walking through town."

She blinked at him. "You brought a change of clothes? For me?"

"You turn into a bear sometimes," he said. "It seems to be extremely hard on your wardrobe. I thought..." He trailed off, slightly horrified because she looked like she might cry. "Are you all right?"

"I'm fine," she said thickly. "Thank you. This is...it's very kind. Nobody outside the sisterhood has ever...well. Thank you." She turned away and shrugged into the robe. It was thinner material and probably didn't do much about the cold, but there was only so much room in a pack after all.

"Are you sure you're all right?"

"Yeah. Yeah, I'm sure." She looked at him, her eyes too bright, and squared her shoulders. "Now. What do we do about Stachys?"

"I feel that could have gone better," said Clara, around sunrise.

"Saint's balls," muttered Istvhan. "You're telling me."

Stachys had not wanted to leave. In fact, he had refused to leave, had crumpled into a wailing heap, and when Clara had put a soothing hand on his shoulder, he'd tried to bite her. Attempts to comfort him failed. Attempts to reason with him failed. Stachys believed that He would come back and if Stachys wasn't there...well, Istvhan couldn't quite make out what he was afraid of, exactly, but something. Possibly the man simply missed his creation as desperately as a parent missed a long-lost child, or possibly He would be angry and would do something that made merely cutting off the sculptor's hands seem trivial. Possibly both.

The only thing he was sure of was that they could not get Stachys out of the house without half-killing him in the process.

"We could still kill him," Clara offered again.

Istvhan groaned. "I'm tempted," he admitted. "But the Rat might be able to get a lot more useful information out of him. And the only way we're getting him to the Temple by force is if he's catatonic and we're history's greatest monsters."

Clara grunted. "So what do we do now? Report back to the Rat?"

"All we can do." Istvhan rubbed his eyes. They felt gritty. He and Clara had dragged branches over the bodies as best they could, but anybody visiting Stachys would be able to smell them and locate them in short order. *Although I get the impression that he doesn't get too many human visitors.*

"Should one of us stay and stand guard?" said Clara. "I don't know how often these things check in with each other, but they're bound to notice if one comes out and there's a half-dozen dead clay things here." She frowned. "And by that, I suppose I mean you, because the bear might just run away again. It has very strong opinions about things that are too rotten to eat that still walk like people."

"Which would mean sending you back to the Rat alone," said Istvhan. "I don't like the thought of that."

"A long day's walk through inhabited countryside," said Clara. "Oh no, whatever shall I do. A beach plum might eat me."

He glared at her. "I'm not worried about the inhabitants, it's the people who might be looking for you."

"You *do* know I spent the better part of two decades walking back and forth along the canal alone, carrying valuables?"

"Were any of the ruthless local government factions trying to have you kidnapped for blood sports at the time?"

She scowled and looked away. "We don't *know* that anyone in Morstone is looking for me."

"We don't know that they aren't. And if so, it is potentially very, very bad."

"Fine, fine." She lifted her hands and let them drop. "I accept that it's a risk. Is it more of a risk than letting Stachys stay here alone?"

"We'll impress the need for swift action on the Bishop," said Istvhan, rising. "Let's get moving. The sooner we go, the sooner we can take baths with actual soap and get this smell out of our hair."

If they had had to walk all the way back to Morstone, Clara would have probably given up and gotten a room at an inn. But the next town over had an early morning ferry and Istvhan dumped coins into the pilot's hand until she agreed to take the two of them on board.

The other passengers were clearly early-morning people taking wares to market. They were loaded down with baskets and boxes and in one case, three cages of live chickens. Clara and Istvhan, soggy and smelling very strongly of something very bad, were obviously not locals. They went as far downwind of the others as they could and tried not to look like very large people who had just destroyed a great many animated corpses.

"Well, I feel inconspicuous," murmured Istvhan in Harshek. Clara noticed that he was carefully *not* looking at the water.

"I think the chickens are staring at us," she said.

"I'd probably stare at us too."

"Surely people fall in the river all the time." Clara tried to adjust her cloak. The wind off the river wasn't warm and her damp robe barely provided modesty, let alone warmth. Unfortunately, despite her best efforts at scrubbing, the cloak had very obviously been present for something dreadful. The burnt, rotting smell was ground into the wet fabric and combined badly with the smell of wet wool.

She noticed after a minute that Istvhan had turned a bit more green than the smell could account for, and realized her mistake. *Right. He doesn't like deep water.* "Not from the ferry," she said hastily. "Just, you know, showing up soaking wet and all."

"We'll get where we're going and change clothes," said Istvhan.

"Before I ruin any more clothes, I'll need a..." Clara drew a blank on the word *bath* in Harshek. She could see the word in her head, carefully illuminated by Sister Sigrid, but for the life of her, she couldn't remember how it was pronounced, and the more she thought about it, the more the word seemed completely unreal. *Oh gods and saints, I am so tired. I am too old to stay up all night any more, piling changes on top of changes...* "Person-laundry," she said finally, because that made more sense than *bath*, which was clearly not a word and had never been a word.

Istvhan stared at her. She stared back. "Bath?" he said.

"Is that how you pronounce it?"

"I thought it was until you asked me. Now I don't know either."

"I'm very tired."

"So am I." He rubbed his face. "We used to do forced marches. Thirty-six hours and I could still fight. Now I stay up for twenty-four and have a minor skirmish and I feel like I've been trampled by a bull."

"Getting old is a terrible thing. They say that beats the alternative, though."

"I'm not sure. I never used to hurt myself sleeping."

"Oh gods, yes. You sleep wrong and your neck goes out for a week." She shook her head. "I'm amazed that sleeping on the ground didn't lay me up permanently." He smiled. His eyes wandered across her face and Clara thought vaguely that she must look absolutely dreadful. "I know, I look like I'm three days dead."

"You're beautiful," he said, with absolute sincerity.

She looked away, embarrassed. He'd meant it, too. *Paladins, dammit.* They said you were beautiful on the inside and they really genuinely believed it. It wasn't fair. You couldn't *not* love someone like that. *How am I even supposed to try?*

Fortunately for her heart, and the chickens, and the other passengers, the pilot called for Morstone and they docked at the outskirts of the city. She and Istvhan pulled up the hoods on their cloaks — the smell inside Clara's was truly horrifying — and made their way from the docks to the Temple of the Rat.

CHAPTER 36

One thing that you could give the Rat's people over many other commanders that Istvhan had ever worked with was that they listened and then they acted. They didn't tell you that it was impossible or that you were overreacting. They didn't tell you to calm down. They asked intelligent, clarifying questions, and then the well-oiled machinery of the Temple went into action. Istvhan told Faizen that he and Clara had located the wonderworker responsible for the smooth men, that he required watching, and that he needed to be brought to the Temple as quickly as possible and that more smooth men would be coming.

"Time," he said, "is of the essence."

Faizen nodded. "We do not have many fighting men available," he said. "But we will find a way. Are you able to accompany us back, if we arrange a carriage?"

He traded a look with Clara. "Yes," he said, feeling exhaustion gnawing at his bones. "I am, at least."

"I will," said Clara. "Though if you can spare me five minutes and a bar of soap, it will make everything much easier."

Faizen smiled. "It will take substantially longer than five minutes to arrange for transport. It will take several hours, even working as swiftly as we can, to arrange transport and to call in a healer that I would trust with men's minds." He held up a hand to forestall Istvhan's protest. "But if you give me clear directions, I can have someone there within the hour. Not to fight, but to hide and watch. If these smooth men do come for this wonderworker, our watcher will tail them as far as he can, and give us an idea where they take him. Will that be acceptable?"

"The best I can ask," said Istvhan, "and more than I hoped for."

"Then both of you, go to the bathing room in the healer's quarters, and I'll set things in motion."

The bathing room in question was, as it turned out, the one the healers used on people with body lice or particularly contagious diseases. Apparently their smell precluded using the other facilities. It was not warm, but the water went directly out a grate on the floor and into the river. Clara and Istvhan went in, were handed soap that smelled strongly of pine tar, and set to scrubbing.

"I want you to know, Domina," said Istvhan, "that the only reason I am not ogling you like a schoolboy is because I am so tired that I can barely think. The spirit is willing but the flesh has been badly treated."

"Oh, good," sighed Clara. "You keep seeing me naked and I had yet to return the favor, and now I'm afraid that if I turn my head too fast to look, it'll fall off."

"Honestly, given the breeze coming up through the grate, I'm grateful. I am not exactly at my best."

"And I am?"

"*Your* breasts don't shrink in the cold."

"My breasts haven't shrunk since I hit puberty." She dumped an ewer of tepid water over her head. The healer's assistants were trying to heat more, but someone was giving birth in the next room and mere scrubbing took a distant second place. Occasionally, a scream would echo through the walls, reminding Istvhan that everything could be much worse. "Seriously, I dropped so much weight during my illness, and not an ounce off my chest." She lifted the offending articles of anatomy in her hands and Istvhan felt his cock attempt to stir, take note of the temperature, and go back into hiding.

"My sisters would sympathize enormously," he said. "Two of them are built to the same scale you are, and their complaints are frequent and passionate. I have learned to agree politely."

"Wise man."

It took a ridiculous amount of the harsh pine tar soap to get the smell out of Istvhan's hair, and even more to get it out of his boots. In the end he wasn't sure if he'd succeeded or if the smell of pine tar just masked it, but he'd take smelling like freshly sealed boards over smelling like rotten flesh and burnt hair any day.

Clara, meanwhile, vanished from the shower and returned wearing a fresh robe and a fresh cloak and carrying an armload of clothing. "Your aketon is drying, but they don't think the surcoat can be saved," she said.

Istvhan sighed. "It served me well. What have we got?"

She handed him a robe akin to hers. He shrugged into it, feeling naked without his chainmail. *Well, if someone stabs me here in the Temple, we have problems already.* "All right, let's see how they're doing."

"The watcher has already left," reported Faizen, when they made their way back to his office. "They'll ride a relay there. It shouldn't seem too unusual, since couriers take messages that way all the time. The last stop, that's the one that will have the most chance of being remarked upon."

"I don't think the smooth men are interrogating people," said Istvhan. "Most of them can't actually talk. I just don't know how long before they realize the guards are gone. We could be extremely lucky or extremely unlucky, there's no way to tell."

"All is in the hands of the gods," said Faizen. "The mind healer is on his way, and we'll see how our luck falls."

Istvhan woke.

Clara was in his arms, moving rhythmically against him, and for a moment he thought that all his erotic dreams had come true.

Admittedly, in his dreams he hadn't been wearing pants or chain-mail, but that sort of thing could be dealt with. And the rhythmic motion had been rather more of a hard slide and rather less of an irregular bumping, accompanied by loud clattering. And his head hadn't hurt quite so much. And—

Clara let out a loud snore against his shoulder. Istvhan opened his eyes. His dreams always involved her being enthusiastically awake. This would not do at all.

He focused his eyes and made out the faces of Faizen, the mind healer, and her apprentice, all sitting on the bench opposite him. *Right. We're in a coach of some kind. And I am clearly exhausted and so is she.*

Clara let out another snore, woke herself up with it, and jerked upright. "Sorry," she muttered.

"I dozed off myself," he admitted. The mind healer wore a small smile. She was a plump, silver-haired woman with a kind face. Her apprentice was a raw-boned young man, nearly as tall as Istvhan but far skinnier. With his shock of thin, pale hair, he strongly resembled a nervous stalk of wheat.

The carriage wasn't bad. It was probably a mail coach that had been repurposed for other things, and it was fast rather than smooth, but no worse than many coaches Istvhan had ridden in. It was, however, built for smaller people. He and Clara were both sitting with their legs drawn up and turned partly sideways, to try and give the three on the opposite bench space.

It was always a bit awkward to know what to say in coaches. You were all so close together and you never knew if you were making too much eye contact with the people on the other side, or whether you should have a conversation or not. Istvhan had used this fact to his advantage a time or two — if you could get someone talking, they were likely to keep talking to fill the space, and it was sometimes remarkably easy to get them to confess something. On the other hand, if you didn't want to talk, it was hard to avoid it. You could usually stare out of the windows, but the windows in this case were shuttered to keep the cold out, so he could only catch tiny glimpses of the countryside.

"How far away is this place?" asked the apprentice.

"I only know how far away it is in on foot," said Istvhan.

Clara cocked her head. "How long was I asleep?"

"The better part of an hour."

"Then, if we've kept this speed, we should be changing horses soon. Then not much farther at all."

"Good to know," said the apprentice. He smiled sheepishly. "Although given what you've said about these clay people, I'm not sure I'm in a hurry to get there."

They went back to trying not to stare at each other. The wheels hit a bump and jostled Clara against Istvhan. He wondered how she felt about that. *You have permission*, she said last night. Oh god. Why did there have to be a river and a pack of murderous golem heads between them and a convenient bed?

"I keep trying to think of something more to tell you," Clara said to the healer. "Something I've forgotten that you'll hear and say, 'Oh, I know exactly what's going on!' and it'll all be easy after that."

The healer chuckled. "Would that it was that easy. But for every easily recognized disorder of the mind, there's a hundred that vary wildly from person to person. You've done well, but I'll simply have to meet him."

Unfortunately, it was not so easy. When they pulled up to the ceramic works at last, the door hung open and the chimney was no longer smoking.

"You're too late," said a voice over their head. Istvhan looked up, startled. A man came down the tree that overhung the road, slithering down the trunk as easily as if it were a ladder. He had dark skin and long black hair pulled back in a tight queue. His feet were bare and looked as hard as horn. "They came and got him about an hour ago."

Istvhan swore. Faizen sighed. "Did you see which way they went?"

"To the river, and got on a boat. I followed them that far. Then I figured I'd come back here and warn you." He grimaced. "When you said those things looked weird, I thought it might be an exaggeration, but...Lords of the Deep, that was *not* something I wanted to see."

"Was the man injured?" asked the healer.

"Not that I could see. He was crying and asking if someone was mad, but none of them ever said a word. That bit was bad enough, but..."

"What happened?" asked Istvhan.

"The damnedest thing I've seen, and I served on three ships and saw things out there that nobody's ever seen on land. I was up this tree, thinking it'd be a good place to watch, not really expecting much, when a whole group of them showed up. They were wearing hoods and hats and things, and I couldn't really make out the faces at first. They didn't talk, just stood there for a minute, then went poking around in the bushes. Finally, one of them comes back holding something...swear I thought it was some kind of big goblet at first, with a weird stem on it. They all stood around, almost where you're standing, and started dipping their hands into the thing and pulling out some kind of clear jelly. And it stank. I could smell it from up in the tree and I was afraid I was gonna be sick and they'd spot me. Hard to stay hidden when you're puking your guts up. You may think I'm exaggerating, but it was worse than cutting into a whale."

"Oh, we know," said Clara. "Not the whale, but the rest of it."

"Yeah, figured you might. Anyway, the goblet or whatever was hollow, and they were taking this jelly out. Then they'd eat it off their fingers. That's when I realize that they've all got the same face, and none of them have hair under the hats." He swallowed. "Then the one holding the thing turns a bit, so one of the others can reach it, and I realize the goblet's got a face on it, and it's just the same as theirs, only with a big chunk knocked off the back."

"One of the heads," said Istvhan grimly. "You have to smash them or they'll just find another body to put it on. The stem's a spike they drive down into the neck."

"Young man," said the healer, with some asperity, "you cannot just drive a large piece of clay into the neck. It's full of bones and cartilage. It's not empty space." The apprentice put his hands to his own neck, as if testing its solidity.

"I know that and you know that," said Istvhan. "But I've also seen the corpses they leave behind, so what we know doesn't seem to apply here."

The healer scowled. "*Magic,*" she muttered, in much the same tone that she might say "syphilis."

"Their heads are hollow," said Istvhan. "Sometimes we find some clear goo on the bodies, or on the severed heads. It seems to be what smells. But I had no idea they ate it. I had no idea they ate *anything.*"

"Yeah." Their informant looked slightly green. "I don't know if that was its brains or what. Anyway, once they'd all eaten the stuff, they just stood there for a bit, not saying anything, and then one tossed the broken head into the bushes and they all went into the pottery. And a few minutes later, they came out with a human. I guess that's the guy you were after. He didn't want to go, I'll tell you that much, but after seeing what they were, I didn't much feel like trying to stop them."

"You did the right thing," said Clara.

"You're kind to say so, ma'am, but it's hard to see a man get dragged off and not help."

"Eating the jelly," muttered Istvhan. "What was that for?"

"There's burial rites where the deceased's family ceremoniously eats their brains," offered Faizen.

"And it's not a good idea," said the healer tartly. "Might as well eat raw pork while you're at it."

"I didn't think they were the sort of thing that cared about burying the dead," admitted Istvhan. "They aren't really alive in the first place. They're just popped out of a mold. And if you kill one, the others don't get angry or sad or anything, so far as anyone can tell. Obviously they can think, but they're...I don't know."

"It may not be burial," said the healer. "Whatever this substance is, they could be deriving some other benefit from it."

Their spy scratched the back of his neck and said "Truth is, it seemed like they knew what to do after they ate it. Before, they were all just kinda wandering around 'til the one found the head, and then they went all together, like."

"Like they learned something from eating it?" said Faizen doubtfully. "Is that possible?"

The lanky apprentice opened his mouth, closed it again, then said, almost apologetically, "Could be...uh...no, forget it."

"No, no, tell us," said Clara. "We're grasping at straws here, one more straw is fine."

"This is probably silly." He wrung his hands.

"Young man," said Clara, sounding very much like a nun, "if you do not spit it out, I shall be cross."

He gave her a panicky look, eyes rolling white around the edges. "Uh, uh — my Da kept cows. And when the ladies — when they — uh — when it's getting close to breeding, you know, the bull — he's always tasting — when they urinate, you know—"

"I did not know that, and I wish I still didn't," said Istvhan, to no one in particular.

"But Da says it's how they tell that the lady's ready. That there's something in the urine. He learns it from the taste." His ears were turning scarlet. "Anyway, I thought maybe the jelly here, maybe there was a taste to it and it told them something. But that's probably a bad idea."

"No, that's quite an interesting thought," said the healer. She tapped her upper lip. "There are things to be learned from many excretions. You can taste milk and know if the cow ate garlic. And healers can taste a patient's urine and know if they have a particular wasting sickness by the sweetness. Perhaps they were deriving some information from tasting their fallen associate's...ah..."

"Head goo?" offered Istvhan.

"Not the term I would have chosen, but yes."

Istvhan wished again that Doctor Piper from Archon's Glory was here. The doctor knew more about dead bodies than anyone he'd ever met, and was the expert on the smooth men's physiology. *He'd love this. Just the kind of experimental question to really get him interested. Although it might end with him eating head goo, and no one wants that.*

"Maybe it told them how he died," offered Clara. "Then they knew they had to take Stachys away with them, instead of just posting more guards."

"Anything's possible, I suppose." Istvhan sighed. "I'm sorry, everyone. I seem to have dragged you all here far too late. We have been very unlucky."

"Let's see if there's any clues in the house," suggested Faizen. "All may not be completely lost."

Unfortunately, the room did not bear out his optimism. It looked mostly the same as when they had left. The bench that Istvhan and Clara had sat on had been overturned. Istvhan could not remember if they had done that, or if it was a sign of further struggle.

"I don't think he fought them," said Clara, echoing his own thoughts. "The place mostly looked like this already."

"Someone who he felt safe with, then?" asked the apprentice.

"Or someone who frightened him more than leaving." The healer shook her head. "From what you've said, it sounds like this creation of his has some significant hold over him. Fear. Love. Both, perhaps."

"Love? For the creature that cut off his *hands?*" The apprentice's voice actually cracked on the last word and Istvhan felt himself age several subjective decades.

"People," said the healer, giving the young man a look that told Istvhan that he wasn't the only one feeling suddenly old, "are rarely straightforward. And they will accept terrible injury from people they love, and tell themselves that the depths of the pain proves the depth of their love. Eventually, you'll stop being surprised."

The apprentice hung his head. "Sorry, mistress."

"I can't possibly diagnose someone I've never met," said the healer. "It's bad form and I might as well throw a rock and hope I hit the correct malady." She folded her hands inside the sleeves of her robe, a gesture that Istvhan was so used to seeing from Clara that it was briefly surreal to see from a stranger. "That being said, if you weren't absolutely certain that he was in serious danger or posed a serious danger — or both — I would have strongly opposed removing him from his home. He clearly felt safe here, or at least safer than he did leaving it. Wherever they took him, he's probably frightened out of his wits."

"I *knew* we should have killed him," muttered Clara under her breath.

Istvhan was thinking something of the sort and kicking himself for it. *Damnation. He unleashed a scourge that I* know *has killed dozens of people, possibly hundreds. And I got cold feet at the last minute and talked myself out of it. Because I no longer believe in my own rightness. Because I'm starting to question all those people I killed under the god's influence.*

I should have listened to Clara. If you can't trust a nun to be your moral compass...

They filed glumly back to the wagon. Their tree-hopping spy climbed inside and Istvhan and Clara followed. The apprentice closed the door to the pottery and banked the fire. "If he comes home," the young man said, "it should still be waiting for him."

CHAPTER 37

Ethan's galley, with its wall of beds and its warm hearth, had never looked more inviting. Maude croaked at them from somewhere behind the woodpile.

They both sat down. Weariness and guilt hung over Istvhan like a cloud of fog. He began mechanically stripping off his hauberk, hoping he could get it off before he fell down.

Clara reached out and touched his arm. "Istvhan."

He looked at her.

"Stop beating yourself up. You were trying to do the right thing. Paladins don't murder people in cold blood."

"Maybe they ought to, when the alternative is a horde of smooth men roaming the earth."

"In which case they'd no longer be paladins. I don't know what they'd be."

"Bishops, probably," muttered Istvhan, thinking of Beartongue. But the Bishop of Archon's Glory was not god-touched, she was simply a ruthlessly capable administrator. The Rat called lawyers and priests, not paladins. Beartongue believed in fairness and decency and justice, but Istvhan suspected that she was not above helping those things along with a well-placed knife or spot of blackmail as required.

"Either way," said Clara. "It's in the hands of the gods now."

"I used to *be* a hand of the gods," said Istvhan.

"Fine...fine..." She ran her fingertips over his bicep and he stiffened, both figuratively and, if she kept going much longer, probably literally as well. *Oh gods, not now, I'm so tired, I wouldn't manage more than a bump, a squirt, and a post-coital tickle...*

"Domina, if you're trying to distract me, I am very willing to be distracted. But at this moment..."

"What?" She blinked at him, then at her hand, then she actually blushed. Istvhan watched, charmed. "No! I mean...*yes*. But not until after I've slept for about twenty hours."

"Oh good," he said. And then he found the strength to lean over and kiss her, and even if there was no energy left for passion, there was enough of a spark to warm him all the way down to sleep.

Clara woke with the gratifying sensation of having slept at least half the day away. Her tongue felt like flannel and her muscles like wet clay, but by god, she had *slept*.

She was coming back from using the privy when the door to the galley opened and Istvhan appeared, carrying a board covered in cheese, bread, and sardines. "I don't know if you're as hungry as I am, but I figured that it was a safe bet."

"Bless you," said Clara, her stomach growling. "You are a prince among men."

"There's tea on the hearth."

Clara gave a jaw-cracking yawn. "What time is it?"

"Middle of the night, I think. So I suppose this isn't quite breakfast. I haven't been up for very long either. Food was just my first thought."

For the next few minutes, the only sounds were of two people devouring heroic quantities of food. Clara had changed too many times in the last twenty-four hours and her body demanded payment.

When the roar of hunger had been muted, she slumped back

against the wall, holding a third cup of tea. "I am going to be half sardine by weight by the time we're done in Morstone."

"At least it's not beach plums."

"There's that."

They sat in companionable silence, digesting. Maude made an indignant croak somewhere in the woodpile, probably annoyed by the activity at this late hour. Clara turned her head, grimaced, and rubbed at her neck. The crick in it from sleeping on the coach had not gone away. Instead it appeared to be set in concrete. "Getting old is the worst," she said. "When I was young, I could fall down a hillside, shake myself off, and be none the worse for wear. Now I sleep wrong and I'm hunched up for a week."

"I know," said Istvhan, with the passion of someone who had his own collection of trick joints and hostile muscle groups. He scooted to the edge of the bed-platform and gestured to her. "Here. Sit and I'll rub it for you."

Clara, no longer being of an age when she could fall down the aforementioned hillsides, was also old enough to know that when handsome men offered to rub your neck, there was only one way the evening was going to end.

Last chance. Last chance to step back with your heart even slightly intact.

She looked at Istvhan, sitting in the warm glow of the hearth, his upturned hands on his knees. His arms were bare and his shirt gaped open at the throat, far enough to reveal the long flat planes of muscle. The line where his shoulder muscle dipped into his bicep made her want to howl like a dog.

You know it's too late for you. It's been too late for a long time.

She rose, not trusting herself to speak, and knelt in front of him. He set his thumbs on either side of her spine and began to massage the muscles there, sliding farther down until the tension in her neck was gone and had been replaced with a rather more urgent tension a good deal lower.

He leaned forward and kissed the back of her neck, and she closed her eyes.

"Tell me what you are thinking, Domina," he said against her hair. "Tell me, so I don't guess wrong."

I'm thinking I'm in love with you, you absurdly decent man. I have fallen in love and it's worse than it ever was before, because you know what I am. You could be my lover and my partner and we could be so good together, and when you finally walk away, it will destroy me.

She said none of these things. If she did, she might force the loss to happen right now. He *was* decent, and he wouldn't lead her on just to bed her. *If I'm going to lose him, I damn well better get a night of pleasure first. Several, if possible. Half a dozen.*

So instead she stood up and faced him and let her robe fall down from her shoulders to her elbows, and said "I think that I want you very badly."

Those dark eyes went wide. He rose to his feet as well. *"Domina,"* he said, as if the word were an obscenity or a prayer. *"Yes."*

She was beautiful. She was beautiful and strong and she was in his arms and Istvhan was fairly certain that his cock was hard enough to pound tent pegs. *Pace yourself,* he thought, *you aren't as young as you used to be.* His cock ignored him.

He took both her hands in his, kissed each knuckle, and breathed on the tender skin of her wrists. She shivered and he tugged her backwards, towards the bench, until he could sit down on the edge. She was still wearing the bodice under her robe. They'd fallen down so quickly the night before that she hadn't undressed completely. He unlaced one side and ran his fingers across the crossed red lines the lacings had left on her skin.

"Clara," he said, drawing the words out. "You are magnificent." He leaned in and kissed each red line, feeling the softness of her skin against his lips. He would probably have marks as well by the time this was done. At least, if they did it right.

He wanted to bury his face in her breasts and make love to her right on the spot, but if he did that, it really would be over in a few minutes. She deserved better. Hell, he'd waited so long for this, *he* deserved better, too. So he denied himself, slid the fabric free without touching her skin, and instead lifted his hands to her hair. "May I?"

"Yes."

She sat between his knees, on the edge of the bench, while he unbraided her hair and slid his fingers through it. It smelled of...well, of pine tar soap, honestly. His probably did too. He set his lips against the nape of her neck, feeling her skin against the roughness of his cheek. "Damnation. I should have shaved."

"I'll forgive you this once." She slid her hands up and down his thighs, which was the only part of him she could easily reach. Istvhan was just congratulating himself on their positioning when she managed to slide her arm between them and began attempting to unlace his breeches behind her back.

"This is very difficult when I can't see the ties," she muttered.

"Yes, but you certainly have my attention, Domina."

"What, only now?"

"You have had my attention for weeks. Since you walked into my tent with nothing but a sword."

She turned in his arms and kissed him, hot and hungry, passionate enough to make him think that he'd had her attention for just as long. He kissed her until he thought he might drown, while she figured out the ties and began to loosen them. *Oh, Saint's teeth, this won't last long if she keeps that up...*

He came up for air and caught her hands. "Much more of that and I will disappoint us both."

"I doubt that highly."

"Your faith is touching, but now that I have you, I would much rather take my time and do this right." He ran his lips down the line of her neck, across her collarbone, and then lower, down to the place between her breasts he'd touched once before.

She stiffened as he reached it, her breath catching. "Easy," he whispered against her skin. "Easy, Domina. I've got you."

A shudder went through her. Istvhan prided himself on making women quiver, but this was the wrong kind. He looked up and caught a flicker in her eyes of the wrong emotion entirely.

He lifted his head. She had gone suddenly, alarmingly still. "Domina? What's wrong?"

She turned her face away from him, and when he reached up and ran his thumb across her lower lip, it trembled.

"You're frightened," he said. The words sounded completely mad when he said them aloud. She was here, in his bed, of her own choice. She'd kissed him in the inn hallway with none of the hesitancy of inexperience. And yet he had trained himself to recognize that look and it struck him like a splash of cold water.

She did not deny it.

Frightened? Now? But what happened? What's different?

And then he knew.

"I know your secret," he said. "That's the difference, isn't it? I know what you are."

She pulled away and rose. Istvhan let her go. He suddenly did not know what to do with his hands, so he draped them over his knees and watched the firelight run across the edges of her skin.

"I'm sorry," she said.

"I'm not. I'd rather know." *But knowing means I've gotten too close, doesn't it? It means that I could really hurt you.*

...it means someone did *really hurt you, doesn't it?*

Istvhan had a sudden desire to find this hypothetical man, pick him up by the throat, and have a long conversation.

Clara pulled her robe up over her shoulders and knelt on the hearth, poking the fire up. It didn't particularly need it, but Istvhan recognized a distraction when he saw one. "It's not so easy," she said, not looking at him. "Plenty of men say they want a woman who's an animal in bed, but in practice, not so much."

"Plenty of men are idiots."

"Ah?" She turned her head. The light reflected just slightly wrong from her eyes, a flash of green instead of red. "And you will not fear that if you make me angry, I will turn into a bear and tear you limb from limb?"

"I've made you angry on several occasions already, as I recall. In fact, I stabbed you once."

Her laugh was stifled but genuine. Istvhan had never in his life thought that he would bless his past self for stabbing a nun, but apparently the world had gotten very strange when he wasn't looking. "So you did," she said. "I'm not sure it counts, though."

"Please don't make me stab you again to prove that I find you desirable."

Her shoulders shook, but not with fear this time. "Oh St. Ursa, no, no. No more stabbing."

"Thank the gods. I don't mind a good argument as foreplay, but not when live steel is involved." He got off the bed and came to sit beside her at the hearth.

She narrowed her eyes, studying him thoughtfully. "No, no, I see what it is. You see a hurt you think you can heal. It's like paladin catnip, isn't it?"

That blow was so precise that Istvhan was surprised he wasn't bleeding, but he had no intention of letting her know that. "Believe me, if I could fix more of the world's hurts by making passionate love to a beautiful woman, I'd be a very happy man."

She raised an eyebrow at him.

"Clara..." He let the word trail off his tongue like a caress, and saw her soften, just a little. "Clara, do you truly think you need to be hurt for me to want you? I grant you, I am what I am, and we do tend towards heroes and martyrs, but I try very hard to avoid being either. And honestly, I don't know that anyone really wants to bed martyrs." *Which is half the reason that the Bishop sent you on your way, isn't it? She said she had no desire to become a duty.*

Oh. Huh. He'd been a little hurt by that, in truth. Not a great deal, just a sliver that had pricked at him more than it ought to. Until he spoke the words out loud, he hadn't realized how right the Bishop had been. The hurt smoothed itself away and left a vague sense of foolishness in its wake.

Perhaps that realization lent him some kind of strength. He

reached out and stroked his thumb across Clara's cheekbone, and she did not pull away.

"I would prefer you not be a martyr in bed," she admitted.

"What about a hero, then?"

She rolled her eyes, but she also leaned her cheek against his hand. "You do think well of yourself."

"Give me a chance, Domina," he said, pulling her close. He would take exasperation over fear any day of the week.

She sat in the circle of his arms, bolt upright. Not quite relaxing. Not yet. He trailed his lips along her jaw and down her throat, feeling the quiver, trying to soothe it. It would be all right. He would drive out fear with passion if he had to. He plucked at the opening to her robes. He could still remember the softness of her breasts from that night in the cave, and he desperately wanted to see if his memory was accurate.

She shifted just a little. He felt her soften against him. He slid his hands under the fabric, reaching. There. Yes. The weight and the curve against his fingers. Saint's balls, his memory had failed him completely, this was so much better.

The door slammed open. Clara and Istvhan leapt apart as if they'd been caught doing something indecent, which they had, but not nearly as indecent as Istvhan had been hoping. Clara snatched at the throat of her robes, pulling them closed.

Ethan stood in the doorway with his arms full of dripping jars. If he even noticed the state of their clothes, it wasn't obvious. "You've got to help me," he gasped. "There's men coming to raid the safehouse. We have to save the newts!"

CHAPTER 38

Well, this is my own damn fault, thought Clara grimly. *If I had just thrown myself on his cock like a sensible woman, this would be an amusing anecdote that happened afterwards. But no, I had to get cold feet halfway through, like a shrinking virgin afraid he won't respect me in the morning, and so we had barely started when suddenly, newts.*

If only he hadn't been so damned careful about it. So tender. So very much *himself.* Her illusion of losing herself in mindless lust had been completely shattered. She hadn't been able to forget for an instant that this was Istvhan and she was hopelessly in love with him. Every touch felt like an assault on her defenses.

She gazed across the dark alley. Like most of Morstone, it was built of wood, and it turned and twisted with very little concern for straight lines or lighting. She could only just make out Istvhan as a bulky shadow to her left.

Ethan had not been sure who was going to raid the safehouse, other than men employed by the Sealords. He wasn't even sure which Sealord was behind it, or why. Clara was glumly certain that she and Istvhan were the cause, but all she could do was shove down the guilt and carry jars. And watch for enemies. There were no apparent enemies in the ally, which seemed like a damn shame because she was frustrated and half-aroused and would have welcomed a chance to punch someone deserving in the head.

"Well," she said. "Here we are."

"Indeed."

"Frustrated and covered in newts."

A gusty sigh came from the shadow. "I try to be a considerate lover, Domina," said Istvhan, in the tones of a man confessing to a great crime. "I work very hard at it. I would give you pleasure a dozen times over before I took mine. It is a matter of craftsmanship."

"Mm-hmm," said Clara, shifting the extremely heavy sack over her shoulder. Dozens of jars full of water clinked and sloshed, probably to the dismay of the amphibians contained within. Despite the lids, moisture was leaking out and spreading down her back.

"But I am starting to think that the gods are trying to keep us apart." He peered around the corner of the alley, looking for the wagon that Ethan had sworn was coming to take the newts to safety.

"I've been getting that impression," Clara said.

"If we aren't being attacked, we're rescuing wayward amphibians."

"We couldn't very well leave them."

"No, we couldn't. But I'll be honest, Domina — at this point, I would take you up against this wall, right here, if it wasn't for the newts, and craftsmanship be damned."

She began laughing. She couldn't help it. "And if it wasn't for the newts, I'd let you do it. This is getting absurd."

"I want you very, very badly, Domina." His eyes were deep and dark and the heat in them was enough to make her forget that her back was soggy with newt-water.

"My dear Captain, the feeling is mutual."

His breath quickened. "Do you suppose if we put down the jars, we could..."

Ethan burst out of the door. "I found her! She'd gotten behind the barrels!" He waved a wet burlap sack at Istvhan and Clara. "I'm so relieved!"

Clara let the thought go reluctantly. "Is that the last one?"

"Yes. We've got all the jars. If some of the Sealords' thugs decide to smash things up, nobody will get hurt."

"What about the fish?" asked Clara.

Ethan looked at her blankly. "What?"

She realized that this might end with her and Istvhan lugging a massive ceramic fishbowl between them, but pressed on anyway. "Will they hurt the fish?"

"No, they're ornamental carp," said Ethan, as if that explained everything.

She looked at Istvhan, who looked as puzzled as she felt. "Are the carp not particularly valuable?"

"What? No, but they're..." Ethan looked back and forth between them. "You don't hurt a *carp*," he said, as if telling a small child not to touch a hot stove.

"You don't?"

"No! The River Giant would rise up from the river bed and avenge the insult!" He paused, eyes going round. "Do you not have carp in your lands?"

"We do," admitted Istvhan, "but the gods do not seem particularly concerned with them."

"How bizarre. They're the oracular fish. If one bites one of your fingers off, it's good luck. It means the River Giant has tasted your blood and taken your sacrifice, and you will be safe on the waters of the river for the rest of your life."

"What does it mean if you get two fingers bitten off?" murmured Clara under her breath, as Ethan went to the mouth of the alley to look for the wagon.

"Stop sticking your hand in the water," said Istvhan, just as quietly.

The wagon arrived, fortunately, before they had to explain to Ethan why they were giggling.

It was a long ride in the wagon, covered in burlap sacks, and Istvhan soon lost track of the twists and turns. He had a suspicion that they did not actually end up very far from where they started, but they took such a roundabout path that he couldn't be certain. *Which is fine. The less I know, the less I can give up under torture, if it comes to that.*

He really, really hoped it wouldn't come to that.

When they finally stopped, they were in a little lane, blocked off on both ends by doorways. Ethan dug his way free of the sacks and handed down jars of newts to Istvhan and Clara, while their host waited in the doorway with a lamp held high.

"We don't know the reasons for the raid," said the woman who ran the safehouse, who had no name that she was willing to give out. "Most likely, they simply got word that the Rat has been busy lately and decided to put us back in our place." She was older, with a tight silver bun, and her left eye was made of sparkling blue glass. "Or it may have nothing to do with us at all, and some bullies simply wanted to blow off some steam. They're allowed to trash a house or two, as long as they don't start fires or leave more than a few broken limbs behinds."

"I worry that they got wind of our activities," said Istvhan. He did not want to go into details about those activities, and suspected that their host would prefer not to know either.

"It's possible," she said. "But it is also possible that they chose a few locations at random. Ethan's affiliations are known, and there was another raid a few streets over, of a fishmonger who the Rat hires frequently. I suspect that we'll hear of another raid before the night is over." She spread her hands, blue light winking from her eye. "We simply don't know yet."

"Don't beat yourself up," said Ethan anxiously. "We got the newts out. That's what matters. If I have to replace a few pieces of furniture, that's nothing much. I don't have much good furniture anyway. The monkeys see to that. As long as the animals are safe, nothing else matters."

"Speaking of which, is there a washroom?" asked Clara. "I'm covered in...errrr...newt-water."

"Yes, of course." Their host gestured. "Downstairs, third door. Please, help yourself."

Istvhan rose as well. "I...ah...also. With the newts."

The woman rolled her good eye. "It was kind of you to help," she said. "He does care very much about his pets."

"They aren't exactly pets..." Ethan began, but Clara was out the door and Istvhan was after her before the explanation was fully underway.

The washroom was small. It had a stone floor. It had an empty washtub. It had moss growing in the corners. Nothing about it was remotely erotic, unless you were extremely fond of moss.

Istvhan had dreamed of making love to Clara any number of times. He would take his time. He would find all the soft, secret places of her body and find every way to bring her pleasure. She would cry out in his arms and tremble and beg for more.

His dreams had not included either the moss or the washtub. This was hardly the sort of setting that one wished to make love to a woman. "Domina..." he began.

She kicked the door closed, grabbed the front of his tabard, and said, "Now. Before I lose my nerve or we're drowned in salamanders or somebody shows up wanting a fight."

On second thought, he could probably make the washroom work.

He flipped the washtub over. She had her clothes off and was working on his. They grabbed for each other, no finesse at all, just tongues and teeth and need. He filled his hands to overflowing with her breasts and groaned against her lips. She pushed her hand between them and her fingers closed over his cock and he nearly jumped out of his skin.

He wanted to do everything right. He wanted to be gentle and maddening and skillful, make love to her slowly, drive her to blazing passion under him. He had been longing for this woman for weeks now, and if there was justice in the universe, he would have had her spread out under him on a bed with silk sheets and a full night ahead of him to learn every nuance of her body.

Instead, he had a stone washroom and a wooden tub and a man

323

obsessed with newts was probably going to come looking for him in the next five minutes and the universe was totally devoid of justice but he couldn't concentrate on that at all because Clara's hand was dragging down his length in a manner that would have brought a marble statue to life. At least if the statue was male.

"Clara," he managed to grate out, "I've got to be inside you. Now."

"Thank god," she said. She went down onto the tub and it was a damn good thing he'd done all those vigils because the stone floor didn't even register as he dropped to his knees behind her.

"Saint's teeth. Saint's bloody teeth. Domina, do you—"

"*Yes.*"

It was the only word he needed. It was more than enough. She cried out and so did he, but he was inside her at last and saints and gods and devils but it was good.

Reflexively, he tried to be careful. The first time, you always went slow and gentle, making sure that everything fit together, finding out what your partner liked and how much she could take. But she bucked her hips back against him, driving him deeper, and she was shockingly strong. Care began to fall by the wayside. He grabbed her hips and she growled with approval and it was still good, it was better than good, the flare of her hips in his hands and the softness and he stopped even trying to be careful.

"Domina..."

"Harder," she gasped, pushing against him.

Something broke loose inside him. He didn't have to worry about frightening her. She could tear him in half if she wanted. Istvhan gave himself up to the moment. Their bodies slammed together with bruising force and both of them wanted more.

Then the washtub broke.

Clara nearly pitched forward into the wreckage. Istvhan held her up with both arms and...well, his cock felt load-bearing at the moment, but it probably wasn't. She started to laugh and squirmed free and he said, "Are you okay?" and then she turned and dragged him down on top of her, still laughing. He met the softness of her body with the hardness of his own. *Not yet. Not until she's ready.* He slid his hand down between them, working at her flesh, cursing himself for not knowing what she liked or how she liked it, but he must have done something right because her body suddenly clenched around him, once, twice, and then he could no longer hold back. Her nails dug into his back and he cried out her name and collapsed over her as if he'd taken a mortal wound.

"Well," she said, after a few minutes had passed and he had remembered how breathing worked and why he should do it.

Istvhan propped himself up on his elbows. For once, he didn't worry about crushing his partner under his weight, but still, there was a lot of both of them. Her breasts were warm against his chest. "I feel as if I should apologize."

"Of course you do, you're a paladin. You could apologize to the owner of the washtub, if you like. Not to me."

He laughed. So did she, which caused muscles to clench and his laugh turned into something between a yelp and a groan. "Sorry," she said.

"If I don't get to apologize, neither do you." He rested his forehead against hers. "I would very much like to do that again," he said, "but perhaps more slowly and not on a stone floor."

"That would be wonderful." She stroked her fingers down the back of his neck. "Still, I have no regrets."

"My only regret is that we will have to explain the breakage." He gazed down at her, suddenly serious. Did she still have doubts? This was the time when they tended to rear their heads, after the passion was done and before the warmth had quite faded away. "Domina...Clara..."

Shadows flickered in her eyes. He lowered his head and brushed his mouth across hers with all the tenderness he hadn't had a chance to show earlier. "It will be well. All of it."

She closed her eyes. He knew he hadn't quite convinced her, but she managed a smile. "Except for the damn washtub."

CHAPTER 39

Clara lay in a small, dark room, with the door closed, and felt her nerves jangling.

The woman who ran the safehouse was trying to be kind. "No one will find you here," she said. "This is the most secure place in the house." And she'd made up a very large pallet on the floor, which was helpful, because none of her beds would have fit Clara at all.

It was just so very small and the door was between her and the rest of the world. It felt like a cage. And Istvhan was housed separately somewhere, because of course they hadn't said they were a couple and there was no reason that the woman would assume they were and Istvhan had lied very smoothly about the washtub, much more smoothly than a paladin should have been able to lie.

Maybe they weren't a couple. Maybe Clara was the one making assumptions. And now she was alone in the dark, and the warm afterglow of love had turned to nerves and wondering if he had been disappointed or if everything would be awkward now or if, having finally had her, Istvhan would be off to other conquests.

The bear did not like her fretting. It liked the darkness and the quiet but it had learned to fear cages and it stirred uneasily in her mind, wondering if it should smash the door down, and that would be much harder to explain than the washtub.

She got up and unbolted the door. It was still dark in the hallway, even though dawn had to be breaking. She could see a little damp light through a crack in the boards near the end.

"Clara?" whispered a voice somewhere in the hall, followed by a knock. "Clara, are you in here?"

Istvhan. Her shoulders sagged with unexpected relief. He was here. She wasn't alone. If she was in a cage, she had someone to watch her back while she fought free.

Shuffling footsteps and another knock, a little closer. "Clara? Are you in here?"

"Are you just going from door to door?" she whispered.

"Oh thank the gods." Istvhan's bulk eclipsed the crack of light. "Yes, I was going from door to door, trying not to bother anyone. I've found two storage closets and the privy."

"I'm down this way."

She heard the boards creak as he moved closer. "I didn't know where they'd put you. I was worried."

They stood inches from each other. Clara cleared her throat. "It's not a very big room," she said, "but there's probably room for two people. If they were good friends."

She could hear his voice rumbling in his chest. "I would say that you and I are very good friends, wouldn't you?"

"I like to think so." She reached out and caught a fistful of his shirt and tugged him back, toward the doorway. Somehow, despite having two people in it, the room seemed less confining. She didn't even flinch when he closed the door, though he left it unbolted.

"Now, then..." he said, stretching out beside her. "As delightful as our interlude with the washtub was, I think I would prefer to try that again, more slowly, and with less furniture."

"It's very dark," she said, which came out almost like a protest.

"That's all right. I shall simply have to do everything by touch."

His hand rose to her face, slipped down her neck and across her collarbone. She swallowed hard, feeling the ghostly trail of his fingertips across her skin, awakening feelings more complicated than mere lust.

"I'm glad you came," she said, to break the silence. "It was starting to feel like a trap here, and the bear was starting to think about breaking out."

His hands paused. "That would certainly be inconvenient, yes."

"Not the sort of thing our hosts are used to worrying about."

"Do *I* need to worry?" he asked. "Not about the cage, but you said once that strong emotions bring out the beast. Hungers. Does that include sexual hungers? Should I be prepared to backpedal very quickly and offer you a truffle?"

She raised an eyebrow, even though she knew he couldn't see it in the dark. "You really don't know if I'll turn into a bear in the middle of sex, and you were still willing to take that chance? Really?"

"I have known women that I would wrestle bears for," said Istvhan. He sounded very sincere. "You're one of them. It's just that in all the other cases, I expected to have to go looking for the bear, instead of having one delivered."

Clara snorted. "No, no. That's not a concern. Unless a fistfight breaks out in the middle of the bed. You, um, don't smell that interesting to the bear."

"I feel strangely insulted."

"Don't be. Male bears in rut mostly smell like meat and piss."

"Oh, you should have known me in my teen years, then."

She started laughing. He pressed his lips against her shoulder, and she could feel him smile against her skin. "Enough dark thoughts, Domina. I am still wide awake, and this time, I intend to take my time and do this properly. For both of us."

Istvhan woke, for the second time that month, with his head buried in someone's cleavage. Unlike the first time, he knew exactly where he was and who he was with. Admittedly, she was still a nun, but that didn't seem to matter nearly as much as it used to.

This is a very fine way to wake up. I could get used to this.

"Are you all right down there?" asked Clara.

"I am having a moment."

"Yes, I see that. Can you breathe?"

"Air is for the weak."

She chuckled. "Well, as long as you're enjoying them."

"They are glorious beyond measure."

"I'm glad someone likes them. They make it very hard to run and my back usually hurts."

"Hmm. I do not want you to be in pain, Domina. I shall go everywhere in front of you and hold them up for you to spare your back."

"*That* won't attract attention at all."

"I shall challenge anyone who looks at us askance to a duel. Two duels. Ten duels."

"I'd think one duel would be sufficient."

"I like to be thorough."

They might have gone on in this increasingly silly vein for quite some time — Istvhan was more than willing — but someone knocked loudly on the door and instincts took over. He rolled to his feet, grabbing his sword, just in time for their host to open the door. She was carrying a lamp and bright daylight spilled through the doorway behind her.

Many women would balk at suddenly confronting a large naked man with a sword, but she was made of sterner stuff. She looked him up and down, raised the eyebrow over the glass eye, and said, "Ah."

"Apologies," said Istvhan, lowering the sword and attempting to look less naked. Unfortunately, there were limits to how much you could modestly cover with a blade. He heard Clara smothering laughter behind him.

"You could have simply told me," the woman said. "I could have made up a second pallet in here."

"I didn't know myself," admitted Istvhan, who already felt guilty about lying over the washtub and couldn't quite bring himself to compound the falsehood.

"Then my congratulations. There is food in the main room,

though I suggest you dress to eat it. The benches are old and may have splinters." She set the lamp down, nodded to Clara, and pulled the door closed.

"There goes the least impressed woman I have ever met in my life," muttered Istvhan.

"I imagine running a safehouse does that to you."

After a quick washing up, they finally entered the main room. Faizen was waiting for them.

"We have confirmation," said Faizen, without bothering with greetings. "Our spymaster is working on details now, but it seems very clear. Approximately a dozen women, mostly older, were delivered as a group to the colosseum eleven days ago, under the seal of the Shipbreakers."

Istvhan felt Clara go very still next to him. Her breath went out in a woosh, as if someone had punched her in the gut. "A dozen," she said hoarsely. "There were more. Who has died? Are they certain of the numbers? Do they have descriptions?"

Faizen was already shaking his head. "Nothing so clear, and nothing so clear cut. That's an estimate only. There may be more or less."

"Alive," she said. For the first time since he had known her, there were tears in her voice. "Praise Ursa, some of them are alive."

She swayed a little on her feet. Istvhan wrapped his arms around her and pulled her close. She said something against his collar, but he could not make out the words, muffled as they were by cloth or weeping or both. He wondered briefly if there was a chance that this emotion would be too much and if he would find himself holding a bear against his chest, but these were minor concerns in the grand scheme of things. He merely held her and stroked her hair and murmured things that did not matter in the slightest.

"I'm sorry," she said, almost inaudibly, when she finally pulled away. Her eyes were red-rimmed.

"It's all right," he said. "I did the same when I found that some of my brothers had escaped the carnage of the temple." She nodded to him and wiped at her face with the back of her hand. "Although the Rat priests kindly provided handkerchiefs then."

Faizen cleared his throat and waved a square of linen at them. Clara gave a tiny choke of laughter and took it.

Conversation was stilted, to say the least. Istvhan and Faizen carried most of it. Clara sat at the table, staring at the food, one hand rubbing her chest.

Istvhan put an arm around her shoulders. "Eat," he said, in the paladin's voice.

She glanced up at him, her eyes narrowing. "I know what you're doing," she said.

"I know you do. But eat something anyway. We are going to have to come up with a plan, and that is never easy on an empty stomach." She grimaced, but took a piece of bread and began to gnaw on it, without much enthusiasm.

Faizen nodded. "When you're done, I'll take you to the spymaster. He'll tell you everything we know."

It was a long trip, made longer by another uncomfortable ride hiding in the wagon, although Istvhan made it rather more entertaining by whispering dirty jokes in her ear until she blushed. Neither of them spoke of the sisters being discovered alive, and she was glad of it. She was already too unsettled. A little straightforward lust was much more welcome.

The night before had been extremely lustful, but no less unsettling. She'd wanted it fast and hard again, a quick physical release untroubled by emotions. But Istvhan stubbornly refused to be hurried, whispering soothing words and stroking her skin, and she yielded at last.

The gods have mercy, it had *meant* something. Not just physical passion. It felt like love and that was terrifying. It would be far too easy to read love into his tenderness in return. She was glad to step back from that brink, even if it involved questionable jokes about milkmaids and watermelons.

They were ushered into the office of the Rat's spymaster again, and this time he offered chairs to everyone. He gave his name as Halishi. Istvhan didn't think anything of it, but Clara tilted her head sideways. "Like in the parable?"

Halishi's chuckle was almost silent. "You are well read."

"My convent illuminated manuscripts. One of our sisters was fond of the more obscure tales." She glanced at Istvhan. "St. Abvu escaped martyrdom by telling his enemies that he was in the wilds hunting halishim. They went out to look for the beasts, but they cannot be found, and so while they were trying to find the halishim's hunting grounds and thus St. Abvu, he fled across the water."

"Ah," said Istvhan. "A wild goose chase."

"Something of the sort. Although geese actually exist and the same cannot be said of the halishim."

"So far as the world is concerned," said Halishi, "I do not exist either. And someday I will retire and take another name and my replacement may be Halishi instead."

"You've been saying you were going to retire for a decade," said Faizen.

"And perhaps in another decade I'll actually do it. But you know how it is...you see a job and you are the one who knows it best, and it is very hard to step away." He nodded to the last member of the little group, a bony woman with muddy brown hair and a nose like an eagle. "Perhaps I'll make you take over."

"Avert," she said, holding up three crossed fingers in a clear warding gesture. "You won't get me in that chair that easily."

"And what may we call you?" asked Istvhan.

"Sparrow." She smiled. "Also not my real name."

"I would hardly expect as much."

"Sparrow's the one who brought us most of the intelligence we have available," said Faizen. "If anyone can help us figure out how to get your sisters out of the colosseum, it's her."

"Thank you," said Clara.

"Don't thank me yet," said the woman, her smile fading. "I can't see a way out yet myself, unless your sisters can fly. But that's what we're here to figure out."

"Then let us get down to business," said Istvhan, hitching his seat forward. "Show us the maps."

CHAPTER 40

It took the better part of an hour to go over the problems. Despite Halishi's claims that the spy network inside the houses of the Sealords was not particularly good, the maps seemed very clear to Istvhan. So did the difficulties.

"Getting in is easy," said Sparrow. "Load up a wagon full of deliveries and you can ride inside to unload it. Getting out again, once there's been a jailbreak...that's the hard part. They'll simply pull the bridge to the main city and leave everyone stuck on the island. After that, they can literally go floor by floor and throw anyone that they don't recognize into a cell. They did it once before when a group of prisoners who were set to be tiger bait managed to overpower a guard. Only two escaped, if you can call it that, when they threw themselves into the sea."

"They didn't survive?"

"The current comes from the north, not the south. Another month from now and we'll be seeing chunks of ice going by. This time of year, they'd survive...oh, maybe twenty minutes in the water, if they were good swimmers. The Sealords didn't even bother to send out boats. They'd be swept south and the first beaches you'd come to, *if* you managed to break out of the current, are held by the Sealords as well. All they had to do was station a few guards on the docks there and watch to make sure they didn't somehow grab hold of a piling."

"Could a boat come and pick us up?" asked Istvhan.

"A boat that holds over a dozen? Not without being noticed and filled full of arrows." Halishi shook his head. "You have all my sympathy and the bishop's aid. But I can't ask one of my people to commit outright suicide."

"And I have no idea how to steer a boat," muttered Istvhan. He thought of cold dark water, a force that could be neither persuaded nor beaten, and shuddered. "Clara?"

"No. I can manage a barge on a canal for a short period, but that's a far cry from this."

"Sheer cliff on the north side," said Sparrow, tapping the map. "No luck there. There's a water stair on the inland side and they bring goods through it, but that will definitely be closed off. Even if you fight your way to the dock there, and tried to ferry all your people out..." She shook her head. "You can't get a boat back upriver without them seeing it. They'd just raise the chains at the river mouth. Part of the reason Morstone's never been invaded."

Clara put her elbows on the table. "Tell us about the interior first. What are we looking at?"

"They'll be held here," said Sparrow, tapping a layer of the map. "They're in the beast area, which is probably why we've heard about them at all. It was strange enough for there to be a group of middle-aged women in a beast cage that people talked."

"Of course," muttered Clara, "they don't dare keep them where one might change and break the bars." Her voice and eyes were flat and Istvhan ached for the emotions that she must be clamping down right now.

"The best time to free them, if we can manage it, will be after the beasts are fed the night before," said Halishi. "They treat the animals very well, at least until they have someone cut them to bits." His smile held no humor in it. "That means darkness, and while there will be guards and general patrols through the area, if you can take down the watchers and the attendants, you'll just have to get them out without one of the patrols raising an alarm. The second best time will be right before they are due in the pit. No one will be surprised that they are not in their cell, and while someone will come looking for them much sooner, it will perhaps be thought that they are being moved somewhere, not that they have escaped. And you have an excuse for moving them through the hallway, at least for the first hall or two, if you encounter a patrol — tell them you're going in through a different door, because the beast door will give away too much."

Clara nodded. She traced her finger from the beast level to the inland dock, over and over, her eyes shadowed. Istvhan wondered what she was thinking. "Can this route be done?"

"There is one portcullis," said Sparrow, "but it has levers on either side, with locking mechanisms, and it is only meant to keep beasts in, not someone who can throw switches. There are guard patrols, but no checkpoints. They expect human prisoners to escape, not..."

"Not beasts," said Clara, still in that soft, flat voice. Sparrow and Halishi winced. Istvhan reached out and took her hand, but her fingers were cold as ice.

"Once at the water stair, you would only have one direction to defend against," said Halishi, tapping the corridor that led onto the docks. "But as we said, there's no way to get a boat into the river from there. They've got towers with archers on either side of the bridge. They can't hit the water stair because of the angle, but you've got nowhere to go but the sea. And any craft that handle the sea is a target for more archers above."

"A craft, yes," murmured Clara. She moved over to the map that showed the coastline and the bulk of the island, drawing her finger from the inland side of the island, down, along the coast.

Halishi looked up suddenly, nostrils flaring. Sparrow was already shaking her head. "Don't even think of swimming. You'd freeze."

"A *human* would freeze," said Clara. "But I have stood in fresh snow melt up to my chest and flipped fish onto the banks with my paws." She tapped the water stair. "My sisters and I will swim for it. If you can arrange for a bonfire on shore...say, a mile south...we will make our own way off the island."

"We can do that," said Halishi. "But they cannot leave the bonfire lit forever without attracting attention. You must get them all out at the same time. Once the colosseum locks down, you will have no more than an hour, and perhaps less."

Clara nodded. "Bears are swifter in the water than humans. I doubt most people realize how much swifter. And they will not be expecting us to swim."

Something chill and hard sank into Istvhan's bones. The dark water at night, impossibly cold, impossibly deep, the current sweeping them south... "Are you sure?" he said. His voice wanted to crack as if he were a boy. He swallowed and forced it to obey him. The paladin's voice. The calm one. *You do not add your fears to her burdens.* "There will still be archers."

"Dark bear, in dark water, at night," she said. "If they can hit us, they deserve to." She frowned, looking up at him. "But we'll still need to find a way to get you out."

Fear was not the only burden that he would not add to hers. "Don't fret for that, Domina," he said. He could not use the paladin's voice for this, because it was not entirely true, but he managed a smile anyway. "Get your sisters out. I'll make my own way home."

He made love to her fiercely that night, as if she were already slipping away from him and by passion alone he could win her back. In a sense, perhaps, she was. Istvhan could feel her retreating, pushing back the emotions that threatened to overwhelm her, and even knowing why she was doing it, it felt as if she was pushing him away as well. He did not know how to bridge the space between them with words. Anything he said would come out wrong or would threaten the fragile equilibrium that Clara was trying to maintain. Instead, he tried to fill the gap with his body, wringing pleasure out of both of them until they were tired and sated and sore.

"Mercy," she said, as he rolled over to face her. "I am middle-aged and another round will kill me."

"I'm as middle-aged as you are," Istvhan said, amused. He brushed the hair back from her face, letting his fingers linger against her cheek.

"Yes, but you seem to have forgotten that fact."

"You inspire me to great acts, Domina. Also, I had quite a large breakfast this morning."

She swatted at him. "Must be the beach plums."

"It was *not* the beach plums. Bah." He caught her hand and flattened it against his, playing with the fingers in the way that lovers had done for a thousand years and probably would for a thousand more. "Look at you."

"Don't start in about my dainty fingers again."

"Compared to me..."

"Compared to you, everyone in this city is dainty." She shook her head. "God, it was no wonder they got wind of us. A pair of giants roaming around, what else were they going to think?"

Istvhan chuckled. "It's a very cosmopolitan place. I didn't think we'd stick out that much."

"Yes, but it's a port city. Sailors tend to be wiry and short. The occasional giant for muscle, but you mostly want people who can climb rigging and fit under these damned doorways." She waved toward the lintel. "Plus the locals all run about five-six. I was afraid I was going to break the chairs at a couple of those inns."

"It wasn't the chairs I worried about, it was the spoons." Istvhan shook his head mournfully. "Did you notice how short the handles are compared to the bowls here? I was afraid I might accidentally swallow one."

"What an ignominious death. 'Here lies Istvhan, Paladin and Hero, choked to death on a small spoon.'"

"I was really hoping for more of a death-and-glory charge at the end, I'll be honest."

She sobered. "Well, you might get your chance in a day or two."

He propped himself up on one elbow. "Do you want me to be comforting or tactical?"

"Tactical, if you please."

"It's not the worst plan I've ever seen. We know a great deal about the territory, and you and I are more than a match for most. But I'd be lying if I said that I thought the odds were good. There's just too many of them."

"Yeah, we'll probably all die. But I have to at least pretend we'll succeed, or I won't be able to do anything at all." Her smile was wry and self-deprecating and Istvhan didn't believe it for a moment.

"Domina, that's a load of bull. You'd storm the gates alone if it was the only thing you could think of to do." He paused, then added, "And I'd be right there beside you, so I guess that makes two of us."

She met his eyes and suddenly the look was too intense. The two of them, together, against all enemies. It felt too right. It felt like an echo of the godhead that he'd never thought to feel again, the belief that he was standing in the one place in the universe where he utterly belonged.

Next to her.

He had to look away, and so did she. His chest felt tight and he understood why she was always rubbing hers.

Do you feel the same? When all this is over, you'll go back to your convent. And I...what will I do? A group of nuns who can turn into bears hardly needs me to escort them. Although I could smooth the road for you, certainly with the Arral.

He wanted to offer. He wanted to believe that she felt it too. *And if she doesn't? And if you make her think about it now, at this moment when the last thing she needs is more emotions? To confess to her that you think about a future with her? What if the only reason she was able to bed you was because she thought it would not last?*

It would be the depths of selfishness to throw himself at her feet two days before the battle and demand that she deal with his feelings, on top of everything else. So he yawned instead and curled up around her, and felt her body molded against his as if they had been made to fit each other.

I don't fall in love, he'd told Doc Mason. He'd been telling the truth, or so he thought. He had his brothers and his work and the drive to make the world a little better before he died. That had always been enough. He'd never needed more.

I could go back to that life. I could pick up where I left off.

He tried to imagine bedding another woman. Doing the whole dance again, watching a stranger's eyes to make certain that they weren't physically afraid. Constantly watching himself, never letting go completely, the whole world too fragile, too damn small.

Just thinking about it was exhausting. But that wasn't love, was it? *You are my friend and we understand each other and the thought of bedding someone else makes me tired? Saint's balls, try to put that in a love letter, see how far you get.*

Hell, he couldn't even say that he'd die for her. He was a paladin. He'd die for almost anyone. It was part of the job description.

I trust you to watch my back. I have enormous faith in your competence. I want you to be happy. I want to carry extra robes around in my pack in case you need them and I want you to eat the beach plums I won't eat and I want to wander around the world with you and complain about the size of the silverware and I'm afraid that you'll go back to your convent and you won't need me any longer and I'll be so glad that you're happy and so damn miserable that you're not beside me.

Clara fell asleep long before he finished brooding, and he breathed against her hair and wondered what would happen to them.

CHAPTER 41

A messenger came for Istvhan in the morning, telling him that he was summoned to the Temple. Even though the message said that it was not an emergency, he didn't linger. Once he arrived at the main courtyard, though, he wasn't sure who had sent for him. He gazed across the crowd of people, wondering what was going to go wrong now. A very pregnant woman caught his eye. She appeared to actually be in labor. He couldn't do much about that, so he got her a chair, and thus was occupied when someone came up behind him and said, "Well, the Rat's letting just anyone in here these days."

"Galen!" He spun around and grabbed the other man's shoulders. "Galen, you made it!"

"Don't sound so surprised, Boss, I'm not completely incompetent." Galen embraced him briefly, a ferret hugging a mountain, then stepped back. "I was much more worried about you. Is Clara...?"

"All in one piece. Saint's blood, so much has happened." He rubbed his forehead. "What about your people?"

"All good. Brant's delivering his barrels now. We'd have been here two days ago, but Brindle rescued an ox. They're at the South Gate."

"Rescued a...no. Not here. Let's get a drink and I'll get you caught up. And you can get me caught up. Everyone will be caught up."

"Judging by the look of this place, nobody's been caught up for a while." Galen shook his head. "What a madhouse."

"They're doing the best they can under the circumstances," said Istvhan. "They're working miracles, frankly, given..." He had to stop, because the pregnant woman had just let out a bellow and clutched at her belly. "Oh no. Madam, can I help you somehow?"

"You can get this baby *out of me*," she hissed.

"Squeeze my hand," he said, offering her two fingers. She gripped them like grim death.

"So I'll just go get that drink and bring you one, shall I?"

"That would be for the best."

"Bring me one too," growled the pregnant woman.

"Make hers a double," suggested Istvhan. Galen saluted.

A healer came out, swore, timed the contractions, said, "It'll be a bit yet, we'll clear a bed," and went away again. Istvhan told the expectant mother a long, rambling, mostly-true story about one of his sisters, who thought that she still had a few days left and had gone out to check on her flock of sheep because one of the ewes had steadfastly refused to give birth, and had ended up flat on her back under a tree with a sheepdog as a midwife. "The damn ewe lasted three more days. But my nephew was healthy and happy and is now taller than I am, so believe me, you'll do fine."

She fixed a gimlet eye on him. "Get me the drink or the dog. I don't care which."

"The drink is coming."

"And stop telling me stories."

"Yes'm."

"I will piss on your foot if you tell me another story."

"Noted."

Galen returned just as the healers had finally cleared a bed. He ceremoniously handed the woman one of the low bowls they used in Morstone for wine, and Istvhan helped prop her up through the door and down onto the bed, while she drained the bowl. Being now completely superfluous to the process, he and Galen took themselves out and left the woman in the hands of professionals.

"Well, that was a good deed done," said Galen.

"Easy for you to say. I can't feel my fingers. She had a grip like a snapping turtle." He took one of the remaining bowls and took a sip. It was, of course, beach plum. "All right. Let me fill you in…"

They found a quiet place, a meeting room about the size of a large closet, and Istvhan ran down the entire saga from leaving to their arrival at Morstone. "But we found Clara's people. We've got a plan…" He briefed Galen on the general outlines.

"You're breaking into their colosseum?" Galen nodded to himself. "Right. Give me a few hours to get everything sorted here and get some food in me, and I'll be ready to go."

"You are *not*," said Istvhan. And when Galen looked mutinous, he added, "That is an order, dammit."

"Strictly speaking, we're only a little bit military. You can't exactly have me court-martialed. What is Beartongue going to do, cut my pay?"

Istvhan rubbed his face. Bishop Beartongue insisted that the paladins draw a stipend, but the fact was that none of them were particularly materialistic. A life spent mostly on the road in the service of the god had impressed on all of them the importance of traveling light, and even now that they had mostly settled in one place…well, Istvhan's brother-in-arms, Stephen, considered it a huge splurge if he bought two skeins of yarn that actually matched. If Galen owned anything more than his sword and his armor and the kit to care for them, Istvhan would be surprised. *I don't even know if he's got a third pair of drawers for formal occasions.*

"You can't come with me because you've got a different job to do. I'm just damn glad you arrived in time to hear it from me, not the local clergy."

Galen raised a skeptical eyebrow. "Appealing to my sense of duty is usually a winning proposition, but I'll be the judge."

"We found the person who made the smooth men."

Galen inhaled sharply. "Go on."

Istvhan plunged into that tale as well. He did not spare himself in the telling, either in how the tide had risen against the smooth men or in how he had failed to kill Stachys when he had the chance. "He's out there somewhere now," he finished. "And you can either wait here to see what the Rat's people turn up, or you can go back to Beartongue and tell her what you've learned. It might be enough to get some more temple muscle back up here, though the gods only know what that would do to the local political situation."

"That's for the higher-ups to decide," said Galen. "We're just the muscle." He smiled wanly. "The mostly unstoppable berserk muscle, I grant you. Though it sounds like they'd need a lot more than the seven of us to destabilize this place."

"Mmm. Yes. Well, in any event. You have got to make sure word gets back about this wonderworker and the smooth men. I know the Rat will do what they can, but they're stretched absurdly thin here. They've dropped damn near everything to help us, but..." He waved a hand in the general direction of the mass of people in the courtyard.

"I saw on the way in. You're right, though, they are working miracles, given what they're up against."

Istvhan leaned back. "So what about you? How did you fare after we left?"

"Oh, nothing so exciting. The hunters came back with crossbows, and I told them you'd left and pulled the tarp back off the wagon. They couldn't very well pretend I'd shoved the two of you into barrels, and they didn't relish a fight against all of us, so they went away again. After that, it was a straightforward trip." He paused. "Except for the ox."

"How did *that* happen?"

"We were in some little town off the trade road and ran into an ox that had balked. The drover was beating it — not just a tap on the flanks, but really beating it. The ox wasn't moving and this fellow was getting madder and madder." He grimaced. "You hate to see anybody beat an animal like that, but it's not like I know what to do with livestock. But Brindle pulled up the mules and threw Brant the reins and was on the drover like a terrier on a rat. Got the stick away and started asking him how he'd like a gnole to beat a human instead."

Istvhan put his face in hands. "Oh god, I can see it now."

"Yup." Galen took a slug of wine and wiped his mouth. "The drover wasn't any too pleased but he'd obviously never seen a gnole before and didn't know whether to spit or run away. And then I was right behind him, of course. I was just going to suggest the drover step away and cool down, but Brindle said he wasn't leaving an ox with a human like that. So then I realized we were probably about to commit cattle rustling right there on the main road and was trying to figure out how we're going to get away with it, when Brant showed up. Pulled out his purse and counted out money on the spot, told Brindle to unhook the ox from the cart, and that *ended* the matter."

Istvhan raised his eyebrows at that. "Odd man, but his heart's in the right place."

"There's probably a hundred acorns planted between here and the mountains. And we made the rest of the trip with an ox tied to the back of the wagon. It moves about half as fast as I walk and Brindle dotes on it."

"So shines a good deed in a weary world?" offered Istvhan.

"Something like that. Oh — also Andrel left once we were out of the mountains. Demanded his pay, said he wasn't going any farther with us."

Istvhan winced. Once your hired men started deserting, it often spread like wildfire. "How did everyone else react?"

"At that point, I think we were all glad to see the back of him." He shrugged.

"Think we'll have to worry about him?"

"At the moment, no. Unless you already know about the sisters, going around telling people that a man on your last job ran off into the woods with a werebear nun is a hard sell. I suspect he's getting good and drunk and sulking a bit. But I'll see that the Rat doesn't hire him again. Are you and Clara sleeping together yet?"

The question came in the exact same tone of voice and caught Istvhan by surprise. "Ah...I...how is that your business?"

"Just wondering if I have to start shopping for wedding presents, that's all."

Istvhan snorted. "Yes, we are, no, you shouldn't. It's probably nothing. And if it's more than nothing, we're about to do something stupendously dangerous in two days, which may render it all moot anyway."

"Look me in the eye and tell me in the voice that it's probably nothing," said Galen, who was easy-going and good-natured and knew very well how to place a knife.

Istvhan stared at the ceiling.

"Mm-hmm. You sure you don't want my help? I can send Brindle back to the Bishop..."

"And who's going to guard him and the mules? And the ox? We've paid off all the mercenaries. No, I need you to take word." He sighed. "And I suppose we probably shouldn't meet again. If they catch us, they'll come for any known associates, and if we're seen together..." He spread his hands.

Galen scowled, stood up, and tried to pace. He could only get about four strides in the little room, so he sat down again, clearly frustrated. "I don't like this."

"I'm not exactly thrilled myself."

The redhead looked at him, looked at the ceiling, looked back at him again, and then checked his bowl to see if there was any wine left in the bottom. "Fine. We'll do it your way." He drained what was left down to the dregs, grimacing. "What do they make this stuff out of?"

"Beach plum," said Istvhan, rising to his feet. "You don't get used to it."

CHAPTER 42

On the last morning, neither of them slept late. There was no banter. Istvhan sat up and draped his wrists over his knees. He missed Ethan's galley and even Maude the toad, who might have provided something harmless to talk about, but Faizen had not thought it prudent to return them to Ethan's safehouse. (Ethan himself had appeared briefly to tell them that the damage was minimal and indistinguishable from monkeys or something called a kinkajou, whatever that was.)

He turned and saw Clara looking up at the ceiling. Without thinking, he leaned over and placed his palm between her breasts. She inhaled sharply and he imagined that he could feel the roiling of emotions under his hand.

"Clara—"

"Don't," she said. She wouldn't meet his eyes. "Please don't. Not now. I can't handle it."

He swallowed. "I never meant to add to your burdens, Domina."

"I know. And if the world was different..." She sat up. "In another life, maybe we'll meet on the canal, and I will be a trader and you will be a mercenary and we will fall into each other's arms."

Istvhan wanted to ask her about this life, and whether there was any chance of that happening now. But she had asked him not to, and to force the conversation would be cruel. *More than cruel. Perhaps dangerous for us both, if she cannot keep the beast on a leash when we break into the colosseum.*

"As you wish, Domina," he said, and they rose together, to dress and prepare to storm the Sealords' gates.

Getting into the colosseum was easy. Clara's nerves screamed that it was too easy, that it should have been hard, but it wasn't. They sat on the back of the wagon with the barrels, both of them wearing laborer's clothes and slouched down to look smaller. Istvhan's mail fit under the coarse tunic and Clara had her hair stuffed into a hat. They had elaborate backstories worked up, just in case, but all they did was show their passage chit to a bored-looking guard and the wagon rumbled over the bridge without a second glance.

"I expected it to be much harder," she whispered to Istvhan.

"They're more concerned with keeping people in than out, I suppose. And they bring so much food in daily..." He shrugged. "The transition to the actual cell levels are going to be where things get hairy. That's where they actually patrol."

He wasn't wrong. They carried barrels into the kitchen and simply walked off afterward, into the hive of activity there. No one looked at them until they reached a set of stairs leading down.

"These?" murmured Istvhan.

"They're what I remember from the map."

They went down the stairs. There was a wooden door at the bottom, barred from their side.

"It's bound to be guarded," she said. Istvhan executed a complicated wiggle, unhooking the short sword that had been lying along his back. Clara took hold of the bar and waited for his signal.

The guard on the other side said, "Hey! What are you—" and Istvhan's sword took him in the throat.

"Subtle," said Clara, looking down at the man and the blood now painting the walls.

"I didn't want him to raise the alarm."

"I think anybody who uses this door is going to be more than just alarmed." She stepped back to avoid standing in the growing puddle of blood.

"Look on the bright side," said Istvhan, "it keeps us from worrying if we need to hide the body." He stepped over the corpse, and hurried down the hallway. "Did you have another plan?"

"I thought we could talk to them. Try to deceive them."

"Interesting."

"I somehow thought you had experience with stealth missions."

"Domina, I'm a *berserker*."

"Perhaps you gnawed your shield very quietly?"

He gave her a wry look over his shoulder. "Cross corridor up ahead. Wait here."

He crept to the crossing, looked both ways, then gestured for her to join him at the end. "Not a lot of cover."

"They both attach to the corridor that we want, if memory serves. That one should have alcoves, although the map wasn't clear on how big they were."

"Pick a direction."

"Left."

They went left, around a turn. There was another guard at the end of the corridor, facing them. "Let me handle this one," muttered Clara, stepping forward, while Istvhan held the sword out of sight. "'Scuse me, sir, we're looking for the storerooms. We're supposed to pick up a bag of fennel seed, but we've gotten turned around..."

"This isn't food stores," said the guard. "You've gotten very lost. Go back the way you came and up two flights of stairs."

"But we were just up there and they told us to come down three flights," said Clara.

"I still think we got an extra flight in there," said Istvhan helpfully.

"Oh, this place is a *maze*."

"Regardless, you're in the wrong place. Man on the door shouldn't even have let you in," said the guard, rolling his eyes. "Go back the way you came."

"Isn't there a shorter way?"

"No."

"But if we really have to go down another flight, there should be a set of stairs past you, and then we could—"

"*No.*"

"But—"

"Go back the way you came," said the guard acidly. "Don't make me call a patrol to have you marched back."

"Ugggh," said Clara. "I'm going, I'm going...wait, did we come from the right or did we go straight?"

The guard made a frustrated noise and took several steps toward them, gesturing. "You had to have come from the stairs."

"Well, I *thought* we did..." She took a step backward, which led the man out of sight of the cross corridor, and then, fresh out of ideas, laced her hands together and clubbed him on the back of the neck.

He went to his knees. Istvhan stabbed him helpfully.

"Don't gloat," she said, glaring at the paladin.

"Domina, I would *never*. Shall I put the body with the other one?"

"Sure, why not?"

There was less blood this time. Clara mopped up as much as she could with the man's tunic while Istvhan dropped the body with his comrade's corpse.

"I took their swords out so it'll look like they stabbed each other."

"Will they buy that?"

"Can't hurt."

They crept down the corridor again, looking for a place to hide.

"I'm sorry," said Istvhan a few minutes later, looking at the bodies scattered at their feet. "Did you want to try to talk to any of these?"

"Hrrwufff."

"Was that sarcasm? Do bears do sarcasm?"

The look the bear gave him indicated that while bears might not, Clara certainly did. A moment later, her body shuddered and became a good deal smaller and less hairy. She stood up and Istvhan handed her what salvageable clothing he could find. One of the guards had been carrying a loop of rope, which made a serviceable belt for the battered robe. He pulled off his tunic and offered it to her. It left his armor rather distressingly obvious, but it made her look rather less like she had exploded out of her clothes, so that was probably a wash.

"They're going to know we're here," she said, pulling the tunic over her head.

"I think that ship sailed a while ago." Istvhan nudged one of the bodies. "They didn't even bother to ask who we were or where we were going, they just charged us."

"You had a bear with you."

"I would ask a man with a bear where he was going."

"...I suppose that's fair."

"No, I'm guessing they've found the bodies." He grimaced. "This is a really dreadfully good design from a security standpoint. Everything funnels into the guard levels and then through a couple of choke points on those levels. All you need is a handful of patrols to hold the whole thing."

A shout went up somewhere behind them. Someone else had found the last set of bodies. "Intruder on the floor!" they bellowed. "Intruder!"

"Well, shit," said Istvhan conversationally. A paladin and a bear could take down a remarkable number of people, but he was limited by not being berserk and Clara was limited by not being able to stand up in the hallway.

"Alcoves around the corner," she said, breaking into a run.

"Your ability to memorize a map astounds me, Domina."

"I'm a trader. It's what we do."

"And here I once asked you if bears could read maps."

"Yes, well." She peered around the corner and presumably saw no one, because she did not slow. "They're not very good at remembering landmarks or cardinal directions, unfortunately. There!"

They reached the alcoves. They looked at the alcoves. They looked at each other. They looked at the alcoves again.

"They looked a lot bigger on the map," said Istvhan.

"They're where the privy drains from upstairs cut through the walls," said Clara. She managed, by turning sideways and inhaling, to wedge herself into one, but Istvhan couldn't see her getting out again in a hurry. "Well, damn. I suppose we just keep going—"

Nearly a dozen men appeared at the end of the hallway.

"No," said Istvhan, very quietly, "I'll keep going. You stay here."

"What? What are you doing?"

"Surrendering," he said. "Get your sisters out."

"What?"

"Hush, Domina." He raised his sword in salute to the oncoming guards. "There's far too many of them. This is where we part ways, and may all the gods look after you."

Clara wedged herself as far back in the alcove as she could, straining her ears to hear what was happening.

Now? Now?

No. Don't change, she thought. *Don't. There are too many of them, and if you try to change in this hole, you'll get stuck like a cork in a bottle. And that means you cannot panic, no matter how much you want to.*

She heard the voices of the guards, Istvhan answering them. She heard a jangle of metal and a crack of fist on flesh.

Calm. I am calm. I am quiet. I have faith that Blessed St. Ursa will set me on the right path.

"Gentlemen," said Istvhan louder, sounding both pained and somewhat bemused. "I suggest that you do not continue. I am a paladin of the Saint of Steel. If I go berserk, I will try to kill all of you. Perhaps you will kill me. I imagine neither of us desires that outcome."

Clara could picture his face and his expression as he spoke. She shoved her hands in her pockets and her fingers closed over something small and hard. The acorn of the emperor oak.

The one in charge said something else, somewhat muffled.

Istvhan said, "Look for the trail of dead men. I did that alone. I would be very good in your gladiatorial pits, I think. That is why I have come."

Clara still couldn't make out his captor's voice, but caught the phrase *job interview* in scathing tones.

"I enjoy killing," said Istvhan pleasantly. "I enjoy killing men. I would enjoy killing all of you. Nevertheless, if you put me in the pit with a sword in my hand, I will enjoy that even more, and there will not be nearly as many...repercussions."

His tone was absolutely chilling. Clara was used to paladins being poor liars, but apparently Istvhan had not been informed of that. *Remember how calm he was on the road? How easily he covered for their mission? You always knew.*

The tiny, traitor voice in her head whispered, *You know you can't trust anything he said to you to get you in his bed.*

That didn't matter now. The only thing that mattered was that Istvhan had come with her into the heart of the enemy's stronghold and he was sacrificing himself to save her. *He could leave me behind with a kiss and a tickle and a "You know it would never work," after this is all over, but he's here now and* this *is the important thing.*

Another crack of fist on flesh. Istvhan grunted.

Now? Now?

Blessed Saint Ursa... But Saint Ursa seemed very far away. If She protected her chosen so well, why had all the other sisters been taken? Why was it left to Clara? Why was she left listening to a man give himself up to the enemy to save her? A man who had cried out her name in passion and left safety behind to help her? What good was St. Ursa, if he died?

What good had Istvhan's god done him, in the end?

She clenched her fist over the acorn and felt the tiny point on the end dig into her palm.

Faith. Faith made material. Brant does not know if what he plants will ever grow. He has faith that it will anyway, though he will never see it.

Saint Ursa, Saint of Steel if there is anything left of you that listens, save this man and save my sisters. I will follow this road to the end, even if it means my death, but don't make me watch him die.

Another guard ran up. Clara flattened back into the alcove, but he didn't look in her direction, just skidded past. "Sir," he gasped, "sir, the other patrol's dead. All of them. Like they've been torn to pieces."

Whoever the man in charge was, he let out a growl that would have done the bear proud. "Just you?" he asked. He must have turned to face the new arrival, because his voice was less muffled.

"Berserkers," said Istvhan, "are not known for our ability to work well in groups."

A bark of amusement. "You'll go in the pits either way. Maybe we'll feed you to a tiger to warm up the crowd."

"As you wish."

"Bring him," snapped the leader and then with clanking and grumbling and Istvhan saying, "Now, now," in a chiding tone, like a teacher to a misbehaving pupil, the group went off down the hall, leaving Clara alone.

She sagged back against the alcove wall, wiping at her face, and it was a long few minutes before she could bring herself to move.

CHAPTER 43

They put him in a cell. It was a fairly average cell. Istvhan had not been in a great many of them in his life, but it was neither a hole in the ground filled with rats nor a luxurious stateroom with armed guards. Distinctly middle of the road. The door was made of metal bars rather than being solid, which let a fair amount of light in, presumably so that prisoners could be assessed at a glance for suitability in the fighting pit.

He put a hand through the bars to try and find the locking mechanism, and discovered that it was out of reach for anyone with shorter arms than an orangutan. *Can't say I'm surprised. They have a lot of experience with this, I'm guessing.*

He tested each of the bars for weakness. There was none. He checked the flagstones in case anyone had politely left a secret door or hidden compartment. No one had been so courteous. The drain for waste was firmly cemented in. Given a sharpened spoon and a couple of months, Istvhan could have chipped his way out, but his captors had not thought to provide the spoon, either.

There was a rope hammock in the cell, as one might expect in such a nautical city. It was even long enough to accommodate Istvhan, which was impressive. He upgraded his opinion of the cell slightly.

And then, since there was nothing he could do and the alternative was to sit up and fret, he climbed into the hammock, prayed to all the living gods and one particular dead one for Clara's safety, and went to sleep.

Clara was impersonating one of the cleaning crew, by the simple expedient of picking up a bucket and walking off with it. She had tied her robe up with the loop of rope and washed the blood off her face. Fortunately, on her non-descript clothing, blood was indistinguishable from any other set of stains.

There were cleaners everywhere, once she was inside the main complex. No one looked at them twice, probably because there were simply so many *people*. The colosseum complex was a small city unto itself. Clara passed a floor full of gladiators working out, a floor that appeared to be sleeping quarters for workers, and two more full of cells sized to accommodate a human. She tried to calculate how much filth that many prisoners would generate, on top of the blood and dirt from the gladiators, on top of housing for the staff, and came up with an absurdly large amount. *No wonder there's people with mops everywhere you look. And we started halfway down the complex. The upper quarters are probably housing for higher ranked officials, and such people generate an ungodly amount of housework.*

The floors that had prison cells were guarded. Cleaners were still going in and out, but Clara did not know if they were on a schedule or known to the guards. She wanted very much to go check for Istvhan, but getting herself thrown in a cell would help no one, least of all him.

She told herself this three or four times. *And if you do find him, how will you break him out? This isn't like the beasts, where hardly anyone will be watching.*

He sacrificed his freedom for your sisters. Don't throw that away.

She did not seem to be moving. She was rooted to the spot,

washing a section of wall that was probably now clean enough to perform surgery on.

Once you find your sisters, you can come back for him. If you set a bunch of tigers loose, that will be enough distraction for any number of guards.

That finally got her moving again. She picked up the bucket and hurried to the next set of stairs, looking for the runs where they kept the beasts.

"You. Paladin."

Istvhan looked up, startled. The speaker at the bars was so nondescript that he suspected she worked at it. Colorless hair, colorless eyes, shapeless clothes. If she had not been at the door of his cell, which automatically rendered her the most interesting thing in Istvhan's world, he might have overlooked her completely.

"Will you speak with me?" she asked.

"My social calendar is not particularly full," said Istvhan glancing around the cell. In addition to the lack of sharpened spoons and escape tunnels, no one had included any reading material. He would have given a great deal for a scandalous broadsheet to pass the time.

"You *are* a paladin, aren't you?" she said. "Saint of Steel?"

"How did you know?" asked Istvhan, not seeing the point of denying it.

She shrugged. "The Sealords have eyes and ears," she said, "and there are few enough berserkers about. Word is that a Saint came in as part of a caravan a few days ago, and now you are here and claiming to be a berserker. And enough men are dead that I am inclined to believe that claim. It does not take an expert to put two and two together."

A Saint came in as part of a caravan. They must have gotten word of Galen, somehow. Someone talked. Istvhan decided not to correct her impression. It might yet work out in his favor. "Then I fear you have the advantage of me, madam."

His flirtation earned him a colorless smile. "The Saints of Steel are said to be the elite."

It was his turn to smile. "We have our moments."

She nodded. "You will fight in the pits, then?"

"It is what I came to do."

"Why?"

The best lies were made of truth. Istvhan licked his lips. "My god is dead," he said. "I am a weapon with no master. Most of my comrades chose to die when the God did, but I choose the manner of my death. And I heard you had a necromancer working here. To die and take such an enemy with me..." He gave her his most feral smile.

She did not rise to the bait. "They say that a Saint of Steel cannot be defeated in battle."

"We can. If you throw enough bodies at us." That was no lie.

She nodded. "Tomorrow is the new exhibition," she said. "Antony's drowgos are expected to carry the day again, but the Shipbreakers have brought in something new. Something strange enough that Antony is nervous."

Something like a convent full of werebears, I expect.

"It is in the interest of the other Sealords that Antony's control of the pits be broken. Whatever Shipbreaker MacLaren is planning, a little assistance may be useful. You will go to the pits immediately beforehand. The drowgos are meant to warm up on you before they face MacLaren's champion. If there are fewer drowgos afterward than Antony expects, that will serve all of us well. Will you do this?"

"Do I have a choice?"

Another fleeting, colorless smile. "Many men fear the drowgos. They are dead men, after all."

"I do not fear the dead," said Istvhan. "In my experience, the living are the ones who cause problems."

She nodded to him. "The roster will be changed, then. And you may learn how much trouble the dead can cause after all. And perhaps Antony will learn how much trouble can be caused by the living."

She began to turn away. Istvhan raised a hand. "May I ask a question, madam?"

Colorless eyes met his. "Perhaps."

"When I get to hell, who shall I say was my benefactor?"

She smiled. "Perhaps you'll find out before you get there."

The run stank of urine and fear and the boredom of beasts. The bear did not like it. It was the smell of a thousand traps, layered all together. *It's not,* she lied to it. *It's not. It's just a foolish human thing. We are free. Hush.*

Something roared, practically in her ear and Clara staggered back to the opposite wall. The bear growled and Clara locked it down with iron will. *It's nothing, it's nothing, it can't get to us, not now, hush, hush...*

"New here?" asked a sympathetic voice. Clara looked over and saw a wiry older woman. "Sent you to muck out stalls and didn't warn you?"

"They asked if someone wanted to do it and I...I like animals..." she said weakly.

"So do I," said the woman, "and this is a terrible place for that, if you ask me." She offered Clara a hand up. Her grip had surprising strength in it. "Don't mind him, that's just Crabby."

"Crabby?"

The woman gestured at the tiger who had roared. He was standing full length with his paws on the bars. Stretched out, he was taller even than the bear. "Crabby. He's got a fancy-ass noble name, but we call him Crabby. Don't worry about him attacking you, he mostly hates men." She steered Clara past the tiger's cell, well away from the bars. "Stay away from the bars, though, he likes to spray. They all do, actually. That's your job today, cleaning piss off the walls and the floor. Glamorous, huh?"

Clara managed a smile. Now what would a timid cleaner who likes animals say...? "Doesn't sound much different than cleaning the men's privies."

The tiger-keeper laughed. "And they're a damn sight better behaved, too. Look, you see the gutter on the floor there? Stay behind it and you're safe from anything but piss and noise. Don't go over that gutter, though. Not your hands, not your head, not any part of you. Otherwise, if they can get a paw through the bars, they might be able to reach you."

Clara's gulp was not entirely feigned. "Any others I should know about?"

"Stay away from the ape cage," said the woman. "They aren't keeping apes in it right this second, but they've got an amazing reach on them, and they'll throw nasty shit. The door's solid, not barred. It's at the far end." She waved around the curved semi-circle of the run.

Aha! Clara consulted the map in her head. The ape cage. That would be where her sisters were being kept. "Do I just mop, then?" she asked, hiding her excitement.

"Mop to start. If you somehow manage to finish that before lights out, you can work on emptying the muck buckets at the base of the gutters, but the piss has been piling up."

"When is lights out?" Clara was beginning to think that this place never slept. She was fairly certain that it was already early morning, and her sense of time passing screamed at her.

"About two hours before they start the fights, so the beasts are rested. Though we don't have to send any of them out to get slaughtered tonight, thank the River Giant." She sighed. "If you have any questions, just give a yell. I'll be on for a few more hours."

Do you happen to have a dozen nuns locked in a cage? This did not seem particularly safe, no matter how friendly the woman was. "Thank you," said Clara instead. "You're very kind." She kept her head down, filled her bucket at the nearby trough, and began to scrub.

It was hard work, but not particularly difficult. Most of her attention was spent trying to keep the bear from making trouble. The animals yelled or roared or screamed, according to their natures, and she scrubbed up their leavings and thought calming thoughts and wondered how long until lights out.

Her world narrowed to scrubbing, flagstones, and piss. It seemed like an eternity, but eventually a keeper began turning down the oil lamps and said, "You can stop there," as he passed.

"I'll go out the other side," she said, and waited to see if he'd protest. But apparently this wasn't unusual or even noteworthy. "Don't get pissed on," was all he said, and went to the next lamp.

She went to the far end of the run, stepped out the door, and waited, watching through the barred window. A keeper did a quick walk-through, then came out the door. Clara busied herself scrubbing the floor at the entrance and he immediately apologized for tracking dirt through, then went off, whistling.

And that was all. She watched for nearly twenty minutes and saw no one else. When the coast outside was clear, she slipped back inside the run.

Keys to the cages hung on the wall beside the entrances to the beast's run. Clara had had another moment of doubt when she saw them — *this is too easy, why aren't they hidden?* — but practicality overwhelmed it. You wouldn't hide the keys to a tiger's cage. The tiger couldn't very well steal them. And if something did go wrong, and someone locked themselves into a cell or if an animal injured itself, you'd have only seconds to remedy the matter. You wouldn't keep the keys locked up like you would for human prisoners. You'd keep multiple copies and you'd keep them in easy reach.

Blessings on your shaggy head, Saint Ursa. Clara grabbed the key ring. In the dimness, she could not make out any labels on the keys, or perhaps they weren't labeled at all. She sorted through them by touch as she hurried down the darkened run, back toward the ape cage.

Beasts watched her as she passed. A cat gave a coughing snarl. She heard something else, too, a distant thundering, though she did not know what throat it might have come from.

She was most of the way to the cage, the sound still growing around her, when she realized that the beast that made that cry was human. Above her, through layers of wood and stone, the crowd was beginning to roar.

CHAPTER 44

Istvhan heard the roars of the crowd through the walls. He wondered how long it would take for their initial bloodlust to be sated, how long until someone came for him. If anyone did.

I have only the word of a well-informed stranger that the roster has been changed at all. And only luck to protect me, should that captain of the guard see my name and decide to change it back.

Assuming the captain had the rank to override the woman he had met. Which was an interesting question all on its own, and not one that Istvhan had sufficient information to speculate on. *I am caught in the wheels of a vast political machine, and I have only the faintest idea of where the levers are located.*

The roars went on, occasionally falling, more often rising to a crescendo. *Killing their way through the warm-up acts?* He was just wondering whether to call out for a guard when one came to him. The jailer had a ring of keys in hand. "You're pit-fodder tonight," the man said. "Are you going to come quietly?"

"Probably," said Istvhan. "I'm bored. A pit fight sounds like an improvement." He put his hands through the bars and the man manacled them together, then swung the door open.

"Do I get a weapon?" asked Istvhan, as he was marched along the run.

"Aye, you do. Better show for the crowd that way." His jailer steered him toward a wall covered in weapons. None of it was of particularly high quality, but there was an extraordinary variety. "Pick your poison."

"May I handle the bastard sword on the lower left?"

The jailer did not uncuff him, but took down the sword. "Elliot's got a bolt on you," he said, jerking his chin to another man, who sat on a chair with a loaded crossbow, pointed very clearly in Istvhan's direction. "Don't get funny and he won't have to use it."

"I should not dream of it." Istvhan hefted the sword as well as he could, given the manacles. It wasn't a good blade, but it had weight, and after the first two or three assailants, you were pretty much using the edge as a club anyway. And he didn't trust any of the shields on the wall to hold up to a direct hit. "This will do."

As he walked toward the ramp that led up to the fighting floor, he caught a glimpse of a colorless shadow against the wall. She stepped forward, gesturing for the keys, and his jailer handed them over immediately, obedient to whatever authority she possessed.

"When you get to hell," she murmured, "you may tell the Lady of the Waters that the Dovekies still keep faith."

Istvhan bowed to her, very deeply, and went up the ramp, prepared to sell his life dear.

He'd been in a lot of fights in his life, but this was the first one that Istvhan could remember that came with an announcer.

"And now, gentlefolk, spectators of the sport, we have a challenger who fought his way into a prison cell! Claimed to be an elite swordsman in his own country. Let's see what the drowgos think of that!"

I don't know if I hate this or if I want one to follow me around for all my fights. Istvhan scanned the crowd. The seats rose high overhead, with the very top open to the sky, though it was nighttime and torches provided all the light. The seats were jammed full, presumably with the wealthiest closest to the bottom and the rabble stuck high in the nosebleed section. There were seven boxes studded around the amphitheater in the bottom row, each with a large sigil on the front. Three represented stylized diving birds, the others a collection of waves, ships, and swords. *One for each Sealord, I suspect. Is that one Antony there?*

His suspicions were confirmed a moment later when the announcer shouted, "Still undefeated, Sealord Antony's drowgos!" and the man in the box stood up, punching a fist at the air. He was a young, rather rat-faced man, with thinning hair and a sailor's wiry muscle. It was the person next to him that caught Istvhan's attention. He wore a dark hooded cloak and sat far too still, but it was more than that. Something screamed at Istvhan to pay attention, that this was *bad,* this was *evil,* this was *important.*

Paladins of the Saint of Steel had never been known for their finer sensitivities. Istvhan was no better at spotting a demon than the next person, and far worse if the next person happened to belong to the Dreaming God. But every half-buried sense of the uncanny that he possessed was suddenly screaming at him, and the cloaked figure was the locus.

If that's the necromancer, he's a damn fool. He's dressed like a cliché and he shouldn't be out here anyway. Unless he has to maintain a visual link to his dead bodies.

Two doors opened on opposite sides of the arena, and figures filed in. The crowd screamed. Istvhan took a few steps backward, darted a glance behind him to make sure that none had come through the door behind him. They hadn't. Just these, then, at least at first.

"Dredged from the bottom of the sea and animated with the desire for battle! They feel no pain and no fear! They do not know the meaning of defeat! Can any man actually kill them...*twice?*"

He hadn't needed an announcer to tell him that. The drowgos were most definitely dead. Istvhan had fought far more corpses in the last few days than he ever wanted to fight again, and it did not take an expert to see that these were more of the same. Water dripped from their clothes, smelling of brine. The skin that he could see was green-ish-black and had a waxy appearance. All of them seemed to have normal heads, or at least as normal as dead men could get. There were six of them and three had shrouds that covered their faces, but the others were eyeless and swollen, with blackened tongues protruding from their mouths. They wore winding sheets and shrouds and ragged clothing.

Well. The longer I last, the longer Clara has to get away. Let's see what I can do.

Six. Two with tridents, the rest with various swords and cutlasses. Not insurmountable, with the battle tide on him. Not great odds, nonetheless. If they fought as a unit, he'd be in deep trouble.

Istvhan took a deep breath. The battle tide was rising, a red haze pulling at the edges of his vision. *It is time,* he told it. He stopped holding back and let it rise.

"Sisters?" whispered Clara, peering through the barred window of the ape cage. "Sisters, are you there?"

Oh please, let them be there, let me not be in the wrong place, let them not have moved them before the fight...

Rustling. Shifting cloth. And then a familiar voice said, uncertainly, "Clara?"

The hard, knotted space in her chest felt as if it had been struck with a hammer. She clutched the bars. "Sigrid? Is that you?"

"Clara? But you're dead!"

"No, I'm not, I'm really not." She choked on something between laughter and tears. "I didn't die. Some Arral found me — oh, it doesn't matter! I'm here now and we don't have much time. I'll get you out." She fumbled with the keys and slid one into the lock. They were huge, heavy things and the locks were massive. The first one didn't turn, and she tried the next. The keys jangled on the ring. One of the tigers gave a coughing snarl at the sound and another cat roared from farther down the block, until the whole row rang with echoes. *Blessed Saint Ursa, they've probably learned that the keys mean it's feeding time...*

"Are you all right?" asked Sigrid, through the door.

"I've just got to find the right key."

And then she stopped, because something very sharp and very cold was prodding her in the back.

Very slowly, she turned her head.

One of the tiger keepers stood four feet away. He had a wicked spear with a crossbrace on it, set directly against her kidneys.

"I don't know how you got out," he said, "but I'm guessing you're one of them. Do you know what this thing I'm carrying is?"

"Bear spear," said Clara, her mouth dry.

"Exactly so." He put a touch of pressure on the weapon and she felt it slice through the cloth of her robe. The sides would be razor sharp, designed to slide through muscle and shield fat. "There was a fashion for bearbaiting a few years back. Me, I say that's a damn waste of a fine animal, but I haven't forgotten my business."

Clara swallowed. A soldier or a guard, she would have been confident in overpowering. They were used to fighting humans. But this man worked with animals every day and he was doing everything right. "If you let us go, I'll give you anything you want."

He shook his head. "There's nothing you can give me. Put your hands on the door."

She obeyed. "Please," she said, not taking her eyes off him. "Please, you must know this is wrong. We're nuns. We've been kidnapped. This is not right."

"No, it isn't," he said. He looked as old as she felt. "It's not right when it's tigers, either, or bears, or men. But I've got a granddaughter and I'm all she's got left, and if you escape on my watch, I'll be the next one in the pit." He whistled, not looking away, and another keeper popped out of a tiger cage a few doors down.

"Uh, sir, is there a problem?"

"Yeah," he said. He still didn't take his eyes off Clara. "Go round up the rest of the keepers. One of the beasts is loose."

The drowgos did not fight as a unit, but as six individuals, which was why Istvhan was still alive. He'd already learned that cutting their heads off didn't do anything. It just meant that he was fighting something headless. They were stumbling and not particularly agile, but they were still very much in the fight. He settled for lopping off their sword arms, which seemed to confuse them. The bodies were obviously well decayed, and cutting off their arms felt more like hacking through a block of hard cheese than flesh.

I shall simply have to take off their arms and legs until they can no longer get at me, he thought, and his thoughts were incredibly slow, rolling through his skull like stones, while his body moved with the speed of the tide. Sometimes time skipped sideways and he would find himself dragging his sword out of something's body without quite knowing how he got there. He found that he was actually relying on the announcer to tell him how many he had damaged.

"And he's gotten the arms off another one! They may not be dead, but they won't be taking a swing at him any more!"

I have got to hire one of these guys... There were three armless drowgos now, and he was working on the fourth. He had gotten one of its legs off and its hand at the wrist. It did not seem pained, but it fell over and began crawling after him. The battle tide rolled over him again. Everything was so slow. The movements of the enemy were clumsy and took so very long.

One of the ones without a sword arm came at him, trying to catch him in a one-armed hug. He danced out of the way, but there was a second one behind him and it actually got an arm partway around his waist. It was cold and wet and had the same soft, bloated feel as the leg he'd ripped off the smooth man days earlier.

He'd never been violently ill when the tide was upon him. His shred of remaining consciousness was deeply relieved.

Istvhan slammed the butt of his sword against the drowgo's chest, not expecting it to do anything but shove the creature back. Instead, he heard a strangely familiar hollow crunch.

The drowgo collapsed.

Even through the red haze across his vision, Istvhan thought, *What the hell?* It sounded like clay. But that made no sense at all. He got out of the way in case the thing was only stunned, but it lay unmoving on the sand.

Another was approaching, carrying a trident, and he backed away, out of range of the downed one, and waited to meet it, still puzzling over the sound. *That didn't sound like bone. How is that possible?* He had already chopped one's head half off, and it was flesh he cut through, too-soft and bloated from drowning, but definitely flesh. None of them had an extra head sticking out of their backs or shoulders.

The new drowgo had reach, but it was so slow. No faster than a human. The battle tide was swift and merciless. He had years to step past the thrust of the trident, to grab the shaft in his free hand and yank forward, pulling the drowgo off-balance, just so that he could angle it and shove backward. The butt of the trident hit it in the chest and he heard another crackle of breaking pottery and it collapsed, lifeless. The crowd howled, a distant roar like the sea striking rocks.

Istvhan fought free of the tide. It was probably foolish but if he was right, it changed everything. He kept hold of the trident, dug the tines into the wrappings over the downed drowgo's chest, and pulled.

Under the winding cloth, there was a shirt. Under the shirt — shit, shit, another one was coming, he didn't have time but he had to know — there was a gaping hole, black-ish green at the edges, the inside coated with grave wax.

Inside the hole, there were a dozen shards of broken pottery.

Clay hearts? Do they have clay hearts? *That would make a certain kind of sense, but Stachys never said anything.*

He uncoiled, leading with the sword stabbing straight into the next one's chest at the approximate level of the hole. A foolish move, one that no smart warrior would have tried on a human opponent. The ribs would knock your blade aside, and if they didn't, you'd have his torso permanently affixed to your sword, and presumably all his friends and maternal cousins would come running while you had a foot on his sternum, trying to pry him off.

No ribs. Another crackle of breaking ceramic. Another one down.

The one crawling toward him was the obvious target. He took off its other arm and rolled it over with the trident. It snapped and kicked at him. He pinned it down with the trident through the neck and pulled its shroud aside.

...oh.

It wasn't a heart.

The head of a child, cast in clay, snapped its jaws at him and opened its mouth in a soundless snarl.

CHAPTER 45

Clara had hoped to be reunited with her sisters as a liberator. Instead, she was shoved unceremoniously through the door on the point of a bear spear. The door slammed and left her blinking in the gloom.

"Clara," said Sister Sigrid, and folded her arms around Clara's shoulders.

"I was trying to rescue you," she said, feeling tears coming. "Oh god, I was so close, it's so stupid to get caught *now...*"

Sigrid patted her back as if she were very young. "We're all together again. That's worth something." Then she stepped away and there was another hug and another and even though she'd failed, they were *here* at last, after so long...

"Clara!"

"Late as always, I see."

"I thought I'd never see you again."

"I'm so glad you're alive."

"We all thought you died!"

She tried to answer all of them, but Saint Ursa only knew how coherent she was. Towards the end, she was just nodding and sobbing and unable to form any sentence at all.

"Is...is everyone still alive?" Clara asked, when she could get control of her voice again. She looked around the cell, her eyes adjusting to the gloom. The ape cage had been hastily converted to a kind of dormitory, with hammocks slung above and below and a table with food and drink. She tried to count bodies and gave up. "Where's the Abbess?"

"The Abbess didn't make it," said Sigrid gruffly.

Clara felt her heart clench. "The wagon was too much for her?"

"It wasn't the wagon. But how did you get here?"

"What do you mean, it wasn't the wagon?"

One of the two novices began to cry. Sigrid put her hand against the door as if trying to keep the world out. "We spent two weeks at a manor house a little south of here. The man that the raiders handed us over to demanded that we change, to prove that he wasn't being swindled. The Abbess refused. Said that we were not animals to perform for their amusement. So they hurt her until we complied."

Clara inhaled sharply. "Hurt..."

"She died of her wounds."

"We should have obeyed her wishes," said Sister Emilia. "We lowered ourselves to change, and for what? It didn't save her."

"If we'd done it sooner, it would have," growled the Sister Apothecary.

"It's done," said Sigrid. "It doesn't matter now." She looked at Clara, and Clara read in her eyes that it mattered very, very much and Sigrid was holding her temper by the barest shreds. "Do you know where we are?"

"Morstone," said Clara. "And we're about to be sent into the fighting pits."

Dismay ran through the assembled sisters, but Sigrid only nodded. "Tell us what you know, then."

Istvhan could hear the crowd screaming, could see another legless drowgo crawling toward him, but he couldn't look away. The sculpture in the dead thing's chest was no larger than his fist and there was something dreadfully misshapen about it. The forehead bulged over the face. Its eyes were far too widely spaced and had been sculpted closed, like a monstrous fetus.

Bizarrely, his first reaction was relief. This wasn't necromancy. This was evil, but it was a simple, straightforward evil that he understood. No one was dragging the dead back from their endless rest. The drowgos were not undead, they were simply dead flesh being driven forward by a wonderworker's magic.

Stachys told us. He said that he'd been angry when he made the last mold, that it wasn't right. And I thought he meant that it didn't work right, but no, he meant that what he'd created wasn't right. It wasn't something that could pass on the street. Maybe it was his way of trying to stop what his creation was doing.

Poor fool. That thing he created just found another way to use it.

The crawling thing jerked and twisted on the end of the trident. Istvhan smashed the clay child's face with his boot heel. The drowgo went limp.

He yanked the trident free and made his way across the sands, pinning each of the crawling drowgos and stomping down on its chest. Only one survived. He hauled the wet cloth off it and saw that the hole was in its belly instead, the clay head jammed in upside down, half-buried in a tangle of blackened viscera.

Don't puke in front of the enemy. Don't give them the satisfaction.

"He's done it!" screamed the announcer. *"He's killed them! Through the heart, every time! The swordsman's strategy pays off!"*

He stalked toward Sealord Antony's box and flung the trident down. It landed upright and quivering in the sand. *"Well?"* he shouted. *"Have you got any more?"*

It was absolutely grandstanding and the crowd loved it. Antony turned an ugly shade of mottled red and pounded his fist on the edge of the box. The hooded figure next to him turned their head and gazed down at Istvhan from the shadows of their cowl.

You're no necromancer. You're Stachys's great creation, aren't you? You found a way to get bodies supplied for you. I'll bet diamonds to dogshit that you're harvesting the bodies of the people you kill in the arena. Maybe soaking these overnight so they swell nicely, and jamming one of your nasty little heads into their guts. Oh, what a fine deal that must be. Every fight humans lose, you win.

He wondered how many previous gladiators had figured out that the little clay objects were controlling the corpses. *Did you just bury them under a wave of bodies, then put another head on top of them? The drowgos are undefeated, so no one's lived long enough to pass word. And from the crowd, it probably just looks like I'm destroying their hearts.* The heads were so small and the walls were so high. As long as the drowgos left no survivors, and as long as he kept the people who cleaned up the bodies happy, Antony could keep going indefinitely, feeding bodies into the smooth men's mill.

The crowd showed no sign of letting up. Istvhan waved to them, thinking what a disgusting group of people they must be, to enjoy watching beasts and men be torn to shreds by the corpses of their countrymen. *You know, in some countries, they just have oiled naked men wrestle each other and nobody raises the dead at all.*

"Enough, Antony," called another of the Sealords, rising to his feet. He was an old man with a pouched, sagging face and thinning hair. His box was decorated with the sigil of a ship caught in a mailed fist. Shipbreaker MacLaren? An odd title, but the gods only knew how the Sealords named themselves. *Impressive that I can hear him so well over the crowd. This place must have been designed for the acoustics.*

"If your drowgos cannot handle one solitary swordsman, give someone else a turn. I've champions of my own to put in the ring."

Antony's voice was strangled with rage. "This was barely an opening act! We sent in a handful to give him a fighting chance. My drowgos will take him and your pititful champions both, like they've taken all the others!"

"Let us see, then," said MacLaren, and sat down. He made a casual gesture toward the announcer.

"From Sealord MacLaren, of the Shipbreaker Clan, appearing for the first time in the arena...the Sisterhood of Saint Ursa!"

The crowd cheered, but Istvhan suspected that they would have cheered at anything at this point.

And this is where they find out that Clara's broken her sisters out of their cell. I hope.

"From the barbaric South, far across the mountains, a tribe of sisters known for their savagery! It is said they capture men for mating, then kill them when they're finished! But how will they fare against Morstone's own menace from the deep?"

If I somehow live through this, I am going to tell Clara so many stories.

The tension grew. The announcer fell silent. Istvhan dared to hope, and kept his eyes fixed on MacLaren. *Any minute now, a runner is going to come in and tell him...any minute now...*

He heard the doors creak wide behind him, and he turned.

A dozen women were pushed through the entryway, in a tight little knot. They were mostly middle-aged and older, but two teenage novices clutched each other's arms, terror written across their faces.

No.

Oh no.

Gods, please.

And at the front of them, the person in the world that he least wanted to see at that moment.

Clara met his eyes, her expression bleak, and shook her head.

The crowd did not know what to make of a group of frightened women, no matter how the announcer had billed them. There was some scattered cheering and a lot more muttering and confusion. Istvhan did not delude himself that they wouldn't be delighted as soon as there was blood on the sand, though.

He walked toward Clara. An older women, nearly as tall as she was and built along similar lines, moved to get between them, and Clara hastily put out an arm.

"You shouldn't be here," he said.

"Neither should you."

"Yeah, well..." He looked around at the entry doors. Any minute now, the drowgos would start pouring in. "Listen, this is important! They're smooth men! They've got a clay head inside their chests. Smash those and they go down."

Clara's eyes went wide, but she didn't waste time with questions. "We'll have to fight," she said over her shoulder. "These things aren't alive. There's a clay thing in their chests. Smash it and they die."

The door began to slide open. He gripped the haft of his trident, wondering how many of the nuns had heard that and understood it. Wondering how much of a bloodbath he was about to witness.

The big woman beside Clara turned to another woman next to her and said, "What do you do?"

"Smash the clay thing in their chests," said the second woman. Both of them grabbed two more and repeated the question. Drowgos began to emerge from the doorways, lining the walls of the pit. The dead men stood arm's length from one another, ringing the colosseum. The crowd's muttering began to turn to cheers as the pit filled with dead men.

"Must we fight?" asked a voice at Istvhan's elbow. The woman was old and frail and white-haired. "We have refused to change for their amusement, and now..." She raised one hand to the crowd.

Saint of Steel, whatever is left of you, White Rat, if you'll hear me, Saint Ursa if you exist — please, please let them not be determined to be martyrs. I'll die with a glad heart for them, but let it have some meaning. "If you do not fight, dead men will tear you to pieces," he said.

Clara's voice was flat and eerily uninflected, as if she were distracted by something of great importance. "I know this man. I will fight beside him."

The big woman said, "Not alone."

"Sigrid, the Abbess didn't want—"

"The Abbess is dead," said Sigrid flatly. "Don't ask me to watch the novices go the same way."

The drowgos finished filing in. Doors slammed shut with a hollow ring of metal. Istvhan turned in a circle, seeing dozens of the dead men, evenly spaced in a ring around them.

He turned back to Clara. Torchlight woke green fires in her eyes. "We will not recognize you as beasts," she said. Her jaw was tight and he realized at last that she was holding off the change with the very last of her self-control. "Get as far away from us as you can."

Sealord Antony brought his arm down in a slashing motion, and the drowgos charged.

CHAPTER 46

Istvhan knew one of the drowgos was coming up behind him and so he turned, catching its raised cutlass on his sword and punching the creature in the chest, hoping to find the hole. His fist struck ribs, but they dipped sharply to the left, and his second blow found the clay head. The drowgo collapsed and he spun away from it, took off another one's arm — *oh god it's so spongey I hate this so much* — and then found himself behind the line of drowgos.

He looked over their heads and saw the Sisters of Saint Ursa.

Clara had changed while his back was turned. So had the woman beside her. He watched the transformation move across them, like a fire catching, first one, then another, each of them standing up taller and taller, shapes flowing and changing into beasts, the novices half-grown juveniles, the rest as large as any bear he'd ever imagined.

The noise of the crowd changed abruptly. It did not become silent, but the roar became a hiss of indrawn breath, as every spectator saw what was taking place.

In that sudden hush, he heard the little old woman standing between two massive she-bears say, "Oh, *bollocks*," and then she, too, was changing.

How odd, thought Istvhan, feeling very detached, *it doesn't seem to have any relation to how big they are as humans.* The old woman was a silver-muzzled giant, a third again as large as Clara.

The drowgos were incapable of astonishment or surprise. They did not slow, but waded into combat, striking at the bears with sword and trident. One of the novices was cut down almost immediately. Then Clara and Sigrid hit the wall of drowgos like a hammer. Bodies flew. The crowd went mad.

Telling them to go for the chest may have been overly precise. The bears fought like...well, like bears. They smashed drowgos down and flung them aside. Paws larger than Istvhan's head laid open terrible gashes in the rotted flesh. The problem was that these blows were not particularly fatal unless they hit the right place. Istvhan had his back to the wall and watched as the silver-muzzled bear tore a drowgo's head from its shoulders, whereupon the drowgo stabbed her anyway, or tried. It had much the same effect as Istvhan's initial attempt to stab Clara, but it enraged the bear even further. She reared up and slammed her paws down on the drowgo, which crushed it to the ground and apparently took the clay head with it.

If the bears had fought as a unit, they could have made short work of the enemy. But most of the bears wanted to run away instead of fighting, and only turned when they had been pressed up against the wall. Only a few seemed to retain enough human presence of mind to know that they had no choice but to fight. Clara and Sigrid and the silver-muzzled old woman were the best of the lot, scything down the enemy like wheat, but they took blows from their own panicked sisters as well as the drowgos themselves.

To get in the way of the bears was to risk death. To stay out of battle was to let the nuns die.

It was not even a choice at all. Istvhan saw a knot of drowgos descending on the remaining novice and waded into the fray.

Time slipped sideways. He lost his sword somewhere. He had a vague memory that one of the bodies had been fresh, not old, and when he hewed into the thing's ribcage, the bone had locked onto the blade. Well, it hadn't been a very good sword anyway. And now the bear was in front of him and two drowgos and the bear was trying to climb the wall in a desperate panic to get away.

The drowgos, he told the tide desperately, *it is the drowgos we want, not the bear.*

The tide did not answer. It rarely did. And it had finally seen enough of the bears to begin to understand how to fight them. *The face,* it whispered. *The eyes, the nose. The body is armored. Strike the face and blind it first...grab the trident from this drowgo, shove it in front to take the blow, then aim for the eyes and it will rear back...*

No! Istvhan did take the trident from the drowgo, by the simple expedient of chopping its arm off, but he fought the tide, hooking the shaft over the monster's neck and hauling it backwards. It squashed unpleasantly against him but it lost its footing, and he smashed the butt of the trident down into its chest, hammering away until he found the hole and the clay head controlling it.

The second drowgo lifted its blade to cut at the bear's legs — *again,* he thought, there was already a splatter of blood on the sand — and Istvhan flung himself between them. He caught the thing's cutlass on the trident and slapped at its chest with his free hand, trying to find the hole, not finding it, it had to be somewhere, come on—

The tide wrenched him suddenly to one side, sacrificing his left shoulder as it did. The drowgo's cutlass slammed down and he felt his collarbone creak with the impact. Not broken, but he was going to have a devil of a time lifting his left arm for a while and why had the tide pulled him aside when—

The drowgo came apart and a paw larger than his head smashed through the space where he had been standing. Something roared, louder than the crowd, directly in his ear.

Up, up, get it on its hind legs, you probably can't go through the belly there's too much fat and hide there, try the throat, hit it in the face with the trident first—

He feinted with the trident and the bear snarled, lashing out. He jerked out of the way just in time to avoid having his head ripped off. Somewhere very far away, Istvhan could hear himself screaming, but the tide was over his head now, his vision red around the edges and the pain in his shoulder like a goad and he was made to kill and keep on killing until nothing else moved on the sand and the beast was *in his way.*

A cut opened up on the bear's muzzle, and presumably he'd made it. His left arm was numb. The bear struck again and knocked the trident spinning out of his hands and he staggered backward, groping for the cutlass the second drowgo had dropped and if he could get it and get in low, perhaps he could open up the belly after all, he didn't dare go high, the bear would catch him in a hug...

He got the cutlass. He was moving too slow, but the bear wasn't striking him again. Why not? What was it waiting for? The tide clawed at him, trying to drive him forward, and then the bear shook its head as if to dislodge a fly and took a step back and growled and the tide wanted him to press the advantage and he lifted the cutlass, waiting for his moment.

They faced each other across the sand, beast and berserker. Istvhan could not tell if the sound he heard was the crowd or the roar of the tide in his ears. The bear shook its head again. Everything was red, red with pain, red with blood, but there was something he was supposed to remember, a word beating in his brain, a name...

"Domina?"

The bear's growl was so deep he could feel it through his boots.

What was this feeling? Why did he look on a beast with claws like daggers and think of a body under his and a voice laughing in his ear? Why was he thinking of *beach plums,* of all things?

There might be drowgo still alive. Certainly there were other bears. He was in mortal danger and the tide knew it, but he fought his way toward the surface anyway and suddenly everything clicked back into place.

"Clara," he said, and threw the cutlass down.

The bear took a step forward and rose up on its hind legs and Istvhan gazed up at his death and took a step forward to embrace it.

She shivered and dwindled and then she was human and she walked forward into his arms.

The drowgos were dead. Most of the sisters had become human again. Sigrid was the last to change, standing on her hind legs and gazing at the crowd with small, fury-bright eyes. But then she, too, dropped to the ground and shivered into human skin, and it was only a group of bleeding women picking up the rags of their clothing while some of them wept. There were three dead bears on the sand.

Istvhan retrieved a long knife from the sand and stood beside Clara, trying to watch the doors in case more drowgos were coming. The announcer was shouting, but all he could hear over the crowd was "defeated at last" and "victory." The dead bears did not feel like victory.

He looked up, and the noble in the Shipbreaker box was standing, waving his fists in the air as if he had personally defeated the drowgos. Antony was gone.

"Do they let us out now?" asked Sigrid, coming up beside them. One of her arms dangled awkwardly at her side.

"I've no idea," said Istvhan. "That arm looks bad."

"Broken," she said. "Little bastard got one of their damn pitchforks into my leg and twisted right as my weight came down on it." Istvhan and Clara both winced.

Clara bled from a half-dozen cuts, none of which looked particularly serious, even though the sight made Istvhan want to find Sealord Antony and carve him up like a ham. *I should probably do that anyway, just on principle.* He wondered if he could tear off some of his tunic and mop up the worst of it.

"Don't fuss," said Clara, watching the crowd.

"I wasn't fussing."

"You were absolutely about to start. Anyway, what happened to *your* arm?"

"A drowgo, obviously. I don't think it's broken, but don't ask me to do any heavy lifting for a bit." He shook his head. "I take it you didn't get out."

"They caught me as I was opening the door," she said. "Sheer bad luck. One of the handlers never left the cell block. He was in the pen with the goddamn tiger, if you can believe it."

"I'll believe anything. Saint's teeth, are they ever going to let us out of here?"

"Door's opening," said Sigrid laconically.

Istvhan braced himself for another onslaught, but the only things in the doorway were two men, who waved them forward. "Come on!" one called. "This way!"

"Do we trust them?" asked Sigrid.

"No, but what are we going to do, keep standing here until everyone goes home?" said Clara reasonably.

Istvhan walked forward, sword held down. If they were carrying chains, he'd kill them both, and anyone who came after them. But they were not. In fact, one clapped Istvhan's shoulder and pumped his fist in the air. "That was amazing! I've never seen anything like it!"

The sisters followed him, leaning on each other. Istvhan emerged into the beast run and there were at least a dozen people there with food and water and what looked like medics with a bowl of water and a stack of cloths and everyone was beaming at them like...like...

Like you won. Like you were gladiators and they expect you to be proud of your victory. They cannot possibly have their heads this far up their own asses. Can they? Do they not understand that we're prisoners?

Apparently they did not. A beaming woman pressed a mug of water into his hands. The medics descended on Sigrid, clucking their tongues. Other people brought cloaks and draped them over the sisters' bare shoulders. Clara met his eyes over their heads and she looked as baffled as he felt.

"Sir, are you injured? That arm looks a bit rough. Can you move it?"

"I'm fine," he growled.

"Yes, I'm sure you feel fine," said the medic, "but that's just the adrenaline talking. If you can get your chain off, I'll take a look and wrap it up for you."

"Give me just a minute," said Istvhan. "I need to get some more water first. I'm parched."

"Yes, of course, sir."

He began to move toward Clara, but before he had gone more than a few steps, a familiar voice said, "Well done, everyone!"

Istvhan froze. It wasn't possible. *He can't be that big a fool. He can't have actually come down here to congratulate people he locked in cages. He can't.*

He turned, very slowly, thinking that he must have mistaken the voice. After all, he'd only heard it shouted above him in the arena, the acoustics surely must have lead him astray, it couldn't really be...

Shipbreaker MacLaren beamed at him.

He had three bodyguards behind him in a wedge, but he was shaking hands with medics and keepers and smiling with all his teeth. "*So* impressive! A great victory over Antony's monsters! Well done! This will shake things up, my goodness, yes!"

There are ten werebears here and one berserker. And he is shaking hands. And his guards are letting him do it. Have they all taken leave of their senses?

"Once you're all done here, we'll see about getting you to better quarters," said MacLaren, "as befits champions!"

"This is madness," murmured Clara in his ear. "Isn't it? I'm not wrong, am I?"

"Completely. I almost want to grab someone and remind them we're prisoners."

She huffed a laugh. "I suspect they'd remember in a hurry if any of us tried to leave."

Istvhan scanned the crowd. The beast keepers looked far more alert than the guards did. *Maybe they aren't quite sure what to do with people rather than animals?* Still, if the nuns tried to bolt, they'd undoubtedly get involved. "If I cause a distraction, can you get them away?"

"Depends entirely on the distraction."

He nodded. He wasn't quite sure what the distraction was going to be himself. He could stab MacLaren with a cheerful heart, but that might just result in guards going for everyone. *I suppose I will have to improvise.*

The Sealord looked up at him and his smile faltered. It occurred to Istvhan that he was probably looking incredibly grim, so he tried to soften the expression by bowing to the Sealord. *Stern, but proud. Try to look stern but proud.*

...what the hell does stern but proud look like? Am I supposed to do something with my eyelids?

Whatever his eyelids were doing, apparently they satisfied MacLaren. When he straightened up, the man was beaming again. "You're the one the Dovekies sent in, aren't you? Good man, good man. Not that my lovely ladies couldn't have handled it on their own, eh sisters? Eh?"

The Sisters of Saint Ursa were dead silent for a minute, and then someone — he thought it might be Sigrid, said, "Woo?"

"Ah — yes, quite." It seemed to occur to MacLaren rather suddenly that he was standing in the beast run, not congratulating the usual sort of gladiators. A trace of concern crossed his face. "Well, should be going. Just wanted to come down and congratulate you all on a fine victory. Antony is probably crying in his rooms right now!"

Istvhan sensed his window of opportunity slipping away. *Right,* he thought, *I can't wait to see what I do next.* And then he drew his knife and leapt at MacLaren.

CHAPTER 47

Apparently what I'm doing next is taking a hostage. Huh. How 'bout that?

He wasn't in the habit of taking hostages. Paladins generally frowned on that sort of thing. *I suppose this will be a learning experience for everyone.*

MacLaren was skinnier than he looked under the robes, his body all bone and aging sinew. Istvhan got the knife just behind the man's ear, his bad arm wrapped around MacLaren's neck. The pain in his shoulder made everything go briefly red, but as long as the Sealord didn't struggle, he could present a convincing illusion of strength.

Obviously he had no chance of living through this. He knew he had no chance. Keepers were already grabbing spears and nets off the walls. MacLaren gurgled against his arm. "Stop him! *Stop him!*"

"I wouldn't get any closer," Istvhan said, holding the knife in a businesslike fashion. "One nick under the ear here, and he'll bleed out before you get one of those spears in me." Across the crowd, he saw Clara's face, mouth hanging open in surprise, and then saw a sudden hardness settle over her features. *That's right, Domina, you know I'm a dead man now, but you'll use this, I know you will.*

"You can't kill me," gasped MacLaren. "If you kill me, they'll kill you. And if you don't kill me, there's nothing stopping them from

385

killing you anyway." He choked a laugh at Istvhan's elbow. "You're a dead man either way. Guards!"

Tough old bird, I'll give him that, even if he's a damn fool. One of the keepers stepped forward, lifting the spear.

"Poke me with that thing and I'll cut off his ear," said Istvhan, setting the knife against MacLaren's ear. He did not approve of torture in either a moral or practical sense, but he approved even less of being stabbed with spears.

"Don't listen—" MacLaren ordered. The keeper moved forward. Istvhan pushed the blade down a quarter inch. The man's voice suddenly went up an octave and blood squirted against Istvhan's chin. "Stop! *Stop!*" The keeper froze.

They formed a horrible tableau, the keeper, the white-faced crowd, most of them jostling for position, trying to see what was going on. At the back of the crowd, Clara and Sigrid were ushering the other sisters into a group and everyone was looking at him and no one was looking at the far door and Saint's blood, it was working, he just had to hold their attention a little longer. What would hold their attention, though?

Inspiration struck. "I have demands!" Istvhan cried.

One of the medics stepped forward, holding up his hands in a peaceful gesture. "Everyone calm down. This doesn't have to end badly. We can resolve this."

Blessed are the peacemakers, thought Istvhan, *for they will buy us time.*

Several of the sisters seemed to be arguing. From Clara's expression, Istvhan could tell that she was about to start swearing. MacLaren's breath rattled in his chest, blood pouring down the side of his head. Could a man bleed out from having his ear cut off? Istvhan had no idea. Hopefully not, or at least not quickly. *Not unless he's a hemophiliac or something.* Somehow, it did not seem appropriate to ask.

"You'll...never..." gasped the Sealord.

"Maybe not, but do you really want to convince me of that while I'm holding this knife?"

The Sealord gurgled something. There was so much blood. God, he hated head wounds.

Apparently Clara had won the argument, whatever it was. Most of the sisters had vanished around the curve of the beast run. Sigrid had her good arm around the novice, who was clearly overwhelmed, and was herding her away from the crowd. "Now, what are your demands?" asked the medic.

That's...a damn good question, actually. Hmm.

"What's the easiest way off this miserable rock?" he asked.

The medic's eyes flicked to one side. Istvhan set his back more firmly against the wall. "Don't think I don't see you over there," he said to the keeper who had been trying to angle into his blind spot. "He loses a little more ear for that." He barely twitched the knife but MacLaren screamed again. Istvhan felt ill. Sigrid and the novice were out of sight now, thank all the gods.

"We can get you a ship," said the medic.

"Which I have no way to crew," said Istvhan. "No. You'll get me two fast horses and a sack of coin. And an escort across the bridge and to the north wall." He yanked the knife free — MacLaren moaned — and pressed it against the man's throat. "Anybody tries anything, I'll start taking off more bits."

"Two horses," said the medic. "Yes. Of course."

"Good horses. No nags."

"No, of course not." The man took a step back. "If I give you my word, will you allow some of these people to leave? It's very crowded in here, I think you'll agree."

Istvhan mentally called down a thousand blessings on the man's head. "All the women can go. Healers too. Through that door," he said, jerking his chin toward the near door, farthest from the way that the sisters had gone. "You lot! Find rooms and shut yourself in. I start seeing too many people in the halls when I leave, and I'm going to get nervous, you understand?"

"Please do as he says," said the medic over his shoulder. "Murine, Ly, get the others out of here."

Two of the women began herding their fellows toward the door, in almost exactly the same brisk fashion that Sigrid and Clara had used. Istvhan felt a pang of amusement at the sight.

When they were out and the hall had fallen silent, the medic turned back. "Now..."

Istvhan wondered how long he could possibly draw this out. MacLaren's breath was rattling and his own arm was in so much pain that if the Sealord had tried to break free, he might have succeeded. *Sooner or later he's going to pass out, or one of the guards is going to get brave. Clara, I hope you're moving fast.*

"And no one's coming after me once I leave," said Istvhan. *Might as well wish for a thousand dancing girls and a kingdom while I'm at it.*

"Of course not," said the medic, who probably also knew that this was an impossibly silly request, but was determined to keep him talking.

"And a letter of safe passage through the—"

A roar sounded from around the corner, shockingly loud, and then another. A cat screamed, high and dangerous. And above the cries, he heard Clara's voice shouting, *"The beasts are loose!"*

Throwing the doors to the beast cages open was a good way to get yourself killed, and Clara was anticipating it with every instant. The bear was not happy at all, but the bear was also very tired and completely done with fighting, and that was the only reason that she was able to bring herself close enough to the cages to unlock the doors.

She wished them no ill. She thought it was a great crime that they were locked in these cages and made to fight. But letting them out was the only distraction she had available, and at least this way, they'd be killing people complicit in their captivity, not prisoners.

As it turned out, though, the biggest problem was that the beasts just didn't want to come out. They had their familiar cages, most of them had been fed recently, and there was a lot of noise and yelling outside the bars. One of the leopards snored at her. *This is not a distraction,* she thought grimly. *How the hell do we rescue Istvhan like this?*

She sure as hell wasn't leaving him behind. He'd saved all their lives by suddenly snatching MacLaren. All the other sisters were in the hall already, with Sigrid ready to slam the door shut if the beasts turned toward it. But none of the animals were moving! For that matter, she didn't even know what the things in the slimy water pit were, or if there was anything living in there at all. For all Clara knew, she had just tried to summon the bathing area to the attack.

Blessed saint Ursa, she thought, *do something! Please!*

She saw a bucket of fish and dumped it out on the ground in a splash, hoping that the smell would entice someone out, and turned toward the last cage.

Crabby hit the bars with a snarl that shook her to her bones. "Good tiger," she said hoarsely. "Good boy?"

He dropped to all fours, turned his back, and sprayed extravagantly all over the floor she'd spent so long cleaning. Clara dodged out of the way but felt her bare foot splash in something warm. *Thanks, Saint Ursa. No distraction, and now I get to make a death-or-glory charge to save Istvhan with one foot soaked in tiger piss.*

Unless...

"Nice tiger," she said, slammed the key in the lock, and turned. She yanked the door open so hard that it hit the wall and bounced with a rattle of bars, but she was already bolting at top speed for Sigrid.

Crabby understood doors. Doors were either closed, and thus unbreakable, or open. If they were open, you went through them very fast before a human stopped you.

He understood doors so well that he didn't even bother testing the one that slammed closed after Clara. Instead, he turned away and saw that all the *other* cage doors were open.

The tiger's roar filled the beast run, and suddenly none of the animals were sleeping.

Clara peered through the barred window, saw Crabby loping

down the run, saw that a leopard had come out to investigate the fish. The leopard saw the tiger, and then Crabby had something to *chase*.

She cupped her hands around her mouth and shouted a warning to the other end of the beast run.

"It's suicide to go in there," said Sigrid, as she yanked the door back open.

"Probably."

"Right." Sigrid stepped inside with her. "Let's see how big a mess we can make."

Istvhan cast an eye over the remaining crowd. Keepers, guards, and a couple of men who apparently were just there to serve drinks and bring clothing. When the leopard came around the corner, the servitors screamed. The keepers immediately decided that nothing involving humans was nearly as important as the animal coming toward them, and then the tiger came into view and a collective groan went up among them.

"Get out!" shouted one over his shoulder. "Crabby's loose! Get out, but for the love of god, don't run—"

It was too late. The servitors broke and ran. So did one of MacLaren's bodyguards. Another tiger poked its head around the corner, apparently to see what all the commotion was, and saw humans running away.

Every one of the beasts in the cages knew that you were supposed to chase humans when they ran away. They'd been whipped and harassed until they learned. Humans were prey. Admittedly, they were mostly prey when you were out on the sand in the loud room full of more humans, but even though this was the wrong room, the humans were running and there was a blood smell, and most big cats were not known for their fine handling of nuance.

Istvhan had his back to the wall and the tiger passed so close to him that he felt the wind ruffle his hair. A wave of smell hit him, meat and urine and predator, and then the tiger had the running guard down and casually bounced his head off the ground with one giant paw.

"Who all is out?" shouted a keeper.

"All of them!" cried a voice from farther down the run. It sounded like Clara.

Four wild boars with massive foreheads and underslung tusks rounded the corner. "Oh fuck," said one of the keepers.

Istvhan decided that it was probably time to leave for healthier climes. He flung MacLaren into the arms of the two remaining guards, shoving them backward toward — well, it was big and had spots and Istvhan was not going to try to work out the finer points of species identification at the moment — and began moving along the wall, looking for an empty cage to hide in. The spotted cat of unknown provenance did not appreciate having a person land on it. It swatted and hissed. One of the guards, braver or more suicidal than his counterpart, tried to stab the cat. It appreciated this even less.

Moans and yowls drifted down the run, and then something that sounded like a monstrous yawn: "Gyraaaaannnnnhhhh..."

"Was that the *hippo?*"

The boars charged. Three keepers had spears. There were four boars. The math did not work out well for the humans. Istvhan waited until all the tusks were pointed in the opposite direction and slid past the fray with his heart in his mouth. He saw a cage with the door open, apparently empty, and threw himself inside. Nothing attacked him. He swung the door closed and waited. *Clara, wherever you are, get the hell out of here!*

"I told them the boars were a bad idea," said a voice sadly. Istvhan looked up and saw that there was a man in the cage opposite him, also holding the door closed. He was the oldest looking keeper Istvhan had seen, and the paladin guessed that you didn't get to be an old beast keeper without a certain degree of sense. "I told them and told them. Cats are predictable. Boars aren't."

Another spotted cat sauntered past, in a kind of I-was-just-going-this-way-for-no-particular-reason amble. The keeper watched it go, shaking his head. "Does that one eat people?" asked Istvhan.

"They all eat people, son. That's the only reason they're here. In the wild, though, no. But it would eat a boar if it could get it."

"Maybe you can answer a question for me," said Istvhan, fully aware that he was in a cage, holding the door shut, talking to the enemy, who was also in a cage holding the door shut, while wild beasts rampaged outside, and that this was among the more desperately surreal conversations of his recent life.

"Son, I don't seem to be going anywhere."

"What the hell *was* all that? One minute we're locked in cells and the next we're conquering heroes and you just...expect us to forget about the cells?"

"What? But you *won* the *fight.* Against Antony's drowgos. Those things have been ruling the arena for months!"

"With nuns kidnapped from a convent!"

"But they won!"

They stared at each other through the bars in mutual noncomprehension.

"You're not from Morstone, are you, son?"

"No."

"Maybe that's why," said the keeper. "Look, the gladiators start out as prison scum. Fodder for the fights. I'd fire any man who treated my beasts the way that those people get treated. But if they live through it and they win, they get treated right. Better than right. At the higher levels, you get whatever you want. Wine, sex, adoration. That's why they fight, yeah? You win, you get *everything.*"

"I'm not sure that nuns really care about wine, sex, or adoration."

The keeper sighed. "Neither do the beasts," he admitted. "It ain't right to make them do it, but the fights have gone on longer than you or me and they'll keep going long after we're dead."

"So MacLaren genuinely expected us to just shake hands and be happy we'd won," muttered Istvhan. He'd dealt with some strange cultural blind spots before, but this one was so vast that he didn't know whether to laugh or scream.

"A Sealord coming down to talk to the rabble like us?" The keeper raised his eyebrows. "He was trying to honor you. Real man of the people. Gets his hands dirty and everything." There was a note of bitterness in the old man's voice, and Istvhan couldn't tell if he was being sarcastic or not.

I am on the edge of a vast political machine, he thought again. *And this man has seen part of it and has opinions and if I am lucky, none of what he knows will matter at all and I will get the hell out of here as soon as the beasts are done rampaging.*

"Have you got a smoke?" the keeper asked finally.

"No. And even if I did, how would I get it to you?"

The man sighed. "You wouldn't, but a man can dream."

There did not seem to be much more to say to that.

Istvhan was starting to wonder if the beasts had all moved on or if everyone was simply dead, and considering actually poking his head out of the cage when Clara appeared, hurrying in his direction. "Istvhan!"

He made frantic gestures at her. "Be careful! They're all loose!"

"This side's clear, except for a couple who aren't leaving the cages unless they get dragged out. Come on!"

Istvhan let the door swing open and joined her. The change of angle let him see that the keeper was not actually alone.

"There's a big...really big...snake in there with you."

"Yeah, that's Clutch. He's harmless. He ate a goat earlier this week, he won't bother anybody for a while." The keeper glanced over his shoulder to where the snake lay in a quiet coil. "You could take a nap in here if you wanted."

"...I'll pass."

Clara paused as they drew level to the snake's cage. "Well?" she said, in a colorless voice.

The old man shook his head. "Go on. They can't pin this one on me." Something flickered across his face and he added, "I know it was wrong, Sister. I know. I didn't do it because I thought I was doing right."

She nodded once, grimly, and tugged Istvhan back up the run.

CHAPTER 48

Sigrid was waiting for them. Her eyes were bright and she had a huge grin, despite her arm being in a makeshift sling that probably hurt like the devil. "Couple of critters wanted to go out this door. We let them, so long as they went left instead of right."

"Critters?" said Istvhan.

"I'm no expert. Looked like a bunch of red dogs with black tails. I growled at them a little and they decided left was just fine."

"Dholes," said Istvhan. "That's...fine. I'm sure it'll be fine. Actually, I'm not sure of anything. How far away is the dock?"

"Two flights down, through a guard level," said Clara promptly. "Then we're in the loading area." She steered Istvhan out the door and to the right, where the rest of the nuns were pressed against the wall. Sister Emilia was twittering over Jan the novice, and the Sister Cellarer had grabbed a spear at some point and was holding it in a menacing fashion.

"Will we have to fight more of them?" asked Sigrid.

"The guards were not particularly friendly before," said Istvhan. "Nor inclined to listen."

"I've got maybe two more changes in me," said Sigrid. "I doubt the others have more than one."

"We'll let them save it for the water, then," said Clara. She was already worrying how Sigrid was going to manage the swim with her arm broken, and what to do with Istvhan. *No. Focus. You've gotten this far. Do the next thing and worry about it when you get there. There may be a boat, or you may figure something else out.*

"Nice work with the old guy," said Sigrid.

"Paladins aren't supposed to take hostages," said Istvhan morosely.

"Yes, but you didn't keep him, so it's probably fine."

The corridors were not empty, but since the sounds of roaring were already echoing through the halls, no one seemed to have any interest in stopping them. In fact, two more people in servant's livery joined them. "Where are we going?" whispered one.

"Away from the screaming," Sister Emilia said, patting the man's hand. "You stick with us, you'll be fine." He looked reassured. Clara wondered what he'd think when everyone else turned into a bear.

They reached the stairs that funneled down to the guards. Istvhan looked at her. "Any thoughts?"

"Let's try subtlety."

The guard at the foot of the stairs was already looking jumpy, and the appearance of a large group of unauthorized people didn't help. He put his hand on his sword hilt. "No farther."

"Don't be an ass," said Clara, striding toward him. "Haven't you heard what happened?"

"Heard what...?" He clearly didn't want to draw on her, but he also didn't want to let her past, so he ended up skipping backwards in front of her. "What are you talking about?"

Istvhan shoved his way forward. "There's been a breach. All the beasts are out."

"What? *All* of them?" The man blanched. "How is that possible?"

"Damned if I know, but they are. The big tiger, you know—"

"Crabby," said Clara helpfully.

"—he's out and a bunch of boars. They're clearing the halls as fast as they can, but we've got to get these people to safety."

"But — I—" He looked at the crowd pouring down the steps. "I can't let you—"

"Get your ass back on the stairs," said Istvhan, "and watch for tigers. We'll get them clear."

"Watch for *tigers?*"

They left him standing in the middle of the hall, staring up the steps, his throat working.

The actual guard patrol was a little more difficult, but only just. "Who's your superior?" demanded the captain. "Who authorized this?"

"Authorized? You blithering idiot, there's a pack of *wild boars* charging around up there! Who authorized *them?!"*

The captain set his feet. "That's as may be, but I can't let you past without orders."

Clara looked at Istvhan. Istvhan looked at Clara. There were six of them, although the five behind the captain were staring up at the ceiling, as if boars might fall through at any moment. Could they take six? Probably, but not without someone getting hurt. She was already tired from the drowgos, and the adrenaline was bound to wear off eventually.

And then Sister Emilia pushed her way past Istvhan and planted herself in front of the guard captain. The tiny old woman put her hand on the startled man's chest — that being as high as she could reach — and said, at absolute top volume, "There are *tigers* loose upstairs, and *you* want to stand here *waving your dick around? We've got wounded!"*

The captain said, "Um?"

Wisps of white hair flew around Emilia's face, animated by her fury. "A tiger grabbed my leg!" She yanked up the edge of her robe to reveal a bony shin, marred by a single slash mark. Clara was pretty sure it had been from a drowgos's blade, but it wasn't as if anyone could tell the difference.

The captain said, "Er?"

"I got away from it by the grace of the gods and this brave man here hitting it and *you* want to pull a sword on him? When he got us all down the stairs and *away* from those beasts? What is *wrong* with you?"

"Ma'am—" said the captain, who was clearly made of stern stuff indeed, "I understand but my orders—"

The novice burst into tears.

Jan was fifteen and she cried as only a teenage girl on a mission could cry, with hitching sobs that joined into a rising wail. Sigrid steered her alongside Clara and released her arm with a whispered "Atta girl!" The novice stumbled forward alongside Emilia and latched onto the captain like a limpet.

"W-w-why are you doing this?" she sobbed against his tabard. "We were *attacked* and — and — people are *dead* and there's all these *animals*—"

The captain said, "Oh shit," and patted her awkwardly on the back. He looked up with panic in his eyes.

"Now you see what I'm dealing with," growled Istvhan. "But if you want to take charge of them, I'll go back and get another load—"

"No!" The captain began trying to disentangle the girl from his tabard. "No, no, if it's — ah — an emergency—" He eyed the group crowded into the hall and evidently decided that no one was storming the fortress with old women and servants. "Why don't you just take them down and we'll — err — guard the rear—"

"Good choice," said Clara. She raised her voice. "All right, everyone, orderly fashion, two at a time, these nice men are going to see that no beasts come after us, keep moving…"

They reached the stairs down. The guard there buckled before Sister Emilia had even finished yelling. "Yes'm. Yes. If the captain said it's okay, then yes, of course. Sorry to bother you."

"Didn't know you could cry on command," said Clara to Jan, as they went down the stairs.

The novice managed a smile. "I don't do it much at the convent. Worked a treat on my Da, but the mistress of novices just says to get it all out and I'll feel better when it's over." She snorted. "Given…everything…today, it wasn't hard though."

"No, I imagine not." Clara squeezed her shoulder. "I'm sorry about Ari."

Jan nodded. "Me too." She dredged up another smile, although it trembled at the edges. "Your friend there saved me. They were going to get me, too. I didn't even think about fighting, I was just trying to climb out. I knew I couldn't climb that wall, but I kept trying anyway."

"I know," said Clara. "It happens to all of us sometimes."

They reached the bottom of the stairs. It seemed bizarrely quiet. People were rolling barrels and moving crates, just as if there weren't wild animals loose on the upper levels. *Maybe they don't know?*

Istvhan took the lead, grabbing a woman who looked like a supervisor. Clara caught the words "beasts" and "escape" and "don't want a panic." The supervisor stared at him in astonishment for a moment, then swung into action, clapping her hands. "Everyone! There's been a problem on the upper levels, so I want you all to go to the cheese cellar and wait there until we get word, understand? Quick, quick, now! Quick like a fish!"

"Thank you," said Istvhan gravely, as the people unloading responded, mostly with groans about the inconvenience. None of them seemed terribly alarmed, though. Sister Emilia detached the two servants from the group and sent them on after the supervisor.

"And you?" asked the woman, looking over at the nuns.

"We've got wounded," said Clara. "We'll probably send people along in a few minutes, but we've got to make sure they get treated first."

"No healers down here."

"We can't very well go back up. We'll work something out."

The supervisor nodded. Clara recognized the look — a problem had been identified as not *her* problem, and therefore she could move on. "How long should this take?"

"I wouldn't think more than an hour or two," said Istvhan. "I'll go check with the guards upstairs once we're done and bring word."

"Thank you. We can't afford to get too far behind, you know." She nodded, then began herding the stragglers towards a door, and presumably, the cheese cellar.

"Now what?" asked Sigrid in an undertone. "Do we have to fight even more people?"

398

"Only a few, I think." She sniffed the air. The smell of seawater was coming strongly from a double-wide hall ahead, which squared with her memory of the map. "This way to the docks."

There were three guards on the docks. Clara started trying to think of a cover story, and then Sigrid simply turned into a bear, roared once, and smacked the nearest one over the side with her good paw.

"Subtle," said Istvhan, and stabbed the second one, then kicked him into the water for good measure.

"Oh hush," said Clara. The third man was gaping at them in pure astonishment. Sigrid advanced. He tried to shout an alarm but only managed a kind of limp squawk, then jumped into the water himself, which was possibly the most intelligent thing he could have done.

"Right." Clara clapped her hands, aware that she sounded not unlike the supervisor. "Bear form, everyone. This is where we swim."

One of the older women — Istvhan didn't know her name — was the first one in. The water level was a few feet below the docks but apparently bears did not fear diving. She hit the water with a great splash. A moment later her head popped up, fur soaked against her skull, and she began swimming south without looking back.

"That simple, then," said the young novice. She turned to look up at Istvhan. "Thank you for saving me."

"Of course," he said, which was probably an inadequate response. She smiled at him, and then she was a young bear scrabbling over the edge and into the water behind her sister.

"Right," said Clara. "I was hoping for a boat." She looked around the dock, her hands on her hips.

"I'm going back," said Istvhan.

"What?"

"I can't go with you. I'd drown. Or freeze. And I'd rather die here with a sword in my hand."

She stared at him. "Okay, but you don't have to go back! Go hide in the cellar, talk your way out..."

He shook his head. "You don't understand. Stachys's creature is here. It — he — is working for Antony."

Clara inhaled sharply. "Oh," she said after a moment. "Oh, that makes sense. You saw him?"

Istvhan nodded. "If I have a chance to cut the head off the snake..."

Clara looked toward the water, obviously torn. The old woman was herding the remaining sisters to the edge of the dock. "I..."

"Go with your sisters," he said. Even the slap of water against the dock and the cold wind off the water of the bay was making him queasy. "Get them out. Your part is done."

Her eyes were full of anguish. He heard a splash as a bear hit the water, then another. "Istvhan..."

"Go. They won't keep the beacon lit once your sisters start to arrive. You don't have any time."

She looked behind her again.

"You belong with them, not me," said Istvhan desperately. "You know you do."

For a moment he thought she was listening. She half-turned away. And then:

"Well, that's a load of horseshit if I ever heard one," said Sister Sigrid, and slapped him upside the head.

"Ow!" said Istvhan.

"Uh?" said Clara.

The two of them drew together, gaping at the nun. Sister Sigrid put her good fist on her hip and glared at the both of them. "'You belong with them, not me,'" she mimicked, in a high-pitched voice that somehow sounded both nothing like and uncannily like Istvhan. "Horseshit. If the two of you get any more in love, I'll puke on the floor right here. Clara, did I raise a damn fool?"

Clara's lips twitched. "I think you must have," she admitted.

"Well, then I suppose it's up to me to fix it. Come on, then, let's find this drowgo master. My arm's broken, I can't swim out of here, and I want a pound of flesh for what those bastards did to poor Ari."

"The others—"

Sister Emilia cleared her throat. The tiny old woman was the only one still on the dock. "They're in," she said. "I'll go last."

"Don't wait for us," said Clara. "The people at the bonfire are with the Temple of the Rat. They'll help you."

"Follow us when you can, then," Emilia said, "and may Blessed Saint Ursa watch and keep you." Her form flickered and then a great grey-muzzled bear rose up, twice Istvhan's height, turned, and lumbered off the dock and into the water.

"Do you know where you're going?" asked Sigrid.

"Haven't the foggiest," said Istvhan. He did not know whether to shove Clara off the dock or crush her to him and kiss her senseless.

"Then let's get moving, shall we?"

CHAPTER 49

They hurried back down the corridors they had just passed through, which were by now completely empty. The guards were gone. Istvhan guessed that they had gone upstairs to help with the escaped beasts, rather than risk another encounter with weeping girls.

The beast level was eerily silent. That seemed like a bad sign.

"We'll take the nearest stairs up," said Clara. "But I'll be a little lost once we get there. I didn't memorize all the levels."

At one cross corridor, they saw bodies. Something dark and shaggy was gnawing on one. The trio moved on quickly.

"Can they really have killed them all?" whispered Istvhan.

"Maybe. But the animals are valuable. I can't imagine they'd just kill them when there's a chance they might be contained." Clara shrugged helplessly. "More likely they've just gotten all the humans out of the way or behind doors, and now the beasts are wandering around and seeing what's interesting."

"I almost don't know whether to hope for them to be recaptured or not," Istvhan admitted.

"Neither do I."

When they came up to the gladiator level, a man in servant's livery was standing at the head of the steps, staring at a blood stain on the floor. Istvhan didn't think it was one of their stains, but it was hard to tell these days.

"Can you help us?" Istvhan said. "We're looking for where they keep the drowgos." The servant narrowed his eyes and Istvhan waved forward. "There's been an escape. Animals got out, and they've blocked off the beast runs."

"I heard the shouting, aye. The captain told me to stand here, but he didn't say what to do if something showed up. What got out?"

"A tiger and some bears," said Clara. "They're trying to round them up, I heard."

Istvhan nodded to her. "I was over that way and ran to help but... bears." He looked down at his sword and gave a self-deprecating shrug. "Might as well stab the things with a toothpick."

"Anybody hurt?"

Clara shook her head grimly. "From what I've heard, there's been a lot of injuries. They got out of the run."

"Did one of 'em get you?" the man asked, gaping at Sigrid's arm.

"Nothing so dignified," said Sigrid. "Fell on the damn stairs trying to run away. The keepers told us to go find the drowgos because...ah...."

"They're hoping to use them to herd the beasts," said Istvhan, stepping smoothly into the gap. "Animals don't like the smell, I guess? But I don't know where I'm going. I only ever saw the gladiator side, and not for long. Can you help us?"

The man relaxed. "Oh, aye, certainly. It gets confusing if you're only ever on one side or the other." He pointed down the hall and rattled off a list of turns, ending with, "And you can't miss it."

"You're a life saver," said Istvhan, saluting with the sword. The trio hurried around the corner.

"Good plan." Clara nodded to him. "Subtle, even."

"I had a most excellent teacher."

"The teacher had a most attentive student."

"If you two don't stop flirting, I'm going to be ill."

"Sorry, Domina."

"Hmmph."

The door looked like all the others, but there was a familiar scent in the air, a stench of burning hair and rotten milk. Istvhan halted. "This is the place," he muttered.

"Saint Ursa have mercy," said Clara. "Sigrid, you know how to kill them?"

"I got the gist. Go for the clay bits."

"Right." Istvhan pushed the door open.

His hunch paid off. Almost, he wished it hadn't.

It was the mirror of the beast run, a semi-circle, though this one had no cages. There were dozens of drowgos laid out on the floor, in long lines, like bodies laid out after a battle. Hooded figures stood among them. When the door opened, the figures all turned, in eerie unison, to look at the intruders. Istvhan recognized the tallest among them at once. He had seen that one before, at Antony's side.

They stared at each other, the trio of living humans and the ranks of the dead. Smooth men moved to the tall one's side, spreading out behind him like an honor guard.

But that was not all. Slumped in a corner, shivering and sick, flanked by two smooth men, was Stachys.

"Well, well, well," said the hooded figure. "Look who came to join us." His voice was terrible, the voice of something that should not have ever been given the ability to speak. It was guttural and lungless and it made the hair stand up on Istvhan's arms. But it was also smooth and cultured, all the accents landing precisely where they should. The combination made Istvhan feel as if his ears were going to start bleeding.

The hooded figure pushed back his cloak. He was a smooth man. Istvhan had expected that. Not merely a head, this was a sculpted bust with skin sewn up over the edges, drawn tight with thick black thread. His skin was waxy and desiccated and he smelled strongly of spices.

"You're not rotting," said Clara.

The clay head smiled. "No," he said. "It was so inconvenient, always having to find new bodies. But they have so much salt in this city, do they not?" He spread his arms and Istvhan saw the long line of stitching down a narrow, sunken chest. His pectoral muscles were flat and sunken and also had that strange, waxy shine.

"Saint's breath," said Clara. "You've salt-cured yourself." Sigrid swore softly behind them.

"A crude form of mummification, but an effective one. And it keeps me from relying on anyone else to stitch me into a new body more than once a year or so." He tilted his head. "Now why are you here? You killed many of my kin in the arena, did you not? Did you think that you might finish the job?"

"I have been hunting you across half the continent," growled Istvhan. "You murdered dozens of people in Archenhold."

"I did nothing of the sort. Others of my kind did that." He shrugged, the clay moving like flesh, the black threaded skin at the edges stretching against the waxy muscle of his chest. "Many of us went out in the world. We were looking for a place where we might live. Do not your own people do that as well? And sometimes kill those you find there?"

"Sometimes," said Istvhan. "We don't ride their corpses around later, though."

"We are, by nature, parasitic on your kind," the bust said pleasantly, in that hollow, horrible voice. "We require your dead. In the end, this local arrangement is the best one we have yet found. Your people were always going to die in the pits. I am merely making sure that those deaths do not go to waste."

"You're a monster," said Clara.

"As are you. I saw what you did in the pit, you and your kinswomen." He smiled. He had a beautiful smile, a young god sewn onto the shoulders of a monster. Stachys, at the height of his powers, had been a genius, there was no denying it. If the gods had been kind, they would have dropped a rock on the man's head before he unleashed his genius on the world. "I suppose you will try to kill me now? After chasing me across the continent?"

"That's the plan," said Istvhan, who really saw no point in lying about it.

"And when you die, your bodies will be used by my kin." His smile grew and it had teeth in it, and there was something not quite right about the teeth — maybe Stachys hadn't sculpted them quite perfectly, or perhaps he had never sculpted them at all. "Perhaps as a bear. I had not thought of putting my kin in animals. The goat was so unsatisfactory. But a kin tiger, or a kin bear...my, what a swath they'd cut in the arena."

"Love..." said a weak voice from the corner. "Love, that's not... that's not right. It's one thing if people are dead, but...but the animals didn't *do* anything..."

"Be quiet," said Stachys's creature to his creator. "No one asked your opinion."

"It's not right," mumbled the sculptor, staring at his clay hands. He looked half-dead already. *God help me, it might have been the kinder thing if we had killed him. At least he'd have died at home and not dragged here to be abused by this monster.*

"You're not wrong," said Istvhan to Stachys, very gently. "It isn't right."

The sculptor frowned up at him. One of his cloudy eyes had gone nearly white, and Istvhan wondered what had happened to him. "Do I know you?"

"We've met before," said Istvhan, giving Stachys his full attention and hoping that Clara was keeping an eye on the bust in his terrible salt-cured body. "You told me all about how you made him. You said it was out of love."

"Yes..." breathed Stachys. "Yes, I remember. Love is what makes it work."

"Oh, so *you* were the ones who killed my kin guarding him." Stachys's creation applauded sardonically. "Well done. It was sloppy of me to leave him out there, I suppose, but he is such a useless thing to lug about."

"And yet you don't kill him," said Clara thoughtfully. "I wonder why not?"

"Sentimentality," said the creature sharply.

"I doubt that." She flexed her hands, as if imagining that they were a bear's paws. "I doubt that very much. I think even you don't know what happens if he dies. I think you know there's a chance that all his magic will die with him. Including you."

Stachys looked from Clara to his creation, then back to Istvhan. "Is that true?"

"Don't be ridiculous," said the creature.

"I think it might be," said Istvhan, in the kindest voice he could manage.

"Oh," said Stachys, and seemed to lapse back into himself, as if he had exhausted his store of words. The two smooth men behind him did not shift, but their flat ceramic eyes stared into Istvhan, unblinking.

"You bore me," said the creature. "Kin, kill them."

The smooth men started forward. Clara held up a hand. "Before I try to kill you," she said, "I have one question."

"Ask quickly," said the creature, as the smooth men advanced. He stepped back, placing them between himself and the three warriors. "If it's interesting, maybe I'll answer it before you die."

"Why did your kin eat that clear goo from inside the clay head?"

A smooth man swung at her. Clara ducked. An instant later, Sigrid was erupting into bear form and its head exploded into pottery shards as she struck it with her good paw.

"Clay," said Stachys's creation, stepping back further, "is far more efficient than flesh. I can know all that my kin know at a taste. It doesn't work on your brains, you may be interested to know."

Istvhan rushed the smooth men standing over Stachys. One's head popped as his knife hilt met it, but the other swept its blade at him, and he took the cut on the bad shoulder. Hot white pain ran down his arm and then it went limp, not merely numb but nearly useless.

The smooth man lifted its sword, and then a bear's mouth engulfed its entire head and crunched down. Shards of pottery flew and the beast dropped the clay, making a gagging noise of disgust.

"You probably don't want to bite them..." said Clara, far too late.

Blood and clear goo dripped from the bear's mouth. It gave Clara a look. Istvhan still did not know bears well, but he had once had a dog give him a very similar look after it bit a porcupine. Clara shook her head sadly, and then there was a visual sizzle and suddenly a great deal less free space on Istvhan's side of the room. The second bear waded into the fray.

Istvhan did not see a great deal of available space, so hung back, holding his injured arm. He tried to curl his hand into a fist and immediately wished that he hadn't. The pain was so sharp and electric that it almost stopped being pain and became something else entirely.

Still, if you were going to fight smooth men, intelligent bears were better than two good arms. It had been hard to know where to aim on the drowgos. The smooth men required no such precision. Smash the head and they died.

Stachys's creation skipped backward as the last of the smooth men shattered against the wall. "My, my," he said, sounding amused. "You've killed my guards. Oh dear. Whatever shall I do?"

The bears either did not understand or did not appreciate sarcasm. Istvhan narrowed his eyes. He knew what it meant when a human enemy gloated, but the living statue did not look quite like a human and did not move quite like a human and Istvhan had serious doubts that he behaved quite the same either.

"Oh, wait. That's right. I have an entire army right here." The creature grinned then, and there was an emptiness in his mouth, as if his throat opened onto a vast pit. "Up, drowgos! Up!"

One of the bears made a nervous clicking sound in its throat, and then, all around them, the drowgos began to rise.

"Pity you didn't arrive about an hour earlier," said Stachys's creation, as his army shambled to its feet. "Before I finished putting the new kin into these bodies. It takes a bit longer on these, because the flesh is so rotten that it doesn't form the connection readily. Still, they should be ready now...ah, there we go."

And then he laughed.

"We killed them once," said Istvhan, with bravado he didn't feel. He fell back toward the bears, watching the corpses sway on their feet. "We can do it again." He tried to do the mental math. They had rendered a number of them completely useless for battle, surely — limbless or torn in half. That left perhaps twenty here, and two bears and one paladin, except one of the bears only had three working legs and the paladin only had one good arm.

The resulting equation was not coming out in Istvhan's favor, so he ignored it.

"There were a great many more of you then," said the creature, echoing his thoughts. "Of course, you did make more than a few of my drowgos useless. Fortunately, I found some lovely replacements."

Three more figures rounded the curve of the run. One of the bears made a sound that Istvhan had never heard from an animal's throat before.

Their heads replaced by the unblinking stare of the smooth men, Clara's three dead sisters stumbled forward into the fray.

CHAPTER 50

"Oh no..." said Clara softly behind him. "Oh no, no, no. Not you. Not this."

"Decided to join us in humanity?" asked the creature. "Or what passes for it, for such as you and I."

Clara ignored him. Istvhan darted a glance back and saw that she had her arm around the remaining bear's neck. The bear moaned and tried to back up, running into the wall and starting like a frightened dog.

Istvhan stepped forward in between the dead women and the living. One good arm. One knife. Twenty drowgos and three former nuns.

No bears to back him up.

He did not blame them. The two werebears were stronger than any human, but strength was useless in the face of love. Very well. He would be strong in their stead. It was what paladins were for, after all.

"No," said Stachys. The potter's voice was very quiet, but the smooth men made no sound, and it fell into that soundlessness like a stone in a pond. "No, love, this is wrong."

"Be quiet," said his creation.

"You can't do this."

The statue rolled its carved white eyes. "And how do you plan to stop me? You've never stopped me before. You just whine and snivel and collapse in a heap and I do whatever I wish anyway."

Each word struck the man like a blow. He flinched repeatedly, lifting his clouded eyes to Istvhan.

"You three first," said the sculpture, waving the three dead nuns forward. The trio advanced. Behind Istvhan, the bear moaned again.

"No," said Stachys again, with a little more conviction this time. He stood up, shaking violently, and staggered forward, as if to place himself between Istvhan and the smooth men. *"No."*

His creation broke into the same sardonic applause that he had used before. "Oh, very impressive. That will certainly work. You, in the middle, hold him and make sure he doesn't hurt himself."

The sculptor lunged.

Istvhan realized too late what was happening and tried to push the man away, but his useless arm refused to obey. The pain was breathtaking but he still tried to turn, pulling his knife hand away. He was too slow. Since his god died, the tide had not been concerned with saving lives, only with taking them.

The knife entered Stachys's belly. The sculptor blinked a few times and said, "Oh...oh, that's not so bad, is it?" and clutched Istvhan's wrist, pinning the blade in place with his own bodyweight.

Istvhan dropped the knife and tried to catch the man as he fell, but Stachys collapsed straight down, dragging the blade upward through his flesh until it struck bone. His creation screamed.

It was a scream that was not-right, the same way that his voice was not-right, a scream that should not have existed from a throat that should never have been born. Istvhan's hearing vanished in a high-pitched ringing and the bear screamed.

He could no longer hear, so he did not know what Stachys's last words were. The man's lips moved, something that might have been a word or a name, and then he died.

The smooth men crumpled. The drowgos went first, collapsing where they stood. The three women went more slowly, first to their knees, then down into huddled piles on the floor.

Stachys's first and finest creation, in his stolen body of flesh and salt, swayed on his feet. He, too, tried to speak, but Istvhan could not hear those words either. He did not say very many, in any event. His clay lips moved slow and stiff and then stopped moving entirely, frozen in a snarl, and then he fell forward. The ceramic bust struck the floor and smashed into a thousand shards and none of the bodies in the room moved, not now or ever again.

Clara felt as if her head might explode from the scream and hardly cared. Her chest already felt as if it had exploded. She had shoved everything down, over and over, so that she could function, but seeing her sisters coming toward her like that...she couldn't. She had dropped the beast's form because she could feel her control slipping. Sister Sara, who took care of the bees and harvested the honey every year. Sister Mel, apprenticed to the apothecary, who sat with Clara when she'd caught the summer fever two years ago. Ari the novice, barely fourteen, never to grow any older at all.

She'd known they were dead, and she'd told herself that she would grieve later, when everyone was safely away. Seeing them walk forward, with those obscenely sculpted heads atop their bodies, was worse than death. *I couldn't save you in life, and now I can't save you again. Blessed Saint Ursa, why would you let this happen to them? Why?*

And then they died and the scream rang in her ears and Istvhan turned and pulled her out of the room so she didn't have to look. He was saying something to her, she thought, but she couldn't hear him.

Sigrid turned human again, and had the presence of mind to grab their clothes. Sigrid was practical. Clara had to be practical too. *Everyone on this accursed island will have heard that scream. Half of Morstone probably heard it. I can't fall apart. I can't dwell. Mourn later. We have to get away.*

The feelings did not want to be shoved away. Istvhan was still holding her upper arms and saying something and the ringing was slowly subsiding but all she could make out was "...right?" *Is he asking which way to go? Is he asking if I'm all right?* She shook her head helplessly at him, touching her ears, and he nodded and held up her robe in that familiar gesture, which threatened to make her start sobbing again for no particular reason.

Not now. Not now. Now we have to get away.

The question of which way to go was answered when gladiators spilled around the corner, holding their heads. Istvhan pointed to the open door and said something, gesturing with broad arm movements, and tugged Clara and Sigrid away. They followed his lead, still clutching their heads.

"Up or down?" Clara heard, although the ringing in her ears tried to distort it.

"Down," she said, hoping that he could hear her. Down had been clear, thanks to the beasts. Saint Ursa alone knew what it looked like up above.

Apparently the scream had done more to cow the animals than any number of men with spears. Even the scavengers had fled from the bodies. Clara led the way toward the docks, not sure what they would do when they got there, but lacking any better ideas.

Sigrid stretched her jaw and grimaced, apparently trying to pop her ears. "Is that it, then? Are we done?"

"God, I hope so," groaned Istvhan.

They reached the provisioning area and Clara saw the bins on the side of the wall and fell on them, ravenous. Raw potato was perhaps a bit much, but there were apples, packed in layers of straw. Sigrid joined her, nearly eating the cores in her haste.

Istvhan looked up the stair worriedly. "I think more are coming."

"Damn and blast," muttered Sigrid, grabbing as many apples as she could hold. "If I change again, I'm not coming out in this life."

Clara felt pretty much the same way. She tightened the rope belt at her waist and shoveled apples frantically down the neck of the torn robe. *If I can get a couple more in me...*

"You should probably get those lumps looked at," said Istvhan, as they fled for a more sheltered spot behind a wall of barrels.

"Apple pox," she said, fishing another one out of her cleavage and biting into it.

"What did I — *crunch crunch* — say about — *crunch* — flirting?"

Clara was about to answer when they heard a door creak and then the footsteps of multiple people on the stairs. She wasn't sure if the metallic noises were from armor or if her hearing was still playing tricks on her, but she didn't like it. *We need to go to the docks. Now.*

"What was that horrible sound?" someone asked behind them. It sounded like the supervisor who had taken her people to the cheese cellar. "Is it safe now? Can we come out?"

"Not sure yet," a man replied. "Someone's broken a group of prisoners out. Has a group of women come this way? And a big man with a knife?"

"Shit," whispered Istvhan. "I think they finally did a headcount."

"Why yes, there was a whole group of them earlier — they said they needed medical attention. They went that way?"

The footsteps grew louder, and Clara picked up the pace. The steps to the dock were in sight. "We're nearly there," she whispered.

"Right," said Sigrid. She turned and planted herself in the doorway. "Get going. I'll hold them."

"What?" It took a moment for Clara to understand, and when she did, she didn't want to. "Sigrid, no! You'll be killed!"

"Don't be a fool," said Sigrid. "I still can't swim. I'll hold the corridor as long as I can."

Her vision blurred. On some level, she knew that Sigrid was right, but when she tried to find calm, it wouldn't come. "I can't lose you, too. Not on top of everyone else."

"*Go.*"

Istvhan saved her. He caught her arm, shook his head. "Let her choose," he whispered. And then: "Domina Sigrid," he said, bowing his head, "it has been the honor of a lifetime to fight beside you."

"You're damn right it has," said the nun who had been like an older sister to her. "Now take her out of here and *go!*"

Clara's face was the color of bone and there were tears streaming down her face. He didn't think she knew they were there. But she kept pace with him, step by step, as they pelted down the stairs, and her expression held the chilling tranquility that frightened him whenever he saw it.

Cold air struck their faces as they reached the docks. Istvhan looked into the churning water and felt his stomach lurch. *I can't swim in that. I can barely look at that.*

"You go," he said, pushing her toward the edge. "I'll go back and help Sigrid."

"The hell you will. I'm not losing you both in one night." She shucked off her robe and stood shivering on the dock. Apples bounced on the boards and fell into the water with a splash.

"Clara, I can't swim in this. Even if I could, I won't know where to go. They'll have put the bonfire out by now," said Istvhan. "They can't afford to wait."

"Probably. Do you trust me?" asked Clara.

Istvhan looked at her, then at the dark water, then at her again. The waves slapped against the piling, black as tar. Cold spray soaked his feet.

"Do you trust me?" she asked again.

He opened his mouth and what came out was, "I believe I am madly in love with you." *Oh. Hmm. Did not expect to say that.*

It's true, though. It's true, and if I die, I want her to know that I loved her. That she was more than worthy of it. That all those times I never fell in love, it was because I hadn't met a woman as strong as she is. He tore his eyes away from the water to meet hers, and waited for her answer.

"That's very nice," said Clara, sounding a touch exasperated, "but do you *trust* me?"

Trust is faith plus predictability. He had faith in her. And his only prediction was that she was stronger than he was when it came to this. *I was strong for you. Now maybe it's your turn to be strong for me.*

"I trust you," he said, still looking at her and not the water. "But I can't make myself jump."

"You don't have to." She yanked the rope belt out of her tattered robe and looped it around her neck. "Grab on. Wrap it around your wrists."

"I'll choke to you to dea—"

"*Do it.*"

Someone shouted from the top of the stairs. It did not sound like Sigrid. Istvhan grabbed the cord, tied it around his bad wrist, looped it around the good one, and gripped it tightly. Clara turned her back to him. "Don't fall off," she said. "And don't let go."

Istvhan would have said something clever, but suddenly she was changing and the cord snapped taut against the bear's neck and god, he was an arrogant fool to have even worried, what man could possibly choke something with a neck that size, and there was another shout and the world lurched and Istvhan and the bear were falling into the dark water.

CHAPTER 51

The water was so cold that at first he barely registered the impact. It drove the breath from his lungs and went up his nose and his first instinct was to kick free and get to the surface. He lost his grip on the rope and if it had not been looped around his wrists, he'd likely have fallen off and never found her again, but then the bear was at the surface and somehow the air was even colder than the water and he was choking and coughing up water and trying desperately to breathe but he couldn't let go of the rope, the rope was the only thing that would save him oh gods oh saints this was it this was the end he should have stayed on shore at least he would have died warm...

The bear swam with her head out of the water and her back mostly submerged. Clara could feel Istvhan's weight and hear him sputtering. How long could he survive in the water? The bear could swim for miles, even encumbered, but he could not possibly last that long. Even the mile south to the headland where the Rat had lit the bonfire would be difficult, and now that the fire was no longer lit, the gods only knew if she'd see it at all.

Don't die, she thought. *Don't die. Hold on. I've got you. Just hold on.*

It got worse. It couldn't get worse, and it got worse anyway. They were parallel to the shore and the waves hit them from the side, in a queasy up-and-down motion. Istvhan retched until there was nothing left in his stomach, then retched some more. The water slapped at his mouth and sometimes seawater got in and then he had something else to puke back up.

He was so cold. His teeth chattered when he tried to close his mouth. He knew he had to hold onto the rope, but he couldn't feel his fingers. Maybe they were still on the rope. Maybe he'd let go hours ago. Had it been hours? Surely it had been.

At least he couldn't feel his bad arm any more. That was worth something. He wasn't even scared by the terrible numbness, because everything was going numb now. Maybe it hadn't been so bad. Certainly not as bad as the cold and the seasickness.

He retched again, helplessly. He could still see the bear's ears in front of him, so he hadn't let go. That was good. He couldn't let go. That was the only thing he could remember any more, that he absolutely couldn't let go.

The bear had swum for what seemed like ages. It hated the sideways slap of the waves, but whenever it tried to turn toward shore or out to sea, the annoying voice in its head started telling it no and pushing it back. It was annoying. Bears didn't get seasick easily, but it was definitely thinking about it.

The voice said that there was a headland and maybe that was true, but the bear didn't know why it couldn't just turn and go up on shore here. The voice was yelling about people who would be angry, but that was absurd. People were tiny. The bear was large. If the bear wanted to be on the shore, what could the tiny people do to stop it?

Still, the voice understood things that the bear didn't, like fire and how to get out of cages. It would keep swimming and trust the voice, at least for now.

Istvhan was hanging onto the rock in the ford. He hadn't let go. If he held on long enough, his brothers would find him once the battle was over. He just had to keep holding on. The water was getting in his mouth and his nose and things were so dark but at least he wasn't cold any more. He was starting to warm up. That was good. His brothers would surely find him, even in the dark. He had faith.

His last thought, as the darkness closed over him, was to wonder where his god was, and why he could no longer feel Him.

The bear came up on shore, dragging its burden behind it, and shook. Water flew in all directions. Clara came forward, convincing the bear that its work was done, and it retreated, grumbling.

She realized her mistake immediately, as Istvhan's full weight landed on her back and she went to her knees. The wet rope seared across her throat and she gagged.

Once she'd gotten the rope over her head, she rolled over, reaching for Istvhan. Tiny pebbles crunched painfully under her knees. "Istvhan? Istvhan, are you..." *Alive?* she wanted to say, but didn't quite dare.

He was ominously silent. She did not see in the dark as well as the bear but his skin looked terribly pale, pale like one of the drowgos. When her fingers closed over his wrist, he felt as cold as the sea.

"Oh no," Clara said, and rolled him over, hammering on his back. "Breathe, you bastard, *breathe!* Don't you dare die!" Dear god, he'd told her he loved her and she'd said "That's very nice." How was she supposed to live with that?

Calm, she thought. *Calm down and do something practical. You have to be calm.*

She reached for calm and found...nothing. Only panic and despair and mourning for Sigrid and her sisters. Only shock and horror at how they'd died, and under that, long months of holding on and coping and waiting and now it was over and there was no calm left in her and Istvhan was cold, so horribly cold, and if she lost him now, she might as well just walk into the sea.

"Breathe, dammit!" she screamed. *"Breathe or I'll kill you!"*

"Motivation, that's the ticket," said a familiar voice from the dark. "I've always said you can never underestimate the value of motivation. Nevertheless, my dear, I would stop punching him in the back like that. There's not likely to be any water left in him, and his kidneys will thank you."

Clara lifted her head and blinked toward the voice. Was she hallucinating? "Doc Mason?" she whispered.

"The one, the only, accept no counterfeits or imitations." The traveling salesman went down on his knees beside her. "You might have saved us all a good deal of trouble if you had simply mentioned that you were working with the Rat, my dear."

She gaped at him. He set his ear against Istvhan's chest, listened for a moment, then cackled. "Yes! There we go. Heart still beating. He's just as cold as a miser's heart, that's all."

"The fire," she said, looking around. There had been a dull orange glow on the headland and she found it again, the remains of the bonfire after it had been smothered.

"Not enough to warm a minnow, I fear. I was tasked with seeing it extinguished and keeping watch for any stragglers. Now, now, don't despair. The best thing for hypothermia is body heat. Carry him to the wagon and we will wrap you both in blankets and you can lend him some of yours." He was working as he spoke, getting a knife under the rope around Istvhan's wrists and cutting the soaking cord free.

Clara got her arms under Istvhan and staggered to her feet. The man was dead weight and she was exhausted, but damned if she was going to give up when he needed her.

The wagon seemed an eternity away. Mason kept up a constant stream of chatter the entire time, and she was grateful. It was so dark, or perhaps the despair in her chest was growing to cloud her vision. Her vision was graying out around the edges and she navigated by following the sound of his voice. "...your more ursine qualities, Domina, were a surprise, I confess. No, no, I'm not scolding. I don't know that I'd have told me either. Still, quite a surprise. And of course, once Halishi mentioned your names, well, you could have knocked me over with a feather..."

By the time that Clara heard Tolly saying, "Clara? Is that you?" she could barely see anything but sparks. She managed the steps by memory alone, banging Istvhan's knees on the doorway — *if he lives through this, a few more bruises probably won't matter much* — and set him down on the floor. "Blankets," she gasped, swaying.

Tolly slid past her and unleashed an avalanche of quilts. It took the last of her waning strength to get Istvhan stripped and bundled into them and then she simply collapsed on top of him.

"There you go," said Doc Mason. "Just...err...lie there and think warm thoughts, yes?"

"He's so cold," she mumbled.

"You don't swim your way out of Morstone without losing a bit of body heat. Now lie still and keep quiet. I'm sure someone will be along soon to ask why there was a bonfire here, and I shall have to bemuse and bemaze them." He patted the blankets. "All will be well, my dear. You'll see."

Clara hoped he was right. She was certain that she would not rest until she knew Istvhan was going to pull through. She remained certain of this as the wagon door slammed and then exhaustion crept up and hit her over the head.

"Really," said Istvhan, his voice somewhat muffled by female flesh, "I fear I have gotten used to waking like this. You may be stuck with me."

Clara shot bolt upright, spilling him onto the floor. *"Istvhan! You're alive!"*

He squinted up at her. "Did you think I was dead? Were you doing something strange with my corpse?"

"No, I — you were so cold — Doc Mason said — I was afraid—" She knew that she was babbling and didn't care. She wrapped her arms around him, which meant that he had his face planted in her breasts again. He didn't seem to mind, and at least that way he couldn't see that she was crying.

"How do you feel?" she asked, when she had wiped the tears away and freed him from her cleavage.

"Terrible," he said cheerfully. "My head's pounding and my wrists feel like they've been flayed. Did we get away, though?"

"I think so. And Doc Mason showed up, and told me that we should have just said we were working for the Rat."

Istvhan's laugh turned into a groan as he put a hand to his head. "I might have known."

"Indeed you might have," said Doc Mason, opening the wagon door. "The Rat and I have been old friends for many years. A traveling salesman sees everything and goes everywhere." He peered at Istvhan. "You know, I have a tonic that will fix that headache right up."

It took a few hours to treat everyone's injuries — Istvhan's wrists really had been flayed, and his shoulder was a massive bruise, cut in places where the chain links had been dug into the skin. Clara had gotten off lightly by comparison, with only a few cuts from the drowgos' blades, already thoroughly washed in seawater. The worst was a rope burn across her throat that made her look as if she had only just escaped a hanging. She was also, once again, without clothes. But eventually she and Istvhan were both wrapped in blankets and propped up with cups of tonic-laced tea, and Tolly had finished fussing over them both.

"We shall drive south a little way," announced Doc Mason. "Your sisters are waiting there, and Faizen is watching over them."

"Did they all arrive?" asked Clara.

"All but one named Sigrid," said Doc Mason, looking at her anxiously.

Clara had to pinch the bridge of her nose and take a deep breath. Istvhan gripped her free hand in his. "She stayed behind so we could get away."

"Ahhh." Doc Mason removed his hat and held it over his heart. "May her courage be remembered as long as the stars."

"Did anyone come looking for escapees?" asked Istvhan. He didn't let go of her fingers.

"Not as such, no. I suspect they will eventually, but it will be some time before they remember how well bears swim. And by then, hopefully, we shall have you well on your way." He beamed at them both. "Now sit and drink tea and warm up. I shall get you south in due time...and possibly sell a little tonic in the process, hey?"

He shut the door. Clara slumped against Istvhan's shoulder, and he leaned against her in return.

"We did it," she said. It made almost no sense to her. She couldn't seem to get her head around it. "We actually did it."

"We did."

She started to cry then. She hadn't meant to, but it was all still there and now that she did not have to do anything, it welled up. Joy that Istvhan was alive was mixed with grief and both of them were almost too much to bear.

He put his good arm around her and did not ask foolish questions. Eventually she ran out of tears, if not of grief, and could pull away, saying, "Well, now I look terrible and your blanket is soggy."

"You are beautiful. More beautiful than I am, at the moment, when I look like a drowned rat."

She managed a laugh, scrubbing at her face. "You look very handsome."

"Ah, Domina, I see your eyesight has suffered as well." Istvhan laced their fingers together. "I had been thinking, you know..."

"Oh?"

"If you're going back to your convent, Domina, you could maybe use a couple of mercenaries on the trip. Perhaps even to help you figure out how to raid-proof your convent once you get there. No one wants a repeat of the last few weeks."

She felt a smile tugging at her lips. "Mercenaries? Or paladins?"

"I suspect that I could arrange both."

"Are you sure you want to? I've already dragged you all over the countryside, into pit fights, nearly *drowned* you..."

He shuddered. "Fortunately, I don't remember a good deal of that last one. Just being cold and holding on."

"You must have been terrified. I know you hate water."

"Do you know, I wasn't?" His dark eyes held hers. "I knew if I held on long enough, someone would come for me. And it was you."

Clara looked down at their interlocking fingers. "You know, you said something to me right before we went into the water..."

"Did I really?"

She peered into his face. "Do you not remember?"

"Hmmm...I do seem to recall baring my soul to a woman who said...what was it, now?"

"Oh god." Clara untangled her fingers so that she could put her face in her hands.

"*That's very nice*, I believe she said."

"I wasn't expecting it! And I was a little distracted!"

Istvhan began laughing. "Well, there were a few things going on. Would you like to try again?"

"Can we?"

"Domina," he said, his voice serious but his eyes dancing, "I am quite hopelessly in love with you."

"Oh good," she said. "I'm in love with you, too. Very much so."

He kissed her then, and she kissed back, and eventually Doc Mason thumped on the roof to yell that they had better not be canoodling in his wagon, but neither of them minded at all.

ABOUT THE AUTHOR

T. Kingfisher is the vaguely absurd pen-name of Ursula Vernon, an author from North Carolina. In another life, she writes children's books and weird comics. She has been nominated for the World Fantasy and the Eisner, and has won the Hugo, Sequoyah, Nebula, Alfie, WSFA, Cóyotl and Ursa Major awards, as well as a half-dozen Junior Library Guild selections.

This is the name she uses when writing things for grown-ups. Her work includes horror, epic fantasy, fairy-tale retellings and odd little stories about elves and goblins.

When she is not writing, she is probably out in the garden, trying to make eye contact with butterflies.

 twitter.com/ursulav

ALSO BY T. KINGFISHER

As T. Kingfisher

A Wizard's Guide To Defensive Baking

Paladin's Grace

Swordheart

Clockwork Boys

The Wonder Engine

Minor Mage

Nine Goblins

Toad Words & Other Stories

The Seventh Bride

The Raven & The Reindeer

Bryony & Roses

Jackalope Wives & Other Stories

Summer in Orcus

From Saga:

The Twisted Ones

The Hollow Places

As Ursula Vernon

From Sofawolf Press:

Black Dogs Duology

House of Diamond

Mountain of Iron

Digger

It Made Sense At The Time

For kids:

Dragonbreath Series

Hamster Princess Series

Castle Hangnail

Ingram Content Group UK Ltd.
Milton Keynes UK
UKHW021319100423
419923UK00021B/99/J

9 781614 505303